The Englishman's Boy

The Englishman's Boy

Guy Vanderhaeghe

Picador USA New York

The author wishes to express his gratitude to the Canada Council and the Saskatchewan Arts Board for financial assistance received during the writing of this novel.

Picador® is a U.S. registered trademark and is used by St. Martin's Press under license from Pan Books Limited.

Library of Congress Cataloging-in-Publication Data

Vanderhaeghe, Guy, 1951–
        The Englishman's boy / Guy Vanderhaeghe.
            p.   cm.
        ISBN 0-312-16823-3
        I. Title.
    PR9199.3.V384E54   1997
    813'.54—dc21   97-15518
                                                CIP

First published in Canada by McClelland & Stewart Inc.

First Picador USA Edition: September 1997

10 9 8 7 6 5 4 3 2 1

To Montana Dan Shapiro,
a true-blue man to ride the river with.

" 'Historicism' (the science of history) scientifically speaking, is the affirmation that life and reality are history and history alone."

– BENEDETTO CROCE

"History is the record of an encounter between character and circumstance . . . the encounter between character and circumstance is essentially a story."

– DONALD CREIGHTON

The Englishman's Boy

E ven from such a distance Fine Man could smell their camp, the
fried-pig stink of white men. He took up a pinch of dirt, placed
it under his tongue, and made a prayer. Keep me close, Mother Earth,
hide me, Mother Earth. It was light as day, the moon's bright face a
trader's steel mirror, the grey leaves of the sage and wolf willow shining silver, as if coated with hoarfrost. Under a full moon, it was dangerous to steal horses – even from foolish white men.

One of the wolfers rose from his blanket and stepped away from
the fire. The one with the ugly hair, red like a fox's, he stood making
his water and talking over his shoulder. A noisy man lacking in dig-
nity. It must be a poor thing to be a wolf-poisoner, to be ugly, to eat
pork, to hate silence. There was nothing to envy these people for,
except their guns and horses.

The red-haired one rolled himself back up in his blanket and lay
like a log beside the fire. "Say goodnight to Jesus," said one of the
other men wrapped in blankets. They all laughed. More noise.

Fine Man felt Broken Horn's body relax beside him and knew
Horn had been covering Red Hair with the "fukes," a sawed-off
Hudson's Bay musket, the only gun they carried between them.
Broken Horn was edgy. Fine Man sensed Horn no longer believed in
the promises and the truth of his dream.

In his dream, there was heavy snow, biting cold. Many starving,
shivering horses, coats white with frost, had come stumbling through

the high drifts to crowd the entrance of Fine Man's lodge. There the grass of spring pushed up sweet green blades through the crust of the snow, tenderness piercing ice, and gave itself to strengthen the horses, even though it was the black months of winter. Fine Man read this as a power sign that somewhere there were horses wishing to belong to the Assiniboine. But Broken Horn did not trust Fine Man's sign any more, and Fine Man did not trust Horn with a gun in his hand.

Suddenly the white men's horses began to mill about, hopping in their hobbles like jack-rabbits. Powdery dust rose like mist, to hang swirling and shaking in the moonlight. Fine Man shifted his eyes to the fire. But none of the lumps under the greasy grey blankets raised a head, their ears were deaf. How did white men distinguish their corpses from those who had only gone to sleep?

The herd broke apart, horses turning and spinning, bumping one another like pans of ice in the grip of a swift current. A moment of complete confusion, rumps and heads bucking above the dust, then the strong current found a shape and stood alone, a big blue roan, broken hobbles dangling from its forelegs, teeth bared, ears laid back.

Lit by the moon, the roan was stained a faint blue, the colour of late-winter-afternoon shadows on crusted snow. Coat smooth as ice, chest and haunches hard as ice, eyes cold as ice, a Nez Percé horse from beyond the mountains which wore snow on their heads all the year round, a horse from behind the Backbone of the World.

When he saw him, Fine Man knew the promise of the dream was true and he rose from behind the juniper bush to show himself plain to the winter horse. Broken Horn's sharp intake of breath through the teeth was a warning, but Fine Man gave no indication he heard him, his ears were stopped to any sound except the singing inside him, the power chanting in him. He stood upright in the moonlight, upright in his Thunderbird moccasins with the beaded Bird green on each foot, upright in the breechclout his Sits-Beside-Him wife had cut from the striped Hudson's Bay blanket. He gazed down at his hands, at the skin of his muscled thighs, at his belly, and understood. White moonlight was his blizzard, a blizzard to blind the eyes of his enemies who lay frozen to the ground in the grip of his medicine-dream, drifted over by the heavy snow of sleep.

He edged toward the horse, addressing him in a soft voice, politely. Fifty yards to his left, the fire was rustling, hot embers cracking like nuts, spitting like fat. Behind him, Horn lifted himself to one knee, swiftly spiking three arrows in the ground near where his bow lay, and aimed the fukes at the sleeping body of a wolfer.

"Little Cousin," said Fine Man in a soothing voice, "Little Cousin, do not be afraid. Don't you recognize me? I am the man you dreamed, the man with the lodge of plenty. I am the man you led your brothers to." He stopped for a moment. "Take a good look at me. There is no harm in my hands," he murmured, displaying empty palms to the roan. Turning and pointing to Broken Horn, crouched with his musket levelled at the sleeping white man, he said, "That man there came with me to find you. Some of your brothers may choose to live with him – if they so decide. It is for them to choose." He stepped forward lightly, words rustling lightly. "Cousin, you are a beautiful being. I do not say this to flatter you. The white man rides you with steel spurs and a steel bit in your mouth. This is not how to sit upon a beautiful being – with cruelty." They were face to face now, he and the blue roan. He removed his left moccasin, the moccasin of the heart side. "Feel, Cousin, there is no harm upon my feet," he said, reaching up carefully to gently stroke the roan's nose with the moccasin. He pursed his lips and blew softly into the left nostril of the horse, who snorted Fine Man's breath back in surprise, shaking his head from side to side.

"Now you know there is no harm in my heart. Now you know that I am the good man who you dreamed. Tell your brothers," Fine Man coaxed.

Broken Horn was signalling him desperately to come now, leave this place, clear out, but Fine Man was making his way carefully and deliberately from horse to horse, showing each his knife before severing the hobbles. When he finished, he returned to the blue roan, stood at its withers, took a fistful of mane and walked it away, his legs matching its forelegs stride for stride. Hesitantly, the other horses followed the man and the blue roan, nineteen horses strung out in a winding procession through buck-brush and sage, black shadows stark on the ground, edges sharp as a knife-cut.

Without haste, they picked their way across the river bottom and to the feet of steep, eroded hills which, washed in the cold light of the moon, became reflections of moon's own face, old and worn and pocked and bright. Fine Man led the blue horse up the first hump of hill, the others filing behind, hooves daintily ticking on loose stones, gravel cascading loose and running with a dry sigh down the slope. He paused, his hands resting on the blue roan's withers; the string of horses paused too. Below, Fine Man could see an elbow of the Teton River poking through the cottonwoods and the tongues of the white man's fire darting, licking the dark. A sudden breeze sprang up and fanned his face, luffing the mane of the blue horse, stroking and ruffling the surface of the water so it flashed and winked in the moonlight like the scales of a leaping fish.

He and the blue horse began their descent then, down into the belly of a narrow coulee twisting through the scarred and crumbling hills. The other horses trickled down the slope after them, filling the coulee as water fills the bed of a river. One by one they dropped from sight, tails switching, heads bobbing, ghostly gleaming horses running back into the earth like shining, strengthening water.

The fire died amid the charred sticks, the moon grew pale. The stream of horses flowed north to Canada.

2

I typed four names. *Damon Ira Chance. Denis Fitzsimmons. Rachel Gold. Shorty McAdoo.* I sat and stared at these names for some minutes, then I typed a fifth, my own. *Harry Vincent.*

I did not know how to continue. It's true that once I was a writer of a sort, but for thirty years I've written nothing longer than a grocery list, a letter. I went to the window. From there I could see the South Saskatchewan River, the frozen jigsaw pieces bumping sluggishly downstream, the cold, black water steaming between them. A month ago, when the ice still held, a stranger to this city would have had no idea which way the river ran. But now the movement of the knotted ice, of the swirling debris, makes it plain.

So begin, I told myself.

History is calling it a day. Roman legionaries tramp the street accompanied by Joseph and Mary, while a hired nurse in cap and uniform totes the Baby Jesus. Ladies-in-waiting from the court of the Virgin Queen trail the Holy Family, tits cinched flat under Elizabethan bodices sheer as the face of a cliff. A flock of parrot-plumed Aztecs are hard on their heels. Last of all, three frostbitten veterans of Valley Forge drag flintlocks on the asphalt roadway.

This is nearly thirty years ago, 1923 to be exact, and I am a young man standing at a second-storey window in the script department of Best Chance Pictures watching extras drift by in a yellow light creeping towards dusk – shooting suspended for the day. I am waiting for a man by the name of Fitzsimmons, waiting anxiously because a visit from Fitzsimmons is not to be taken lightly. Returning from lunch today I found this terse message on my desk.

Dear Mr. Vincent,

Please be so kind as to wait upon Mr. Fitzsimmons at the close of office hours this day.

Yours sincerely,
Damon Ira Chance

The office cleared out two hours ago and there is still no sign of Fitzsimmons. Even though I suspect the possibility of a practical joke, I stay put. For one thing, the letterhead (reading "Office of the President and Chairman") appears genuine. I don't intend to jeopardize a seventy-five-dollar-a-week job, not with the expense of keeping my mother in the Mount of Olives Rest Home.

History having disappeared from sight, my gaze turns to the jumbled vista of the studio lot, twenty-five acres of offices, workshops, streets of every kind – French, Spanish, Russian, Chinese, Wild Western. What I can't see from my window, I know, having walked through it often enough.

All of this make-believe is held in quarantine by a ten-foot fence and a gate which trumpets in black iron scrollwork: Best Chance Pictures. When I first came to work here eighteen months ago the gate trumpeted Zenith Pictures, but then Damon Ira Chance bought it from Mr. Adilman and the name changed, along with a number of other things.

From the beginning, Damon Ira Chance was an enigma. Nobody knew anything about him. People assumed that the surname Chance had been adopted for the sake of the ringing phrase, Best Chance Pictures. If Samuel Goldwyn could steal a name for business reasons, what was stopping anybody else? Then one of the trade papers published a story identifying Damon Ira Chance as the son of Titus Chance. For over forty years Titus Chance's name had been mentioned in the same breath with the likes of Carnegie, Gould, Rockefeller, Morgan, and Mellon. Although not quite as rich as these plutocrats, his wealth was considerable, very considerable. During the Civil War the family textile mills had made a bundle supplying uniforms to the Federals, and when peace came, Titus Chance shrewdly reinvested war profits in oil, steel, railroads, banking. The old man survived well into the new century and at his death his money had passed to his only child, Damon Ira, an obscure figure, a middle-aged Henry James character who had spent most of his life living abroad in Europe. Unlike a Henry James character, however, Damon Ira Chance promptly took a large part of his inheritance and bought a movie company with it.

It is on this man's orders that I am waiting for Denis Fitzsimmons in my dog-kennel office. There's not much to amuse me here, a desk, a typewriter, a coffee can full of pencils, a three-shelf bookcase holding Dreiser, Crane, Norris, London, and back numbers of *The Smart Set*, which my friend Rachel Gold browbeat me into subscribing to because it is edited by her idol, H.L. Mencken.

Rachel has an office just a short way down the corridor, a much more magnificent office befitting a head writer. In it there is a long table for writing, a six-shelf bookcase, many ashtray stands, a cabinet with a broken lock holding bottles of bathtub gin, and a big sofa for thinking and napping on.

I tell myself five more minutes and then I'll leave. Five minutes pass and then another five. As it grows dark outside, I see myself in the windowpane, a tall, thin, gangly, big-nosed, big-eared young man nervously smoking and fidgeting with his wire-rimmed spectacles. A very ordinary, common young man whose only uncommon feature can't be detected in the glass at the moment. My limp.

I sit as minutes become hours, checking my watch, chain-smoking cigarettes. Then, sometime after ten, I hear a car pull up, followed by the creak of the stairs which lead up to the gallery that runs round the offices on the second floor, finally the tread of heavy feet outside my office door. Suddenly, Fitzsimmons is here, looming in the doorway without having bothered to knock. Six feet four, maybe two hundred and seventy pounds, he stands there breathing heavily through an open mouth, all bulging shoulders, barrel chest, tree-trunk legs threatening to burst the stitches on an expensively tailored double-breasted suit. Seen up close, the meaty florid face breaks down into a riverine system of tiny red veins and spidery tributaries, a knob of mashed nose, a large, froggish mouth spiked with the kind of tiny baby teeth that belong to a six-year-old.

He draws a couple of wheezy breaths and says, "I got held up. Business." Then he takes out a handkerchief and begins to mop his sweating face, his cranium of closely cropped hairs, orangey-red like the pelt of an orangutan. "Some fucking paradise, this California. Never had so many fucking colds in my life." He blows his nose into the handkerchief.

"Drink orange juice," I say. "It's supposed to be good for whatever ails you."

Fitzsimmons's eyes scan my office; he doesn't look at me. "If it isn't colds, it's the fucking clap. All these actresses got a dose of the clap. You telling me orange juice will cure the clap?"

I'm not about to tell this man anything.

"If it would fix the clap I'd ship a couple of boxcars back East. I got plenty of friends in New York could make use of it." He laughs, a strange laugh that grates and pops explosively, like gravel being ground in the jaws of an adamantine mill. He stops all at once, as if he has forgotten why he's amused. "Let's go," he says.

I follow him down the stairs, his bulk rolling like a storm cloud. We get into the waiting Hispano-Suiza and drive off. Aside from the sound of Fitzsimmons sucking his teeth, we wind through deserted streets in silence. Contrary to what you might expect, in the early twenties Hollywood was a ghost town after dark. For the original inhabitants, mostly retirees from the Midwest, a high old time might consist of a game of gin rummy, cranking your own ice-cream maker. The film colony was not much livelier. Most movies were filmed in natural light and that meant rising at dawn and shooting until dusk so as not to waste precious hours of sunshine. Early to bed and early to rise. Even as we pass down Hollywood Boulevard I can see that all the stools at a lunch counter are empty, a lonely waitress staring out the window at our big car as it rolls by.

When I finally summon the courage to ask Fitzsimmons where he is taking me, all he says is, "To see Mr. Chance."

This is a very big surprise. Nobody, or almost nobody, ever gets an audience with Chance. In the nine months since acquiring Zenith, he has earned the reputation of being a recluse, *Photoplay* dubbing him the Hermit of Hollywood. At his own studio he is merely a rumoured presence, rarely if ever seen. Now and then someone catches a glimpse of him standing at his office window on the third floor of the administration building, then the Venetian blinds snap shut and he is swallowed up from view. On very special occasions, some of the Hollywood aristocracy, a great star, or important director are summoned to his sanctum sanctorum for tea and cake, a decorous private audience. This is not the usual Hollywood practice; all the rest of the studio bosses are hands-on men, a presence on the lot. At Universal, Carl Laemmle is known as Uncle Carl, a chipper gnome who chats with property men, grips, electricians, stars, and directors alike. Louis B. Mayer is a man incapable of passing a pie without sticking a finger in it. He shows directors how to direct and gives acting lessons to great stars. Fall over and die like this. Roll your eyes like this when you drop. And lemme see the whites. Often he breaks down in tears, moved by the brilliance of his own performance. "The D.W. Griffith of actors" they call him at Metro, but only behind his back because Louis B. Mayer hits people. The illustrious list of people he has socked includes Erich von Stroheim and Charlie Chaplin.

But Mayer's is not Chance's style. He is aloof, patrician, resented. In nearly a year, the closest I have got to my boss is at his single recorded public appearance, the premiere of his first production. I had been the rewrite man for titles on *The Orphan Maid* and was vain enough to attend the picture's opening to see just how much of my work survived final cutting.

I was having a cigarette outside the theatre when the plum Hispano-Suiza I am now riding in drew to the curb and Chance and Fitzsimmons stepped out. Pandemonium broke out. Flashbulbs erupted. Reporters and cameramen began to jostle and shout, "Look this way, Mr. Damon!" "Hey, Hermit!" "Cheese please, Mr. Chance!" There he stood, a bewildered little man, weak eyes blinking, his thinning, wispy hair appearing to stand on end as the camera flashes throbbed epileptically on his starched shirt front and pale, stricken face. With reporters and cameramen nipping at his flanks, he looked like a penguin set upon by savage dogs, panicky, defenceless.

And then Fitzsimmons seized him by the elbow and started to thrust his way through newspapermen, to violently hack a path through the mob to the lobby. There were yelps and curses as the big Irishman shouldered people aside, trampled on their toes. I saw him slap a camera out of someone's hand, heard it smash on the pavement. In seconds, the two were safe inside. Meanwhile, the disgruntled press swore and milled about on the sidewalk. Who the fuck does that big ape think he is anyway, pushing me? I got a press card. Nobody but a cop pushes a press card around. I'll put the fix in on this picture. I'll get his picture a write-up he won't soon forget.

Damon Ira Chance did not forget. *The Orphan Maid* would be his last premiere for a very long time.

Nobody can quite figure the relationship between Chance and Fitzsimmons. It is an inexhaustible topic of speculation. Rachel Gold describes them as Jekyll and Hyde; fold their personalities together and you have Louis B. Mayer. It is her theory that Chance is the sentimental Louis B. dreaming pictures in his tower, while Fitzsimmons is the violent and ruthless Louis B. who hits and threatens people. Together, she claims, they might possibly make one successful movie producer.

She may be right. There's no doubt Fitz frightens people. He is the trouble-shooter, the hands-on man at Best Chance Pictures who relays orders from on high, hustles technicians, reads the riot act to stars and directors. He need only walk onto a set, expensive brogues creaking ominously, and a fearful hush descends. I'll never forget the day he took the director Bysshe Folkestone aside, one big arm laid across his shoulders like a cross, walking him from the eighteenth-century Devonshire cottage where Folkestone was shooting to a tract of the

Sinai on a nearby set. We all stood watching from a distance. It was like a silent movie without subtitles and musical accompaniment. After a few words from Fitz, Bysshe started to wave his arms; his face, in turn, registering outrage, innocence, perplexity, while all around the two of them work continued, trucks dumping sand and workmen with shovels and rakes scrambling frantically to mould desert dunes to recreate ancient Egypt.

Bysshe kept talking and Fitz kept refusing to look at him. Fitzsimmons stood trickling sand from one enormous hand to another, back and forth, back and forth, eyes riveted on the stream sifting down from his fist. And Folkestone ran on too, unwilling to see that the big Irish egg-timer was measuring how long it took for him to cook. After three or four minutes, Folkestone realized Fitz wasn't listening and began to run down like a wind-up toy. His once emphatic and confident gestures became uncertain and tentative. In the end he shrugged half-heartedly; his arms fell to his sides; he fell silent.

Fitz began to dust the sand from his palms, still without looking at Bysshe, contemptuously, one hand slowly wiping the other. Folkestone stood waiting. The cleaning of the hands went on and on. Even at a distance, from where we stood, you could feel the cold cruelty of this pantomime. Nobody could have stood it for long. The meaning was perfectly clear.

Folkestone broke away and began to stumble out of the desert, sinking to his ankles in the sand. Lurching out of Egypt and into Devonshire he kept going, sand leaking out of his pant cuffs on to the paper turf. We all suddenly became enormously interested in our cameras, our clipboards, our costumes. Fleeing around the corner of the papier-mâché stone cottage, Folkestone groped blindly for some support and brushed a painted canvas backdrop, shaking a slight disturbance into a mild English sky.

The next day a new director was at work.

The powerful Hispano-Suiza is now throatily purring up into hills which have been beset by a recent boom in house construction, a rash of thirty-room haciendas, Italian villas, and Tudor mansions thrown up helter-skelter by Hollywood's finest in the mad race to outdo their box-office rivals. Mary Pickford and Douglas Fairbanks have set the standard with their hunting-lodge home, "Pickfair," run with a modest staff of fifteen servants. Now everyone else is straining to gain ground on the reigning King and Queen of pictures. Harold Lloyd has bought a sixteen-acre estate, "Greenacres," with its own golf course and an artificial waterfall spotlit at night with coloured lights. And in the near future, John Barrymore will buy King Vidor's "Bella Vista," over the years expanding it into sixteen buildings and forty-five rooms, adding two swimming pools, a trout pond, a skeet-shooting range, an aviary, a library of first editions, and a trophy room housing the only dinosaur egg in private hands. His guests will also have two bars from which to imbibe – one an English tavern, the other a "Western" saloon dismantled and shipped down piece by piece from Alaska.

According to Rachel Gold, this lunacy is not like the inspired lunacy of Buster Keaton, who can frequently be seen driving a thirty-foot bus in an admiral's hat – a bus expressly built for him by the Fifth Avenue Bus Company and equipped with two drawing rooms, an observation deck, and bunks for six. Keaton, she says, knows how funny bad taste can be; the rest of them don't.

It is a very strange world into which Fitz is steering the Hispano-Suiza, a world half-wild, half-artificial. Rabbits scutter into the road and flicker in the headlights; coyote eyes glitter and slink in the ditches. Most of the hills are still undeveloped, bald and blank, overlooking nothing, just as the canyons open on nothing. And then the car headlights will suddenly pick out an unexpected expanse of stone wall, your eyes will jerk from the eyes glowing in the ditches to graze the roof of a Norman farmhouse, a turret, a Tudor chimney. Then the impression of Europe dissolves and you are back in a lunar landscape of parched hills where owls glide through swathes of incandescent light. The powerful car bores on, headlights fanning scrub, the dirt track behind us writhing with dust.

Suddenly, the hood swings left, noses through an iron gate, and the Hispano-Suiza rolls up a long drive. Ahead of us lies a Tudor manor, its imitation thatched roof humped like a haystack against the sky, a few of its leaded windows showing light. This is "Mina," the house which Howard Adilman named for his wife but never finished before Damon Ira Chance bought Zenith and, along with it, accommodations befitting a movie mogul.

Fitz draws up to the front of the house, turns off the motor, and motions me out. He uses a key to let us in the door. There is a long entrance hallway which leads into a barren reception room. Our footsteps echo as Fitz leads me to a staircase curving up to the second floor. As we go up it, over my shoulder I catch a glimpse through an open door of what appears to be a ballroom. It is entirely empty except for a single ladder-backed chair standing precisely in the middle of the marble floor under a huge crystal chandelier. I see no signs of servants, hear no off-stage noises – no phonograph playing, no doors opening or closing, no voices – the whole vast house is silent and still. We pass down a corridor lined with closed doors. The corridor is painted starkly white, just as all rooms we have passed through have been painted white. So far I have seen no paintings, no rugs, no photographs, no furniture, except for the one lone chair stranded on that vast floor. My heart has begun to beat dully, heavily, and my mouth has gone dry.

Fitzsimmons stops, knocks softly on one of the doors. A voice calls to enter and we do. Chance sits on a sofa with his back to the door, facing a screen hung on the opposite wall. This is the first furnished room I have encountered in my passage through the house. One wall is filled with floor-to-ceiling bookcases and a sliding library ladder; another is covered with maps of the western United States; the last has a huge leaded window looking out on to the night. There is a projector mounted on a trolley standing near the sofa, three armchairs covered in chintz, a gleaming oak floor, and a mahogany liquor cabinet behind whose doors bottles gleam.

Fitz says, "What was it tonight?"

Chance doesn't bother to turn around when he answers. "*Judith of Bethulia.*" The voice sounds tired. Then he musters energy. "I want you to make a note, Fitz. In this movie Griffith put Bobby Harron in

13

a tunic. Big mistake. Harron has terrible legs. See to it that none of my directors puts a male lead into a short tunic until you've inspected his legs. Nobody else but you."

"Got it."

"Not a mental note, Fitz. A paper note."

Fitz takes out a note pad and scribbles. "I brought Vincent," he announces as he writes.

"Please introduce us," says Chance, still not bothering to turn around. With Fitz's hand on my elbow I find myself being steered to the front of the sofa where a man in a three-piece oatmeal tweed suit is sitting. His thinning hair is neatly brushed, the clothes are elegantly cut, his brown brogues are polished to a chocolate richness. He might be a professor at an Ivy League school – a professor of good family and substantial private means. His tailoring, his grooming are all that they should be. Only his grey complexion falls short of the mark, the unhealthy colour of a man who never sees much sun.

"Mr. Vincent," he says, "how good of you to come and see me on such short notice. Please sit down," he says, patting the sofa beside him. "Too bad Fitz couldn't have got you here earlier, you could have joined me in viewing one of Mr. David Wark Griffith's films – an older one, but then I don't find that Mr. Griffith ages."

Fitzsimmons says, "You ought to take a holiday from the Griffith. Look at something different for a change." Towering over us, he sounds and looks a bit like a disapproving parent. "I want to get preached at, I go to church," he adds.

"Fitz prefers the Keystone Kops, Chaplin, Keaton, Harold Lloyd," Chance explains cheerfully.

"Fatty Arbuckle, that's the guy who really makes me laugh."

"Nobody is laughing at Mr. Arbuckle any more, Fitz. My word, no. The joke's on Mr. Arbuckle now."

What Chance is referring to is a sexual scandal that rocked Hollywood only the year before. A starlet, Virginia Rappe, died as a consequence of a drunken party in the comedian's hotel room in San Francisco. Accusations were made that Arbuckle had raped Miss

Rappe with either a Coca-Cola or champagne bottle (some said an icicle) and ruptured her bladder, resulting in peritonitis and death. Much of America stirred with anti-Hollywood hysteria, pulpits rang with denunciations; there were reports of women attacking the screen when Arbuckle comedies were shown and Wyoming cowboys riddling them with bullet holes. Despite Arbuckle's acquittal in a series of trials, Paramount cancelled the jolly fat man's three-million-dollar contract and junked three of his pictures already in the can. Suddenly, Fatty Arbuckle had become Starving Arbuckle, a star who couldn't get work.

"And thanks to Mr. Arbuckle we find ourselves saddled with that insufferable Hays," says Chance. "Not the man I would have picked for the job, but then Messrs. Zukor, Loew, Goldwyn, Laemmle, Fox, and Selznick did not consult me. I am not part of their cabal."

His dismissal of Hays takes me aback. Hays, the little man with bat-wing ears and rodent teeth, is uniformly detested by writers, actors, and directors, regarded as a tool of studio heads, a way of disciplining troublesome "creative" people. So it comes as a great surprise to hear a studio head disparage him.

Fearing possible government censorship of the movies in the wake of the Arbuckle scandal, industry leaders quickly hired President Harding's former postmaster general, Will Hays, to clean up Hollywood's image. What came to be known as the Hays Office immediately issued dictates prohibiting carnality on-screen or off. Morality clauses were soon a feature of studio contracts; unseemly private behaviour could get you fired, or the vague clause could be used as legal grounds to get rid of people causing other problems.

"I grant you," says Chance, "that there may be a philosophical justification for censorship. If we claim that Shakespeare and Milton improve the mind, then it is only fair to assume that inferior goods may damage it. But censorship for business reasons is another matter. And if we must have it, I would prefer the censor to be able to distinguish between the good and the bad. Mr. Hays does not set my mind at rest on that point. As owner of my own movie company, I did not expect to be dictated to by a small-town Hoosier whose aesthetics were formed by the Knights of Pythias, the Rotarians, the Kiwanis, the Moose, and the Elks. That is not why I came to Hollywood."

Before I can stop myself, I ask him the question all of Hollywood has been asking behind his back. "Why did you come to Hollywood, Mr. Chance?"

"Why, to assist Mr. Griffith in his great work, Mr. Vincent. To make American movies." He pauses, studies my reaction. "The look on your face suggests you are not sure what I mean. You are thinking, Aren't all movies made in Hollywood American movies? They are not, Mr. Vincent. Think of Mr. Lasky returning from Europe to hold a dockside conference to announce he's corralled the best writers England can boast – James Barrie, Arnold Bennett, H.G. Wells, Compton Mackenzie, E. Temple Thurston, Max Pemberton. How can English writers author American movies? And then Samuel Goldwyn hires Maurice Maeterlinck to write pictures for him because Monsieur Maeterlinck owns a Nobel Prize for Literature. I hear Goldwyn keeps him on hand to introduce to distinguished visitors as, 'The world's greatest writer. He works for me.'"

Fitz abruptly says, "Who wants a drink?"

"Denis recalls me to my duties as a host. I have been remiss. As you see, I can get carried away," Chance apologizes, offering a smile. "We have some very good Scotch that some of Fitz's friends got us from Canada. Or perhaps you would care for something else?"

"Scotch and water is fine."

"Soda with mine. As usual, Denis."

He turns back to me as Fitzsimmons busies himself mixing drinks.

"You see, Harry . . . do you mind if I call you Harry? You see, Harry, I want to make pictures rooted in American history and American experience. Just as Mr. Griffith showed us how to. I'm tired of all these people making movies about Marie Antoinette. Prisoner of Zenda stuff. Chocolate-coated kitsch. Costume dramas, knights and castles, Robin Hood. Why not a film biography of George Washington instead of Henry VIII? Do you see what I mean?"

I nod. Fitz serves the drinks, then retreats to a chair in the corner. All but his shoes and pant legs vanish in shadow.

"That is what I mean when I say I wish to continue Mr. Griffith's work," Chance explains with just a touch of smugness.

It is hard to remember that Griffith only died in 1948, five years ago. I don't suspect the name means much to anyone now, except the most avid film buffs. He died an alcoholic, guiltily ignored by the very business which he pioneered, a neglected, pathetically grandiloquent figure. But for about a decade he dominated movie-making in a way no one has since, or is ever likely to do again. He began to direct when movies were shot with a stationary camera as if they were stage plays, actors and actresses making exits and entrances. It was Griffith and his cameraman, Billy Bitzer, who take the lion's share of credit for inventing the vocabulary of movies – close-ups (audiences wanted to know what had happened to the actors' feet), rapid cuts from scene to scene and character to character, the "fade-out," the "soft focus," tracking cameras. He even used a variation of colour photography, printing night scenes on blue stock, day scenes on yellow. It was Griffith who first demanded that movies be regarded as art and Griffith who gave some credibility to the claim they could be. He produced some of the first Hollywood spectaculars with *The Birth of a Nation* and *Intolerance*, as well as small, intimate movies like *Broken Blossoms*. His pictures were a reflection of their maker, a mixture of bombast, hokum, sentiment, and high artistic purpose.

Griffith was an obsessive eccentric and one of his obsessions was history. He employed a large staff to research his period dramas and dunned archaeologists and historians for blurbs to advertise the "accuracy" of his movies. But his obsession with history went further. He argued that the motion-picture camera would end conflicting interpretations of the past. Eventually all significant events would be recorded by movie cameras and film would offer irrefutable proof as to what had really happened. Vast public archives of documentary movies would make history democratic; by viewing the evidence, citizens could check the facts, know the truth for themselves.

In the early years Griffith was always surrounded by admirers; people who never thought to laugh when the great man propounded his naive theories, or wore kooky straw hats with holes cut in them to prevent baldness, or declaimed ornately like a hillbilly Shakespeare. To them he was always Mr. Griffith, the Genius.

This is the man Chance begins to lecture me on in a style sounding a bit like an address to Congress. He says that he has made an intense study of Griffith's films, pondered them, and drawn conclusions. Griffith is the man who has given America to Americans. America had cried out for bread and received stones until Griffith came along. It was *he* who had answered the cry for bread *with* bread, filled America's spiritual emptiness *with* a vision of itself. He was able to do this because he was a simple, self-educated man who had never forgotten his roots in backwoods Kentucky, a man with similarities to that other self-made genius, Abraham Lincoln. If it had been Griffith's misfortune to go to college, some half-baked professor would have made him ashamed of who and what he was, filling his head with Henry James's traitorous nonsense about the ineffable superiority of Europe. Instead, Griffith had sat at his father's, the old Colonel's, knee, absorbing his stories of the Civil War, retelling them in *The Birth of a Nation* with all the passion of someone who felt he had been present at the great battles, the touching surrender at Appomattox. This primitive, rugged self-confidence had produced an American *Iliad*, and the American people had responded to it the way the Greeks did to Homer, responding to the poetry of *conviction*. Chance tells me this with a conviction which seems at odds with the rumours of his life spent abroad, as if a Henry James character were launching an attack on James himself.

He breaks off suddenly, as if embarrassed by his passion and enthusiasm, gives me a sly smile. "And then there is something else Mr. Griffith taught us by example. How to make a profit from fact. No motion picture since has approached the profitability of *The Birth of a Nation*. It was pure genius on his part to advertise his motion picture as fact. Americans are a practical people, they like facts. Facts are solid, they're dependable. The average American feels foolish when he enjoys a made-up story, feels sheepish, childish, a mooner, a dreamer. But entertain him with facts and you give him permission to enjoy himself without guilt. He needn't feel swindled, or hoodwinked, a hick sold a bill of goods by a carnival barker. He prefers to feel virtuous because he's learned something useful, *informed* himself, *improved* himself.

"You mark my words, Harry, there'll come a day when the public won't swallow any of our stories unless they believe them to be real. Everybody wants the real thing, or thinks they do. Truth is stranger than fiction, someone said. It may not be, but it's more satisfying. Facts are the bread America wants to eat. The poetry of facts is the poetry of the American soul.

"Of course," he qualifies, "the facts in picture-making must be shaped by intuition." He pauses dramatically. "I learned that at the feet of Bergson. I am a Bergsonian," he declares, a little like Aimee Semple McPherson might declare she is a Christian.

I haven't the slightest clue what a Bergsonian is, but it sounds vaguely like Theosophy, or something worse. "A Bergsonian?" I say.

"Before the war I attended his lectures at the Collège de France in Paris. A mesmerizing philosopher. His lectures were packed to the rafters – society ladies, students, writers, artists. Admission was by ticket only. I was one of those privileged to be admitted. Bergson taught that received ideas, habit, routine, turn a man into an automaton, a robot. What distinguishes a man from a robot is not intelligence – presumably a machine might some day be constructed that could outperform a man in the rational faculties – but intuition. The intellect, Bergson says, is designed to apprehend the external world but cannot plumb the inner world of things. It's the wrong tool, Harry. Intuition has its roots in our deepest being, a being we are scarcely aware of, and because we are scarcely aware of it, it remains our truest, most uncorrupted self. My intuition, my will, is the clue to my hidden self. Through intuition it is possible for me to penetrate whatever shares my fluid and changeable nature – other human beings, all art . . . history. Analysis puts a man outside the thing he studies, while intuition puts him inside. Analysis therefore renders partial knowledge while intuition renders absolute knowledge."

"Very interesting," I say.

Chance scrutinizes me with a searching look. "Don't gainsay intuition, Harry. After all, it led me to you."

I shift uneasily on the sofa. "How is that, Mr. Chance?"

"I had a feeling about you. I used to watch you crossing the road. There was something about you. . . . One day I pointed you out to Fitz and asked, 'Who is that young man?' He didn't know your name. I told him to find out and bring me your file. When I read it, everything fell into place. I learned you were a scriptwriter, that you knew shorthand, that you had worked on a newspaper."

"That's right."

Chance turns to where Fitz sits in his dark corner. "Denis, bring the bottle and join us in a toast." The shadows part as Fitz wrenches himself up out of the chair and into the light; the floor groans under him as he makes his way to the sofa and replenishes our glasses. Chance lifts his whisky tumbler. "To the picture I hope Harry is going to help us to make. To the poetry of fact." Our glasses chime against one another, we drink. I don't know what it is I'm drinking to and so I feel counterfeit, ridiculous, but it's good whisky, not to be wasted. Chance stares down into his glass and says, "Fitz has heard rumours about an old man, an extra and bit player in Westerns. It's said the cowhands regard him as a tin god, the last bull buffalo of the old West. There are a lot of stories afloat about him. If he's the genuine article he could be the basis for my movie of poetic fact. If Colonel Griffith gave *The Birth of a Nation* to his son, this old man may give me the picture I want to make. I do not overestimate the potential. Think of Al Jennings," he says.

I do. Al Jennings was an Oklahoma lawyer who had gone off the rails and taken to robbing trains and banks until captured by United States Marshal Bud Ledbetter in 1897. After his release from the big house, he parlayed a reputation as a rough, tough, and hard to bluff desperado into a career in Hollywood. Riding his new celebrity hell-bent for leather he offered himself as a candidate for Attorney

General in his native state, running under the confidence-inducing slogan, "I was a good train robber and I'll be a good Attorney General." Failing in this campaign, he made a bid for the Democratic gubernatorial nomination where he made a shockingly good showing. Now, his political career on hold, he was back in Hollywood making more movies about – Al Jennings. And he wasn't the only Western outlaw who had made hay with his notoriety. Emmett Dalton of the Dalton gang starred in *Beyond the Law*, a picture which in 1920 broke box-office records in New York and Los Angeles. Even the legendary Wyatt Earp had a walk-on in Allan Dwan's *The Half-Breed*; but a one-eyed old man didn't have much future in the acting business. He did, however, temporarily bask in a kind of reflected glory. Among his pallbearers at his 1929 funeral were the Western idols William S. Hart and Tom Mix.

"I see," I say, "you intend to make this man the next Al Jennings."

"Better. Al Jennings produced with money. Al Jennings turned into art."

"All right," I say, "but what do I have to do with Al Jennings and art?"

"You were a reporter. Reporters are supposed to be good at tracking people down."

As a reporter on a small-town newspaper like *The Sentinel* I didn't have much trouble tracking down the newsmakers. A walk down Main Street got you to the mayor; next door to the mayor was the office of the local constable. They furnished the newspaper with hard news. Nor did it take much digging to discover the woman who had grown the potato with the startling resemblance to Theodore Roosevelt. I don't say any of this, of course. It would sound flippant.

"I think what you want is a private detective. Not me."

"No dicks," Fitz growls. He has been quiet so long that this intervention startles me.

"I concur," says Chance. "A man who sells information is not entirely trustworthy. He may sell it to somebody else. I would prefer to enlist a man who shares my ideals. Besides, there is more required than simply finding this man."

"What else?"

"We'll want his stories taken down. I understand you know short-hand, Harry?"

"Yes."

"Part of your education as a reporter?"

I shrug. "I quit school when I was fourteen – to help my mother out. I went to work clerking in a grocery store. I thought night-school commercial classes were a way to improve my prospects – typing, shorthand, bookkeeping, that sort of thing."

"Very good. When you find him I want you to interview him; I want every word taken down and delivered to me. And there are other things in which your good judgement and experience would be invaluable. Would he be an asset in a publicity campaign? Would the press and public take a shine to him?" Chance hesitates. "Is he co-operative? Co-operation will be important. You know what I'm say-ing, don't you?"

"Yes."

"Good. And don't forget, if we are successful, at some stage this raw material will need to be shaped into a scenario. Who better qualified to write the scenario than the man who got the story from the horse's mouth? Up until now you've worked only as a title-writer. It would be a great opportunity for you, to write a big picture, wouldn't it, Harry?"

We both leave that question unanswered because the answer is obvious.

"So who is it that I'm supposed to find? What's his name?"

Chance raises a cautionary finger. "Don't take what I'm about to say amiss, Harry. But before I divulge his name I need some assur-ances from you. A promise that what we have discussed here will remain absolutely confidential. This is a matter for the three of us in this room and no one else. I am aware of what my reputation in this town is. The pampered son of a rich man, dabbling in pictures, a rank amateur. For that reason, I prefer my affairs kept private. If what I'm up to were made public, my enemies would twist it to make me look ridiculous. I won't be made a laughing stock."

"I can keep my mouth shut," I assure him. "But they'll want to know what I'm up to in the office. It's impossible to keep anything quiet in the office."

"This job won't require you to work in the office. Stay away from the office. At least for the time being."

"That in itself will raise questions –"

Chance interrupts forcefully. "Fitz will arrange things in the office. None of that need concern you."

"Fine. Let Mr. Fitzsimmons take care of it. But I still need to know who I'm looking for."

Chance leans forward, picks up a can of film lying on the floor, waves it at Fitzsimmons. "Denis, put this in the projector for us. There's a good fellow." Fitz does what he is told, deftly and efficiently; in moments all is ready. "Out with the lights, Fitz. Let us begin!" Chance cries gaily.

The projector starts to whir, the lamp beside us is extinguished, the film begins to jump and twitch on the screen. What we are looking at seems to me raw, unedited footage of the dime-a-dozen Westerns that every studio in southern California churns out like sausage. None of the title cards have been inserted and this makes the story hard to follow. This is what I make of it.

There is a trial. An ill-favoured fiend is convicted of something on the testimony of a beautiful young girl. A handsome officer of the law embraces her ardently as the villain is carted off to his cell, shrieking imprecations and struggling in the grasp of his jailers. Next, there are shots of a wagon train and of the lovely young woman sitting on a wagon seat, apparently singing, her lovely face tilted up to the sky. Then – a jailbreak! Gunplay, honest citizens shot down like dogs in the street, horses galloping, swarms of dust.

Later, the villain kneeling beside wagon ruts, shaking his fist, presumably swearing revenge to the same sky the heroine serenaded. Followed by night. The wagon train encamped in a circle, a blazing fire, a geyser of sparks, eerily luminous smoke shuddering up into the black sky. Three men saw soundless fiddles, a boy twangs a silent jew's-harp, a mute concertina snakes back and forth between hands. Men in big boots swing women in calico dresses and poke bonnets.

I can feel Chance stirring on the sofa beside me, his body tense with anticipation. I glance over at him. He is staring at the screen with such intensity that his soft, full face is as rigid as a granite Buddha's. Suddenly he springs to his feet, gives a sharp, nervous tug to his trouser legs and skips to the screen. The hot white light of the projector glazes his features, giving him the queer, fixed look of a ceramic doll.

The camera cuts to a little dog, jigging on its hind legs. Round and round it hops, tongue lolling. An old man joins in the dog's dance, capering in a spry, lock-jointed way, waving crooked arms above his head. The dog leaps against his legs, barking and barking, noiselessly.

"Him," says Chance, holding a finger up to the face on the screen. Seemingly on his command, the camera cuts to a close-up. The old face swells, filling the screen the way a dream fills the mind. A huge, eroded face. He's laughing now, the old man, the white stubble of his beard standing up like bristles on the back of an enraged hog, the deep eye sockets black and charred-looking, as if they had been burned into the face with a red-hot poker. "Him. His name is Shorty McAdoo. Find him for me, Harry."

It is after three o'clock in the morning when Fitz and I leave Chance's house. There are many things to discuss and plan. I am to have a car placed at my disposal. I am to have an expense account. I am to have an increase in salary from seventy-five dollars a week to one hundred and fifty dollars a week. I am to find Shorty McAdoo and get his story. I am to do this without revealing who I am working for.

When he bids me goodbye, Chance says, "My regrets at keeping you so late, Harry. But I do not sleep well. I sometimes forget that others are not accustomed to the same hours."

"You'd get more sleep if it wasn't for the speech-making in the middle of the night," says Fitzsimmons disapprovingly.

"It is not speech-making," Chance answers sharply. "It is thinking aloud. Thinking aloud, Denis."

Fitz, reproved, shrugs.

Going down the long white corridor that morning, descending the long curved staircase, I feel the same anxiety I experienced earlier. In the midst of the silence, the starkness, I become too aware of myself. I watch my hand slide along the banister, my foot plant itself on the next step. Out of the corner of my eye I catch the ladder-backed chair isolated on the cold marble floor of the ballroom, the strangeness of its position.

3

Seeing as it was unseasonably fine that morning of April 16, 1873, the swells took the opportunity to cut a figure by promenading to and fro on the hurricane deck of the *Yankton*. The stern-wheeler had been due to depart Sioux City, Iowa, at ten a.m. sharp, but loading one hundred and eighty ton of freight and ten cord of wood to fire the boilers was taking longer than expected. A number of the topside gents flashed pocket watches in the pale spring sunshine and rattled souvenir gold-nugget watch fobs from the Montana gold fields to illustrate their impatience. The remainder strolled about with a grave and stoical air, frock coats unbuttoned to display paisley waistcoats and brightly checkered peg-top pants stuffed into knee-high boots. Like clockwork, they lifted their hats to the same two ladies they kept meeting on their circuit around the pilot house, or paused to lean out and launch impressive arcs of dirty brown tobacco juice into the dirty brown waters of the Missouri.

Down below, on the levee, a crowd of several hundred jostled feverishly, clutched by the excitement which always accompanied the season's first run to Fort Benton, head of navigation on the Great Muddy. Well-wishers called goodbyes to relatives and friends jammed solid against the rails of the lower deck; children and dogs blundered about in the blind alleys of legs and skirts; roustabouts traded rustic sallies with departing deck hands. On the fringes of the crowd an old blind black man, hat in outstretched hand, sang with much fervour

26

and little profit until a teamster driving a freight wagon swore to peel the skin off his back if he didn't haul his black arse out of the way. The tatterdemalion's tiny granddaughter led him away by the sleeve.

The sun climbed higher and the twin stacks of the *Yankton* belched black smoke and sparks into the mild spring sky as she built a head of steam. Several shrill warning blasts were loosed on the boat whistle, summoning all aboard, and the ladies flagged the air with cambric handkerchiefs and piped falsetto farewells, farewells suddenly overwhelmed by the ear-splitting squeals of a stray pig entangled with two dogs, one with its teeth sunk in the sow's hindquarter, the other in her ear.

Then the Englishman sailed into sight, parting bedlam like Moses the Red Sea, sauntering coolly up the gangplank in the latest word in bicycling suits: tweed coat, braided trousers, Hessian boots, bowler hat, glories which momentarily stilled the multitude and cast the boys on the upper deck utterly into the shade, one of whom grimly remarked, "The things you see when you ain't got a gun." Behind the Englishman, stooped under a load of gun cases, Gladstones, and pigskin valises, plodded a young tough in broken-down boots, his face half-hidden by a wide-awake hat gone green with age.

Once these two were safely aboard, the crew smartly shipped the gangplank and to tumultuous cheering and a continuous shrieking of the boat whistle the *Yankton* began to forge its way upstream, the entire boat vibrating with the effort of its engines, pulsing and shuddering like a living thing as it beat against the current. Slowly, Sioux City shrank from sight and the brown boredom of the Missouri spread itself before crew and passengers, a monotony relieved only by the menace of snags and sandbars, by rapid shifts of weather and sky. The boys on the hurricane deck buttoned their coats as the breeze freshened and hurried down to the lounge to uncork a jug of bourbon and inaugurate a month-long game of poker.

Despite making an unfortunate first impression, the Englishman, whose name was John Trevelyan Dawe, proved to be popular with passengers and crew. He lost money at poker with equanimity, stood drinks with aplomb, made gallant and edifying conversation with the handful of ladies who qualified as respectable. When inquiries were made as to what he was doing in this part of the world, Mr. Dawe declared he was a sportsman, come to trophy-hunt. He talked a good deal, but interestingly, so his volubility was forgiven.

Some of the gents, particularly the Southerners, didn't approve of his referring to the white boy as his manservant. In their opinion, if he wanted a servant he ought to have hired himself a nigger. Their displeasure, however, was somewhat alleviated when the Englishman complained that the boy refused to shave him, brush his clothes, or black his boots. The gentlemen told him this wasn't England. In America, niggers came in only one colour – black. The Englishman said that if this was democracy, it was outrageous.

The boy, however, did condescend to keep his employer's hunting gear in good order. Most afternoons he could be found sitting outside their cabin surrounded by the Englishman's armoury, sharpening knives and hatchets, cleaning and oiling the Colt pistol, the Winchester, the Henry, the Sharps breechloading buffalo gun, the Westly Richards tiger gun. The frock coats were mightily intrigued by this latter example of British gunsmithing. As the boy worked, the gun-fanciers clustered around him and loudly debated the merits and demerits of the two-foot-long .65-calibre barrel, of the one-ounce ball it fired, of the ingenious spring which regulated the trigger pull.

One week out from Sioux City, Dawe propped this cannon on the railing of the second deck, drew a bead on a lone bull buffalo a hundred yards distant on a cutbank overhanging the Missouri and fired a shot that spun the Englishman on the deck boards like a dust devil. The smoke cleared. The bull stood on the promontory, motionless as a statue on a pediment. Limey marksmanship and Limey guns were hooted. Then, suddenly, in mid-hoot, the buffalo crumpled up like brown butcher paper balled in an invisible hand, pitched headlong over the cutbank, ploughed down the slope in a fanfare of uprooted willow and bounding stones, sliding to rest in the shallows of the river, a hole over its heart big enough to put your fist in. As one of the gents said later, "You shoot a tiger with that, the only way you going to get you a tiger rug is hold a quilting bee and stitch the bitty pieces together again." With one shot the Englishman vaulted from curiosity to celebrity. Someone even reversed policy and bought *him* a drink that night.

The *Yankton* proceeded upriver, slow and unstately. Often she ran aground and had to "grasshopper" herself off sandbars with short bursts of power to the stern wheel and winches attached to long spars planted in the muck on either side of the bows. There were other delays. High winds forced her to lay up. The boiler burned through and had to be repaired. A deck hand fell overboard and drowned; his corpse had to be retrieved and buried. Ten days out from Sioux City, a herd of buffalo turned the channel black and bellowing and solid, so solid a man could have walked from bank to bank, using their backs as stepping stones. Passengers broke out guns and whisky and soon the *Yankton* was cloaked in shifting clouds of blue gun-smoke, lit with orange muzzle-flashes like a painting of the battle of Trafalgar. The gents on the hurricane deck poured fire down into the river, levering their Winchesters like pump handles, ejected casings making brass rainbows as they arced into the air. Some of the great beasts passed so close to the boat that men in steerage hung over the rails, touching the muzzles of their rifles to their humps as they fired. Dozens of the dead spun in the grip of the current, streaming tributary blood, the wounded roaring as they were sucked downstream. Hunters ran frenziedly from starboard to port, struggling for one last shot, whooping and swearing and jostling for vantage, throwing spent rifles to the deck and drawing revolvers which they emptied into the dark, struggling mass. And all the while, a prospector pranced about the deck, sawing "Dixie" on a fiddle, as the bodies swept by, like sandbars torn loose from their moorings.

The further the boat journeyed up the river and the closer it drew to its ultimate destination, the more vexing delays became for those on board. Frequent halts were made to take on fuel, either at the yards of "woodhawks" or, between stations, to land parties to cut wood. When men were landed, the captain saw to it that they were accompanied by an armed guard for fear of hostiles, a guard for which the Englishman always volunteered himself and his manservant. Once ashore, the Indian-fighting gents who had blown hard on the hurricane deck about the scalps they had lifted turned uneasy, bickering about whose turn it was to deploy himself as a lonesome lookout on the fringes of the cottonwood groves. Dawe's sweet-tempered and smooth-as-butter manner sawed on their nerves, seemed a reproach to the ants scurrying in their pants. They put it down to his ignorance of the kind of devious, heartless, sneaking, despicable, dirty foes Indians were. It grated on them the way he talked, booming his way through the willows with that plummy, toney voice, like he was bugling for Peigans, trumpeting them in for the kill. He made everyone edgy, everyone, that is, except the skinny kid beside him who had no other handle than "the Englishman's boy." No one had troubled to ask this boy his name, and if they had, an answer was no certainty. The Englishman might have known it, but nobody ever heard him use it. Dawe just called him "boy."

Dawe's boy had the gaunt, cadaverous look of the rural poor, of the runt who has sucked the hind tit, who has been whupped with horse-halters and stove-wood, anything hard and hurting that came to hand. His anthracite eyes did his talking for him. They said: Expect no quarter. Give none. He owned a face white and cold as a well-digger's ass. He didn't string more than five words together at a time and no one could place his accent. He was seventeen but looked fifteen, stunted by a diet of bread and lard and strong tea. Everyone took him for a runaway from some hard-scrabble, heartbreak farm. Out West, his kind were thick as ticks on a dog.

He made quite a sight armed with the Englishman's fine guns, a lethal scarecrow with pearl-handled Colt revolver tucked into the pocket of a patched jacket, chased Winchester cradled in his arms, a bandolier of cartridges draped over his shoulder. He walked with a hunter's tread in his rotten boots, heel-toe, heel-toe, alone through the drifted leaves, the budding trees, deeper into the thickets, the voices behind him starting to shimmer and blend with the ringing of the axes, the rasp of the saws. When he found a suitable tree, he climbed, Winchester tied around his neck with a leather thong, light and nimble and easy, stepping higher and higher up the branch-rungs, up to his roost in the last bough stout enough to support him. There he clung, swaying in the wind, scanning the dun plains heaving themselves off into the distance, watching for Assiniboine, Sioux, Peigan. There he clung, smiling. He had heard one of the fancy men ask the Englishman why he had brought the kid ashore. Could he shoot? Because unless the Englishman knew he could shoot, there was no point bringing him. "I don't know if he can shoot," Dawe had said. "But I do know he'll stand and fight."

The Englishman's boy wasn't a smiler. Even with the moon standing brave and blue between the funnels of the *Yankton*, the hard prairie stars glittering ice-chips, the boat rocking in the ebb and lull of the water, he did not treat himself to a smile, especially not when dancing. The quality liked niggers and white trash like him to grin when entertaining. "Fly them heels, boy!" they shouted. He flew them. But he handed around no smiles. From the waist up he was rigor mortis, plank-stiff, arms nailed to his sides, poker-faced. But below, the greasy pant legs flapped and bucked, the skinny legs jerked and twitched, the boots drummed the deck boards louder and louder. "Buck and wing!" the women cried, and the coins, white as frost, began to skip and bounce about the blurry boots. Around and around he spun, showing himself to the whole encroaching circle like a damn hurdy-gurdy girl, cutting licks and capers on the deck, faster and faster, outracing the wheeze of the mouth organ, the scrape of the fiddle, outracing the faces looming dizzily at him against a background of dark water, dark sky, faces glaring white-hot in the light of kerosene lamps.

Fill your eyes, you sons of bitches. Throw your money. This poor whoreson's a-dancing on your grave. Believe it.

Hung there suspended between a desert sky and a desert earth, ears humming with wind, alert and predatory as a hawk, he smiled. The Englishman knew him if nobody else did.

4

I have a face and a name. With these, my pursuit of Shorty McAdoo can begin. But the first business I have to take care of the morning after my meeting with Chance is my mother. I telephone the director of the Mount of Olives Rest Home and order her moved to a larger room, one with plenty of sun and plenty of windows she can spend her time cleaning. Thanks to the miraculous doubling of my salary, I can afford to do it.

My mother had a hard life and one of the hardest things in it was my father. Because he was a labourer in railroad construction, we saw almost nothing of him from the time the frost went out of the ground until it went back into it. That suited me just fine, but in the winters we paid for it, having a lantern-jawed bully to contend with day after day, the three of us trapped in a cramped apartment where my mother and I went around on tiptoe so as not to provoke him. The only time I ever saw his hardness shaken was when he was drunk. Then he would sometimes go terribly maudlin, cry and beg for forgiveness after he hit my mother, or take me up on his knee, rub my face raw with a two-day growth and blubber about my lameness.

At last, one winter when I was ten, he neglected to come home to Saskatoon for the winter. We had been abandoned. My mother took this very badly; worry about money always made her desperate. She took work cleaning houses and we stumbled along from one financial disaster to another, often rescued by municipal relief, or church charities. All this took its toll, and during the next four years her behaviour became increasingly erratic and odd. Often, when she should have been at work, I would come home from school to find her lying despondent on the couch, all the curtains in the apartment drawn, the place cloaked in stale darkness. If I talked to her, she wouldn't answer; if I coaxed her to eat, she refused. I began to spend more and more time away from home, mostly in the public library where it was warm and the old-maid librarian treated me kindly. In the beginning, I read biographies of poor boys who had made good like Thomas Alva Edison, Henry Ford, and Andrew Carnegie, seeking to discover the key to the money that would rescue her. But in time, like her I too lost hope, and as an escape turned to reading Walter Scott, Robert Louis Stevenson, G.A. Henty.

By the time I turned fourteen, the writing was on the wall. My mother was no longer remotely capable of holding a job and I quit school to help support us. I started as a stock and delivery boy in a grocery, gradually working my way up to clerk. I liked school and resented leaving, but my despair was not total. Queen Victoria had not been dead so very long then, and the nineteenth century had wrapped a warm muffler of sentiment around the hearts of school-marms, Dickens having made cripples touching and lovable. I hated those female teachers whose faces went sweetly vacuous and temporizingly benign when they turned to me. Although they didn't mean them to, those looks thrust me on the outside. Outside became a state of mind. Maybe that's what Chance's intuition detected in me, that, and a sense of grievance. Because of Chance, for the first time in my life I felt myself gratefully moving to the centre of something important, admitted to an inner circle.

In 1914 war broke out. If a bum leg ever had a silver lining, my luck was that being crippled preserved me from the slaughter in Flanders, probably saved my life. There seemed to be no luck that could save my mother. With every year that passed, her condition worsened, apathy and depression now alternating with periods of wild, frantic activity. Returning from work, I would find all the furniture in the flat piled in the middle of the floor while she "housecleaned," scrubbing everything in sight with a crazy, fixed determination. One day I came home to discover the building in an uproar; she had let herself into a neighbour's unlocked apartment and "house-cleaned" that, too, going so far as to burn some of Mrs. Kenzie's dirty laundry in a barrel out back. The police were called, she was brought before a magistrate, and committed to the North Battleford Hospital for the Insane.

A year later, I left Saskatchewan, the doctors telling me her case was hopeless. On my final visit, as she sat on a ward surrounded by forty other female lunatics, she asked one thing of her son. To buy her a new dress so if I happened to lose the memory of her face I would be able to pick her out by her clothing the next time I visited.

I headed for the States in the winter of 1919, hungry for a future. For the next couple of years I drifted around the Pacific Northwest doing odd jobs, the longest of which was working on a weekly newspaper in a small town in Washington. Then *The Sentinel* went under and I hit the road again, making my way to Los Angeles. It was there that Rachel Gold tossed me a life jacket. I was living in the YMCA and limiting myself to one meal a day, bacon and eggs, the cheapest hot meal on the lunch-counter menu, when a woman climbed up on a stool beside me and struck up a conversation about the book I was reading, Jack London's *The Iron Heel*. That in itself was unusual; back in those days, even in the Babylon which the American public presumed Los Angeles to be, women didn't strike up conversations with strange men. It wasn't long before I learned just how unusual a woman Rachel Gold was. She was the first "new" woman I had ever met, a woman on the pattern of Anita Loos and Dorothy Parker, wittily cynical, tough, intellectual, and very pretty. She came right out and asked what I thought of the book, a novel that predicted the destruction of the labour movement and a takeover of the United States government by a fascist organization. I said I found it farfetched. In seconds, she was contradicting me, squirming restlessly on the counter stool, tugging and twisting fistfuls of her lacquer-black hair, cut short in the Clara Bow style, looking like a woman trying to shake, to wring ideas out of her brain. I didn't argue, only laughed and shrugged. Who else did I read? she wanted to know. What did I think of Mencken? In minutes, we found common ground in an admiration for Dreiser and Norris. As she talked she radiated a kind of alertness, an electricity that made it impossible to take your eyes off her. She was small, quick in speech and gesture; her dark brown eyes were quick too, flashing her judgements a split-second before she spoke them. She was vulgar and funny; she made me laugh. Of Dreiser she said, "He's the greatest American novelist not writing in English." She mentioned her second husband, "A guy," she said, "who always looked good spending somebody else's money at the race-track." She had no conception of privacy and when she asked me what I did, her charm prompted me to tell her the truth. I said I was out of work. At the end of an hour, she butted out her last cigarette, hopped down off the stool, and thrust a tiny white hand at me. "Rachel Gold," she said. I gave her my name and we shook hands. She wanted to know where I was staying; I told her. "Well, be seeing you," she said as she swung out of the lunch room, a little woman of five feet, owner of bewitching hips.

The next morning there was a note for me at the desk of the YMCA with an address – if I was interested in a job. This is how I became a junior scenarist at Zenith Pictures. As impossible as it sounds, things like this happened in Hollywood in those days. The whole business was shaking down into what it was to become, and while it did, everything was provisional, raw, sketchy. Plumbers like Fatty Arbuckle and laundresses like Mabel Normand became overnight stars. People learned on the job; there were no such things as qualifications, except knowing somebody. The person I knew – scarcely knew – was Rachel Gold, a scriptwriter who I had no idea was as respected, as sought-after in Hollywood as Elinor Glyn, Frances Marion, and Anita Loos, women who then wielded more power behind the scenes than any women in Hollywood have since.

On Rachel Gold's say-so I got hired. But as she said, "Around here you get one kick at the cat and you better hit it square in the ass, or you'll be out of here tomorrow." I became a protégé of hers, an unofficial assistant. It is often said of men that they divide women into virgins and whores and I believe Rachel Gold did something similar with men; to her they were either *mensches* or gigolos. A *mensch* was a man you could talk to but wouldn't sleep with, and a gigolo was a man you could sleep with but wouldn't want to talk to. Her first husband, a Jewish optometrist, whom she had married when she was seventeen, was a *mensch*. Her second husband, a Gentile from South Carolina, the man who impressively and caddishly decorated race-tracks and gambling dens, had been a gigolo.

In Rachel's eyes, I definitely fell into the *mensch* category and that made it possible for her to work with me. A lot of my time was spent vetting books for her scenarios, horrifically bad melodramas she couldn't bring herself to read. If I said a novel had potential, then she would read it. The rest of my time I wrote titles, the cards flashed on-screen to help the audience follow the plot of the movie. My first day in the writing department Rachel Gold gave me her crash course in the art of scenario-writing, delivered in the Menckenian rhetoric she often affected when talking about the movie business and the Booboisie it catered to. "There is only one principle of successful comedy-writing – Kick Authority in the Ass," she declared. "When the Posterior of Power is clutched in agony, all the little people from Mobile to Minneapolis are convulsed with hilarity. So kick him, My Little Truth Seeker, kick him." On writing subtitles for the historical epics then in vogue, her advice was, "For anything prior to 1600, be it Babylon or Tudor England, crib the King James version of the Bible. This satisfies the nose-pickers in Chattanooga who can read, although sometimes they get confused and believe they're conning the word of God, which can later lead to confusion in tent meetings. For American historical costume dramas, the Declaration of Independence is an unfailing model for the speech of the quality. When it comes to frontier gibberish I merely reproduce the kitchen-table conversation of the relatives of my former husband. The Gentile one."

"The true test of any scenario," Rachel was fond of saying, "is to read it to a cameraman. Cameramen are invariably Irish and invariably drunk. If they can grasp the plot, the moral, the *theme* of your simple tale through an alcoholic haze, you can be assured you have struck the proper intellectual level. If one of these sons of the Emerald Isle happens to weep upon hearing your masterpiece, what can I say except – El Dorado! A word to the wise. Never consult a story editor about your script. Story editors are people who once harboured higher literary ambitions – such as writing fiction for one of the better women's magazines. A house divided against itself cannot stand, Vincent, and story editors are cracked from top to bottom, conscience-stricken souls who berate themselves for selling out for a mess of pottage. They are whores who delude themselves they only lent their cherries, not irretrievably lost them. I, on the other hand, know exactly who popped me, when, where, and for how much."

I owe a lot to Rachel Gold. I owe her the seventy-five-dollar-a-week job that allowed me to bring my mother down from Canada, to place her in the Mount of Olives Rest Home. And now because of the train of events she set in motion I find myself more than a scenarist; I find I have become a detective.

5

After a passage of thirty-two days, the riverboat *Yankton* made Fort Benton. When the mountain steamer hove round the bend, the whole town, warned by the smoke she had shown on the horizon, was turned out to greet her, to celebrate the breaking of the winter's siege. For three weeks there had been no tobacco, no flour, no dried fruit, no molasses, no bacon to be had. Minnie Rifle Whisky, watered, and then revived with cayenne pepper, was selling a dollar a glass at the only saloon with stock. For two weeks the whole country, Indians, independent traders, trappers, mule-skinners, bullwhackers, had fore-gathered in Benton to await the arrival of supplies.

Now the cannon in the old adobe fort boomed a welcome which clapped and echoed in the river valley as young bloods whooped lathered horses up and down the riverbank, firing pistols in the air. On the levee, merchant dignitaries waited in a knot of sombre black coats and high-collared white shirts, Old Glory at their side, the flag doleful for want of a breeze. A French priest or two, a Methodist preacher, clerks, the better tradesmen, dowdy ravens flocked together in black. Ranged behind them, trappers and whisky-traders, bear-greased hair to their shoulders, bristling with guns, dressed in stinking linsey-woolsey shirts and buckskin trousers, boots and parfleche-soled moccasins, kit-fox caps and store-bought felt hats. Faro dealers and freighters, bar-keeps and crib girls, sin and civilization all met on a riverbank. And Frenchies, Métis from Canada, Creoles from the mouth of the Mississippi, interpreters, oarsmen, cordeliers in hooded capotes and beaded moccasins, wide sashes cinched tight at their waists. And their wives, women of every Plains tribe, a few in the white woman's calico dress with blanket leggings peeking out from under the hem, the rest in soft ivory buckskin, Boston shawls around their shoulders, gimcrack brooches pinned to their bosoms, moon faces shining. A little further to the rear stood Peigans from the big encampment which had gathered outside of Benton to trade winter buffalo robes, one hundred and fifty lodges sprawled out on the flats, ringed by vast herds of grazing horses, the cook-fires hazing the air with thin blue smoke and scenting it with the aroma of fat meat cooking, the nights throbbing with the firefly light of hundreds of lodge fires, pulsing with drumming and the piping of elk effigy whistles as young men paid court to girls of marrying age. To salute the *Yankton*, these bachelors had dandified themselves with their best weasel-fur fringed shirts and daubed their faces with ochre, white clay, bright Chinese vermilion. As the captain strode down the gangplank to shake hands with functionaries of the I.G. Baker Company and the passengers spilled off the boat in unseemly haste, wading through the river mud for the town, the Peigans watched the ceremonies of the white man with a dispassion bordering on contempt.

The last passenger to disembark was John Trevelyan Dawe, carried off on a blanket by three crew members and his boy. They slung him into the wagon bed of a teamster, packed his luggage tightly about him, and spread a coat over his face to keep the sun out of his eyes.

"What's ailing your friend?" the driver suspiciously asked the boy. He didn't like the way the Englishman's teeth chattered and clicked.

"Ague," said the boy.

"Sure 'tain't mountain fever?"

"I said her once," the boy said, putting his foot to the wheel and boosting himself up on to the seat beside the teamster. "You got your trip money. Move them skinny mules."

Soon they were rumbling down Front Street, the Englishman rattling and groaning on the wagon bed. Front Street wasn't much, white dust and a ramshackle collection of log, frame, and adobe buildings, a thoroughfare littered with horse droppings, torn playing cards, and chamber-pot slops that Fort Benton's sporting women tossed out their bedroom windows. Wild-eyed men wandered in and out among the wagons and horsemen, on the verge of being ridden down or driven over. Bursts of cheering and the energetic thumping of bar-room pianos by saloon "professors" announced the broaching of the first whisky barrels, which had been galloped posthaste up from the *Yankton* by buckboard. Merriment was epic and general. In a situation of robust supply, the price of whisky had plummeted to two bits a shot.

The proprietor of the Overland Hotel was loath to let a sick man on the premises, saying it was bad for custom. For a time the Englishman's boy stood silent. Then he said, "Nothing worse than fire for business."

The owner wanted to know what he meant.

"Never know about fire," said the boy. "Comes out of nowhere sometimes, like a thief in the night."

He got his room. For three days the Englishman alternately shook with a bone chill or swam in a greasy sweat slick as melted butter, the fever frying him like pork in a skillet. The boy never left his side, God's rightful angel of mercy. His own Pap had died of a like complaint, fire and ice, his spleen swelling like the Englishman's, rising below the ribs hard as a piece of oak, bulging out in what was dubbed the "ague cake."

In snatches the Englishman's boy would doze on the floor, waking when Dawe commenced raving and thrashing on his straw tick, hollering for some woman called Nanny Hooper. The Englishman's boy had seen his share die, and it was frequent they called on their mamma in the testing time, the hour of travail, travelling back to the years of the milk-titty. But the Englishman just bellered for his Nanny Hooper, whosoever she might be when to home.

The second night came the convulsions. Straddling Dawe's chest he rode the bucking pony, grabbing fistfuls of hair to pin the flailing head to the pillow while the Englishman's face slowly turned black, his eyes rolling back in their sockets, his heels beating a frantic tattoo on the hard mattress.

The third night there was nothing left to do but sit on a hard chair and listen to the sound of the ragged, hoarse breathing wind down. Towards two in the morning Dawe suddenly cried, "Nanny! Nanny! Nanny!" in the high voice of a little child, then he curled himself up on his pallet and died. The boy straightened the limbs, washed the body, tied the jaw shut with a hanky, closed his eyes. He didn't know what a dead Englishman required in the way of a leave-taking so he sat back down on the hard chair with his hands on his knees and sang "Amazing Grace" to the naked white body, the aubergine face and yellow eyelids.

Going through the deceased's effects he was surprised to find so little real money, only forty-five dollars in gold coin. He had heard Dawe say a line of credit was arranged for him at I.G. Baker Company, but a dead man couldn't draw cash nor goods and the Englishman's boy was owed two months' wages.

He appropriated Dawe's tweed jacket and bowler. Both were sizes too big for him, but he could wear the hat by stuffing the sweatband with the old newspapers which the Englishman had refused to throw away because he said they spoke to him in the soft accents of home. The boy pulled on the jacket and examined himself in a yellowed mirror. With the cuffs turned back it would serve. Warm and a hard-wearer. He slipped a box of revolver cartridges in his left-hand pocket and a box of cartridges for the carbine in his right. Last of all, he crossed two bandoliers on his chest, buckled on the holstered Colt, and slung the Winchester over his shoulder in its saddle-scabbard. As close as he could calculate, with some generosity allowed for the risks he had taken nursing the Englishman, this was what he was entitled to. The rest of the Englishman's worldly goods and possessions he left behind.

The owner was not on duty, a night clerk nodded in a chair. The boy tapped the counter with his knuckles and asked to settle up. The bill came to fifteen dollars for three nights' lodging, six dollars for meals delivered cold to the room, five dollars for a bottle of whisky he'd dosed Dawe with when he was taken with the chills. Twenty-six dollars. Computing the inconvenience of a corpse, he handed the desk clerk forty, and kept back the last five of the Englishman's ready money for himself.

The clerk asked if the fourteen dollars extra was on account for his friend, was he staying on?

"Until you bury him," said the boy. "I took what's owed me. The rest of his guns, his personals – they're yours now."

"You ain't leaving a dead man on premises!" the clerk shouted after him as he went through the door. "Here, you! Stop!"

The boy walked on. He figured they'd do all right burying Dawe, it had to be purely profit. There were silver-backed hairbrushes and a gold watch up in that room. There were shirt-studs and rings in a jewellery case, fancy guns, drummer's clothes. He could've taken his pick of it all and gone out a window, but creeping and crawling wasn't his line. He remembered what the Englishman had said about him down the Missouri, that he'd stand and fight. If it wasn't for the sake of those few words he wouldn't have stopped a minute with the dying man – the truth be known, he hadn't liked him much. His Pap had taught him his lessons about rich men. The soft words of a whore and a whore's hard heart, hand in your pocket. Still, the Englishman had spoken him his due, allowed he had spunk, and was owed his due in return.

The Englishman's boy went out into false dawn, presentiment of morning, the big coat and big hat and the expensive guns rendering him ridiculous and a shade sinister at the same time. The night clerk came to the door of the Overland Hotel, ready to press his point, but seeing him there lit by the light spilling from the doorway, dwarfed by another man's clothes, dwarfed by the long shadow rooted to his heels and stretched in tortured protraction across the pale dust of the street, he felt a sudden unease and hurriedly turned back inside.

The door slammed and the boy sniffed the cold air, looked deliberately up and down the street. A few horses were still standing saddled and tethered to hitching posts outside the saloons, looming in the pearl-grey light like the strange horses that galloped through the last days of the world, the horses his mother had read to him out of the Bible. The boy walked on as the horses snuffled and nickered and tossed their heads in apprehension, walked on past the silent, shut-tered hurdy-gurdy houses and saloons, past I.G. Baker's and T.C. Power's big trading concerns, past a livery stable, a blacksmith shop, a bunkhouse for bullwhackers, walked on with the numbness induced by three days of sleeplessness, propelling one boot mechan-ically in front of the other. It was a short street in a short town and soon he had walked himself out of it and into a wilderness of space, the forlorn sweep of sky and land offering the final proof he was trapped in this town. There was nowhere to go. He had no horse. The *Yankton* had left town as soon as she unloaded and headed back downriver. In any case, five dollars wouldn't have bought him a ticket in steerage, wouldn't buy him much of anything in a boom-town of sky-high prices.

He sat down on a rock, back to the rising sun, and wrapped him-self tighter in the tweed jacket. One thing for certain, he couldn't stomach sweeping out no more saloons, nor sloshing out no more cuspidors, nor being at the beck and call of bar-keeps, piano players with two left hands, frail sisters, and soiled doves. He was done with all that. Sooner starve like a dog in a ditch than be whistled up by the likes of them. And he knew ditches, had more than a winking acquaintance with them in the two years since his brother put the run on him.

It might be one thing to swallow a whipping at the hands of your Pap, but he didn't figure that whipping rights had passed along to Dan with the farm when the old man died. Seeing as his brother was four years older and forty pounds heavier, he'd took it for a while, but then one day when he'd had enough, he'd done Dan with a shovel, whacked his head good and sound, same as a nail. One swing to pound him onto his knees, two more to peg him flat and level with the dust. That shovel blade had rung sweet as any church bell to his ears, whanging away on Dan's poll.

So there his brother had laid swooning in the yard for nigh on an hour, the chickens clucking and cocking their heads at him, eye-ing the blood leaking from his scalp and puddling on the ground. But at last Dan gave himself a shake, climbed to his feet like the risen Lazarus, and reeled for the cabin, muddy gore caked to his face. When he sallied back out with the flintlock, raising the stakes like that, gun against a shovel, what was he to do but fold his hand, cut and run? Now that he owned guns of his own, one at his belt, one at his back, God help any poxy bastard who snicked a bullet past his ear the way Dan had. He was done with showing his heels to any man.

The Englishman's boy turned his eyes over his shoulder and to the river bluffs across the Missouri. There the strong glow of the rising sun lit a mass of shelving cloud so that it appeared a bank of molten lava squeezed from the guts of the earth, each striation distinct and gleaming with a different fire. The topmost layer the rich ruddy pur-ple of cooling slag; then the dim cherry of a horseshoe heated for shaping; then layers of orange and yellow which smelted down to where swollen, bulging hills met the sky in pure white fire. He faced west again where the sun over his shoulder was painting the valley hills with a tenderer light. On the crest of these hills the Englishman's boy could make out three tiny black dots, moving.

They were still so distant he could not make them out, but he pre-sumed they were horsemen. The sun came nudging up behind him, soaring above the folds of the river bluffs. On they came, figures swimming in the waxing light. The Englishman's boy shielded his eyes with his hand and squinted. He wasn't sure, but he thought the three might be afoot. White men didn't go abroad without horses. He took the Winchester off his back and laid it across his knees. The Colt he put no real stock in as yet, having never owned or even fired a short gun before. It was the carbine he trusted because he had been a hunter since the age of seven and a crack shot with a rifle. He sat and waited, hands relaxed on the gun-stock.

By the time the great yellow yolk of the sun was completely clear of the earth, he knew the men descending the slopes to the river flats were not mounted; but it was only God's guess whether they were white or red. At six hundred yards the heads became dots and the bodies tapered. At four hundred yards they still lacked faces. At three hundred yards the heads were blurred, but now he knew they were white men. At two hundred yards they began to resolve into individuals.

Without more delay they were upon him, three men in stinking clothes stiff with grease and blackened with old blood, one of them in a slouch hat with eagle plumes stuck in its beaded band, another who called to mind a flour barrel with legs, the third, a redhead with a wispy beard the colour of a fox's brush and the burned red face and white cracked lips of a man cursed with a complexion unsuited to constant sun and wind. They halted at the rock and leaned on the muzzles of their rifles.

"Morning," said the redhead.

The Englishman's boy nodded warily.

"What's this?" said the stocky one. "Welcoming committee?" He was evidently in an ugly mood.

"Don't pay no mind to Vogle," the redhead told the boy. "He's out of sorts from riding shank's mare. He ain't too light on his feet so's it's a chore."

"Lost your horses?"

"Had twenty head lifted," said the redhead. "Camp's five mile from here up on the Teton. Didn't think there was any need to ride night-herd so close to Benton, but we was wrong. Goddamn Indians would steal horses stabled in your front parlour."

"Ten thousand wolf pelts sitting out there in six wagons and no horses to move them," said the one the redhead called Vogle.

"We can borry teams from I.G.," said the man in the slouch hat. "We'll get them pelts in. I didn't freeze my ass all winter skinning carcasses to get my carcass skinned come spring."

"Not to worry," said the redhead. "We'll get them pelts in right smart and we'll get on the trace of them horses right smart, and we'll spank them red scamps right smart, won't we, boys?"

"Hardwick," remarked Vogle, "I swear to Christ you're happy as a pig in soft shit that them Indians lifted our horses. You're just looking for an excuse to take a crack at them."

Hardwick flashed an uncanny smile. "Happy is the man doing the Lord's work," he said.

"Happy, happy, happy," said the one in the slouch hat. He didn't smile but he spat.

As Hardwick had said, with the loan of six teams and a couple of saddle horses to haze them out to the Teton, the wolfers ran their pelts into Fort Benton right smart. Bumping up Front Street in wagons, they cut a sorry sight, the grim set of their jaws testifying that they knew they were laughing stocks for getting carelessly relieved of their horses on the very doorstep of civilization. In the saloons to which they dispersed, there were sly remarks and winks about infantry and church parades and having to visit a cobbler to get your boots half-soled. That is unless the redhead, Tom Hardwick, happened to be present. He and John Evans were standing drinks all around in an endeavour to recruit a posse to recover the horses and punish the Indians. Both men were well-known in Benton. Most considered Evans an easygoing, affable sort, but Hardwick was held to be a dicey proposition and nobody to mock to his face.

As the day wore on the wolfers got drunker, touchier, and bloodthirstier. There was no stampede of volunteers to help retrieve the horses, and a reluctance to sign on often occasioned charges of cowardice and name-calling, a scuffle or two. Among the wolfers themselves there was resentment against Hardwick for threatening to turn them out of Benton so soon to pursue the horse-rustlers, nipping their fun in the bud after a solitary, cold winter. Philander Vogle, for one, was trying to cram as much amusement as he could into an afternoon at a crib on the line. The crib girls were the cheapest a jump, but they didn't allow you to take your boots off, so Vogle stood at the end of the bed with a bottle in his fist, his pants down around his ankles, waiting for Nature to reassert herself with the wherewithal for a repeat poke. However, the lazy whore kept dozing off in between times – which wasn't much encouragement to Nature.

Throughout the course of the day the Englishman's boy kept moving, drifting up and down the town. He had nowhere to stop, nothing to do, nothing to eat but a box of crackers bought at a general store for an exorbitant price. Left high and dry by the Englishman's untimely death, starvation seemed a probable fate. When he tired of tramping, he perched himself on a wagon tongue or a barrel, the flies and dust from Front Street settling on him as he gnawed his dry crackers and cogitated plans. Maybe he should try to swap his fancy pistol for a double-barrel and shells to keep himself in meat, potting grouse or rabbit or duck. The truth was, no matter how much sense such a scheme might make, no matter how hungry he might get, he knew he was not going to part with the pistol. The pistol made him, for the first time in his life, any man's equal.

When night drew down, Fort Benton grew a good deal livelier even than it was during the day. The saloons poured light and music and drunken patrons into the street where they pissed and fought in the roadway. These fights, noisy affairs with much loud cursing and bellowing of threats, riled the horses tied to the hitching posts to a terrible pitch. They thrashed about, rolling their eyes and tossing their heads until their terror and tension became unbearable. Then they flew at one another, like the men in the street, kicking and biting and rearing until a tether broke and one went careering off helter-skelter down the dark street.

Meanwhile, the Englishman's boy kept on the prowl, sidling out of the way when any particularly dangerous-looking drunk came lurching and muttering out of the gloom. A clear sky spelled that a chilly night was a certainty and staying on the tramp was the only way to keep the cold out of his bones until the livery-stable office closed and he could sneak into the barn and burrow in the hay.

By and by he found himself prevaricating outside the Star Saloon, debating whether or not to invest two bits in a drink. A tot in the belly and a warm place to stop would ease him through the cold hours until it was safe to scare up a place to sleep. It was a thorny, troublesome calculation, money weighed against comfort, but then, through the smeared saloon window, he spied the redheaded Hardwick seated at a poker table. A face he recognized somehow decided him. He went in.

The bar was packed. A fug of dense smoke, animal heat, stale sweat, and rancid grease greeted him as he stepped through the door. The smell of unwashed hide-hunters, mule-skinners, prospectors, and bullwhackers came as a shock after the crisp, clean night air, even to him, who couldn't remember the last time a scrub cloth had touched him. At the far end of the room, behind a low fence with a swinging gate in it, he could see roughnecks galloping hurdy-gurdy girls in dizzy circles to a breakneck air battered out of an untuned piano. Picking his way amid the gambling tables to the bar, he bumped into a man who shot him a drunken, hostile stare. For a moment, the boy couldn't place the stranger and then he recognized the headgear, a collapsible black silk top hat which Dawe had kept stowed in his steamer trunk. Its wearer was none other than the owner of the Overland Hotel, the same man the Englishman's boy had blackmailed into renting them a room.

The boy carried on to the bar, ordered his drink, hooked the heel of his boot on the rail and turned to face the room, glass in hand. The man in Dawe's top hat had his eyes fixed on him. As the boy lifted the tumbler to his lips, a tremor disturbed the surface of the whisky. He held off drinking until it steadied and went smooth as glass, rewarding his coolness with a sip, aware the hotel-keeper had moved in on him, was hovering almost at his elbow.

"You're the son of a bitch who don't pick up after himself, ain't you?" said the hotel man. "Left a corpse in my best bed."

The boy didn't answer. He took another sip of whisky and surveyed the occupants of the saloon.

The hotelier was crowding in, thrusting his face at him. "Left a bill behind, too. Unpaid bill and an Englishman gone high in the heat."

"I settled with your man," the boy said. "You got all was owed – and more."

"You filched the Limey's gear," said the hotel man. "By rights it's mine. I got claim on his chattels. You got movables belong to me." He pointed to the boy's holster. "That fine ivory-handled pistol for one."

"I got nothing belongs to you. The gun is for wages he owed me."

The hotel man smiled. "Wages of sin is death, boy." He brushed back the skirts of his coat and tucked them behind the butt of his pistol. The bravado of a drunken man.

"No wages is starvation and that's death, too," said the boy.

"You goddamn little scut," the top hat said angrily. "Threatening to fire my hotel. You and your Mr. Biggity Big Englishman."

"He couldn't been too big," said the boy. "His hat fits you just fine."

The men nearby were beginning to follow these interesting proceedings. One of them laughed loudly.

Spurred by the laughter, the hotel-keeper cried, "You little son of a bitch! I'll have that gun or I'll have your hide! Depend on it!"

To those looking on, the Englishman's boy raised his voice and said, "This man here is aiming to rob me. You heard him say it. You're witnesses."

The loud announcement attracted attention. Several nearby tables of faro and poker suspended gaming to see how this was going to play out. A portly man in a good coat and good hat shouted, "What you doing, Stevenson? Stealing this sprat's sugar tit?" Everyone around the table guffawed appreciatively at his sally.

"I'm a stranger here," said the boy in a voice which rose above the slackening din. "Whatever falls out here ain't my doing."

Suddenly Stevenson seized him by the wrist of his gun hand. There was no use in struggling. He could sense the power of the man's grip, knew he was not strong enough to break it. He remained very still. Stevenson grinned in his face. "Hello," he said, and suddenly struck him a savage blow to the ear with his fist. The Englishman's boy staggered with the force of it, was jerked up short by the wrist.

Dizzied, the boy said to the room, "I ain't got nothing of this man's. I ain't asking for no trouble." The ringing in his ear made his own voice sound as if it were coming from somewhere distant and deep, the words from his very throat rising out of some unplumbable well.

Stevenson dealt him another blow to the ear. The ear caught fire,

49

the fire sank into his jaw, coursed burning down the side of his neck, running hot in its cords. Stevenson smiled and said "Hello" again. The Englishman's boy could not hear him this time, could only read his lips mouthing the word. The fist cocked again, and the boy dropped his free hand to his boot-top. The hand jumped up with a metallic glitter.

Stevenson's face was all bewildered surprise. He stared down at the knife embedded in his armpit. Then the first shock passed; the steel bit bone like a desperate dog, warping and knotting his face beyond all recognition.

"Leave go my hand," said the boy as he jammed Stevenson up on his toes with the point of the knife. Blood was pouring down the blade like rainwater down a drain spout, soaking the cuff of his jacket sodden and heavy, turning his fingers hot and sticky and reeking.

Stevenson seemed beyond comprehending. Agony was clamping the fingers of his good hand even tighter to the thin wrist.

"Leave go my hand," the boy repeated, twisting the knife hard where it lodged. The knife grating in the joint tore a hoarse screech out of Stevenson and he loosed the wrist.

The pounding piano at the far end of the saloon went silent; the dancers stood still, arms draped around one another; the gamblers sat frozen with cards in their hands.

As Stevenson stood spitted on the knife, the boy pulled the Colt, jammed the muzzle to his head. "Hello," he said between his teeth. The hotel man's eyes bulged. Someone entered the saloon and scurried back out again when he saw what was happening. The hinges of the flapping bat-wing doors wheezed in the silence.

"For Christ's sake, don't kill me," Stevenson whispered hoarsely. "I got a sick wife in Missouri."

Hardwick rose from the table next to the window. The boy swung the pistol on him, Stevenson flinching with the sudden movement. Hardwick spread his hands before him, demonstrating he had no weapon. "Word of friendly advice, son," he said. "You kill him where he stands – they'll hang you."

The truth of this statement contorted the boy's face. He jerked the knife out of Stevenson and drove it, twice, with blinding rapidity into the man's buttocks. The hotel-keeper gave a great hollow groan as his knees gave way under him, capsizing him to the floor in a dead faint.

The boy stepped over the body to where the black silk hat had rolled and trampled it savagely under his dirty boots. No one moved as this was accomplished. "None of this was my doing," he told the room, brandishing the pistol above his head for all to see. "I'm walking now. If this bastard has any kin or friends setting here making plans – you've seen my gun. It's cocked." He took a step toward the door, then pivoted on his heel and kicked the senseless body in the head. "Hello," he said to it one last time.

Now he was moving for the door, the hushed crowd falling back out of his path, falling back from the pistol he carried flush against his right leg, falling back from the strange little figure in the scavenged clothes. He thrust open the swinging doors and strode quickly down the darkened street ten paces, whirled around in his tracks to catch anyone pursuing. He did. Throwing up the pistol he called out, "Stand or I'll fire!"

The figure stopped in the street. "It's Tom Hardwick. Lower your gun." He did. Hardwick advanced. "If you'd been anyplace but where you was," he said, "I'd advised you to kill that man. But there was too much public and it would have looked cold-blooded. There ain't much law in these parts, but there's that much." Hardwick stopped, took a cigar from his shirt pocket, struck a match. He kept on talking around the cigar as he lit it. "You looking to kill that son of a bitch and walk, you ought to put your knife in his belly the second he hit you."

"I give him a chance to back off," said the Englishman's boy.

"Bad policy," said Hardwick. "Don't give nobody a chance." They resumed walking. Hardwick said, "I'd scoot if I was you. That man's a innkeeper and a publican. I never seen a fellow who deals in whisky that was short of friends."

"I can't scoot. I ain't got a horse," said the boy.

"You want to ride with us in the morning I can scare you up a horse," said Hardwick.

For a time the boy walked on without responding. "What would I have to do?" he said finally.

"Whatever circumstances call for," said Hardwick.

Vogle argued against taking the boy. He made the thirteenth recruit and thirteen being the number around the table at the Last Supper, there could be no worse luck. Hardwick said since the only one who'd died on that expedition was the leader, and Vogle wasn't leading nothing, what was he worrying about?

Vogle shook his head. "Thirteen's bad medicine," he said.

"That's the Indian in you talking now," said Hardwick.

6

Harry Vincent, detective, is sitting in a car parked just off Hollywood Boulevard and Cahuenga Avenue, keeping a grey frame
building known as the Waterhole under surveillance. The Waterhole
is a cowboy hangout famous in Hollywood, one part speakeasy, one
part hiring hall. Inside the Waterhole, cowboys play poker and drink
illegal whisky served in china teacups while they wait for picture
directors short of extras to drop by and offer them work. Nobody but
cowboys and directors ever frequent this establishment; tinhorns and
curiosity-seekers are not made to feel welcome in the Waterhole. Even
the cops give it a wide berth and pretend they don't know porch-
climber is sold there. Prohibition may be the law, but the police have
decided meddling with cowboys and their simple pleasures is more
trouble than it's worth.

I've been sitting here for over two hours watching the entrance,
hoping to spot Shorty McAdoo among the patrons who stagger in
and out of the Waterhole on high-heeled riding boots, but no such
luck. There's no use putting it off any longer; the time has arrived to
meddle with the cowboys.

After the hot California sunshine, the shuttered gloom of the
Waterhole leaves me blind. I stand just inside the doorway, blinking,
smelling the place – horse and sweat, tobacco and leather, the rank
fumes of raw alcohol – before I see it. Then I begin to make out
smoke, swirling like fog in the light of a few tin-shaded ceiling lamps,

coiling and curdling greasy yellow under the naked bulbs like milk poured into vinegar. I decipher a crowd of stetsons, the tall hat-crowns wrapped in smoke, toadstools in a shifting ground mist. The toadstools tip back from cards and rose-patterned teacups containing illegal whisky. The glaring light skates down the faces like water down a cliff. They know I'm not a director, so I'm met with nothing but stony, inhospitable stares.

Directors of Westerns like flamboyance, it photographs well, which accounts for the way these boys are duded up. The bigger the hat, the gaudier the costume, the better the chance of being picked for a job. As I wend my way through the tables to the bar, I can sense their hostility; it's a little bit like being dropped into a carnival where all the sideshow attractions resent you for looking at them. And it's hard to ignore the extravagant costuming, screaming for attention the way it does. Beaded Indian vests and brass-studded leather gauntlets, big Mexican spurs with sunburst rowels, chaps of every style – bat-wing, stovepipe, angora – flashy shirts and towering hats, polka-dot bandannas the size of small tablecloths knotted around necks. Street-walkers dolled up to catch the eye of men they despise.

I ask the man behind the bar to pour me what everybody else is having. Apparently everybody else is drinking flat, cold tea. I hold the teacup the way all the cowpokes do, not by the handle, but wrapped in my fist, and nonchalantly inquire of the bartender whether he's seen Shorty lately.

"Shorty who?" he wants to know. "They're all Shorty, or Slim, or Tex, or Yakima."

"Shorty McAdoo."

"I suppose you're going to tell me you're a friend of his."

"No."

"That's good. Because if you did, you'd be a goddamn liar."

"When's the last time you saw him?"

"Four, five weeks ago. Maybe longer."

"But generally he's a regular?"

"Nothing regular about McAdoo. He comes. He goes. Some days

he talks. Some days he don't. Some days he drinks. Some days he don't. I'd call him pretty unregular."

"Where do you think I might locate him?"

The big man pushes himself away from the bar, putting distance between us, folds his arms protectively over a baywindow girded in a filthy apron. "What you want with McAdoo?"

"He'd thank you if you were to point me in his direction. There's money in it for him."

"He ain't given to thanks."

"Then maybe I could do it on his behalf," I say, taking out the envelope of expense money I've been provided with, fishing a ten-spot from it which I lay on the counter. "Where's he live?"

The bartender eyes the money, but he isn't sure. "He ain't going to thank me if you're police."

"It's customary to hire cops with two good legs. You saw me cross the bar."

"It ain't a bar," he says.

"All right, I'll call it a tea shop if it makes you any happier." It doesn't seem to.

"This about that director?"

"What director?" The way I say it he knows I don't have a clue what he is talking about.

"Shorty may be an old man," he says. "But he's a fucking grudgeful old man."

"I don't intend to give him any reason to hold a grudge. Against me or anybody else. I like to be everybody's friend."

He picks up the bill, crushing it in his fist as if he wants it out of sight before anybody notices. "This is all I know. Two months ago somebody said he was bunking at Mother Reardon's."

"Who's Mother Reardon?"

"She runs a boarding house. She likes cowboys. Gives them a preference on rooms."

"Address?"

The bartender takes a stub of pencil from behind his ear, scribbles on a torn envelope. "I ain't promising nothing. It's just what I heard – that he might be there. Cowboys don't stop long in one place."

"I understand," I say.

He passes me the paper. "If you find him, don't bother mentioning me. I don't want no credit on this one."

Mother Reardon's is a shabby little bungalow not far from the empty lot on the corner of Sunset and Hollywood boulevards where Griffith constructed the gargantuan Babylon set for his film *Intolerance*. A hand-lettered sign on a piece of cardboard in the front window says, "Room and Board, Weeklie, Monthlie." The old woman who answers my knock is thin as a straight razor and wears a black dress so shiny it looks wet.

"I'd like to speak to Mr. McAdoo," I say.

"Not here."

"When do you expect him back?"

"Don't. Moved out."

"Do you have a forwarding address for him?"

"Nothing to forward. He never got mail."

I think for a moment, hand on the screen door. "He didn't happen to skip out on the rent by any chance, did he?"

"What's it to you?"

"I'm a business associate," I tell her. "It's possible I might be able to settle any debts. Collect any personal belongings he might have left behind."

A shrewd, cold look passes over her face and then she dismisses the opportunity with a regretful, weary shake of the head. "No, he paid in full. Always did. He's a punctual man."

"Do you have a guess where he went to?"

"No."

"Did he say anything? Give any reasons for leaving?"

Mother Reardon cocks her head, shoots me a look like a bright-eyed scrawny bird. "Business associate, you said?"

"In a manner of speaking."

"Then you ought to know him to be closed-mouthed. Never said

much more to anybody than a word at the supper table. 'Pass the butter.' 'Pass the beans.' That's all he ever asked from anybody, that they
pass him what he paid for."

"So he just up and left."

"That's right. Came out of his room one Sunday morning with his
duffel bag packed and asked what he owed. Left without breakfast."

"On the run?"

"No. He wasn't in any particular hurry."

"I talked to a man this afternoon. He mentioned something about
a director. Did Mr. McAdoo ever say anything about a director?"

"I heard him say a thing or two about directors. None of it good.
I feel the same way. Movie people don't get into my house if I can help
it. They're all whores and thieves. Except for the cowboys. They may
be rough but they're honest."

"Did he have any visitors?"

"A few young fellows came by. Just to sit with him. They admired
Mr. McAdoo. Wanted to hear about the old days. Once I heard him
tell them, 'Don't ask me about the old days. Let the dead bury the
dead. I ain't dead.'"

"What do you think he meant by that?"

"I don't think he meant anything. It's just something an old man
might say."

"Do you know the names of any of those young fellows?"

"No."

"And you have no idea why he left?"

"Could be any number of reasons. Could be money, he hadn't
worked in some time. I'll carry people I trust until they find work.
Mr. McAdoo I trusted, but he never asked me to carry him."

"You mentioned there might be a number of reasons. What other
reasons?"

She considers a moment. "I came in the house the night before he
moved out. I'd been visiting my sister. It was dark. Saturday night the
boys are usually out. I walked in the living room and threw the light
switch. Mr. McAdoo was sitting by the radio." She paused. "He was
crying. That's the last thing I expected to see . . . Shorty McAdoo

crying. He's a tough old bird. I thought, Lord God, what's this? His face was all wet with tears, he wiped them off with his hands. I said to him, 'Mr. McAdoo, are you feeling poorly? Anything I can get you?' He said, 'No, the light coming on so sudden made my eyes burn.' I said, 'Well, let me get you a cool cloth for them.' I went out and ran some water on a washcloth; I knew it wasn't the light. He slipped out before I came back. Maybe he got bad news about family. Maybe he learned he ain't well."

"Anything else?"

She shook her head.

In the next few days I make no more progress. Groping for a lead, I go to the obvious places and ask the obvious questions. I spend an unfruitful afternoon loafing around the Sunset Barn, where a lot of the Western stars stable their horses. It's a popular place for corral buzzards who perch on the rail fences hoping to get noticed by somebody important. For young men who hail from Montana, Arizona, Texas, and Oklahoma, the Sunset Barn is what the drugstore counter was later to become for the corn-fed beauties of the Midwest, the rosy-cheeked milkmaids of Minnesota; it's *the* place to get discovered. They drawl and spit, do rope tricks, and show off their bandy-legged struts. I don't find Shorty McAdoo here, nor do I discover any reliable information as to his whereabouts.

The next day I motor out to Mixville, the ranch where the great Western star Tom Mix produces his horse operas. The ranch foreman knows McAdoo but has little to say about him. He was there three months before doing a picture, but nobody has seen him since. "He's a tumbleweed," he says. "Blows in and blows out." I leave my number and ask him to call if Shorty happens to blow in. The only profit in this wasted day is catching a glimpse of Tom Mix in a lurid purple tuxedo, matching purple stetson and boots, easing himself behind the wheel of his white Rolls-Royce with the fourteen-karat-gold initials TM on the doors. He puts the evening's sunset to shame.

Each night I am required to call Fitzsimmons to make a report on my progress or lack of it. Fitzsimmons wants results and he wants them fast.

"You got expense money – spread it around."

"If anybody knew anything, I would. But they don't."

"How do you know if they know anything until you offer a little fucking incentive? Get the rag out, Vincent. You're getting paid a hundred and fifty dollars a week to get results. A hundred and fifty is a lot of money."

"I know how much money it is, Mr. Fitzsimmons. And the rag was out the minute I signed on. There's a lot of ground to cover and I assure you I'm covering it. It seems everybody has heard *about* Shorty McAdoo but nobody *knows* him. No wife, no kids, no friends. A fucking loner. He could be anyplace, doing anything. He might be dying in some flophouse. He might be making a movie. He might have fucked off to Kansas, or Montana, or Arkansas – anyplace they need somebody to serenade cows from a horse. I don't know. But I'm looking."

"Shit."

"And what's the point of phoning you every night and going through this song and dance? Half the time you're not in. I call a dozen times; I'm up until midnight trying to get through to you. Why can't I call only if I have news?"

"Mr. Chance wants it that way. That's why."

"Then stop chewing my ass. I'm doing my best."

"You think your ass been chewed, Vincent? Your ass ain't even been nipped."

The next ten days I spend bouncing back and forth over dirt roads in the San Fernando Valley, the Mojave Desert, the sierras of Lone Pine, all the favoured locations for dusters. I locate fourteen or fifteen crews employing hundreds of cowboys. I had no idea there were so many cowpokes in Hollywood, but talking to them I learn they've been drifting into town for ten years, jumping off cattle-cars in the Los Angeles stockyards, going AWOL from Wild West shows and rodeos, riding in from the small family spreads which dot southern California. They're all refugees from a vanishing West. The cessation of hostilities in Europe has meant the end of the beef boom, the big spreads in Wyoming and Montana are cutting back herds and cutting loose wranglers. Cowhands wander into Hollywood, chasing rumours that five dollars a day can be earned as stunt men and extras in the Western pictures which Broncho Billy, William S. Hart, Tom Mix, and Art Accord have made famous. Maybe they'll get famous, too. Or at least passably prosperous on five dollars a day, boxed lunch provided. The only problem is there's too many cowboys and too few jobs.

A lot of these cowpokes won't give me the time of day when I mention Shorty McAdoo, maybe because I look like a subpoena-server. Sometimes the young ones, the green boys, talk, but they usually know nothing about McAdoo. To them he's as much a rumour as he is to me. They don't know where he lives, who his friends are. Slowly, it dawns on me that I'm chasing a reputation as much as a man.

On the weekend I drive out to the cowboy star Hoot Gibson's Saugus Ranch to take in the rodeo he throws there every Sunday, sit parked on hot bleacher-boards under a brassy, breathless sky, scanning the crowd for the grizzled, haunted face I'd seen projected on Chance's screen. I don't find it. Delayed by a flat tire, I get back to my apartment late that night, exhausted, my leg throbbing like a rotten tooth. I'm in no mood to phone Fitz. He can wait until morning. Or maybe even until tomorrow night. Fuck him.

I climb into bed and no sooner does my head drop on the pillow than the phone rings. It goes on and on, drilling into my head, then stops. Fifteen minutes later, it starts again. I know who it is. I get up and take the receiver off the hook. On my way back to the bedroom I can still hear the tinny sound of Fitzsimmons, shouting down the line.

At dawn, I drive out to Universal City where more white hats ride the range than on any other spread in southern California. The program feature is king at Universal and the king of program features is the Western, cheap to make and profitable. Uncle Carl Laemmle has many of the biggest Western stars under contract – Harry Carey, Neal Hart, Jack Hoxie, Art Accord, Peter Morrison, Hoot Gibson. Universal City is, as its name implies, a metropolis of sorts, a two-hundred-and-thirty-acre hive with its own police, fire department, street-cleaning crews, shops, forges, mills, prop departments, stages, outdoor sets, and a variety of scenery made to order for Westerns, and Uncle Carl is mayor of it all. This Western factory also has its own herds of cattle, horses, and mules, grazing a huge pasture, ready to serve at a moment's notice. But it also requires a reliable reserve of two-legged stock to work as doubles, stunt men, and extras. Uncle Carl's solution to the problem of ready supply is to construct a big hiring tank fenced with wire to hold cowboys corralled inside the studio gates and out of mischief until they are needed. Anybody looking for employment is penned there until Universal directors give him the nod and cut him out of the remuda for a day's shooting.

I get to Universal City just as the sun is beginning to spread itself on the north Hollywood hills, and already the pen holds forty hands. The scene reminds me of a prison camp, wire and posts, boot-trampled dirt, faces stamped with jailhouse emotions – boredom, apathy, bravado, sullen viciousness. I let myself in at the gate and begin to wander among the men. A small group throws craps on a horse blanket, two play mumblety-peg with a sheath knife big enough to chop sugar cane with; others doze propped up against fenceposts, big hats tipped down to shield eyes from the rising sun. A few stand in silent communion, rolling cigarettes; a number clutch the fence-wires, eyes fixed on the brightening hills as if anticipating the cavalry will ride down from the heights and rescue them.

I drift along, nodding and smiling, trying to strike up a conversation. As the sun warms and starts to take the chill off them, the extras get marginally friendlier and unbend a little, accept cigarettes, pass commonplace remarks about the weather and the promise of the day.

I keep doggedly nudging conversation in the direction of Shorty McAdoo. Finally, in one knot of middle-aged wranglers I manage to awaken some response. One of them claims he's heard Shorty pulled stakes and headed for Bakersfield. Wichita, says another. Somebody contradicts both of them. No, McAdoo's still in the Los Angeles area. The only thing they can agree on is that nobody has seen him on any set or location for at least a month.

"He ain't working because of that deal with Coster," says a fellow wearing a black hat with a silver-dollar hatband.

None of the others seem to know what the deal with Coster is.

"Look at this goddamn place. Not a stamp's worth of shade. Not a dipper of water to be had. Old Shorty had something to say to these high-handed bastards," he mutters. "Said her with a hammer." He taps his front teeth with a finger. "Knocked a few spokes out of Coster's wheel with a shoeing hammer, is what I heard."

"Well, if that's the case," says a fellow in a Canadian stetson, "Coster'll be able to suck dick all the better for it."

They all laugh.

"Story is it had something to do with simple Wylie's brother," says the silver-dollar hatband, tilting his head in a meaningful way toward a solitary kid sitting on a saddle.

"Wylie's twin, you mean," a tall, lanky man corrects him.

"Go on, they don't look no way similar."

"They ain't identical. But maybe they split a brain between the two of them because one's every bit as identical dumb as the other," asserts the tall man.

Everybody turns to look at the kid.

He has been riding that saddle since I arrived, scrunched down on it with his knees up around his ears, secluded in a lonesome corner of the coop. The stray-dog air of him, the wistful, sad-assed, clinging-vine look of him had kept me clear. He looks like the sort of kid that a kind word will stick to you like flypaper.

"Yes," concedes the tall man, "could be it had something to do with Wylie's brother. Because Wylie's setting on Shorty's saddle over there. I recognized it right away. Shorty hung a pair of army stirrups on his rig. Steel stirrups. I recognized a weld on the off-stirrup. Shorty had his off-stirrup mended once."

Before he finishes, I am crossing the tank, hasty and awkward, stiff leg swinging like a gate on rusty hinges. When Wylie spots me coming, he pulls off his hat and crushes it to his chest just the way cowboys do in the movies when the time rolls around to propose to their sweethearts. His jug-handle ears, horse-clipper haircut with haystack top and white-wall temples cut a sorry sight.

"Morning," I greet him.

When he cranes back his neck to peer up at me, his mouth falls open like a nestling begging for the worm. Everything about him is a plea, the timid eyes, the bottom lip chapped raw from hours of anxious sucking. He clamps down on it now, begins to nurse, the corners of his mouth collapsing in little tugs.

"Morning," I repeat. Just a little louder.

He leaves off sucking; the eyes scoot from side to side, avoiding mine. "Yessir," he says.

I poke the saddle with my toe. "I understand the owner of this saddle is Shorty McAdoo."

His panicked eyes cut back and forth between the saddle and my face. He talks very quickly, as if what he's saying is a recitation committed to memory. "He borrowed me this saddle. Them picture men'll hire you sooner you got a saddle your own self. And Miles he got busted up and that was bad and I had to hock my own saddle and so old Shorty he says to me, 'Wylie, you ride this rig of mine for a while. Might turn your luck. It always done right by me,' that's what Shorty said and I been riding her. Rub that luck off her. That's what I been doing, riding her –" He breaks off, looks up to check if I understand, if all is clear.

"But it was only a loan," I say.

He disregards me, plunges on. "Shorty said to me, he said, 'Wylie, you look after this here saddle of mine.' That's what he said, Shorty said." He commences to rock back and forth on the saddle-seat. "Shorty said that. I'm a-watching it for him. I'm a-watching it like a son of a bitch."

"Until he wants it back."

"He borrowed me his own saddle, so's I could get work," Wylie repeats stubbornly. "I found twenty dollar in the saddlebags. I know who put it there. Twenty dollars." The skittish eyes zoom off; he's thought of something else. "Miles," he says, "Miles. That's right. I put breakfast out for Miles. On that table. By his bed. I didn't forget."

"Shorty wants his saddle back. He asked me to collect it for him."

The kid resumes scooting his ass back and forth on the saddle-seat, quicker and quicker, he's riding away. Then suddenly he freezes, both hands lock tight on the horn, knuckles white. It has caught up to him. "He don't," he says.

"Yes, he does."

"He don't want this here old saddle."

"Right now, Wylie. He wants it now. Today."

Wylie blinks so hard his eyelids blur.

"I've got a car parked outside. I'll deliver you. You can hand it over to Shorty personally."

"I ain't even had a horse under it yet," says the kid, jumping to his feet, pulling at the crotch of his trousers. "But if Shorty wants her back –"

"He does."

When we get to the car I inquire of Wylie whether he drives. He nods solemnly.

"All right," I say, "take the wheel. Working the clutch is hard on this bum leg of mine. I don't drive unless I have to."

Wylie takes it at face value. Behind the wheel he doesn't head the car back to Los Angeles as I expect him to, but bucks it out into the wilderness which still clings to the skirts of Hollywood like a burr, racketing us down dirt roads which unfurl lazy pennants of dust under our tires. Most of the countryside we are crossing is unoccupied, state lease land and tracts in the hands of speculators hoping to cash in on the next boom in real estate. But it isn't entirely deserted. Here and there I manage to spot some small frame farmhouse; occasionally we encounter a flivver or farm wagon creaking along the road. Whenever Wylie spies another vehicle, even a couple of hundred yards up the road, he immediately slows to a turtle's crawl and surrenders so much of the thoroughfare he nearly has us in the ditch. When the approaching vehicle has gone safely by he turns a sly look of pride on me. And I smile back my approval of his skilful, life-preserving manoeuvre and wonder how much further we have to go to find McAdoo and whether Wylie has any notion whatsoever of where he is taking us.

Then, all at once, he is talking again, rattling away very fast, something about Running W's and his twin brother, Miles. A Running W is how horses were thrown in movie action scenes before the SPCA got a stop put to it. A Running W worked like this. A post called a deadman was driven solidly into the ground, out of camera view. Two lines of piano wire were run from the horse's fetlocks up its front legs and back underneath the girth of the saddle; the remaining several hundred feet of piano wire were coiled beside the deadman and the ends of the coils snubbed tight to the post buried in the ground. The stunt man's job was to ride a horse at a hard gallop until it ran out of line and the wire yanked its legs out from under it, crashing them to the ground. The Running W killed a lot of horses, hurt and crippled a lot of men. It was not popular with cowhands.

"Miles and me and Shorty we were working for Mr. Coster in the Valley. It's how it happened. The Running W done it. He was bad, Mr. Coster."

"Whoa," I say, feigning ignorance. "Who's Coster?" Any more information I can collect may prove useful.

"The director, the director!" he exclaims excitedly. "All day long he wants this shot. 'Spectacular!' he keeps hollering. 'I want spectacular! Give me some goddamn spectacular!' But it ain't the stunt men's fault. They tried, didn't they? It's the horses, that's what Shorty said. It's the horses. Because they all been throwed lots of times. And they know what's coming soon as them pianer wires get put on their legs. They know. Shorty says they won't run flat out because them horses know they going to get took down hard at the end. So they don't gallop terrible hard. They're smart horses. They been hurt before, them horses. They don't want to get hurt again, do they?"

"Makes sense to me."

"So Mr. Coster keeps trying. One horse and then he tries another horse and another horse and another horse. But Mr. Coster ain't satisfied. He wants spectacular! And the stunt fellers keep going down with the horses and rattling off the hard pan like peas on the bottom of the bucket.

"So Mr. Coster gets the horse wrangler to bring out this big old black gelding – they call him Locomotive – and Locomotive he's never been throwed with pianer wires before so he don't know it and he's a terrible big old horse, a croppy Shorty called him. Know what's a croppy?"

I don't.

"Because somebody cut his ears to warn everybody he's a mean horse, a bad horse, fellers do that, Shorty says, crop their ears. And the stunt fellers they don't want to ride no horse never been throwed – on top of he's mean. And Mr. Coster takes to cursing them all for cowards, gutless wonders he calls them, and all that he calls them, and so they all quit on Mr. Coster.

"So he says to the rest of us fellers, extras and all, he says, 'Who's going to show he's a man? Who's going to ride old Locomotive double the wages?' and I was going to, but Shorty says to me, 'Don't you ride that crop-eared cunt, he's a killer. Stay off him, Wylie.' And I done it, I stayed off that Locomotive but my brother didn't. He rode him."

"Why did he ride him, Wylie?"

"Because Mr. Coster says if he does, next picture he'll give him a part, Miles. And Shorty, he warned Miles, too. But Miles ain't too smart, Miles ain't, and he believed Mr. Coster and disbelieved Shorty. But Shorty knows how Miles is so he helped him anyways, see? Shorty, he thought her all out. He paced off just as far as the pianer wire was going to run out on Locomotive and he marked the spot with a hankerchief, pegged it on the ground and he says to Miles, he says to Miles, he says, 'Miles, when you see that there white hankerchief coming up on you, you kick your feet out of them stirrups because when that fucking widow-maker runs out of wire he'll go ass over tea-kettle and when he does you ain't going to want to get hung up in them stirrups – you going to want to get throwed clear. Throwed clear, understand? Otherwise, you going to smash up bad, like an apple crate. You understand me, Miles? You get your boots out of them stirrups the minute you see that white hankerchief.'"

"Let me guess," I say. "Miles didn't."

Wylie dropped his voice to a whisper. "No, he didn't. Miles was a-spurring Locomotive flat out, they was both going full chisel, and Miles was a-watching for that hankerchief and a-watching for that hankerchief and a-watching for that hankerchief, and then Locomotive wrecked, done a somersault and Miles was planted in them stirrups and Locomotive landed on him flush. He hurt him deep down inside, and Miles he been shitting bloody stool ever since and he don't walk too good."

"So why did he miss the handkerchief?"

"Mr. Coster sent the cameraman to go pick up that hankerchief when nobody was looking. So's he'd get spectacular. Wasn't no hankerchief to see. That's how it was done. I was going to go at him right then and there. I wanted to, but Shorty said no. Shorty said, 'Don't get mad, get even.' That's what Shorty said."

"And I hear Shorty did get even. With a shoeing hammer."

"Croppy," said Wylie, twisting nervously in his seat. "'Mark a bad horse,' says Shorty. 'So's everybody knows him.'" Suddenly, Wylie hits the brakes. I grab the dash and brace myself. The scenery jolts, the sky slants as the car slithers and shimmies on locked wheels through the soft dirt, slides to a stop. A breath of dust sighs into the car, chalks my teeth. A few yards behind and to the right of us a lane runs off the road past a dilapidated mailbox on a drunken post, crosses a skimpy brown pasture scribbled with sage and greasewood, edges up a low knoll and disappears out of sight behind it.

"Almost missed Shorty's turn-off," he announces.

I hold Wylie by the arm, follow the lane with my eyes. At the end of it there must be a house.

"Wylie," I say, "I've got something to confess to you."

I begin by telling him how proud I am of him, how proud Shorty is of him. I say that I hadn't been able to believe anybody in his circumstances would be so incorruptible. I tell him I had argued with

Shorty that he would never see his saddle again, that Wylie would sell or pawn it before you could say Mother Mabel. But Shorty had believed in him. Shorty had said that Wylie was a true-blue man to ride the river with. And Wylie had proved it was true. He had kept good care of Shorty's property, hadn't hesitated for a second when asked to return it, no matter how badly he needed it for his work.

"Let me shake your hand." I shake it. Then I take twenty dollars out of the expense-money envelope. "For your time, Wylie. I was going to prove a point to Shorty, but the point got proved to me. I got to eat humble pie."

"Shorty don't want his saddle?"

"No," I say, "not just at present." I pause. "Your luck seems to be changing, Wylie. You keep rubbing luck off of McAdoo's rig, you may end up the next William S. Hart. Now let me drive. Let me chauffeur one fine man wherever he wants to go."

"We ain't going to see Shorty?"

"Not today. He's busy."

"Shorty don't borrow his saddle to just anybody!" Wylie crows triumphantly, as I turn the car around in the middle of the road. "Not everybody gets to ride Shorty's saddle!"

I offer to take him home but he prefers to be dropped off outside of Universal. It doesn't make any sense because most of the day's shooting will be well under way and none starting. But perhaps he believes me, believes his luck has turned. I drop him off outside the pen, deserted at this hour, a wind scrubbing dust into the air off the beaten earth, scurrying bits of candy wrapper along and sticking them to the wire fence. I watch as he stumps toward it, Shorty's magic humped clumsily on his shoulder, stirrup leathers flapping, stirrups bouncing, his stupid faith that the old man's luck has the power to work a miracle in his own life intact.

7

All thirteen assembled in Front Street, sitting their horses in the early morning grey and quiet, mist curling off the coffee-and-cream Missouri, rising into the still air to hang a muslin curtain between the men and the wind-sculptured bluffs across the river.

It was a force mounted and armed and accoutred without consistency, piebald and paint buffalo runners, blooded bays and chestnuts, Henrys and Sharps and Winchesters and Colts and double-barrelled scatterguns, a Derringer in a coat pocket, skinning knives and Bowie knives, hatchets, a Confederate cavalry sabre hung scabbarded on a saddlehorn, smoke-stained buckskins and bar-stained broadcloth, broken plug hats and glossy fur caps, loud checked shirts and patched linen, canvas dusters and wool capotes, parfleche-soled moccasins and high-heeled riding boots. Every face bearing a different mark of vice or virtue, motive or resolve.

Silence was near complete. The Englishman's boy could hear birds carolling in the thickets down by the river and the horses shifting in the roadway, saddles creaking like the timbers of a ship rocking at anchor, the faint chiming of restless spurs and bridle chains. Someone coughed, but no one spoke. They were waiting on Hardwick.

Hardwick was lighting a cigar. He scratched a match with a thumbnail and his face sprang out at them, bright in the dim surround, like a golden countenance in an old painting. His bay pricked its ears at the crack of the match, sidestepped uneasily when the sulphur burst stinging in its nostrils. Hardwick remained seated, careless and comfortable, reins looped on the horn, hands cupped to the flame. He spoke softly to the horse, checking its restive dance.

For a moment, he drew on the cigar and studied the shadowy cavalry. Then he nodded and, without raising his voice, said: "I got one thing to say to you boys before we commence this enterprise. I don't tolerate a slacker. If one of you thinks he can slack on Tom Hardwick, take another think and fall out now." There came a pause in which he seemed to be taking thought himself. "And I hope there's no cowards among us," he added. "I won't break bread with a coward." He smiled briefly and that was confusing, as if the smile was taking back or amending what he had just said. The Englishman's boy was sure that was not the case. "Well," said Hardwick, turning his horse, "let's move out."

They went up the street at a walk, the slow, sombre pace of a funeral procession, past the shuttered house Fort Benton's merchant prince, I.G. Baker, had built so his wife would not have to give birth to their first baby in the fort, past the ox wagons and trailers parked by the warehouses, past the sporting and gaming houses at this hour black as the heart of sin, past the old adobe fort which had stood godfather to the town, its four massive blockhouses featureless and blank but for the rifle slits in the walls.

Wraiths, they stole out into the country, accompanied by the singing of meadowlarks, the horses steadily warming to their work in the chill morning air. The file lengthened under the blush of sun rising behind them, Hardwick and Evans assuming an air of generalship at the head, the company sorting into a natural order of march, friend falling in with friend, acquaintance falling in with acquaintance, the pack animals and remounts occupying the protected centre of the column, riders at the rear acting as loose herders.

Because they were unfamiliar with the other riders, the Englishman's boy and a hired hand named Hank from a farm between the Teton and Marias which had lost stock too, fell into step with one another. His employer had equipped Hank with a dubious horse and a dubious rifle, enrolled him in the posse to assist in the recovery of his stolen property. Hank looked as if he wished he were in any other line of work than chasing Indians. He talked a good deal, as if talking kept the Indians from peeking around some corner of his mind. The boy wished he would talk less and look to the management of his horse more, a fat white plug with a dirty coat which kept blundering and stumbling about in a slew-footed fashion.

When they arrived at the wolfers' old camp the sun was standing blood-red on the horizon. The camp was marked by a dead fire, a few pieces of charcoal, some fine ash blowing along the ground in a gathering wind. The track of nineteen iron-shod horses was plain as print on a sheet of clean paper. However, Philander Vogle, who had been nominated scout, also espied a faint, partially obliterated moccasin print blended in among the hoofprints.

"They didn't drive them off," he said to Hardwick. "Slippery devils come in and walked them out quiet. That's why we didn't hear nothing."

Touching the brim of his hat, Hardwick saluted the moccasin impression and whoever had left it as a signature on the earth. They rode on.

On the other side of the hills, vistas opened up. It was flat, open country, a barbed-wire fence running parallel to their advance, posts marching off to the horizon like infantry, staking out the Robinson property where Hank worked and horses had also been stolen. The stirring sight of all the posts he had pounded caused Hank to cluck his nag down the line to Hardwick, to point westward and excitedly pass on his information. "There. Over there. That's where they broke the fence. Broke it down and run off Mr. Robinson's horses, by God."

Hardwick said, "Farmer, what's this news in aid of?"

"Why, it's just news, I guess," he said uncertainly.

"It's old news," said Hardwick. "I don't want no news from you except news of where them horses went to. You got any such news?"

"No, no. I don't, I suppose," Hank admitted, crestfallen.

"Then you leave the Indians to us, Farmer. And we'll leave minding the raising of peas and beans and taties to you."

Hank dropped back, deeply chagrined. "He had no business coming down on me so hard. I ought to have thrown it back at him," he said to the Englishman's boy.

"I wouldn't," said the boy.

"Why not?"

"Because I ain't a fool," said the boy.

Late in the morning, a halt was called. Vogle, who had been scouting in advance, returned with a report that a hundred yards ahead he had discovered a dead colt. Recently gelded, it appeared to have bled to death with the effort of trying to keep pace with the fugitive herd.

"That's one of Mr. Robinson's," Hank confided to the Englishman's boy. "He cut him two days ago."

The real news was that where the colt had fallen, the trail forked. The Indians had split the herd and one lot of horses had been driven northwest, the other northeast. Everyone dismounted while Evans, Hardwick, and Vogle convened a council, squatting on the ground.

Hardwick asked Vogle if he could estimate how many Indians were in the raiding party. Vogle said he wasn't sure, but he could find no unshod-pony tracks, which suggested not many.

"How many?" demanded Hardwick.

Vogle shrugged. "Two, maybe three. Can't swear to it."

Hardwick considered a moment. "If there's only two or three, they're from the same band. They haven't shaved off to take their share of the loot home to different camps. They're going to swing back and join up again further north. They're just aiming to lead us on a wild-goose chase."

"So what do we do?" asked Evans. "Split up? Me lead one party of men west, you one party east?"

"I don't like it," said Hardwick. "Not with the head start they've got." He laid a pebble on the ground. "That's us," he said. He traced two lines in the dust with his knife, radiating northeast and northwest from the pebble. "That's them. If they do figure to powwow up north, say here," he mused, laying down another pebble to mark the imagined meeting place, "they've got to hack back from the line they're riding now." He curved the lines to converge on the upper pebble. "The longest way between where we are and where they're going is riding the loop. And if either one of us loses the trail of the scallywags we're chasing, you and me'll be like the fat couple with the big bellies. We ain't never going to get it together."

"Speak your mind," said Evans.

"But if we split the difference and strike due north," said Hardwick, drawing a straight line with the tip of his knife between the pebbles, "we'll make time on them. And sooner or later, no matter where the pebble sets, as long as we keep bearing north, one of their trails is going to cut ours. When it does, we pick it up and go hard after them red rogues."

"If that's their plan."

"There's the kicker. But I'll bet on it."

"All right," said Evans, standing. "We'll ride north."

Hardwick allowed the horses an hour to graze the short, tough grass while the men gnawed hard biscuit and scooped pemmican out of rawhide bags with their fingers. Berries and lard and buffalo meat all scrambled together and poured hot into a leather bag to harden didn't sit well with Hank, who had been raised in civilization, in the East. He said it was like stirring apple pie into your gravy and pork chops. No different. The Englishman's boy held his tongue. Hardwick was listening, watching them.

The man the wolfers called Scotty, a Canadian who had ridden down the Whoop-Up Trail with them from north of the line, pulled a bottle of whisky out of his saddlebags, and passed it around to each man for a swig. He said it was Scotch whisky. The Englishman's boy had never tasted Scotch whisky before, but he drank his swallow and thanked him.

Scotty said, "You're most welcome."

To the Englishman's boy, there was something odd about the Scotchman, a peculiar, unsteady gleam in his eye. He didn't seem to belong with this bunch, seemed not aware of the company he was keeping. He had the Englishman's way of talking. Gentleman's airs. Didn't care to blaspheme. Kept himself spruce and neat. He'd seen

73

him writing in a little book after he finished eating, just how the Englishman did. Journal, the Englishman called his book. The boy could read a little but had never got the hang of writing.

They remounted at noon and rode to the spot where they had seen carrion birds fluttering down for the past hour. Magpies skimmed away and floated back to earth a short way off to wait out the interruption of their feeding. The horses, catching the heavy, sweetish stench of death mingled with the smell of horse, arched their necks, cocked their heads, drummed their hooves, and shied sidelong past the corpse, snorting and nickering. The colt lay stark on its deathbed of wiry grass, stiff back legs streaked with long stockings of rusty blood, eye sockets empty, guts torn and scattered, body encased in a tattered mail of blue flies.

Clear of the corpse they walked their horses on under an impassive sky dappled with handfuls of torn white cloud flying before the wind like cottonwood fluff. Men and horses blinking in and out of the eye of the sun, cloud shadows overtaking and encompassing them and racing on, patches of darkness sailing over the billowing grass like blue boats running before a storm. Antelope and mule-tail, prairie chickens and jack-rabbits, coyotes and fox and grouse started out of the sage, flashed across the emptiness at their approach.

About mid-afternoon, Hardwick took his bearings, consulted his pocket watch, and booted his horse into a brisk trot. Within a mile or two, it became evident that Hank's white nag lacked the staying power to hold the pace. Little by little, the Englishman's boy and the farm hand lost ground until they found themselves lagging in the rear. A gap gradually opened between them and the body of riders. Ten yards, twenty, thirty. When it lengthened to forty, the boy put his heels to his horse and loped back to the column. Hank too closed ranks, but not so effortlessly, and the ground he won back he immediately began to lose again. Three more times the string ran out and had to be wound back tight, and each tightening took a little more out of the white horse. Sweat darkened its belly and patched its chest, lashings of foam flew from its bit, spattering its neck.

No one looked back to see how they fared. Hardwick gave them

74

no quarter for their shortcomings. By late afternoon the breach had widened to several hundred yards. A look of panic crept over Hank's face when he realized that Hardwick was not going to relent, would make no allowances. "Goddamn him, why don't he slack off? He knows we can't keep up."

"I can keep up," said the Englishman's boy.

"I thought we was all in this together," said Hank. "That Hardwick's leaving us as easy pickings for any Indians that's dogging our trail."

"There ain't any Indians dogging our trail. We're dogging theirs."

"We don't know there's no Indians dogging our trail," the hired man muttered. "They might have slipped behind us. Ever think of that? That's what Indians is known for. Slipping behind you and lifting your hair when you least expect it."

The horsemen ahead topped a rise and descended out of sight.

"Look at that," whined Hank. "Now they've skinned out on us entire. We're cold alone and left to fend for ourselves."

"The reason we're cold alone," said the Englishman's boy, "is because of that plug of yours."

Hank's brow furrowed with worry. "I didn't know what I was letting myself in for, signing on with that Hardwick feller. I never did meet a redheaded man you could trust. Every one of them is crazy."

"If you keep up your pissing and moaning," said the Englishman's boy, "I just might ride on and join that redheaded man for the change of company. His talk has got to be a damn sight cheerfuller than what I'm getting here."

With the threat he might be abandoned, Hank went even more squirrelly and apprehensive. He squirmed in his saddle and threw nervous glances over his shoulder. "First rule in the wilderness is stick together, boy. We got to look out for one another. Don't we, son?"

"The only way we'll stick together," said the Englishman's boy, "is if you kick a little more go out of that nag of yours."

"There's no more go to kick out of him," said Hank. "His go has gone and went."

They were climbing the rise. Breaking onto the crest they could see, half a mile away, the posse dwindling on the prairie.

The boy said, "They put any more distance between us, even I ain't going to catch them before nightfall."

"It's a sin to leave a traveller in distress, son. Remember your Bible. Remember the Good Samaritan." Hank put his hand in his pocket. "I got a dollar," he said hopefully, showing it to the Englishman's boy. "It's yours."

"That is one sorry-ass horse and you are one sorry-ass son of a bitch," said the boy.

"It ain't my horse. It's Mr. Robinson's," Hank said plaintively. "And what am I supposed to do? There's no getting blood out of a stone." As he pleaded his case, the Englishman's boy slipped his hand into his boot and fetched out his knife. Hank went pale at the sight of it. "What you setting to do with that knife, son?" he inquired in a tight voice.

"Get blood out of a stone." The boy leaned over, pricked the nag in the haunch. The horse squealed, bucked once, and then broke into a clumsy, wriggling gallop which slopped Hank from side to side in the saddle. The Englishman's boy closed hard and jabbed the terrified animal's hindquarters again. Hank screeched for him to leave off.

But the Englishman's boy did not leave off. He pursued horse and man across the wastes like a banishing Bible angel harrying the exile with fiery sword and implacable visage, a strange white-faced angel scrunched in a big derby hat and flapping coat, blade glittering in his upraised hand. It became clear neither pleas nor curses could deflect him. So Hank stopped his mouth and saved his breath, grimly holding on for all he was worth, like baggage strapped to a mule. They did not lose sight of the wolfers, even though by late afternoon the leading party shrank to a train of ants toiling across a tabletop.

When they rode into the camp on the Marias, the boy was still playing drover, the knife in his hand his goad, the cattle he drove a pale horse trickling thin threads of blood down its haunches and a frightened man rigidly upright in his saddle. The wolfers rose to their feet and gaped in silence. It was a sight for silence. The white horse trotted through the camp as if fire, hushed men, picketed horses did not exist. It did not turn its head. Hank had to rear back and saw the bit to check it from plunging over the bank and into the river. There it stood and shook, head between its knees.

"Where's Hardwick?" asked the Englishman's boy.

One of the men pointed. Hardwick stepped out from behind a clump of willows, buttoning his fly. "Them boys is tardy for supper," he said. "Where's my switch?" The men laughed.

"That man needs another horse," announced the boy.

"Does he?" said Hardwick.

"He can't keep up."

"Ain't that a pity."

"He needs a horse," said the boy.

"Farmer Robinson put him on a horse."

"It's a poor horse."

"It's a poor man," said Hardwick. The boy and Hardwick looked at one another.

"I ain't watching out for him no more," said the boy.

Hardwick shrugged.

"He's scared the Indians is going to catch him if he's left behind," said the boy.

"Then he ought to have stopped at home and admired his favourite cow's ass."

For the first time Hank looked up, roused out of his numbness. "I didn't ask to come!" he cried. "Mr. Robinson sent me!"

"Hold your chat," said Hardwick quietly. "I'm talking to this boy here."

"Why'd you push so hard today?" cried Hank. "What was your all-fired hurry?"

"My hurry?" said Hardwick. He wasn't speaking to the farm hand but to the Englishman's boy. "My hurry? My hurry was to reach water. My hurry was to get my men a sup of hot food before dark come down. Because I don't hold with cook-fires after nightfall. I don't hold with lighting no beacons to plundering Indians. That set all right with you?"

The boy said nothing.

"That set all right with you?" demanded Hardwick.

"Yes," said the boy.

"It don't set with me!" shouted Hank. "And this bad treatment ain't going to set with Mr. Robinson. It ain't going to set with him how that boy used his horse neither. He'll require damages!"

"You keep on hollering," said Hardwick, "you'll catch some damages."

Hank bit his lip and crawled down off the inert horse. "I don't have much appetite," he remarked to nobody in particular. "Even though Mr. Robinson put ten dollars in for supplies I don't believe I'll help myself to my share of that bacon that's frying."

"Second thought he don't need to stop at home to admire no favourite cow's ass," said Hardwick to his companions. "All he need do is look in a mirror."

8

I follow a ridge of starved, stingy weeds running down the middle
of the lane, drive over a rise to confront desolation. A burned-out
house, two walls still standing, the rest a tangle of blackened studs
and joists collapsed in a cellar, fingers stabbing at the sky. I park the
car, walk over. There are tortured lumps of melted window-glass scattered on the ground, heat-twisted nails, wooden shingles gnawed by
fire, chunks of broken, ham-sized, smoke-cured cement. Where the
floor still holds, it supports a scorched metal lamp, a charred sofa.
Tall, rank weeds sprout in the midst of the debris in the cellar, evidence the conflagration was not recent.

Across the neglected brown yard I see the ruins of a barn,
destroyed by fire like the house, heaps of ash and tumbled beams.
In the singed, wasted crossbeams of a windmill, birds flit from spar
to spar, a rusty pipe lugubriously drips water into a trough wearing
a green caul of algae. Turning slowly in an intimidating expanse my
eyes come to rest on a low-slung bunkhouse I first overlooked. A
single window glints in the sun, the rest are masked with tar-paper
eyepatches. A man is standing on the stoop of the bunkhouse watching me. Without acknowledging the intruder, he turns and goes into
the bunkhouse. A minute later, he steps back out in a black jacket
and walks towards me past a stack of rusted irrigation pipe, a hay
rake, a ramshackle, derelict buggy. His stroll is unhurried and deliberate. When he reaches the car he stops, props a foot up on the

bumper and ties an errant bootlace, straightens himself and says, "What you want?"

Shaved and with his teeth in, he looks less crazed than the man in the roughcut Chance had shown me. Considerably smaller, too – five feet four, one hundred and thirty pounds of stringy muscle, tightly wound sinew, bone. A common trick of the camera, to make a man seem bigger than he is. It had come as a great shock and disappointment to me when I started work at the studio and first encountered stars in the flesh. They seemed diminished, ordinary, piddling creatures.

But distortions of the camera aside, there is no mistaking this is Shorty McAdoo. It's the eyes. Bits of bituminous black, countersunk in deep sooty sockets, soft coal smouldering. He isn't wearing wrangler duds, just a pair of drab workman's trousers, a collarless shirt under a black suit jacket that seems to have been his reason for the visit to the bunkhouse. Window dressing for the visitor.

"Mr. Shorty McAdoo?"

"Who wants to know?"

"The name's Harry Vincent." I offer my hand. He doesn't take it. "No reason for alarm," I say.

"I don't feel no alarm," the old man informs me. He looks like one of those over-the-hill jockeys who hangs around race-tracks, a trim, youthful body surmounted by an implausibly ancient face.

"I've been looking for you for more than two weeks," I say. "I was ready to throw in the towel when I bumped into a young man by the name of Wylie."

"Wylie, eh?" he says in a guarded voice.

"You came up in conversation."

"What else come up in conversation?"

I hasten to reassure him. "There's nothing to worry about."

"Fuck worry. What you want, mister?"

"I'm not here about Coster. This has got nothing to do with Coster."

"If it ain't got nothing to do with Coster, why mention it?"

My eyes sweep the bleak, ravaged property. "There must be a reason you chose this particular garden spot to hole up in. I thought it might be Coster. This looks like a convenient place to avoid a warrant."

"Warrant for what?"

"Maybe assault and battery."

"Ain't no warrant out on me. I never done nothing to Coster."

"Don't get me wrong," I say. "Why you're here is none of my business."

He makes a gesture of dismissal. "This ain't got nothing to do with Coster. I just got sick of all that picture shit."

"I think I know what you're talking about," I say. "Some of your acquaintances have been telling me tales about the bad way you're treated."

"I washed my hands of her," he says with a controlled, wintry vehemence. "Been a five-dollar-a-day fool long enough. Fellers shouting at you out of a blow-horn. Couldn't take it no more. I'm done with all that. I reckon to get shut of this place entire. Head north."

"Where north?"

"Canada. Not that that's any of your business. But I got nothing to hide." He pauses. "They got some space there. Was a time a man in this country could go anywhere on God's green earth it pleased him, poor or proud. But the rich men keep putting all us dogs on the leash. Loitering law, vagrancy law. Old man like me can land in county jail for standing on a corner with empty pockets these days."

"Look," I prompt him, "is there someplace we can go and talk?"

"Talk what?"

"Business."

"I don't recollect no business to talk with you. What business I got to talk with you, Mr. Harry Vincent?"

"Give me ten minutes. It might be your ticket up north." I issue this like a challenge and that's how he takes it. He weighs me grimly.

"Come along then," he says at last, turning on his heel for the bunkhouse.

It is terribly still. The burned barn rides along in the corner of my eye, a black blot. I can feel the destroyed house at my back. The sombre windmill scatters sparrows into the air which wheel, shimmer in the sunlight like the leaves of an aspen, and then, one by one, drop back down solemnly on the struts of the windmill, pegs on a clothesline.

The question presses me. "What in Christ happened here?"

McAdoo points his finger at the house, at the barn, at the windmill. "This?"

"Yes."

"I knew the man owned this place, Austin Noble. He and his wife moved out here from Nebraska. Noble'd been a cattle-buyer. They was an old couple, Austin and his wife, didn't have no kids, nothing was holding them in Nebraska; get shut of the winter cold, they figured, eat oranges in California. So they sold up in Nebraska, bought this place; he kept a few horses, she kept a few chickens. Hired a man to farm the rest of the land. They was here about a year and his wife took sick, something about the heart, the lungs." He shrugs. "Might been both. She died. One morning, he gets up, sets fire to the house. Walks out in the yard, puts a torch to the barn. Next, the windmill. Hired man seen it. He run and hid himself in that clump of trees yonder. Austin was making for the bunkhouse but then he must have recollected he had a man living there. He stops in his tracks, takes a pistol out of his pocket, puts in it his mouth, pulls the trigger." McAdoo halts, directs me. "Just over there." He resumes walking. "Property went to a brother of Austin's in Omaha. He figures to sell it to one of them movie studios – they turn it into another Universal, another Inceville – make him a rich man. Big shit ideas. He don't know you going to pass property off on them boys you got to sell scenery. Ain't no fucking scenery to speak of here. But that's right to my purpose. He can set tight in Omaha waiting for an offer and I can set tight here until he gets one."

The bunkhouse must once have housed eight or ten men, but now it's sadly decayed, its footings raggedly fringed with last year's brown grass and this year's verdigris weeds. The only sign of life is the swallows ducking in and out of mud nests daubed under the eaves, scrolling the palimpsest of dusk with their pursuit of insects. McAdoo pushes the door open and I follow him in. Because of the tar-papered windows, a kerosene lamp sits on an apple box at the far end of a room long and narrow as a shooting gallery, the light making luminous the sheets of an unmade bed. German expressionism, I think to myself. A lot of cameramen would give their eyeteeth for that shot.

McAdoo waves me down the room. As he does, his suit jacket flaps open and I glimpse a pistol in the waistband of his pants. He put the jacket on to conceal his weapon. With a man carrying a pistol at my back, the short walk down the room lengthens alarmingly.

Signs of the former occupants have not all been erased. Against either wall, to the left and to the right, the skeletons of iron cots stand, skinned of their mattresses, a pile of old magazines stacked at the foot of one of them. Defunct calendars curl on the walls. I slip by a cast-iron stove with a coal-scuttle tipped beside it.

Halting in the pool of lamplight, McAdoo indicates a wooden chair. "Set yourself," he says, sagging down on his bed. The harsh light shining up from the apple box drills his eyes even deeper into his skull, bathes the bony forehead in a fierce, waxy glow. His face appears on the verge of melting. Putting a hand inside his coat he draws out the revolver and lays it down on the mattress beside his leg. "You armed?" he asks quietly.

"God, no, I'm not armed."

"Don't lie to me."

"I'm not armed."

"Stand up and hold out your arms," he orders. His hands run expertly down my sides, pat my pockets, slide down the inside of my trousers. "All right, set again," he says. "We don't have to think about that no more."

I settle myself gingerly on the chair.

"You got to watch your step in these lonesome parts," he remarks. "I blame these picture people. Every lazy no-account's heard how they'll pay you five dollar a day to stand in a crowd, holler and wave your arms. Easy money, no work, they think. Flame for the wrong kind of moths. A week ago I come in here and some ugly son of a bitch and his head lice is laying in my bed. Drifter. Clear out my bunk,

I said. Know what he done? Give me a big smile, fiddled out his cod and asked for a suck. If I didn't run the bastards off, this place'd be just the same as one of them goddamn downtown missions. I'd be lying awake of a night listening to old men bugger each other. No thanks to that music. This is my home." He pauses. "And I don't recall offering you no invitation."

"Point taken. You didn't."

"That's right. I didn't." He waits.

I light a cigarette, my hands are trembling. I pass McAdoo the pack.

"Obliged," he says. "This is my first in a goodly time." He wolfs down the smoke, makes to return the package.

"Keep them," I say.

He presses them into my palm. His fingers feel like they've been whittled from something cold and hard, like ivory.

"What I mean is, keep them, you're a long way from supplies," I say by way of apology.

"I make out fine. I come here with supplies," he declares. "Coffee, dried peas, beans. I planted me a truck garden, some of it's showing now. There's quail abouts, and rabbit for flesh. I shot a small doe last month. There's still some deer in this country, not many, but some."

"You're living wild then."

"Hell, a roof ain't wild. This ain't living wild."

"Tobacco doesn't grow wild for the picking," I say. "You take it."

He doesn't object this time, just tucks the cigarettes away in his shirt pocket. But I guess he feels his need has compromised him. He says angrily, "I tell you this Hollywood is one sour pot of milk, can hardly see it for the flies." He gets to his feet with a savage jerk of the shoulders and moves to the stove. In a barely audible voice he remarks, "Nothing colder'n a cold stove. Why's that? I get a bad headache I always lay her on a cold stove." He stoops over, presses his forehead to the stove, his hands loosely cupped around the swell of the fire-box. A strange, oddly disturbing sight, as if he is resting his head on a woman's breast, his hands on her hips. Consolation. The old man doesn't stir. I can hear my watch measuring the stillness. Maybe he's faint with hunger.

Alarmed, I rise to my feet. "Mr. McAdoo? Mr. McAdoo? Are you all right?"

The head slowly lifts from the cold iron; the head slowly turns. His voice is gentle, bleak. "What you want from me, son? Who are you?"

The voice beckons me, I feel myself fading out of the lamplight, drifting into the tar-papered gloom surrounding the stove. At the far end of the bunkhouse, I catch a stain of light seeping through the one dirty pane of glass, puddling on the board floor. The swallows rustling under the eaves purl like running water. We are face to face now, the black eyes glitter at me. I say, "I'm not the police."

"Hell, I know that. I weren't born yesterday. I been christened, son."

"I'm a writer."

"Newspaper writer?"

"I used to be. But not any more. I write books now. I want to write a book about the Old West. Everyone tells me you're the man to talk to. That you have the stories. A writer needs stories. They all said talk to Shorty McAdoo if you want the real dope, the truth."

Surprisingly, my little encomium angers him. "I ain't interested in all that old dead shit. I know the truth."

"It's history," I say, lamely. "It's something we all ought to know."

"Then go talk to Wyatt Earp. He's living in the vicinity. He'll put you up to your ass in history. He's full of it."

"I don't want Earp. I want you."

"And I don't want to get mixed up in all that shit."

"All *what* shit?" I demand, exasperated. "What shit are we talking about?"

"Lies."

The two of us stand in the middle of an empty bunkhouse staring at one another. The pool of smudgy light shivers on the floor as, outside, a cloud blows across the face of the sun.

"Lies are the last thing I'm interested in."

"Go away," he says.

"So how are you going to get to Canada? Grow wings and fly? You're broke. I'll offer you good wages just to sit and talk to me. A stunt man gets paid seven and a half dollars a day to risk his neck. I'll pay you that much money to sit in a chair and talk to me. What could be fairer?"

"You pay me seven and a half dollars a day? What kind of stunts do I have to do for a stunt man's wages?"

"No stunts. Just agree to my terms. You'll have to allow me to take down whatever you say – word for word. In shorthand. So that my publisher can read for himself what you tell me, to judge its potential with the public. If he decides there's money to be made publishing your stories he'll negotiate to purchase the rights to them. Any money you receive up until that point will be money paid for your time alone. Do you understand?" McAdoo begins to scrub his face with his hands. I read it as a sign of indecision. "High wages, Mr. McAdoo. Just to tell the story of your life."

"Ain't no story to my life."

"That's not so, Mr. McAdoo. There's a story to every life."

"Tell them yours then."

"You were there. You can provide the straight goods on how it was."

"Hot and thirsty and hard was how it was. Like it always is. Copy that down in your goddamn book."

"Easy money."

"I don't favour easy money. Too much easy money flying around this part of the world. I ain't seen much to recommend it. Nothing so hard as easy money."

"What is it you mistrust? Me? My motives?" I take Chance's expense money out of the inside pocket of my jacket, remove ten dollars and place it on the top of the stove. I am careful to let him catch a peek of how much money remains in the envelope. "I said I'd pay for your time. I've taken a piece of your time, Mr. McAdoo. I've also imposed on your good will and hospitality." We are both looking at the money as if expecting it to kindle on the stovetop. "If you agree to give me more of your time, you'll be paid. You want to call it off at any time, call it off. No strings attached."

"Don't go telling me that," he says, a bitter edge to his voice. "I'm an old whore. Just listening to you talk – my pussy's already sore. I can guess how it's going to smart you ever manage to haul yourself aboard and commence to fucking me full bore."

"No one has any intention of fucking you, Mr. McAdoo. You will get every penny you're owed. In fact, I am prepared to advance you fifty dollars right now. To demonstrate good faith."

McAdoo hasn't touched the money yet, but he's looking. "He's a rich man then – this man you're working for?"

"He is a gentleman of ample resources. More important, I have trust in his integrity."

"My daddy had a saying. We all share and share alike. Rich man has all the ice he wants in summer. Poor man all the ice he wants in winter," comments McAdoo.

"Maybe it's time you had a little ice in summer," I say, flicking several more bills out of the envelope. I put them down beside the ten-spot on the stovetop. "There's the advance I spoke of – fifty dollars. You could take it and run, but I'm banking you're a man of your word."

"And all I do is talk?"

"Seven and a half dollars a day. Payment in full at the end of each and every day. If I feel your stories don't fulfil expectations, I'll break it off. You can do the same. No hard feelings, no recriminations."

"But you going to ask me questions," says McAdoo. "I know it." At the prospect he sounds sorrowful.

"That's right. I'll ask questions. That's my job, persuading you to answer them. But if you won't – there's nothing much I can do about it, is there?"

McAdoo picks the ten dollars from the stove, leaving the fifty where it lies. He holds the ten-spot out to me. "This money I earned today," he says, "take it and buy me some crackers, some cheese, a couple cans of sardines. Buy me some tobacco and cigarette papers.

And canned peaches. I admire the taste of canned peaches in heavy syrup. You buy me all that and bring it back to me tomorrow."

I can barely fence the elation I feel out of my voice. "All right."

As an afterthought, he adds, "You might get me a bottle of whisky. I ain't had a tot for a month." He smiles mischievously. "Whisky might loosen me up for my sermon tomorrow. But if I'm short on money after you get the other supplies, forget the whisky."

"If you are, I'll advance you on the whisky."

"The hell you'll advance me. I'm not going on tick to the company store." He shoves the fifty dollars at me roughly. "Take that back."

I fold the money back into the envelope. "Then we've got a deal?"

"One-day-at-a-time deal. You bring me my groceries tomorrow and we'll talk a while. Try it on for size. See how the pig flies."

"That's all I ask."

We shake hands formally, punctiliously. The swallows returning to their nests as night falls whir louder and louder under the eaves.

"I look forward to tomorrow," I say.

"What I look forward to is them peaches," says McAdoo. "Don't you go and forget my heavy-syrup peaches."

We part at the stove. My hand on the door, I hesitate, meaning to ask, What time should I come? But seeing what I see, I say nothing. McAdoo stands, head worshipfully bowed to the stove iron, in a chill, vertiginous embrace. Behind him, the light in the lamp is flagging, glowing orange in the glass chimney.

I let myself out. It has begun to rain, big cold drops splash down, faster and faster. I hold my coat closed at the throat, hobbling as fast as I can toward the waiting Ford. Despite the burned house, the burned barn, the scorched windmill, I could sing for joy. Besides, the rain is washing it all from sight.

9

The next morning the wolfers began the construction of rafts to ferry supplies, saddles, guns, and sundry gear across the Marias River. One group of men limbed and chopped deadfall while another dragged the logs to the river's edge where Frenchie Devereux lashed them together with rawhide and bits of rope. Hank, who had quit his hunger strike after one night of famine, sat plugging himself with bacon and beans until Hardwick sauntered up to him and handed him an axe with the remark, "Here's an old friend of yours, Farmer. Shake hands."

By early afternoon the pack horses had swum the ford and were hobbled on the other side awaiting reloading. Three rafts piled with goods were launched and poled to the opposite bank, then poled back to freight more cargo. Sediment turned the current rich and thick as liquid chocolate; it ran with a steady, strong force which twisted and twined under the surface like muscle and sinew flexing beneath skin.

With the final load piled on the last raft, Scotty peeled out of his boots and clothes and flung them aboard as it pushed off. He stood naked on the bank with a weird grin pasted on his face, looking like he was ready to embark on some schoolboy prank, devilishly flout all the headmaster's iron proprieties. Frenchie Devereux, Trevanian Hale, and Ed Grace galloped their horses into the river in a sheet of spray, plunging them into a race with the raft, leaving behind the last two of the party, Hank and Scotty. When the boys on the far bank saw what was up, they hopped about waving their arms, hollering, and snapping off pistol-shots into the blue sky as the raftsmen bent their backs to the poles and the riders whooped on their surging horses.

Devereux's horse was a hands-down winner. It came clambering spiritedly up the trampled mud of the ford, the only stretch of riverbank for several hundreds of yards where steep cutbanks did not overhang the water, Devereux clinging to its back like a leech, his shoulder-length black hair and drooping moustache strewing water, sopping buckskins moulded to his lean body. Cantering his wild-eyed horse around the grinning men he shouted, "Frenchie Devereux! He run the buffalo, he! He run the river, he! Goddamn son of a bitch, eh?"

"Goddamn catfish, he!" Hardwick yelled back at him, pointing to Devereux's moustache. "Goddamn Missouri salmon, he! If the whores in Benton got a look at you now, Frenchie, they wouldn't have you in their beds. They'd have you buttered in the frying pan!" All the men hooted and roared with laughter as Hardwick crooked his thumb across the river to Scotty, jaybird-naked in the hot afternoon sunshine. "A whore don't care for no limp catfish whiskers," he said. "She's after the bait old Scotty's dangling."

Just then the Scotchman leapt up on his thoroughbred and rode it bareback into the river, for all the world a schoolbook myth, rider on the frieze of the Parthenon, gleaming white and confident, head of his horse with cocked ears and distended nostrils parting the brown water like a brave figurehead on a brave ship, Hank following gingerly in his wake. Halfway across the river the Scotchman even slipped off the horse, playfully grasped its tail, and was taken in tow for several yards before letting go and swimming the last ten yards to shore, white arms rising and falling in radiant spray as he pulled himself confidently through the brown water.

Meanwhile, Hank's horse had balked in the shallows, swinging its head from side to side in dismay, snuffling the water as the hired man whipped its flanks and drummed its barrel with his heels. Slowly, step by step, the old white horse reluctantly allowed itself to be goaded into the stream, whinnying to the horses on the far bank as the water lapped its belly and chest. Then, suddenly, the riverbed dropped off, throwing the white horse headlong into the current with a mighty splash. For an instant, only the heads of horse and man could be seen, bobbing in the grip of the current like flood debris; then the arched neck of the horse, the chest of the man broke upward, awash in filthy water and fear.

Scotty, reaching the opposite bank, turned, the blue-white marble gleam of his body sheathed in a coat of silt. The Englishman's boy stood in his stirrups for a better look. Devereux swore an oath in French.

Each time Hank swung the horse in the direction of the knot of men waiting on the bank, the plug would flounder vainly for a few moments, then surrender to the current and be swept further downstream. Already rider and horse had been carried past the ford to where cutbanks stooped over the river, sheer faces of eroded clay and exposed tree roots clawing the air, precipices too steep for a horse to scramble up them and out of the water.

The Englishman's boy knew it for bad, deep trouble. Hank knew it too. He kept trying to jerk his horse around and abreast the stream, back to the landing spot. But its head kept swinging downriver like a compass needle north, back to the path of least resistance.

Lifting a white and stricken face to the riverbank Hank called imploringly, "God Almighty, boys! Help me or I'm a goner!"

Devereux, Hale, and the Englishman's boy booted their horses to the river's edge but they shied and reared; having swum it once, they would not take it again. The other ponies, spooked by the rearing horses, trampled about in confusion and balked at entering the stream. One last time, Hank tried to turn the white horse, failed, and despairingly flung himself out of the saddle, chopping the water with short frantic strokes. The Englishman's boy guessed all Hank's swimming had been done in a rain barrel. He was using himself up fast.

Hale shook out a rope and spun a loop into the river. It didn't come near reaching the failing swimmer. Ed Grace and Charlie Harper struggled through the confusion of horses and shoved off in one of the rafts, but in their hurry they upset it and spilled into the shallows, had to watch the clumsy craft spin out of reach.

They all froze in silence. Watched Hank giving out, his arms feebly clawing the river, his tipped face smeared by a glaze of water and sun. Watched the white horse, now under the overhang of the cutbank, squealing and desperately pawing the face of crumbling clay, sliding back down the slippery slope and crashing back into the river. The whole sluggish dream of doom, blind face gasping for breath, sharp burst of birdsong in the willows, heat trembling trapped between cutbanks, the overpowering, sickly-sweet odour of blooming wolf willow, cousin to the musky, cunning, creeping smell of death. The whole slow playing-out of man's bitter nightmare portion.

Then they heard a splash to their right. Saw Scotty in the water, swimming hard. Saw Hank go completely under, all but for one hand scrabbling and tearing at the air for a hold, then shoot back to the surface, buoyed by the last desperate kick of panic, pale exhausted face disbelieving and bewildered. Saw Scotty grab him from behind as he was sinking for the second time, forearm under the jaw, rolling the dead weight on to its back, heading for the bank, shouting, "Kick, man, kick!" Coming on in jerks, slowly, struggling in the unforgiving grip of whatever clutched their ankles, whatever dragged them down, whatever poured water into their gaping mouths, stopped their nostrils, wrapped their limbs in lead and futility. They were ten yards from touching bottom and it was a coin toss. Four men waded out as far as they could and stood tensely waiting. In the terrible expectant stillness they could hear the hollow panting, the groans racking the swimmers, sounds like a woman labouring to give birth. They beckoned, whispered encouragement under their breath as the small waves slapped against them. "Go it, Scotty," they whispered. "That's the lad." "Just a bit more." "Come on, sport."

And then the two were almost within reach, half-under, sunk like water-logged timbers, rolling in the wash. Devereux leaned out, Ed Grace clutching his belt, and snatched a sleeve.

Half-carried, swooning with exhaustion, the swimmers sloshed through knee-deep water. Scotty set foot to solid ground, took three shaky steps and sank to his haunches, sat with head hanging between knees, arms hugging shins. Hank staggered on a little further, arms slung over Devereux's and Grace's shoulders, then dropped to his hands and knees, retched, crawled away from his puke, retched again, and fell on his face, hugging the earth, knotting his fingers in the short grass.

Vogle came riding to the ford along the top of the cutbank, towing the white horse back upstream with a lariat dallied to his saddlehorn. While it had battered itself against the steep bank like a fly against a windowpane, he had managed to toss a noose around its neck. He pulled ashore the stumbling, spent, mud-smeared horse. Hardwick ran his eyes over it quickly, shouldered himself through the gang clustered around Hank, halted over the sprawled figure. He nudged him with his boot, but the farm hand squirmed against the soil, mewling like a baby somebody was trying to pluck from its mother's breast. Hooking a toe under him, Hardwick turned him turtle and Hank lay blinking up into the sun, teeth chattering between blue lips.

"Three blind mice, three blind mice," Hardwick began to croon, bending over Hank like a mother bends over a cradle. "See how they run, see how they run, / They all run after the farmer's wife, / Who cut off their tails with a carving knife." The men threw uneasy, surprised glances to one another as Hardwick sang in a mocking falsetto to the man spread-eagled on the ground. His voice kept rising higher and higher. "Did you ever see such a sight in your life / As three blind mice?" Then, as abruptly as he had begun, he broke off, peered hard into the face of the man whimpering with fear and rubbing the back of his hand back and forth across his blue lips.

"Ever see such a sight in your life as this blind mouse?" Hardwick inquired coldly.

Evans cleared his throat. "You can see he ain't well, Tom. Give the man a chance."

Hardwick lowered himself on one knee beside Hank. "He ain't a goddamn man," he said fiercely. "If the best part of him hadn't run down his momma's leg he'd have been a rat, but instead she had to squeeze out a little blind cheese-eater mouse."

"I feel bad," said Hank. "Real bad. I near drownded."

"You near drownded," said Hardwick. He pointed to where Scotty still sat in a daze, chin on his chest. "You near drownded that man there, who saved your skin. That's who you near drownded, you worthless, no-account, half-a-penny mouse pelt."

"It ain't all his fault," said Evans. "He was riding a unlucky horse."

Hardwick got to his feet and spat. "Unlucky horse? Blind horse is more like it. Dumb son of a bitch's been riding a blind horse since yesterday and didn't know it. Blind mouse on a blind horse."

"Blind horse?" said Evans.

Hardwick strode to the white horse daubed with yellow mud. "Why you think he missed the ford? Why you think he tried to climb that cutbank?" He poked his cigar inches from the nag's eye. It didn't startle. "Stone blind," he repeated.

"Well, I'll be jiggered," said Evans.

"Don't flinch from a lit stogie." Hardwick drew his revolver. "No more than a pistol between the eyes," he said matter-of-factly, raising his arm and firing in one movement.

The white horse crashed to earth like a wall razed in an earthquake. It lay in the rubble of its flesh, legs lashing about in the last gallop, impressing its mark in the mud like a child makes an angel in snow.

"Mind the hoofs, boys," said Hardwick mildly, stepping around the flailing body.

The legs stiffened, the horse shuddered, died.

Already Hardwick was shoving his way through the stunned men. "We lost us time here," he said. "Get the gear on the pack horses. Get Scotty dressed and ready to ride."

"What about him?" asked Evans of Hank. "He needs a horse."

"That's his horse there," said Hardwick, pointing. "If it can keep up, he's welcome."

They rode out an hour later. Hank sat with Mr. Robinson's gun and the gunny sack of bacon which Hardwick had thrown him clutched to his breast. To the rider of each horse which passed, only feet from where he sat with his legs stuck out before him, he repeated the same words in a lifeless voice. "You best not leave me. Mr. Robinson'll have the Choteau County law on you boys. Consider it."

Apparently they had. No one spoke or looked at him. The trim legs of the horses paced by, as elegantly precise and monotonous as a metronome. Then he sat waiting for more legs to pass to which he could speak and there were none. "You don't want to fool with the law," he said. "No sirree." He got to his feet and shouted after them, "You don't want to fool with the law!"

No one looked back, the horses plodded on. There was nothing but the sound of the wind and his own sobbing. He ran after them the best he could, clutching his rifle and bacon to his chest, but it was cumbersome so he let the bacon fall. The figures got smaller and the sky more immense. It was the river all over again, a wider river, horizon to horizon, waves of grass. It was drowning, the wind stuffing itself in his throat when he opened his mouth to shout, the burning lungs.

The last the Englishman's boy saw of Hank he was running and falling, getting up to run and fall again, running and falling. It was a shameful sight and he turned away from it. A little later, they heard three faint rifle-shots behind them, like firecrackers in the wind.

"What's that?" Evans asked, harkening.

"That fool popping his popgun," said Hardwick.

Evans thought for a moment. "He ain't shot himself," he said. "Not three times."

"Don't bet on it. Stupid bastard rode a horse for a day and didn't figure out it was blind. That nester could shoot himself in the head three times. Nothing there to harm."

"I don't know what to think," said Evans diplomatically. "It don't feel right to have left him afoot."

"If we'd left him a horse we'd never have got shut of him. He'd have dogged us like Mary's little lamb."

"Well, he was green."

"Green? So green he don't shit, he drips sap."

"If you say, Tom."

95

"He was a Jonah. Bad luck. Now we're rid of him, we're down to twelve. No more misfortunate number thirteen. Ain't that so, Vogle?"

Vogle nodded sagely. "I don't enjoy no thirteen," he said.

"Jonah or Judas or some kind of witchery J," muttered Hardwick. "Gone now anyways."

As the Englishman's boy rode, he speculated on the old white horse. Trade one pitch-black darkness for another endless night. Where's the percentage? Except he got the rider off his back, now he didn't have to bear around no heaviness in the level black where he lay, or stood, old white horse.

Last thing that horse ever did hear, the crack of the goddamn round that done him down. Never-ending darkness plus never-ending silence. There's a cheat. But minus the misery. Just maybe, minus the misery. It was hard to say, a hard calculation.

Except for this. Better the white horse than him.

And then it came into the Englishman's boy's mind. The old white horse standing in the darkness of the other side and a rider setting on his back, a rider the Englishman's boy could not make out, nor read his face or the meaning of his gestures, but knew only that he was a sign that nothing was different on the other side, only darker and dimmer, and that the rider on the pale horse was again one of their party, the unlucky, the cursed thirteenth.

IO

Within an hour of leaving Shorty McAdoo, I pass on to Fitzsimmons news of my success at finding him. Fitz tells me that he'll let Chance know. Then he says, "Don't ever take the phone off the hook on me again like you did last night, Vincent," and hangs up. I sit down to wait for Chance to call. An hour later, the phone rings.

"Hello, My Little Truth Seeker. Long time no see."

"Rachel," I say warily. I've known sooner or later she would call, but I'm still not ready to fend off the questions I know are coming.

"Why don't we see you at the office any more? Your absence is sorely felt."

"I thought Fitz explained that."

"Fitz said you wouldn't be coming in for a while. I thought that meant a couple of days. It's been over two weeks. What's up? You aren't sick, are you?"

"I'm working."

"Working on what?"

"A picture."

"Don't give me any of that guff. If you are, the story editor hasn't heard about it. And he's the next best thing to God around here, all-seeing, all-knowing."

"There are higher authorities," I say.

"Fitz?"

"I can't talk about it."

"What're you doing for that black-hearted Irish bandit?"

"Not Fitz."

"Who then?"

"Chance."

There's a pause. The line hums in my ear. "Harry, have you been taking your quinine? I believe your malaria's acting up. What interesting hallucinations it produces."

"Don't believe me then."

But she does. "You? Working for the great man? You've actually been to his office?"

"His house." Despite myself, I'm beginning to revel in my glory.

"In the hills?"

"That's right."

"Up there on Mount Olympus? My curiosity is whetted. Details, Harry. Details. Describe, if you would be so good."

"It's just a house."

"There are no houses up there. Only works of art. Tell me, does he have a piece of the Parthenon in it? Like Mr. Valentino?" Deprecating the taste of the Hollywood aristocracy is one of Rachel Gold's favourite pastimes. "Is it foundering under a great weight of Louis Quinze furniture and Sheraton chairs? Does he have dozens and dozens of Fabergé eggs? And what does he serve them with? Did you hear the latest? One of our leading ladies was recently complaining that the caviar she bought smelled like fish. Chaplin said, 'What did you expect? Because it was eggs, it would smell like chicken?'"

I laugh. "No, Chance's house is nothing like that. He seems to live in the few rooms that Adilman decorated before he sold it to him. It's mostly empty."

"Well, we can't take the measure of the man from that, can we? Next and most pertinent question. Houseboy or butler? Remember when Mickey Neilan got the Oriental houseboy and you weren't anyone unless you had a Japanese or Filipino flunky? But now the pendulum seems to be swinging. Genuine English butlers are all the rage. They're better at teaching you what fork to use. I've heard you can't get a booking on an ocean liner – the transatlantic traffic in Jeeveses is filling all the cabins. Rumour is, they're even stacking all those stiff, English pricks like cordwood in the holds to fill the demand. So which side of the question does Chance come down on in the momentous domestic question, East or West?"

"I don't know," I say.

"And you call yourself an intimate of the Great One. Fie, fie."

"I never called myself anything. You did."

Rachel changes gears, abruptly. "So what's the picture, Harry?"

"I can't talk about it."

"Big secret?"

"You might call it that."

"So why you? How come you're privy to the big secret?"

I'm tempted to answer: intuition. But I don't. "You'd have to ask Mr. Chance."

"It doesn't make any sense," Rachel says. "You're not a scenarist, you're a title-writer."

That stings. "Maybe somebody thinks I'm capable of more."

"No, Harry," says Rachel with great seriousness. "You're a title-writer. And for that you can be thankful."

"What's that supposed to mean?"

"That's my secret." She pauses. "Come back soon, Harry. I miss you."

"All right," I say. Rachel hangs up.

I miss her, too. But not in the way she misses me. There's no point to the way I miss her.

Shortly after Rachel leaves the line, the phone rings again. It's Chance. Unequivocally delighted with my results. We must mark the occasion with a small celebration, a late-night buffet. Could I drop by the house about eleven tonight?

Chance greets me at the door and, offering his warmest congratulations on my success, leads me through his stark mansion. After all the barrenness, the dining room comes as an anomalous relief with its high coffered ceiling and walls of dark wood, its tapestries, its long trestle table floating islands of candles, serving dishes, wine coolers, bouquets of freshly cut flowers on a sea of starched white linen, its fire of logs in a fieldstone fireplace.

"This was as far as Mr. Adilman got in decorating his house before I purchased it," says Chance, guiding me around the room. "The table is reputedly thirteenth-century English." He raps it with his knuckles before he directs my attention to the walls. "Mr. Adilman was particularly proud of these Flemish tapestries which he acquired the year before war broke out in Europe. The château in which they had hung for three centuries was destroyed by German shelling in 1914 – like the medieval library of Louvain, he was fond of reminding everyone. To hear him talk, his purchase of these works of art was an act of clairvoyance and disinterested philanthropy. He was extremely disappointed when I did not dicker over the price of the furnishings, item by item. Apparently, he now entertains dinner guests with my naivete, laughing that he turned his Flemish rags over at a hundred per cent profit." Chance ponders the tapestries for several moments, then says, "Some day I will pull them off the walls and let Fitz wipe his boots on them."

I am examining one of the scenes depicted on the tapestries when he utters this bleak statement. A wild pig bristling with spears is in its death throes, red embroidery threads trace showers of blood. Impassively viewing its agony, a noble sits on a white horse, while peasants armed with hunting spears and billhooks crowd around his charger's flanks, apparently cowering in fear of the tusks of the boar.

Chance lays an arm over my shoulder and sets us moving toward the table. I see it is laid with two places. I ask whether Mr. Fitzsimmons will be joining us tonight.

"No, Fitz would be bored with our conversation. Don't misunderstand me when I say this – because no man ever had a more stalwart friend than I have had in Fitz – but his mind is not tuned to abstractions. 'The Hermit of Hollywood'" – he puts the words in self-deprecating quotation marks – "sometimes finds his isolation heavy. A little intelligent conversation centred upon the higher realms is always welcome."

An extraordinarily handsome young Oriental who bears a strong resemblance to the actor Sessue Hayakawa pushes a trolley loaded with food into the room.

"Ah, Yukio," exclaims Chance. "This looks very good, splendid."

We seat ourselves and Yukio begins to deftly lay dishes of shrimp, smoked salmon, oysters on the half-shell, salad, sliced roast beef, warm rolls and butter. Chance lifts his eyebrows, a signal he is about to impart a confidence. "You need not worry about Yukio," he says. "His English is very poor, just the rudiments of housekeeping pidgin." Chance points to the roast beef and says loudly, "Roasty beefy? Top good roasty beefy?" Yukio smiles a beautiful smile and nods energetically. "You need not fear that anything you say in front of Yukio will ever leave this room," Chance assures me.

I am about to tell Chance that such a fear had never crossed my mind when a champagne cork pops and Yukio is filling our glasses. Chance raises his in a toast. "To an enterprise well and truly launched. Thanks to you, Harry." From his chair, he salutes me with a stiff, truncated bow.

We drink. Maybe it's just the first flush of success, but I feel the need to emphasize the difficulty of finding Shorty McAdoo. Eyes modestly fastened on the bubbles spurting in my glass, I say, "Well, Mr. Chance, I won't pretend it was easy. A bit like locating a needle in a haystack. I know Fitzsimmons was losing patience with me but I really don't believe he understood . . ." I look up; my voice trails away to nothing.

Chance isn't listening to me. He's snatching up platters and sweeping food onto his plate, one dish following another with an assembly-line efficiency fit to gladden the heart of Henry Ford. Now my own voice has fallen quiet, I am aware of the frantic scraping of cutlery on china, the muffled thud of discarded plates dropping on the linen tablecloth. Chance's nose is almost in his food, the silence broken only by the crackle of rolls tearing apart in his hands, the soft whistle and pant of his breath as he stuffs his mouth, the clatter of his fork and knife. His face is beginning to glisten with sweat; his bright blue eyes moistly bulge as he chews.

There is nothing to do but eat, but my eyes keep sneakily rising from my dinnerware and snatching glances at my boss. All at once, he primly crosses his knife and fork on his plate. It's as if a machine had finished eating. Yukio whisks it away. I signal the houseboy to take my plate, too. The firelight pulses on the walls, dances on the silverware and crystal. Chance sits completely still, his eyes fixed where his plate has lain, face as blank as the spot he regards. Behind him, an impassive Yukio stands at attention in starched white coat, the only movement in his face the reflected play of the flames leaping and crackling on the fire irons. When Chance finally does lift his eyes to me, there is scarcely a glimmer of recognition in them. His absent-minded smile is the smile of someone politely easing his way by a stranger in the crowded aisle of a trolley car. "The years of study that lie behind this picture," he says.

A log sinks in the fireplace with a sputter of sparks. I shift uncomfortably in my chair, pick up my napkin, lay it down again. I say, "Your study of Griffith?"

My question seems to pull him back a little from wherever he has drifted. He begins to jab the linen tablecloth with the tines of a dessert fork. "No, not just Griffith," he says. "Griffith is only one piece of the puzzle. A small piece." His habitual fluency seems to return. "You might say that for ten years I searched for the pieces to the picture, trying this and trying that – history, sociology, economics, philosophy – looking for useful fragments here and there, testing and discarding. There were many roadblocks; I awoke in many dark woods." He thinks for a moment, sips his champagne. "It is not easy to grope your way to first principles. It is not easy to forsake personal prejudices for the truth. For instance, even as a small boy I loathed my father. His materialism repelled me. But with time, I came to see that he was merely the unconscious and unwitting servant of the chief tendency of the nineteenth century – the drive to increase and bind together material forces. Carnegie, Gould, Rockefeller, their vaunted independence and initiative was all really an illusion, and they the unconscious agents of what the Germans call the *Zeitgeist* – the spirit of the age. These men were simply tools of an evolutionary process of which they were no more conscious than the lowest life form is of its role in the process of biological evolution. And realizing this, I came to pity my father, pitied his blind, mole-like industry, pitied him most because he deluded himself he was captain of his own fate. The growth of great industrial and business trusts, the unification of Italy and of Germany, the war we fought in this country to prevent the disintegration of the Union, the growth of the European empires were all manifestations of the same urge, the urge to combine and consolidate material forces.

"The more I meditated upon my father's life the more I came to understand that every man is the servant of historical forces – that no man can deny the spirit of his age, any more than a fish can renounce the water for the land. But the fishes which know the currents, the pools, and the eddies of the stream they inhabit, these are the fishes who increase their chances of survival. And so do the men who familiarize themselves with the currents of the age to which they are confined. That I was determined to do."

Chance hesitates briefly, a lecturer marshalling his forces for the next onslaught upon the topic. I wait, perplexed. I have no idea what this "spirit of the age" talk is all about. It sounds a bit like the spiritualist, table-knocking-to-get-in-touch-with-the-dearly-departed, Madame Blavatsky, Hindu swami bullshit which finds such a warm welcome in Hollywood. But I'm not sure. Somehow this is different.

"Which brings me to the present," he says. "Before and after the war I travelled extensively in Europe. It was evident to me that the war had unravelled the nineteenth century and everything it stood for. But America has not realized this. In America, business continues as usual. One year of war was not enough to teach us the stern lessons learned by Europe. America's supremacy in the field of industrial production has made her blind to the facts. The war racked Europe with a creative suffering, the travails of a hard and agonizing birth, the parturition of a quickening spirit. While bigger business, bigger armies, more coal, more steel gave the advantages necessary for survival in the nineteenth century, these alone will not be sufficient for success in the new century. In the twentieth century, survival can only be insured by a consolidation of *spiritual* forces." Chance leans forward eagerly in his chair as he delivers this remarkable statement.

Eccentricity is the privilege of rich men. They can afford it. I set my glass down carefully on the table. "Spiritual forces, Mr. Chance? I'm not sure what you mean. Are you talking about the League of Nations? Ethical principles ruling the conduct of states?"

He smiles condescendingly. "No, Harry, the League of Nations is the furthest thing from my mind – Voltaire arguing that primitive impulses and bloodlust can be curbed by an appeal to reason. When I speak of spiritual forces, I am speaking of that side of man which the nineteenth century denied because of its worship of reason and science."

"What side would that be?"

"Intuition, the life force, what Bergson calls the *élan vital*, the irrational. The night world of visions and fantasies and the waking world of fructifying daydreams. The lost primitive. Sudden insight, inspiration, impulse, imagination. *Instinct*, Harry! The flexing, the liberation of the will. The rich, chaotic, creative stew of the unconscious! But I speak only words, Harry, bare nouns, mere shadows of rich and complex impulses which words fail to properly describe." He smiles, as if realizing he is getting too carried away, speaks more quietly. "I don't want you to mistake my meaning, Harry. I am *not* suggesting we turn our back on the benefits science has conferred. Far from it. The question is not the rejection of technological and material innovations; the question is whether we Americans will summon up our as yet unawakened spiritual forces and employ them for proper ends."

"What ends are these, Mr. Chance?"

Chance is not ready to answer my question. He leans back in his chair, relaxing in the warmth of a memory. "Can I describe for you one of the most momentous events in my life, Harry? It occurred in August of 1907 when I bought my first ticket to a nickelodeon. Do you remember what nickelodeons were like in those days? A couple of hundred folding chairs in a failed grocery store, pool room, bankrupt hardware store. Filled with poor immigrants – Irishmen, Poles, Russians, Scandinavians, Italians. Cheap entertainment for a nickel. The foreigners loved the new picture stories because you didn't have to be able to speak English to understand them, pictures told the tale. The nickelodeons had a bad reputation among respectable people; they were rumoured to be dens of vice; people of my background spoke sneeringly of them as amusement for idiots. But one afternoon on a visit to New York my curiosity got the better of me; I paid my nickel and took my seat among the crowd in the dark. The stench was unbelievable! Week-old sweat, unwashed underpants, a cloud of garlic. Sickening. When the picture began, I was convinced it was nothing but idiotic tomfoolery, mind-numbing sentiment, crapulous melodrama. But then something happened, Harry. The hall was mesmerized, and I do not use the word loosely. They were moved. They wept over innocence outraged, they blazed with hatred for the unrepenting wicked. You recall what happened to Erich von Stroheim after playing so many evil Prussians during the war? It wasn't safe for him to go out in the streets. When he was recognized, stones were thrown at his automobile. It was no different that afternoon. If the villain had appeared in the flesh, they would have torn him to pieces, limb from bleeding limb.

"I'd never experienced anything like it. They roared with laughter, rocking back and forth on their gimcrack seats, heaving like the body of some great beast, mindful of nothing but the flickering on the bedsheets nailed to the wall. And as I sat there among them, something began to move in me as well, Harry. I began to feel the wordless pressure of the crowd, the deep desire of the crowd to encompass, to swallow everyone up in a surge of feeling, to bespeak itself with a single voice. And as the minutes flew by, I could feel arise in me a deep longing to lose myself in the shielding darkness, to lose myself in the featureless crowd! And in the end I did let myself go, all the Puritan reserve and self-possession I had been taught from childhood dissolved, gave way like a rotten dam. I found myself laughing, laughing like I had never laughed before in my life! I shook with it, I rocked back and forth in my chair, banging my heels against the floor!

Seconds later I wept, tears streaming down my face! When the crowd hissed their hatred, I hissed my hatred too! Hissed like a snake! A great release of feeling in the darkness, feeling which touched the lost primitive."

He looks pale now, drawn. His fingers toy with a forgotten champagne glass. Another log collapses in the fireplace, releasing a train of sparks, a cataract of glowing embers. He takes out a cigar, places it between his lips, and Yukio is there with a match. Chance takes a few tranquillizing puffs.

"When I left that nickelodeon, I took something important away with me. The knowledge that the new century was going to be a century governed by images, that the spirit of the age would express itself in an endless train of images, one following upon the other with the speed of the steam locomotive that was the darling of the last century and symbolized all its aspirations. I knew that all those Boston Brahmins I had been raised among, the Cabots, Lodges, and Lowells who held themselves aloof from childish photoplays and who forbade their children to attend them, were nothing more than dumb fish insensible to currents which were capable of sweeping them to their destruction. And while they clung blindly to the past, their Irish chauffeurs and gardeners were learning the language of the new century in the nickelodeon, were learning to think and feel in the language of pictures. Have you noticed how many Irishmen direct pictures?"

I don't contradict him and state the obvious, that the Cabots, Lowells, and Lodges still seem very much securely in the seats of power, and that the Irish are still cleaning the Cabot crystal and driving the Lodges around in their swanky automobiles. All I say is, "The only Irishman I know in pictures is Mr. Fitzsimmons."

Chance doesn't register this comment; he's already pressing on. "When President Woodrow Wilson was given a private screening of *The Birth of a Nation*, he declared it was 'History written in lightning.' The metaphor is fitting. Think of what we all remember of that picture. Battle scenes. The assassination of Lincoln. Lee surrendering to Grant. The stirring ride of the Ku Klux Klan. Sitting through

Griffith's picture is like sitting through one of those dark summer nights when a thunderstorm breaks: instants of brilliant illumination when the things which flash before your eyes – a tree waving in the wind, a river in spate, your bedroom chair – burn into your brain in a way they never would in the steady, even light of day. There is no logical explanation as to why or how this happens. Images take root in your mind, hot and bright, like an image on a photoplate. Once they etch themselves there, they can't be obliterated, can't be scratched out. They burn themselves in the mind. Because there's no arguing with pictures. You simply accept or reject them. What's up there on the screen moves too fast to permit analysis or argument. You can't control the flow of images the way you can control a book – by rereading a chapter, rereading a paragraph, rereading a sentence. A book invites argument, invites reconsideration, invites thought. A moving picture is beyond thought. Like feeling, it simply *is*. The principle of a book is persuasion; the principle of a movie is revelation. Martin Luther was converted in a lightning storm, a conversion accomplished in the bowels and not the mind. A lesson for all of us in this business to remember."

I am getting interested in what Chance has to say. It must show in my face; he leans forward in his chair, lowering his voice. "*Birth* became America's history lesson on the Civil War. For the first time, everybody, rich and poor, Northerner and Southerner, native and immigrant, found themselves pupils in the same history class. A class conducted in Philadelphia and New York, in little Iowa theatres and converted saloons in Wyoming. The movie theatre became the biggest night school any teacher had ever dreamed of; one big classroom stretching from Maine to California, an entire nation sitting at Griffith's feet. In New York alone, eight hundred thousand people saw *Birth*, more people than there are students in all the colleges in all the states of the Union. Think about it, Harry. If Lincoln was the Great Emancipator, Griffith is the Great Educator. Whatever bits of history the average American knows, he's learned from Griffith. Griffith marks the birth of spiritual Americanism."

"And what is this spiritual Americanism, Mr. Chance?"

"Perhaps it can't be defined in words, Harry. Pictures come closest to capturing its meaning. I am a patriot. I was raised a patriot and I will die a patriot. But for years I was troubled by the question, Why have the American people produced no great art? The Germans gave the world their music. The Romans their architecture. The Greeks their tragedies. We recognize the soul of a people in their art. But where is the American soul? I asked myself. Then it dawned on me. *The American soul could not find expression in these old arts because the spirit of the American people was not compatible with them, could not be encompassed in them.*" Chance shoots me a victorious look. "You see? The American spirit is a frontier spirit, restless, impatient of constraint, eager for a look over the next hill, the next peek around the bend in the river. The American destiny is *forward momentum.* What the old frontiersman called westering. What the American spirit required was an art form of forward momentum, an art form as bold and unbounded as the American spirit. A *westering* art form! It had to wait for motion pictures. The art form of *motion*!"

"I see," I say.

"And yet," says Chance with the air of a man divulging a great confidence, "everywhere I look, I see little evidence of that spirit in American pictures. Do you know the reason, Harry?" He reaches in his pocket and produces a piece of paper which he lays on the table, methodically smoothing out its creases. "I asked Fitz to do some research for me. Into the heads of the major studios." He begins to read from the paper. "Adolph Zukor and Fox were born in Hungary. Warner and Goldwyn in Poland. Selznick and Mayer in Russia. Laemmle in Germany. There is the answer why the American movie industry is in such a sorry state. Europeans making our movies for us. Goldwyn hiring English writers. Adolph Zukor offering us *Queen Elizabeth*, with Sarah Bernhardt as star. A French actress playing an English queen. Which he follows with *The Prisoner of Zenda.* European kitsch." He refolds the paper and tucks it out of sight under his plate. "The classroom of the American spirit is now located in the movie house. Americans go to the pictures two and three times a week. Griffith made the American *Iliad*, I intend to make the American *Odyssey*. The story of an American Odysseus, a westerer, a sailor of the plains, a man who embodies the raw vitality of America, the raw vitality which is our only salvation in the days which lie ahead. Perhaps Shorty McAdoo is my Odysseus. Do you think it's possible?"

I shake my head. "It's too early to say – maybe."

Chance sits musing. "I have seen things abroad. I have seen Europe rediscovering the spirit of the primitive, the life source by which nations live and die; I have seen them grasping the power of images. Last year Mussolini marched his Blackshirts on Rome and the government, the army folded. The government possessed all the material force necessary to prevail, and yet they gave way to a few thousand men with pistols in their pockets. Why? Because Mussolini orchestrated a stream of images more potent than artillery manned by men without spiritual conviction. Thousands of men in black shirts marching the dusty roads, clinging to trains, piling into automobiles. They passed through the countryside like film through a projector, enthralling onlookers. And when Rome fell, Mussolini paraded his Blackshirts through the city, before the cameras, so they could be paraded over and over again, as many times as necessary, trooped through every movie house from Tuscany to Sicily, burning the black shirt and the silver death's head into every Italian's brain. Imagine if Lenin learns the trick. Imagine what would happen to us."

"You're going too fast for me, Mr. Chance," I say.

"No, Harry," he says firmly. "I believe you understand me. I believe you see beyond what others see. I know what they say behind my back. That I am a man whose father made his money for him. A ridiculous figure, a standing joke in Hollywood. 'He can't make movies, and unlike Kennedy, he can't make actresses either. A eunuch.'"

"No, Mr. Chance," I falsely object, "I don't believe anyone says such –"

He interrupts me. There is a burden of melancholy in his words.

"I wish this cup would pass from my lips. But there is no one else. No one else but Griffith and me to make the pictures this country needs."

The Hollywood style is grandiose. I am used to bombast and inflation, every picture described as "colossal," "magnificent," "unsurpassable," "epic of epics." But the people who make such announcements do not really believe them, you can hear the cynicism in their voices, sense it in their ridiculously purple prose. But in Chance's voice there is a strength of conviction, of sincerity, which is almost moving.

Suddenly Chance looks exhausted. He fumbles for the square of paper under his plate, picks it up, stares at it. Stares at it in the same queer way he had earlier stared at his empty plate, face vapid and waxen. Is it some kind of epileptic seizure?

"Mr. Chance?" I say. "Mr. Chance?" Neither he nor Yukio moves. The houseboy remains standing behind his employer's chair, face empty, blank as his master's. "Yukio," I say, "get Mr. Chance a glass of water. I don't think he's well."

Yukio does not move but Chance does. He raises his hand and holds out the scrap of paper to me. "I'd like you to have this. As a souvenir of the evening. I have no further need of it." He rises from his chair and slips it into my palm, the way an uncle slips a nickel into the hand of a favourite nephew. I mumble an embarrassed nephew's thanks. "Harry," he says, "I want you to know how important this evening has been to me. I do not feel nearly so alone. You believe as I do, that the mind's highest struggle is to interpret the world, in whatever guise that interpretation takes – science, philosophy, history, literature, painting . . ." His voice dies away. He clears his throat. "And we shall offer another. We shall make a great motion picture. Won't we, Harry?"

"Yes," I say. And half-believe it.

"Now, if you'll excuse me, I'm very tired."

We shake hands and Yukio leads me back through the bare house. I feel some guilt that I have not confessed to Chance that he is seeking help for making the great American film from a Canadian. But there is the question of money. And I have found that Americans, by and large, recognize no distinction between us. Why should I?

I start the car and turn down the drive. As I do, my headlights sweep over a set of French doors which open onto the garden. It is only for an instant, but I believe I have glimpsed Damon Ira Chance alone, in that vast marble desert of a ballroom, standing upright on a chair, in the dark.

I I

The rest of the afternoon the twelve rode with the Bear Paw Mountains hovering mauve, abrupt, stonily upright in the east. For the first hour after Hardwick's desertion of Farmer Hank, each man was mindful to keep his thoughts and his counsel to himself. It was dangerous to do otherwise with Tom in one of his black and bloody moods. Still, a number did feel a trifle downcast and guilty they hadn't put a word in for the farm hand, pled the case that he ought to be left with a horse, even a pack horse, in exchange for the one which Hardwick had blasted between its blind eyes. It wasn't consequences with the law they feared, but the verdict of public opinion. In these parts, cutting loose a man on foot to fend for himself could be regarded as a mite high-handed, even if he was cast out in peaceable country and ought to be able to hike back without mishap to his employer's homestead by tomorrow. If he could recross the river.

And yet, there was no denying they were glad to have seen the last of him. If it came to an affray with Indians, settled men were not much use. Nobody knew for sure whether Hank was a settled man who owned a wife and children, but if he didn't, he had the look of a fellow who *wanted* to own them, which was near as bad. You needed to have a little wild Indian rubbed into you to fight Indians. Which was why Hardwick was such a demon for warring with the red bastards – he'd been captured by Arapahos in Wyoming and seen hard use as a slave before he managed to pull foot and escape. Ever since this close acquaintance with the Arapahos, Hardwick had been apt to kill Indians whenever they annoyed him in the smallest particular.

The Englishman's boy, like all the rest, had said nothing about casting Hank adrift. After a fashion, he was sorry for sorry-ass Hank, but watching him near drown the Scotchman confirmed that he was not only a fool, a shirker, and poisonous bad luck, but a man likely to drag anyone who tried to help him six feet under. Besides, the Englishman's boy was in no position to hand around irritating advice, seeing as he had nowhere to take himself except back to Fort Benton, where trouble awaited him. He might smell trouble here, too, but maybe it was trouble that could be dodged. The white horse and Hank surely was a lesson. If Hardwick got down on you, God help you. If there came a time when he scraped up against Hardwick's bad side, he knew now what to expect.

It was necessary to make the best of the cards he'd been dealt, and as things stood, he'd seen worse hands. In a couple of hours he'd be eating bacon and hard bread, which was a damn sight better than his dinner of cracker dust the night before last. He had a warm coat, a good hat, and he was armed. A strong, sound horse was carrying him. All he lacked was a new pair of brogans.

Scotty trotted up. Silt from the river had dried on his face in a fine, pale powder. It lent him a ghastly, otherworldly air, as if he were one of the risen dead answering to the last trump. A ghost with an odd look in his eye.

"I see Harris tweed in this howling wilderness," he remarked.

"Which one's Harris Tweed?" The Englishman's boy glanced about him.

Scotty brushed the boy's sleeve, fingered it covetously. "This is Harris tweed."

"The stuff?"

"Yes," said Scotty. "Harris tweed cut and stitched by a gentleman's tailor."

"Ain't no gentleman wearing it."

"Gentlemen are not commonly found in these parts. The conditions are not favourable for their support."

"The one owned this coat died right enough," said the boy.

The Scotchman sighed. "Misadventures are legion here. Road agents, sickness, storms, snakes, Indians –"

"Deep water with a fool in it."

"Indeed."

They rode on in silence for several minutes. Whereupon Scotty made a mournful request. "You wouldn't consider selling me that jacket, would you?"

"No."

"It's sizes too big for you."

"What's the matter with the coat you got?"

The Scotchman stared down at its travel-stained front. "I suppose it's largely a matter of comparison between the two. I mean to say –" He turned back to the Englishman's boy. "The maker's label on your jacket – what does it read?"

"Couldn't say. Can't read but a little."

"If you would permit me?" They stopped their horses and Scotty short-sightedly scrutinized the jacket lining. "London," he said at last, rebuttoning the jacket like a fond father putting his son in order before Sunday service. "Cruikshank's."

The boy held up the sleeve and showed him where the blood of the Benton hotel-keeper had drenched the cuff. "Spoiled," he said.

Scotty ruefully shook his head, tightened his lips.

They moved on. The Scotchman said, "If I was to claim to have once been a gentleman, would you believe me?"

"I ain't about to call you a liar."

"I ask because you're the only one of these fellows here who has had society with a gentleman. My mother was fond of saying that the definition of a gentleman is one who never inflicts pain." He contemplated for a moment. "On the other hand, it is said clothes do make the man. A Cruikshank coat couldn't hurt," he mused aloud. "Men in animal skins –" He cast a nervous, furtive glance at some of the half-breeds in buckskin. "Well, perhaps they acquire the characteristics of what they wear. What do you think?"

"I never gave it any thought."

"I confess regret at not having spoken up about the treatment of that chap at the ford. But when in Rome . . ." His voice faded off.

"It wouldn't made no difference. I don't believe there's a man among us is up to changing Hardwick's mind."

"Not Evans?"

A harsh bark of derisive laughter.

"I had pinned my hopes on Evans," said the Scotchman.

"Pin 'em on the donkey."

"I believed I detected a strain of common decency in Evans."

"Well, whatever strain's in his friend Hardwick is right uncommon. You can go to the bank on that."

Scotty fell dumb, growing more and more the sad and disillusioned spectre. Nursing, it seemed to the Englishman's boy, thoughts of Hardwick, or disappointment over the refusal to sell him the tweed coat he set such store by. Or maybe both.

～

Crossing rolling countryside in late afternoon, the line of march scattered and ragged as it crawls up ridges and descends into declivities which cup unpalatable water with a white petticoat hem of alkali deposit peeking from under a dirty skirt of mud. Evans and Hardwick outlined in stark silhouette against a sheet of azure sky cleansed of every stain of cloud; Evans and Hardwick dropping out of sight behind a knoll to rise again in vivid resurrection, tiny black figures against a void, only suddenly to waver, to run and dissolve like characters written in weak, watery ink.

The Englishman's boy dozing slumped in the saddle, hat tipped over his eyes, boots dangling loose in the stirrups, hands folded over the horn, horse wearily plodding on, rocking his saddle-cradle like a solicitous mother. Then, the surprise of a distant rifle-shot. The Englishman's boy snapping awake, ears cocking, eyes springing like cats at the landscape. Held breath. A second crack, followed by a faint ringing, like the dying fall of a tuning fork, a sound wavering, dispersing in the blue vacancy.

Scotty gives a shout, rousing his horse into a gallop. The Englishman's boy jerks his carbine from its scabbard, levers a cartridge into the chamber and turns loose after the Scotchman. Ahead, he sees five men spurring hard, rifles brandished in the air. They flounder over a knoll, disappear, suddenly reappear on the face of another barren swell, hounds of dust pursuing their heels. The boy leans into each rise over the withers of the scrambling horse, cocking himself forward in his stirrups; cants himself back in the saddle, toes up, when it drops on its haunches and slithers down a slope in a whirl of dust and pebbles. Up and down they go, two rises, three rises, four. He crests the fourth and suddenly there are no more. They've been rubbed flat. The sky rushes down to a great level span of monochrome – tarnished sage, withered bunch grass, dun dirt. A hundred yards beyond, the five horsemen are galloping to where their companions sit horses ranged along the horizon line like cups pushed flush to a table edge.

As he closes, he can hear shouting, wild cries, sees rifles bristling, horses stamping and wheeling. He reins his lathered horse in beside Scotty, stands in his stirrups to view the shivaree. Thirty yards off, Hardwick is on his horse, head to head with a big bull buffalo.

"Vogle was scouting for Indian trace when he spots this lone bull," a man called George Bell tells them excitedly. "Hardwick bets Vogle he can't take him down from back yonder, one shot with his Sharp's buffalo gun. Vogle lets fly and misses clean. The buffalo breaks and Hardwick snaps off a chance shot. Lucky son of a bitch hits one of his legs and cripples him." He points to the buffalo sidling and backing, shaggy head swinging slowly from side to side like a church bell tolling as Hardwick edges a nervous pony towards him.

Bell grins. "Tom's just hazing that old buff. Playing some kind of bean-eater Mexican bullfighter, I reckon."

Hardwick spurs his fidgety horse towards the bull. The bull lowers his head, lunges. Hardwick skips his horse to the side as the buffalo's leg buckles, crashing him into the dust. There are war-whoops, rebel yells, shrill whistling.

The bull struggles up smeared with ashy dust, panting, maddened, drool hanging like tinsel from his beard. Hardwick slaps his horse forward with a rifle barrel along the flank and the bull bawls, hooks his horns into the earth, gores and rips the prairie, showering dust and dirt over his back, his blunt head.

The men are all bawling, answering the bull. Deep, sonorous bellows. Shouts. "That buffler is in a fine pucker, Tom! He's a-looking to hook you up Salt River, he is!" "Fix his flint, Tom!"

And Hardwick, heeling his horse on, a cold, arrogant look on his face, rifle-stock planted on his hip. The bull dashes for the horse, the smashed leg crumples again and the buffalo capsizes, a blur of flailing legs. The wolfers guffaw, trumpet and bellow. Hardwick steps his horse daintily around the buffalo while the bull strains to rise, great hump and shoulders pitching, wrenching himself up to totter on three legs, fractured foreleg flapping like a broken branch only held together by a shred of bark.

Hardwick presses the jibbing horse to where the bull waits with black, distended tongue and blood-red eyes, shaking his huge head, flinging threads of slobber into his dirty, matted wool, massive shoulders bridling, the curved, polished horns hooking the air. Hardwick, erect in the saddle, eyes on the bull, rowels the horse on. The musk of the bull flaring the mare's nostrils, lifting her head higher and higher on a twisted neck, turning her eyes crazed and white, firing her hind legs into an executioner's drum roll.

They are all shouting now, some in English, some in French. To the Englishman's boy, the Frenchies' gibbering is crazy folks' noise, the babble of the county madhouse. Beside him he can hear Bell shouting frantic encouragement to Hardwick. "Go it, boy! Take him by the tail!"

The heavy head rises, the red eyes stare.

The Englishman's boy ducks at the sudden explosion beside his ear. Hardwick's horse is rearing and Hardwick clinging to her back. An acrid whiff of gunpowder sweeps like smelling salts through the head of the Englishman's boy. The bull is slowly dropping to the earth, a mass of meat and bone sinking slowly under its own weight, hindquarters slumping, head lolling. He subsides into the bunch grass with a groan, a whoosh of dust squirts out from under the collapsing body.

The Englishman's boy speaks to Scotty. Cannot hear his own voice. Scotty does not hear it either. His rifle is still tucked in his shoulder and he is looking down the steel-blue barrel at the dying buffalo. A whiff of blue smoke unravels when he slowly lowers the carbine. Now the Englishman's boy can hear Hardwick shouting angrily, wanting to know who the fuck has meddled in his frolic.

〜

The Englishman's boy has never seen the like. Vogle cuts the throat and the blood pours out thick and hot, a couple of the breeds catching it in tin cups like water from a pump, gulping it down. Devereux steps forward and splits the skull with a hand-axe, dipping brains with his fingers. Others scatter blue and yellow guts in the scramble for the heart and liver; where the intestines have snaked and coiled the grass wears a greasy shine. Charlie Harper slices buffalo hump like it was a loaf of bread.

Hardwick yanks the liver out of Duval's hand. Duval doesn't argue, doesn't object when Hardwick stalks off to hunker moodily on the ground. Holding the liver in his left hand, he grips it in his teeth, saws off a piece of the flesh with the hunting knife in his right. In a loud voice, between bites, he recollects a British hunter who had travelled with the wolfers for a season and had gladly eaten his meat raw. "He wasn't too high-toned and almighty to take his meat rare. Learned to like it and his women the same way – red and raw. He didn't put on no goddamn airs, did he, boys?" says Hardwick, staring at the Scotchman, who has refused to join the feast.

The Englishman's boy makes himself scarce, disappears amidst the hobbled horses.

The Scotchman sits alone on the grass, looking past the bloody banquet. Like a bystander in shock at a train wreck. Refusing to see.

12

The way he ties into the groceries I deliver makes me suspect the old man has been living on jack-rabbit and not much else. He starts with the cheese, paring cheddar from the wedge, shingling his soda crackers with paper-thin slices. Unhurried, steady chewing, a ruminative savouring of flavour, old turtle eyes squinching up with delight. After that, a can of sardines, forked up with the blade of a jackknife, the empty can mopped clean of the last of the oil, polished shiny with a dry heel of bread stored in the apple box by his bed.

"That was some fine!" he exclaims, wiping his mouth, hefting a can of peaches. The fruit ceremonially relished piece by piece, rolled slippery and sweet in the mouth, mulled over. The juice drunk off with a sigh and stately bobbing of Adam's apple in the loose skin of the throat. Last of all, he uncorks the whisky, sloshes it into the tin, rinses the film of sugary syrup around and around, sips and grins, sips and grins his gaunt old man's smile while studying the label, its pictures of tawny, blushing fruit.

I get up and go to the door for a breath of air; it is stiflingly hot in the bunkhouse. I look out at the burned house and barn, the quixotic scorched windmill. This abandoned ranch, this barren portion of earth might be the photographic negative of the Golden State. Hollywood is supposed to be orange blossoms, eucalyptus, jasmine, palmetto palms, pepper trees, geraniums, bougainvillea, roses, poinsettias flourishing wild in the Hollywood hills. Hollywood is supposed to be soft breezes, the languishing blue eyes of swimming pools, the waves of the Pacific rhythmically combing miles of smooth sand. It is supposed to be flowers and flesh, Mack Sennett bathing beauties, Valentinoish males. Longing, clinging, beckoning. That is what California is *supposed* to be. Love, riches, fame, dreams, wild possibility. Not blackened, ruined buildings, a half-starved old man filling himself with sickeningly sweet canned fruit, dust chasing dust, blind windows and rusted locks, suspended action, the camera crank stuck. Suspended action, the failure to find the right key for his rusted lock, is what the rest of the morning turns into.

I don't make much headway because I press too hard. The long frustrating search for Shorty McAdoo makes me impatient of further delay. I feel my life gathering speed, impelling me onward like the compulsive forward momentum of motion pictures Chance talks about.

Forward momentum, however, does not sit well with Shorty McAdoo. I ask a question about Indian fighting and he says, "Only thing them peaches lacked was a dollop of yellow cream. Churn it into that heavy syrup – Lord, my toes curl."

"I'll get you some tomorrow," I say.

He nods slowly, stroking his bottom lip with his thumb.

I back off on the Indians. There is obviously something there, but it isn't for today. I have a feeling about McAdoo, that he wants to talk. At the mention of Indians, his jaw clamped down hard, just the way a recovering alcoholic picks up his pace passing the entrance to a bar.

So I draw back, but keep my pencil and my pad in prominent view. I want him to get used to the sight of them, see them as a natural part of me, ordinary as my ear, or my nose, rob them of any power to turn him self-conscious. I am trying to ease Shorty McAdoo into conversation the way you ease yourself into a scalding bath. My mistake is that McAdoo has been in more scalding baths than I have. I ask easy questions. He replies with teasing answers.

Where was he born? He tucks his tongue into his cheek and examines the ceiling. Couldn't rightly say. He didn't have the papers on it.

Where did he *think* he was born then? He'd never given it too much *thinking*, he says. His mother said she got him from under a cabbage, but never named the patch. She'd been a godly, upright, Christian woman, so he'd take her word for it until somebody proved him wrong. She'd died of gravel and stone of the kidney when he was about seven, so he'd never heard her supply a correction.

What did his people do? Farmed.

Where? Ends of the bloody earth.

What ends of what bloody earth? Made no difference. If I wanted the nearest post office, write down *hell*.

"I'm not checking up on you," I say. "What difference would the truth make?"

"You got it right," he says. "What difference would it make?"

I want to know what made it hell.

"Worked harder and ate worst than the mules."

"What did you raise on your farm?"

"Stones."

Does he have any family living? He shrugs. His daddy is dead. Died when Shorty was twelve, of unspecified complaints. His brother might be dead or alive, might have children, he doesn't know. He'd put distance between himself and hell as quick as he could.

Where did he go? On the wander.

Wander where? No place to speak of. Every place. Just on the wander.

How old was he when he went on the wander? It was a long time ago. Maybe he was thirteen, maybe fourteen, couldn't testify exactly. One day he scooted, just up and scooted. Spent the summer snitching vegetables from gardens, snaring game. If I didn't tell anybody, he'd lifted a few chickens and milked a cow or two didn't belong to him.

After that? After that, this and that. Come first snow, a sheriff arrested him for vagrancy or beggary, some charge along those lines. The county sold him to a farmer who paid his five-dollar fine. He was bound over to pay off the cash owed to Mr. Good Samaritan. Drew a six-month sentence. Worked out to eighty-three cents a month, room and board. Mr. Samaritan figured he'd scamper first chance he got, which was about right, so he chained him up in a cold chop-box every night. He might have starved if it weren't for that chop-box; ate pig feed by the handful, the farmer weren't a heavy feeder of jailhouse help. He was due for release in May but May came and the farmer said he weren't going nowhere. He'd broke a fifty-cent saw blade, had to work that off before he was free and clear, all debts discharged. All right, he'd said. Don't matter. Another month and I'll be dead of starvation anyways. But just so Mr. Samaritan knew. Watch his Christian back waking and sleeping. He didn't care. They'd hang him for it but he'd see the farmer breeding maggots first. So help him God, he'd put a pitchfork in his guts, a chisel in his head, an axe in his back, he'd bash his brains with a rock till they splashed. If he didn't kill him, he'd burn his barn or house.

"And," I say, "what was the result?"

"He give me a cool glass of buttermilk and some warm corn bread – with butter. He put a bit of salt pork in my satchel. He made his nigger take the boots right off his feet and give them to me. A man travels faster with boots on his feet." He sends me a confiding look, his tongue mischievously tucked in his cheek. "You think your rich man going to like that story? That one going to sell?"

"It might, if that isn't all. Tell me you met an angel of mercy on that road from the farmer's house who turned your life around and put forgiveness in your heart. Tell me you went on to found a great business and endow numerous homes for orphans. Is it possible you did any of those things, Mr. McAdoo?"

He smiles to show we understand one another. "Hell no, Harry, I didn't get around to doing none of them things."

I close my pad and put my pencil in my pocket. "Then this was just practice," I say. "I'm a little rusty with the shorthand and you're a little rusty finding the right stories. Both of us will improve as time goes by." I open my wallet and pass him the money. "Let's see how we manage tomorrow."

"Don't forget that rich yellow cream," he reminds me. "A peach ain't a peach without it has some cream."

"I'll remember."

"Yes you will!" he shouts after me as I go out the door. "Yes you will!"

13

The Englishman's boy sat with his rifle cradled across his knees, looking up at the night sky. It was a sight to ponder, those stars. They recalled to him planting time, trudging his daddy's fields, tossing oats from the sack at his belt, the pale seed fanning and speckling the dark loam like the stars fanning and speckling the black nap of the sky. He gaped up at the seed of heaven, the wash of the Milky Way, the single stars winking the hard bitter fire of flint and steel; a crick stitched in his neck. The whole sky turning lazily in his skull, a slow reeling wheel of constellations, of shaking bands and belts of pulsing fire, of sparkly, pricking light.

Fire day and night, the searing flare of midday sun, the brilliant salty light of midnight stars, fire smouldering its way into him through his eyes, scorching him clean, empty. A clean country this, he admired the smell of it, nothing like the odour of the pigsty, the chicken run, the reek of corn souring in the bin, the stench of a hated brother's shit greeting him when he jerked open the privy door of a morning back home. He was shut of all that now.

Here the scent of sage rose hot and aromatic under the pestle of a pounding sun, the fierce wind bearing hints of cured grass, of desiccated, medicinal-smelling earth. If a man opened his tobacco pouch ten yards off, the Englishman's boy's nose wrinkled, everything carried sharp on the cleanly air. Even buffalo chips burned with a tang he favoured over the gassy smell of coal.

But he had no fire now. Hardwick did not allow it. When the shadows surrounding the herd of horses began to play on his nerves and on his eyes, to shake and shudder, he lifted his gaze to the sky. When the sky began to move, to stir and swirl, he dropped it to the screen of darkness.

A fire would have been a comfort to look at.

Maybe it was just the Scotchman's talk that had him spooked. He had begun to talk strange after he shot Hardwick's bull buffalo. The Scotchman said this place was like the land of the old Bible Jews. Heat and sun, wind and emptiness, no nooks and crannies to hide a poor, creeping man. A clear view for the Almighty.

Most likely Scotty was afraid, knew he'd made a mistake trifling with Hardwick's pleasure. When folks went scared, or off their heads, they'd been known to pile on the Bible talk. The Scotchman seemed to be a bit of both. All afternoon he rambled on about the wilderness, his words quick and breathy, forty days and forty nights, whispering preachments of a sledgehammer sun and anvil earth, sinner stretched suffering between the two, beaten and beaten until he broke and shattered like cold iron, or glowed red-hot with vision.

That was the way of the Bible Jews, the Scotchman said, and the red savages. Walk out into loneliness, let the wind tear at you, your tongue parch in your mouth, your belly squeeze around emptiness, until God came calling. The wild God of dreams and visions. "Your young men shall see visions, and your old men shall dream dreams," he preachified. Prophecies hatched by the sun, promised in the Bible.

Voice dropping even lower, he said he had something to tell the Englishman's boy, tell him because the boy hadn't joined the Devil's Sabbath either, hadn't drank the foul cup of blood, eaten of the uncooked flesh. The Scotchman knew them for what they were, oh yes he did, the unholy ten. Staring at the smudgy red on their lips and chins he had seen them slowly change before his very eyes, their clothes rot and fall away, revealing raddled, poxy old women, Death's bright lip rouge smeared on their sucking mouths. Rubbing the dripping meat back and forth between their legs, groaning, then lifting it to their grinning mouths, the communion bread of Satan, covered in a crawling blue green mould of flies. Feeding the evil heart through the evil mouth.

It made the Englishman's boy cold to think of the look on the Scotchman's face when he said that. It seemed he was changing, too, right before his very eyes. The Englishman's boy hankered mightily after a fire. It was three hours to morning and the night's chill was hammering cold steel nails into the marrow of his bones.

He wouldn't have pulled this watch if Hardwick hadn't seen him palavering with the Scotchman. Hardwick, savage as a meat-axe all day, nothing going to his satisfaction, needed to rake somebody. Vogle had failed to raise horse tracks, which meant the thieves hadn't swung back to rendezvous as Tom had banked they would.

Tomorrow was the Milk River, the Medicine Line; beyond it, the English Queen's country, no law, and a mighty congregation of Indians. If they didn't find trace of the horses before the Milk, Hardwick meant to cross the river into Canada and ride north to the Cypress Hills. There was a plentiful crop of whisky posts in the hills, and for that reason the boys welcomed this plan like news of Christmas.

News of whisky didn't set well with the Englishman's boy. Bad luck and whisky made an evil potion. Killing that white horse was a bad-luck deed. He'd have cut and run, except he didn't know where the hell to run to. Behind him in Benton was a stabbed publican, to the west of him a hornet's nest of Blackfoot. He didn't want to bump up against neither.

His eyes were telling lies again, the darkness shaping and changing. Out there in the belly of the night, the old blind white horse and whatever sat its back were stirring, the shadows parting and closing convulsively in the effort to give birth to this presence, to push this dead-white and terrifying thing, inch by inch, into his mind.

This ain't no vision, he told himself, jerking his eyes up at the stars. Get yonder, second sight. Shake loose of me. I don't hanker to be no Jew prophet. Hear me?

14

Shorty McAdoo has been dragging his feet, stonewalling for three days. Every night Fitz phones and shouts curses at me when I tell him I've got nothing usable yet. I try to get through to Chance on my own, to explain the situation, but can't. Now I come home and find this note shoved under my apartment door.

Dearest Little Truth Seeker,

Rachel Gold demands you dance attendance upon her tonight. I shall collect you by taxi at eight o'clock. Dress: tuxedo *and* shoes. Shine the shoes. Since it is doubtful you own a flannel shoe-cloth, have recourse to the same dirty underwear with which it is rumoured you dry cocktail glasses. Apply polish, rub briskly. To shoes, not cocktail glasses. Comb your hair. Shave.

None of this is negotiable.

Yours,
Rachel

I am going to be questioned about Chance. There is no escaping Rachel Gold's voracious curiosity. "Describe Mr. Chance using four and only four adjectives." A parlour game of her invention. Four won't cover the entire territory, she likes to say, but at least they tell you what you really think about someone. I try it now, while I dress.

The four I come up with are *obsessive, mystical, eccentric, ruthless.* Only one of these adjectives really surprises me. Until this moment, I hadn't realized I believed Chance was ruthless. The word doesn't seem to fit a man so shy, but it won't be dismissed either. Ruthless sticks.

These four adjectives lead me to the noun *artist.* Maybe Chance is an artist. Three of these characteristics – obsession, eccentricity, ruthlessness – earmark two of Hollywood's greatest artists, Erich von Stroheim and D.W. Griffith. They are also slowly destroying them. Maybe Chance has the last two ingredients necessary to complete the great artist – mysticism and money.

By now I'm dressed in my shiny tux and my shiny shoes and it's only seven-thirty. I decide to wait outside. It is a warm evening, the street mostly quiet because it is the supper hour. A few cars pass and a few would-be actresses slink by me on the sidewalk, their hipbones thrust out in the mannequin walk which is à la mode. You can imagine them carrying four-foot-long cigarette holders. Mine is a low-end show-biz neighbourhood of unsuccessful vaudevillians, of young men with sleek hair and pencil-thin moustaches, of dancers who undulate their bellies as extras in Cecil B. DeMille spectaculars, of violin players who saw background music to assist actors and actresses in summoning up the appropriate emotions for scenes of clamorous passion. Late at night my neighbourhood is a scene of strange comings and goings, of cars backfiring in the street at three a.m., of drunken cursing, of bottles breaking on the pavement, of women screaming.

A cab swings to the curb. I open the back door and slide in beside Rachel Gold. "How nice it is to be reunited with an old friend after such a very, very long time," she says.

"Three weeks."

She takes a compact out and starts working on herself, trying to obliterate the faint mist of freckles across the bridge of her nose. "Only three weeks? My but how the time flies when one of us is having a good time."

"Who says I'm having a good time?"

"You always had a good time working for me, didn't you?"

Her skin is luminous ivory, her eyes almond-shaped, large, very green. The punch of these eyes had been diminished in black and white, but they still managed to win her several small parts in pictures before she decided to write movies rather than act in them. Tonight she wears a silk flapper dress striped in three varieties of green which causes the exact shade of her eyes to alter in sympathy every time she moves.

"Where to, lady?" the cabbie wants to know.

"Cocoanut Grove."

"Oh, shit." I put my head in my hands.

"Don't be like that, Harry. We need to have a serious talk." She lays her hand on my knee to demonstrate she means it. She shouldn't do that.

"Right, pondering a stuffed monkey's ass will turn anybody serious." I hate the Cocoanut Grove. I hate the famous décor. When maitre d' Jimmy Manos heard the rumour from Rudy Valentino that the studio was getting ready to pitch the artificial palms used during shooting of *The Sheik*, Manos snapped them up for his new nightclub. He added a further charming touch – stuffed monkeys that can be run up and down the palms on a string. The worst is when Manos invites male club-goers to "date" the monkeys. The drunken scramble for apes often leads to brawls. The Grove is famous for its punchups. The tradition began on opening night two years ago when Jimmy Manos personally cold-cocked two stars; sometimes the personnel of competing studios fight pitched battles on the dance floor.

I've only been there a couple of times with Rachel – I couldn't get past the door on my own – but Jimmy Manos thinks Rachel looks splendid, exotic against the Moorish décor. Rachel is good-looking enough to get in even on a Tuesday night, which is the night to be seen at the Cocoanut Grove, the night when Pickford and Fairbanks, Bebe Daniels, Theda Bara, Gloria Swanson, Pola Negri, Barbara La Marr, Chaplin, Ben Lyon, and Nita Naldi come out in force to judge the Charleston contests and provide wall-to-wall glamour.

But this is a Thursday, so there shouldn't be too much difficulty in running me by the doorman. The cab pulls up to the Ambassador Hotel and Rachel sashays us into the Grove, gamine face powdered bedsheet white, black bobbed hair vibrating with energy, dynamo idling, the famous Gold electricity just a hum, occasional crackle, spark, as her hips twitch their way through the tables guided by Jimmy himself. Rachel prepared to run full throttle, sending high-voltage bursts clear through the scalp, that blue-black hair standing on end, screaming, Look out! Gold coming through!

Heads turn everywhere. She is beautiful.

The table is not the best – the Grove is full for a Thursday – but it's private. Rachel pries open her purse and produces two flasks, one of martinis, one of brandy. "Do the honours, dear," she says, and I pour drinks underneath the table. We stare out at the dance floor, all the pretty little things of both sexes cavorting like mad to dance music dominated by horns. Rachel tosses one leg over the other in a flash of silk stocking and starts it pumping up and down like the handle of a car jack. A hand flies up and grabs a hank of hair which she twists, tugs, tortures – a sure and deadly sign she has something she wants to get off her mind.

"What do you have to talk to me about, Rachel?"

She doesn't take her eyes off the dancers. "Yesterday, one of the guys from payroll calls Donner to verify whether the cheque he's cutting you is correct. It's a big jump – from seventy-five dollars a week to a hundred and fifty dollars. He wants to know whether Donner authorized it. Donner says no, there must be some screw-up. An hour later payroll calls and says, "Sorry to have bothered you. The raise came from upstairs." She unclutches the handful of hair, turns to me, takes a drink. "It started people in the writing department talking, Harry."

"Talking about what?"

"They wonder how a title-writer gets his salary doubled. They ask themselves, What's all that money for?"

"Maybe it's none of their business what it's for. Did you tell them that?"

"Some people say it's snitch money." She says this in a level voice, waits for an answer.

"Snitch money for what?"

"Some of the boys think you might be giving the names of any-body who talks union talk." Rachel's politics are vague, but they're definitely what people call progressive.

"You're the only person at Best Chance I've ever heard advocate a union. Do you think I sold you out?"

She leans across the table; the white face blazes in the candlelight. "No, I don't, Harry. But I'm not the one who needs convincing. A lot of people find what's going on with you strange. They'd like an expla-nation for it. Maybe you owe me an explanation because I'm your friend."

"Maybe a friend ought to change her tone if she's a friend. It sounds prosecutorial to me."

"Gibson is the one with the theory that you're selling out the union sympathizers. He says Fitz is always sniffing around about unions."

"Gibson is a burned-out refugee from the old kerosene circuit – he's got melodrama on the brain. I've got a job on a picture, nothing more."

"I told them that. But all the stuff that's happened in the last two or three years makes people very nervous. Hays. The morals clauses in contracts. Private dicks running all over Hollywood bribing housemaids, peeking in windows, reading mail for the studio bosses. The bosses have made up their minds about one thing – there aren't going to be any more scandals. Arbuckle was just the tip of the ice-berg. William Desmond Taylor gets murdered and half of Holly-wood is suspected, big stars like Mary Miles Minter and Mabel Normand. Then the newspapers report Normand has a two-thousand-dollar-a-week cocaine habit. Zelda Crosby commits sui-cide. Dorothy Davenport has heroin-addict hubby Wally Reid locked up in the loonie bin and he dies in a padded cell. One disaster after another. Like Queen Victoria, the Great American Public is not amused; in Des Moines and Poughkeepsie they whisper Sodom and Gomorrah. Panic spreads among movie executives, they wring their hands, they sweat bullets. Does it bear thinking about? Your future, this beautiful industry which you built with your own two hands, this golden goose should be cooked by such irresponsible people? By these schmucks, these schickers, these pishers?" Rachel is rolling now, her hands are waving, her foot is going up and down so fast it's become a tic. "Somebody save us! the moguls cry. We need a knight in shining armour! Find us a sanctimonious, two-faced little prick with a reputation pure as the driven snow! Enter Willie-Puller Hays, the man in charge of President Harding's election campaign, former member of his illustrious cabinet, a shyster with his foot in the Washington door, a one-time legislator who can reassure men of influence, probity, and judgement there's no need for government censorship – Let Willie pull that wire. And how well he does! Remember his famous statement that the potential of the movies for moral and educational influence is boundless, and it is our sacred duty to America's youth to work in concert with their teachers and clergymen to make a wholesome impression on their minds?" Rachel sticks a forefinger in her mouth and mimes puking. "And the studio heads, Zukor and Loew and Fox and Goldwyn and Warner, they all nod their heads in grave unanimity. 'That is so,' they say. 'Let us tenderly mould the minds of America's youth so that they spend their nickels on our pictures. But let us not lead them astray. If we must reveal to them the mysteries of the female body such as – *tits* – let Cecil B. DeMille be the man to do it, tastefully, in an uplifting *religious* picture such as *The Ten Commandments*. Tit-shaking in godless Egypt, that's the ticket. Tit-shimmying, belly-dancing, and butt-waggling raised to a level both educational and moral. Educational in the sense that we can show how people who had the misfortune not to be Americans once lived in utter tit-shaking misery. Moral in that we can show how God is inclined to punish tit-shakers as ruthlessly as Will Hays himself. This is the message we must impart to America's youth! No tit-shaking! No tit-ogling! Unless in a good cause! Such as the moral and educational one in which we are ourselves engaged to assist America's clergy and teachers!'"

A waiter has arrived to take our order. He discreetly hovers, overawed by her vehemence. I signal to Rachel we have company. She hasn't looked at the menu but knows what she wants. What we both want. "Two steaks. Rare. Lots of fried mushrooms. Asparagus."

The waiter flees. Rachel resumes, calmer, quieter. "Hays is making everybody gun-shy. Right now the studios use private detectives to dig up possible scandal, but it's only a short step before we'll be squealing on one another. The Hearst papers may howl about the Red terror in Russia, but it won't be long before the Hollywood terror will teach the Bolsheviks a lesson or two. Maybe the boys in the office think you're informing on their private life to Chance."

I lean back in my chair. "I'm not." I wait to let the statement sink in. "Besides, Chance hates Will Hays as much as any of us."

"This I believe," says Rachel. "A studio head who hates Mr. Hays. Whom they own lock, stock, and barrel. Who is their paid policeman. Where did you get this unimpeachable information from? Who's your source? Mildred in wardrobe?"

"Chance told me himself."

"Oh, yes, I forgot. The man with whom it is harder to get an audience than it was with Louis the Fourteenth chooses to unburden himself to My Little Truth Seeker."

"I don't know if you'd call it unburdening. We've had a number of conversations in the last couple of weeks."

Her eyebrows lift sceptically. "Plural? Conversations?"

Just then, Bill Heidt, a writer at Fox, weaves drunkenly over to our table and invites Rachel to dance. She waves him away like a bad smell. "No time for dancing, Billy-boy. Rachel's feet are firmly planted on the Road to Damascus. A revelation awaits her. Take a hike."

Heidt, muttering, zigzags back to his table of cronies. When he arrives, his failure is applauded with shouts of derision.

"So tell me, what is the nature of your conversations, Harry?"

I know any mention of Shorty McAdoo is definitely out of bounds, but I don't see any harm in gossip of a general kind. "They're not very different from what you and I talk about at the office. He likes to talk about ideas. It's not easy to explain . . . he's a kind of amateur historian and philosopher."

"So what's he doing in Hollywood? In my experience, millionaire amateurs like Joe Kennedy, William Randolph Hearst, and Damon Ira Chance get into the picture business for only two reasons. Prestige pussy and to make money."

I let it out before thinking. "He wants to make the great American movie."

"Such a small ambition?"

"You don't repeat what I just said. You understand? Not a word."

"Tell me more. My lips are sealed." She refills our glasses with gin, a subtle inducement.

"Okay, laugh if you want. The guy uses words like *art* when he talks about movies. He's idealistic. He wants to make films like Griffith."

"Now there's a noble ambition," says Rachel. "To make movies portraying the Negro as stupid, shiftless, and single-mindedly determined to slake his lust with white women. What a great public-relations job he did for the Klan and the lynching industry."

"An admiration for Griffith as artist doesn't necessarily make someone a Klansman, does it?"

"I find the two hard to separate, Harry. But then I'm a little touchy on the subject of the Klan. As a Jew I've got reason to be."

"Don't start tarring me with that brush, Rachel. I'm not defending the Klan. I'm not defending Griffith's film. I am making a point. The point is that a bad man might be a good artist. Example. Byron. Good poet – bad man. See?"

"And what about Chance? What's he? Good man or bad man?"

"From your tone of voice it sounds to me you may have already formed an opinion on the subject. All I've got to say is that he's treated me very decently."

"Maybe I have doubts because of the company he keeps."

"Are you referring to me?"

"No. That bastard Fitzsimmons."

With Fitz, I feel I'm on thinner ice. I light a cigarette. "I'll grant you that Fitz is not an attractive personality. I've had my run-ins with him. He's hard and he's ignorant. In that respect he's not much different from all the rest of the men in charge of studios. How's he any different from Louis B. Mayer?"

"He isn't a Jew."

"I don't know what that's supposed to mean."

"No, I suppose you wouldn't."

"Then maybe you ought to explain."

Rachel holds out her glass for replenishing. "All I've got to say," she begins as the martini splashes into it, "is that when I first came out to Hollywood there were signs up in all the rooming houses. They read: 'No Dogs, No Actors, No Jews.'" She leaves it there.

"And? The signs didn't have much effect, did they? Because there's no shortage of all three in Hollywood now."

"That's right. Hollywood grew to love dogs and actors. You can't beat that Rin Tin Tin. He's swell. But Jews . . . well, Jews aren't as naturally lovable as dogs and actors. Everybody knows about kikes. As Mary Pickford says to Douglas Fairbanks when he's being difficult, 'Careful, Doug. The Jew's coming out in you.'" And poor Doug, he's only half a Hebe."

"So shame on her. But what's that got to do with Fitz?"

"He's an anti-Semite."

I take a drink. "So's Henry Ford. But he's on the record. He bought a newspaper to promulgate his views. Where's the proof when it comes to Fitz?"

"The way he looks at me."

"That clinches it. The way he looks at you."

Suddenly she's very angry, her eyes flash green fire. "I grew up in New York. I know the look, Harry. Don't make light of it. My brothers got called Christ-killers and beaten up by Irish Catholic toughs often enough for me to be able to recognize it when I see it."

"I stand rebuked. All Irish Catholics are anti-Semites?"

"Why are you defending him?" she bursts out. "Why are you cross-examining me? Who do you think you are? Chief legal counsel for the Klan?"

"Point of order," I say. "Fitz would not be welcome in the Klan –

he's a Catholic. Maybe you two have more in common than you think."

The steaks arrive. The waiter manoeuvres them into position in a bristling silence. The band has taken a break and the Grove is as quiet as it ever gets. Rachel and I eat without speaking. When I can't stand it any more I say, "Listen." She doesn't look up. I rap the table hard with the butt of my knife. "Listen!" Her eyes lift, reluctantly. "You've got to believe me, Rachel. They haven't asked me a single thing about anybody I work with. Nothing. I swear to you." I actually raise my hand. All that's needed to complete the picture is a Bible. "I'm not selling anybody out."

Rachel gives me a despairing look, reaches out and catches my jacket sleeve in a white-knuckled grip. Like she's teetering on a precipice. "Don't you get it, Harry?" she whispers fiercely. "I'm warning what *might* happen. To me as much as to you. In a single year I make more money than my father did in ten. And the more money I make, the more I'm afraid of losing it. Chains of gold are the hardest chains to break." She makes a sweeping gesture that takes in the Grove, the diners. "Do you think anyone in this room has even considered they might have to give this up? Even entertained the notion? I started in movies because they were fun. They're not fun any more and I'm still here. Why? Because I got used to good clothes, money, fame of a sort. But I liked it better when we wrote a scenario Tuesday, filmed it on Wednesday. *Finis.* Everybody an outlaw. Patent-breakers, fly-by-night independents, here today, gone tomorrow. Making it up as we went along. You know what, Harry? It wasn't respectable to be in pictures then. A reputable stage actor wouldn't appear on screen; they considered photoplays the kiss of death. Hollywood was the end of the earth, the place that in the Middle Ages used to be marked on maps: "Here Be Monsters." And we were monsters – misfits and crackpots, dreamers and schemers. But slowly, step by step, bit by bit, money transformed us until one day we woke up and found ourselves lords of the earth. Making more money than the President of the United States. Maybe exerting more influence. Our childhood was over, Harry. We were no longer kids dressing up in mother's clothes, telling each other nutty stories and falling all over ourselves laughing. Fifteen years ago you could make a picture for a thousand dollars. Now they put up von Stroheim's production costs on a billboard in New York. He's gone over a million! they scream." She pours herself another drink; the alcohol is showing its effect. "We made stupid movies then. They were fun. Even more fun to make than to watch. We still make stupid movies, but they're not fun to make any more. Too much at stake. Every stupid movie we launch we cross our fingers and pray it isn't the *Titanic*, because if it is, we're all on the deck chairs. The question is, What'll we do to get into the lifeboats?"

Another interloper. Sammy Burns from the Fox table.

"Speaking of stupid movies – here is the king of the stupid movie," says Rachel. "Nobody can write them stupider than Sammy."

Sammy is too far gone to absorb this. "C'mon, Goldie," he coaxes, "cut the rug with old Sammy. Be a peach." He executes a couple of haphazard steps with one hand pressed to his stomach and the other held at eleven o'clock. His face is shining with sweat and his white tie has come undone.

"You be a peach," says Rachel. "Climb in a bowl on your dining-room table and be a peach there, Sammy. I'm not in the mood for dancing."

Burns abruptly halts his solo. "If I were you, I'd be nice to people. You might need a friend when Mr. Eastern Seaboard finishes running his studio into bankruptcy. I know people," he says.

"A word of advice, Sammy," says Rachel. "Modesty becomes you as much as anything can. Aspire to modesty. And the day I need help from you getting a job in this town is the day that Gog and Magog stalk the earth."

Sammy rocks back and forth on his heels. "What?"

"Exactly," says Rachel. "And please tell the other dreamboats at the Fox table not to bother putting themselves on offer here. I breathe my quota of cigar breath at the office. Now run along. This is the adults' table."

Sammy departs in high dudgeon.

Rachel says, "So what are you doing for Chance now?"

"Research."

"Which you can't talk about."

"That's right."

"And after that?"

"I think he's going to let me write the picture."

"That's a big step."

"I know it."

Rachel purses her lips, lifts her glass, "Congratulations. To Harry Vincent, scenarist of photoplays." She notices her glass is empty. "Any more gin?"

I shake the flask. It's empty. "Nothing but the brandy."

"Pour, My Little Truth Seeker, pour."

I do. Neither of us seems to want to take up where we left off. I can feel between us the sour disquiet of stubborn people. I put her behaviour down to jealousy. It irks her that Chance has spirited away her disciple. Although she always thinks herself in the right, she is never so certain that she doesn't value a loyal seconder. For a year and a half I have seconded all her motions in the writing department, and when she laid down the law about Mencken, Dreiser, and Norris, I seconded that too. I seconded her when she expounded her theory of photoplays. I knew no others. It is Rachel Gold who taught me my job.

I don't really know why I defended Fitz. My motives are complicated. I certainly don't like him, or even respect him, while I have loved and admired Rachel from the moment she swept down on me at that lunch counter in L.A. like a wolf on the fold, seizing my heart in her jaws.

I love her in the only way I can, silently, humbly, discreetly, from a distance. I know that she will never be interested in a rail-thin, gangly, bespectacled man so ordinary-looking that to be truly ugly would lend him some badly needed distinction. I do not lie awake at night imagining the impossible, tormenting myself. Not any more anyway. Friendship is the best I can hope for. I love her with resignation.

Perhaps these are the reasons I see her more clearly than is usual in a case of unrequited love. I know she drinks too much, throws herself at pretty, stupid men. I know that her progressive politics (sometimes she calls herself a socialist) collide with her taste for the high life, and that her brittle gaiety and white-powdered face are both attempts to mask Jewish melancholy and ethical rage.

Thirty years later I still do not know why I loved her with a husband's love rather than the blind passion women like her seem to require – only that I did. But I do know what I admired in her. She had no calculation in her. Which is not to say she was ever blind to what she was doing. She understood the consequences of her adventures, was ready to live with them, was ready not to make excuses. Her mistakes were on a grand scale. She made enemies and friends with abandon, embracing both as badges of honour. She carried her head high. Hers was the beauty of courage and intelligence, to be read in her face, in her eyes, in her passionate, grasping, darting hands. She was a passionate, grasping, darting woman. Rachel Gold sometimes confused rudeness with honesty, but never honesty with anything else.

I am thinking these things when I spot William DeShane crossing the floor, headed in our general direction. The look on my face alerts Rachel. "What?" she says sharply. I don't answer; I'm watching him. William DeShane has caught more than my attention; a lot of people are suspending their conversations, neglecting their shrimp and soup and meringues to follow him with a hungrier interest.

William DeShane is a graceful man, capable of sailing across a room without faltering under close inspection because he is confident inspection will find him faultless. At the moment he is attracting more stares than even a great star might expect to attract because the diners in the Grove are industry insiders, and for insiders a star in the making is more fascinating than a star made. Nobody knows just how big William DeShane might get, but the guess is very, very big indeed. They watch to see which table he is headed for, who among them swings enough weight to receive a courtesy call from William DeShane. This is not Tuesday. This is small-fry night.

He stops at our table, addresses Rachel. "Miss Gold?" I can sense him basking in the knowledge that all the eyes in the room are upon him.

"That's right," she says.

"Allow me to introduce myself. My name is –"

She finishes for him. "William DeShane."

He bows. "I am flattered that one of the ornaments of our industry should know my name. It goes without saying that I am a very great admirer of your work."

"Say it anyway. Tell him to say it, Harry."

"Say it." I try to sound as bored as humanly possible. DeShane offers his hand for me to shake. "William DeShane." The palm is cool and dry, a confident temperature. Mine isn't.

"Harry Vincent."

He's no longer looking at me. His eyes are doing a slow pan of the room. I'll give him this. The man is an actor. He imagines cameras everywhere, all on him. It gives me a moment's satisfaction to note that his eyes are a smidgen too close together, that he's one hundredth of an inch short of perfection.

"Would you care to dance, Miss Gold?"

"Excuse us, Harry," says Rachel rising.

There's a way that a woman folds herself into a man when they waltz that is like handwriting on the wall. I can read it in very big letters. Everybody watches them simply because they are a beautiful couple. The *mensch* pays the bill. The gigolo's evening is just beginning.

15

The situation in the Cocoanut Grove the previous night leaves me feeling hopeless and despondent, which contributes to my being late for my appointment with Shorty McAdoo. I find him sitting on the step of the bunkhouse, honing the rusty blade of a shovel with a file. I take shovel-sharpening to be a way of killing time and apologize for being late, ending lamely with the word, "Complications."

McAdoo leans the shovel carefully against the step. "Speaking of complications, friend Wylie's in the bunkhouse."

"What's he doing in the bunkhouse?"

"Setting with his brother."

McAdoo is sometimes a trial to the patience. "Okay. What's his brother doing in the bunkhouse?"

"His brother's dead."

"Dead?" I say stupidly.

"Dead as old Pontius Pilate. We reckon to bury him this morning." He indicates roughly where by pointing off beyond the derelict, ravaged house. "Wylie hauled him out here in a milk wagon." Gauging the look on my face, McAdoo companionably pats the step beside him. I sit. He drops his voice. "Didn't know what else to do with him. Wylie took all the money he had, every last nickel, bought Miles a coffin, had him embalmed – without he calculated a plot was going to cost extra. There Miles is, all dressed up and no place to go. The county would have give him a spot, but Wylie wouldn't have his brother lying in a potter's field. So he freighted him out here."

"In a milk wagon," I repeat.

"Wylie is acquainted with a fellow delivers milk. They pack considerable ice on a milk wagon. They took Miles with them on the route and when they was done deliveries they brought him out to me."

"And the two of you are going to bury him this morning."

"That bunkhouse ain't no goddamn milk wagon. He ain't going to stay fresh. Sooner he's in the ground the better."

We sit on the step, silent. I am thinking I might as well have stayed in bed.

"Can't be helped. I know you was supposed to interview me this morning."

"My publisher is getting impatient. He wants Indians."

"Maybe I ain't got no Indians to deliver."

"That's not what I hear."

"Why don't you pay your respects to the deceased," says McAdoo, turning dodgy as he always does whenever he begins to feel cornered.

"I didn't know the deceased. Never met him."

McAdoo gets to his feet. "You know Wylie. Wylie'd appreciate you paying your respects. And doing it ain't going to scrape no skin off your ass."

We enter the bunkhouse. There is a cheap coffin of some kind of garish yellow wood resting on a bier made of straight-backed chairs. Wylie sits vigil beside it, the brim of his cowboy hat buckled in his hands. The coffin lid stands directly behind him, leaning against the wall.

"Mr. Vincent come to pay his respects, Wylie," says McAdoo. "You remember Mr. Vincent."

Wylie, nodding sombrely, rises from the chair to shake my hand with a church deacon's solemnity. When I attempt to take it back, he holds on grimly, a dog with a stick in his mouth. It seems he wants to lead me up to the casket for a bird's-eye view of the corpse. Given the situation, I haven't much choice.

A young man lies with his head propped up on a satin pillow, his complexion watery blue-white, like skim milk. The only brightness in the face is a feverish red seam where his eyelids close and two red-rimmed nostrils tilting up at us. A thatch of bushy, sandy hair is the deadest-looking thing about him, stiff, lifelessly brittle as dry wisps of summer hay.

"They cut his hair at the undertaker's," Wylie volunteers. "I didn't know they cut hair at an undertaker's."

"What was it?" I ask. Meaning the cause of death.

Wylie looks at me. Looks at his brother. Looks at me again. "On account of the fall he took with the Running W, he busted up inside. Doctor said his liver, something else . . ." He stops. "He looks every bit himself though, don't he?" Wylie still clasps my hand, gaze resting on his brother's face. We stand in a pocket of stillness, onlookers to a greater stillness boxed by the casket. "It would have meant a lot to Brother, you coming," Wylie confides.

I throw a glance at McAdoo, but he is stubbing out a cigarette on the stovetop, eyes downcast. No help there.

"Yessir, yessir, yessir!" Wylie yells suddenly, in a jagged, piercing voice. "You know who your friends are come a time like this! You bet I know my friends!"

"Sure you know your friends," Shorty says calmly. "Now leave go hanging onto Mr. Vincent and screw the lid back down on Miles. Time's come."

He does as he is told. McAdoo motions me outside, leaving Wylie wrestling with the coffin lid.

Back out on the steps all I can do is shake my head. A loud bang is followed by the sound of wood scraping wood as Wylie jockeys the coffin lid back and forth, aligning it to take the screws.

"I told him he could bunk here with me until he found his feet," says McAdoo.

"Ever consider that might be one hell of a long time?"

"Well, I'm riding easy now with my interviewing money," McAdoo says. "Seven and a half a day should be able to carry us both for a time."

"I thought you were saving money to get to Canada."

"Could be both of us'll go north. What's the saying? Two can live as cheap as one."

"That refers to marriage. If there's anybody I wouldn't want to hitch myself to it would be Wylie."

"Oh," says Shorty, "I can keep old Wylie out of my hair. Turn him to trapping quail and shooting rabbits maybe. Have him dig us a potato garden. Have him comfortable up the bunkhouse some. He takes orders like a damn, Wylie does." Shorty turns, calls back into the bunkhouse. "You got her clamped down in there, Wylie?"

Wylie appears in the doorway. "I lost one of the screws."

"Well, give her another look. If you find her, that's good. If you don't, in the long run that don't matter neither."

Wylie goes back in.

"We'll have Wylie tote the light end of the casket – the legs. You and me can take the head," suggests Shorty.

"I happen to have a bum leg."

"We ain't going far. I'd go to the bank on you being able to carry your share."

After some confusion – I have to switch to the left so that I can swing my stiff leg without knocking it against the casket – we get the funeral cortege moving.

Despite his age, McAdoo manages better than I do. I admire the fiercely set jaw, the tendons stretched tautly along the thin, muscular stalk of neck. My arm burns with the strain and I can only make thirty or forty yards before begging for a halt. We lower the coffin to the ground, take a quick blow, and then McAdoo curtly bobs his head, the signal to stoop, lift, and scurry on. We make our way from bunkhouse to burned ranch-house, and then several hundred yards more, stumbling up a low hogbacked rise selected by Wylie as his brother's final resting place.

We set the coffin down. While I survey the scene, Wylie goes back to collect the tools. Underfoot, nothing but floury dust and dusty plants wilting back to dust. The inky etching of the fired house. The

143

horizon a smudgy glare, the sun sucking blue out of the sky with a voracious mouth.

I sit down in the dust. "He could have put him under a tree at least. There's that orange tree just west of the bunkhouse."

"Well," says Shorty, "them Easton boys come from open country. Wylie wanted to give Miles a look in every direction."

Wylie's back with the tools. McAdoo takes the pick from him. "The ground here's harder than a whore's heart. I'll have to loosen it some before you can shovel." He starts to work, rocking back on his heels with each swing, slinging forward onto his toes, shuddering as the pick bites the resisting ground. The steel rings fervently when it strikes a stone. As the blood flushes his face, Shorty falls into a rhythmical grunting, a sweet basso punctuation marking the rise and fall of the pick. Beside me, his knees drawn up to his chin, Wylie monotonously extols the virtues of the coffin he has purchased, its water-repelling varnish, its stainless-steel screws, its zinc handles.

After fifteen minutes McAdoo takes a breather, dripping sweat. "The ground seems to be a mite easier," he says to Wylie. "See if she shovels." McAdoo drops down beside me; Wylie seizes a spade and enthusiastically digs.

I tell Shorty I ought to be going.

"Can't leave now. Not before the service. Wylie'd take it bad."

"Your service has nothing to do with me; I didn't know Miles Easton from Adam. I came this morning for one reason – because I'm paid to collect your stories. Seeing you're occupied, I have no reason to stay."

"You just rest easy," says McAdoo, patting my knee. "Presently we'll have us a few drinks. Send Miles off in grand style."

I get to my feet and start dusting off my clothes. "I'll see you tomorrow – if tomorrow's convenient."

Shorty grabs a fistful of my pant leg, a hard, mineral glint in his eyes. "It ain't convenient," he says.

Shorty McAdoo means it. "Okay, I'll stay. But you owe me some Indians for this one."

Now he has his way, his face relaxes a little. "What kind of Indian would you like me to serve you up? Tame or wild?"

"Wild, naturally."

"Hell, I wouldn't waste no wild Indian on you," says Shorty. "Those wild Indians the army used to jail for scampering off the reservation, directly they was locked up, they shrivelled and died. Wild Indian got to run free. I'd guess you lock a wild Indian up between the covers of a book, same thing is going to befall him. He's going to die."

"Don't get too deep on me, Shorty."

"Hell, if I was a puddle and you stood in it, you wouldn't get your soles wet. That's how deep I am."

The grave is getting deeper. Wylie has taken it down six inches.

"Then I'll have to settle for a tame one. For the time being."

"I knew a middle-aged bachelor name of Harp Lewis married himself a tame Indian. Got her out of a reservation school run by a Methodist preacher," says McAdoo cheerfully.

"Just a minute," I tell him. "Let me get my note pad and pencil out."

"Went to this Methodist and told him he was on the lookout for a likely wife, could the preacher recommend one of his girls? Methodist told Harp to come back in a week for an answer, so's the preacher could take it to the Lord. Preacher took it to his wife *and* the Lord, seemed the two were in agreement. When Harp come back in a week's time, Methodist told him he had but one girl he'd recommend as suitable for a white man, Ruth Big Head. Not much to look at – but housebroke. Preacher's wife took Harp to the schoolhouse and gave him a peek at her through the window. She was a good, straight, strong girl but pocked and pitted some from the smallpox. Of course that wasn't going to put Harp off – he must have been crowding fifty and he knew he wasn't the answer to any woman's prayers. Things were falling into order. Old Harp Lewis coming along just then wanting a woman was fortunate for the Methodists because they'd educated this girl up to where they didn't want her marrying one of her own kind. Christian Indian girls generally backslid and went weedy if they took a buck for a husband. And Ruth Big Head was the biggest success these Methodists had ever had with a squaw and they didn't want their good work dashed. They'd taught her how to bake and sew and wash floors and keep a garden and milk a cow and read her Bible and sing hymns. They told Harp she was as fine a Christian girl as you could shake out of a tree in Boston. 'Sounds good to me,' said Harp. 'I'll take her.' And he did. He gave her father five horses for her, and the Methodist forty dollars for mission work and another ten to marry them.

"Harp oughtn't have had no complaints. What them Methodists said about Ruth was gospel truth. They'd trained the Indian out of her so that most any of the white women in those parts could have took a lesson from her on proper deportment and staying sober. She kept a fine house. Kept herself neat as a pin – always wore a starched sunbonnet and a clean apron. Couldn't keep her out of a church or stop her praying. She was a purely upstanding Indian but for one particular. You couldn't get a pair of Christian shoes on her feet. She couldn't abide them. Said they bit her feet like a dog. Wore nothing but moccasins.

"Now Harp was one of those fellers who are mindful how they stand in the community and he took it hard his wife wouldn't wear shoes. It shamed him his wife should pull up just that much short of civilized. When neighbours called on the Lewises to pay a visit, all the time Harp would be watching them to see if their eyes didn't go straying to his woman's feet. They were married twenty years and every present he bought her – birthday, anniversary, Christmas – was a new pair of shoes. And every new pair of shoes she carted off to the church and put in the relief box for China. Old Harp Lewis must have put new mail-order shoes on many a China Lily.

"It was just in the matter of shoes she didn't satisfy. Harp had six kids off of her and people said they was the most mannerly, politest kids you could wish for. And people give her the credit for the raising of them, too. Of course, she had such a reputation as a righteous Christian by then it slipped folks' minds she was an Indian. They overlooked the facts, you might say. Harp, who wasn't much given to darkening the door of a church, used to say he was the heathen in the family. But he weren't. There weren't but one Indian in the Lewis clan.

"Winter of 1910 or thereabouts, Harp come down with the pneumonia. He was an old man by then, in his seventies, coughed the life out of himself. Ruth Lewis tended him and prayed over him day and night for a week. Hardly slept, hardly ate, end of it looked like a brown ghost. When Harp died she closed his eyes and walked out of the room. No weeping, no wailing. Her oldest boy give her a few minutes to be alone with her grief and then followed after. Found her in the kitchen. She'd already sawed the little finger on her left hand off with a butcher knife. Blood all over. She was working on the little finger on the right when her son came in. Halfway through the bone."

"Jesus Christ," I say.

"I think she was a Crow," says Shorty. "Crows'll do that when family dies, take a piece of flesh off themselves as a sign of mourning. Finger, piece of muscle, flesh for flesh. The preacher threw a roaring fit about it, reminded Mrs. Lewis the body is the temple of the Holy Spirit, that what she done to the temple was wrong, unholy wrong. She didn't buy it. He might as well have tried to talk her out of her moccasins, for all the effect it had. Wouldn't admit a speck of wrong or harm in what she done. She didn't wear no shoes to Harp's funeral either." He pauses. "She gave old Harp two fingers for love. And she was a tame Indian. Makes you wonder."

Working in shifts, we get the grave dug by early afternoon and return to the bunkhouse. Shorty builds a fire in the stove and heats some water. We all have a good wash and, after, Shorty and Wylie shave with McAdoo's straight razor. Wylie's shirt has a torn sleeve so McAdoo gives him a clean one of his to wear and then slaps the dust out of Easton's trousers with a broom until he judges him presentable for a funeral. Then he tells Wylie to sit on the bed and keep out of his way while he fries us some bacon, onions, and potatoes. We are halfway through dinner when a gritty rattle shakes the bunkhouse in a spasm of wind. Shorty looks up from his plate, listens. Another sharp gust follows, flying grit pings on the single windowpane, and a trembling hum fills the bunkhouse as the wind ebbs in a slow, sobbing withdrawal.

"It sounds like it's turning dirty out there." Shorty pushes away his plate. "Soon as I dress, we best go." He retrieves a box from under his bed, and takes out of it a black frock coat, the kind of coat nobody has worn since the turn of the century. The coat turns him angular, turns his shoulders and elbows sharper, his face more harshly lined, his eyes more unflinching. He becomes a daguerreotype from the last century, one of those stern, severe faces that their descendants can feel weighing them across the chasm of years, judging them small, insignificant, unworthy people.

"Comb your hair," says McAdoo to Wylie.

We go out bareheaded. Wylie, his hair glistening with water, his rooster-tail dabbed down with a bit of soap, McAdoo with a coil of rope in each hand. A hot wind claps a burning hand over my mouth and nose robbing me of breath. In the slack, sallow sky the sun burns wanly behind a veil of blowing dirt. Tumbleweed bowls by and the low brush heaves and surges all about us. We lean into the wind and push it like a stalled vehicle, slowly, one step at a time, past the ruined house and up the slope to the waiting coffin, our hands shielding our eyes.

McAdoo demonstrates how to buck the coffin into the grave, a rope through each of the corner casket handles on the diagonal. When the wind suddenly drops, we can hear the casket knocking the sides of the grave, creaking and groaning, the handles threatening to tear loose. Trying to brake the last couple feet of drop, the hemp sears my palms and I almost get jerked into the hole. The coffin lands with a hollow bang. McAdoo swears, peers into the grave.

"It's all right," he shouts, making himself heard above the wind. "She held together."

We thrust our shovels into the heaped ground, filling the grave. When we lift them, the dirt blows off the blades in tawdry streamers, whipping into our faces. The very air is flavoured with earth. It coats my lips and teeth, I taste it souring in the back of my throat, feel it rawly scratching in my eyes. Everywhere dust is lapping and pluming the land, moving toward the horizon like the creeping, ragged smoke of wholesale destruction. McAdoo stiff-backed in his black coat, Wylie with the burial ropes knotted in his hands, and me. Three figures ghostly and obscure in the shifting, earthly smoke.

So begins the interment of Miles Easton, with a grey smudge rolling across the landscape, edging into the sky like a nasty stain. With this and a memory of the grief of that other stranger, of the funerary rites of a Crow woman, who cut a part of herself away to join whatever she had lost.

The wake lasts past midnight, past a bottle and a half of whisky. Wylie Easton lies collapsed on one of the bunk beds. He has cried himself into a drunken sleep, racking sobs and rage. Now his mouth hangs innocently open like a slumbering child's, his chest rising serenely and falling softly. Outside the wind is drumming against the bunkhouse like a stormy sea against a breakwater. McAdoo has lit a coal fire and left the stove door open for the light it throws, a pulsing illumination which, like the wind, billows and recedes. We are both far gone in drink and strange melancholy reveries. I keep remembering last night and Rachel. McAdoo and I haven't spoken in half an hour and scarcely moved except to reach down to the bottle between us on the floor, to swig from it and carefully replace it on its spot. For the first time, I see on McAdoo's face the brutal, haunted look which marked it on the film clip at Chance's house.

He drains the dregs of the bottle, sets it down on the floor, topples it with a push of a finger. The bottle rolls across the temporary silence in the room; the wind is in a lull.

"Dead soldier," says McAdoo and jabs at it with his toe. It rolls some more.

I feel like shit. My leg is throbbing with that old, familiar, sick, steady ache. I happen to be carrying a bag of marijuana Rachel gave me for my birthday. She said when the pain in my leg got too bad to use it. When I put it in my pocket this morning I thought I would be using it for other reasons, but now I think the time has come to roll myself some relief. McAdoo watches me.

"You ever use this?" I ask, lighting up.

"There ain't much I ain't used in my time – or used me. Pass it on."

I hand him the bag and ease smoke out of my lungs. "Vipah," I intone to the glowing end of the joint.

"I spent a winter in Mexico once," Shorty says. "I smoked more of this than ever I smoked tobacco that winter. I preferred it to that Mexicali liquor shit, worm in the bottle."

"You've been around. Seen some things," I say, encouraging him to talk.

"I seen some things," he agrees in an expressionless voice. I wonder if he isn't seeing them again, wonder if his eyes aren't directed inward, directed back in time. They are hooded, secretive. He puts the twist of reefer in his mouth, sucks deeply. We sit holding the smoke captive in our lungs, McAdoo so still he hardly seems human in the light of the banked fire.

"You've done some things," I say again, prompting.

"I done some things." His eyes meet mine. Suddenly, the pool of ruddy light in which we huddle acquires the privacy, the intimacy of a confessional box, drawing us closer together, making us one against the shadows in the room, one against whatever they might obscure and shelter.

I nudge him on. "Christ, Shorty, it's been a long day. Don't send me home empty-handed."

He doesn't answer.

"Give me a few wild Indians."

"You're a driving man, Vincent."

"That old world's gone. You can bring it back for us. Raise it up like Lazarus from the dead."

"Preacher Vincent," he says.

The wind moves outside, dark and elemental, like the life I imagine the man before me has lived. For an instant, I hungrily grasp at the wilderness McAdoo holds clutched inside him, not for Chance's sake, but because of my need.

"Tell me," I whisper.

Just then Easton stirs on his cot. He rises up on his elbow and stares at us with a sleep-blinded face. "Shorty, Shorty," he calls, like a child waking lost in a strange bed.

"I'm here, Wylie. Go back to sleep. It's all taken care of," says McAdoo soothingly.

Wylie sinks back down on the bed. We listen to the slow steady breath of sleep move like a sweeping broom in the pauses of the wind.

McAdoo turns his face back to me. "I'm taking him to Canada with me. It's his best chance. I been to Canada," he says. His voice changes, as if he is speaking out of a cavern. A cavern of regret, or sorrow. "I went Indian up in Canada."

"You mean you lived with Indians there?"

For a minute, he doesn't speak. I sense the dumb misery of an animal gnawing its leg in a trap.

"Here's where you go Indian." He puts a finger to his temple. "Up in your head. Indian is a way of thinking. Lots of them Eastern boys riding at the studios *play* at cowboys and Indians. They learned Indians reading those boys' books – maybe same kind of book you asking me to help you write – books tell you how to do sign language, show you how to chip an arrowhead with a deer horn, make a war bonnet out of turkey feathers. Books don't make an Indian. It's country makes an Indian."

"How does country make an Indian?" I ask quietly. "Tell me."

He reaches out with his boot and closes the door of the stove. The light in the room shrinks to a few bright slivers threading through the dampers. The glowing end of the reefer travels up to his face and flares there. The cavernous eyes, the stark cheekbones. His voice hard, deliberate, distant. "Five months I went alone out there. Never spoke a word to a soul. Kill your meat and find your water. No coffee, no tea, nary a lump of sugar. Ever know a white man went five months without bread, or biscuits, or beans? I done it.

"I'd soured on folks, wanted shut of them, but lonesome country breeds lonesomeness. I sung every song I knew trying to drown out the Indian talking in my head. Every day I heard him plainer and plainer. The country done it to me. The sky was Indian sky, the wind was Indian wind, every last thing I laid my eyes on was cut to fit an Indian.

"I taken myself away from my own kind; I'd sickened on white folks. I seen a sign of them, seen bull teams, seen freight wagons, I hid. Only trail I followed was animal trail. I seen a hawk, I followed the hawk. Hawk passed me on to a deer, I followed the deer. Deer tipped his horns to the sun, I followed the sun. I rode forty miles some days, east, west, north, south, I wasn't bound for any particular place. Watered my horse in the Frenchman, the Saskatchewan, the Oldman, the Bow, the Big Muddy. I covered some ground. Kept moving."

My pencil is moving under cover of darkness, too, scratching out a story offered under cover of darkness. I turn the pages of the notebook quietly, marching my shorthand across the paper by feel. My eyes grow accustomed to the dark; I dimly make out the old man on his chair, head held upright, the reefer steady now, its bright point hung down the side of the chair.

"Lived that way for a month, went sick. Suffered the bone ache and fever, the bloody shits. One day I found myself squatting by a buffalo wallow, buck naked and white as peeled willow. Looked up and saw a four-o'clock sun, didn't know how it got there. Didn't know where my clothes was. Heard myself . . . singing. Next I knew, it was night. Standing out in the bare prairie in the middle of the most godawful storm you ever seen, but now my clothes had climbed back on me. Thunder booming and the sky cracking like a bad plaster wall, booming so hard your ears near bleed, yellow-green cracks of fire running ceiling to floorboards, whole world shaking and burning like a house falling down around your head, timbers snapping, floor giving way under your feet, roof buckling.

"Two balls of ground lightning come rolling towards me, skipping and flaring over the short grass, crackling, jumping like drops of water in a hot skillet. The hair on me jumps up straight all around my head, I lift my hands to cover my eyes to shut out what's a-going to blast me to Kingdom Come . . . there's a hovering blue light all around them hands . . . like sundogs circling round the sun. I feel myself lifting, boots dangling above the ground.

"Sky opens up. Rain drives me back down, knocks me side to side, pounds me so hard it's going to tear the rags I'm wearing right off me, shred and peel them off my bones like wet newspaper. Can't catch my breath the rain's driving down so hard, I'm breathing rain. She's like standing in a fast-running river, white water boiling over my head, and on the banks of this here stream, big old green tree trunks of lightning are waving in a white wind, forking their roots down into the ground to reach the very hubs of hell.

"Of a sudden I'm stinging all over, cold bees are at me. Hail. She's making a sound like a scythe cutting grass, blood roaring through your head. There ain't no cover but my horse. I throw my coat over his head and duck under his belly. The stones are drumming on him and he begins to squeal like a stuck pig, you never heard the like of it.

"God knows how long I listen to that squealing. I squat under him with my arms wrapped around my head to shut out the sound of it, just rocking back and forth. Then, all of a sudden like, she's hushed, dead quiet. The scythe's done cutting, the blood's done roaring. No more lightning, no more thunder. I can feel the cold rising off the ground, see the pale ice steaming. I come out from under that horse on all fours. I crawl. Don't know where I'm going, don't care. Hail's crunching like broken glass, biting into my knees. Everywhere's white and frozen, mist smoking off the ground and me creeping through it, sweating fever and fear, bawling like a baby. I creep and crawl, looking for a hidey-hole to worm myself into, some place to curl. Then my limbs won't carry me no more and down I drops on my face in the hail, me mumbling into the ice and the thunder muttering off in the distance.

"I wake round dawn, the sky apple-green and me nigh right in the head, but wet and chilled and shaky. I suspicion laying in the hail drew the fever out of me. Only now I ain't laying in hail I'm laying in melt-water. Slathered in mud. I pick myself up out of the muck and look for my horse. No horse. He's made tracks with my saddle and my rifle.

"There's a blow of black despair for you. I sink back down into the mud, can't pick myself out of that wallow. I'm whipped.

"The sun keeps climbing, the mud dries stiff on my face, my hands, my hair, my clothes. And I just sit, can't rouse myself. Until I hear horses. Good Lord, maybe I been saved. I look up from studying the mud caked on my trouser legs and what do I see? Three Indian bucks making towards me on their ponies.

"I shake myself up then, by the Jesus, shake myself up and go for my pistol. But there ain't no pistol to hand. All that capering the night before jogged it loose and it'd gone missing somewheres. I cast about every which way but all I see is puddles with sunshine slanting off them, hail-beat grass, and mud-holes. No Colt. The only weapon stands between me and those Indians is a knife.

"They're on me now. Rein their ponies up in my face and investigate me Indian-fashion – poker-faced and solemn. I must've been a study. Raggedy-ass white man in clothes a beggar of a fort Indian wouldn't wore. Hair all matted and twisted up in mud like a mop, rest of me crusted over with a acre's worth of God's good earth.

"They was right handsome boys, all done up for a party, paint and feathers. The one I figured for the leader of this expedition was straight as a gun barrel, a fall of that blue-black Indian hair hanging down to the small of his back, half his face painted yellow and the other half red, necklace of brass bells hung round his neck that went tinkle-tinkle every time his horse pawed the ground.

"He points to me, says something to his friends in Indian gab. The way they laugh ain't encouraging. He shoulders his pony into me and taps my hair with his quirt. In a big, loud voice he puts what I take to be a question. I'm guessing something along the lines of, What you doing spoiling my air and my scenery?

"By the Christ, thinks I, by the Christ. These lads are Blackfoot. I'd heard plenty of how they done woodhawks and hunters along the

Missouri. They didn't leave no pretty corpses. Lot of dead men with their own dicks stuffed in their mouths.

"Red and Yellow Face gives me another flick with his quirt and makes some remark to his boys that sets them laughing fit to bust a gut. I suspicion what's funny is me plastered in hog muck. Man'll do most anything to save his precious skin and I did. Down I goes on hands and knees, sticks my rump in the air, lets loose a squeal to wake snakes, and starts rooting like a pig in his pen. Lord, the look on those Indians' faces. They'd never seen the like. But when the surprise slid off them they howled with laughter. That was a favourable sign. Nobody likely to murder you when they're laughing at you.

"Old Red and Yellow Face was pointing at me and saying the same word over and over. The other two kept nodding their heads yes, yes, every time he said it. I speculate Old Red and Yellow Face was a man of the world, been to the white man's forts, seen his pigs. Every time he said the word, I nodded and grinned and grunted all the louder. I even pitched myself in a good-sized mud-hole and rolled for him, wriggled on my back, all four trotters up in the air. Your Indian's got a natural contempt for the pig, but this was right up their alley, watching a white man do pork proud.

"What they didn't know I was up to, rooting through the slop on my hands and knees, wiggling my hams, was I was looking for that revolver of mine. Playing pig got my snout close to the ground. And when I found that Colt, I aimed to knock Red and Yellow Face and his brethren off their ponies like they was turkeys setting on a rail fence.

"So I kept oinking, and praying, Please God let me lay hands on that gun. Once or twice I thought the boys might be losing interest so I sat up on my haunches like a fat old boar and made windy, wet farts with my lips, or flopped my hands up alongside my head like they was pig ears. When they was roaring with joy I'd get back on the hustle again, covering ground looking for the Colt, the Indians heeling their horses behind me, not wanting to miss nothing.

"My spell of sickness had weakened me considerable though.

Wasn't long before I was feeling mighty dogged out, but I says to myself, Keep moving, you got to keep moving until you get that gun. Over and over I said it. And that's what I done, went on sinking my wrists in gumbo, the mud sucking the strength out of me, leaving my arms so wearisome heavy it was all I could do to pull them free. Keep moving, I said, you got no hope but that gun.

"Everything squeezing in, your eyes begging for a flash of shiny metal, and this noise in your head like a saw whining through wood. And that's the sound of your own breath, but you got to keep moving, keep moving. Your eyes start to haze, like blood dripping into water, one drop at a time, each drop spreading, and the water going misty, then cloudy, then bright, until there ain't nothing but bright blood, and then you get a new notion – that that noise is the sound of a saw chewing through your heart, the blood spurting deep down in you with every stroke, slowly inching up in you until you drown in it, drown in your own heart's blood.

"And I did. I drowned. Keeled over. Sank. I had strength but for one thing, fumble for that knife in my boot top. Pick away, pick away went my fingers but they wouldn't close on it. Then I knew it was all over. Just lay there panting, hog waiting to be butchered. Lay with my face in the mud and waited for them to come, do what they done to those woodhawks on the Missouri, cut me down to size one piece at a time.

"It was unholy still. A still kin to the still of an empty house, but bigger and stranger. Empty world, it said. I waited. Nothing come. I rolled over, staggered to my feet. I'd have swore there weren't another soul in a hundred miles. Indians was gone, like smoke in a wind.

"Couple of hours I walked in circles looking for my pistol. Where there's three Indians could be more. Found my hat. Found a dead prairie chicken laying where the hail had killed it. Sight of that, hunger came over me so fierce I pulled the feathers off it, ate it raw where I stood. It'd been one long stretch since I'd took food.

"Found my hat, found the chicken, but never found the Colt. When candle-lighting come, I turned south and tramped for the border.

Walked like a dead man. Walked all night. Sun rose and I found the third thing, my horse stepping south too."

There is a long pause. I hear him suck at the reefer but no light shows; it has gone out in his fingers. I lift my pencil from the paper but he starts to talk again, his voice no longer deliberate and hard, but mournful and echoing like it had begun.

"Them old-timey, genuine Indians used to go off solitary in the wilderness so's to find their creature spirit," he says. "That's where they learned it, in the wilderness."

I ask what he means by creature spirit.

"Creature spirit," he reiterates. "Spirit they shared with some creature – grizzly spirit, elk spirit, coyote spirit, crow spirit. Hardship and the country taught them it." There is another pause. "What you make of mine?"

"Your what?"

"You ain't been listening, have you?" he says.

～

The next morning I type up a transcription of the interviews. In the end, I send only the last one because it has about it the ring of naked honesty that Chance is after. I believe it marks progress, shows how McAdoo, under my prompting, is slowly moving nearer and nearer to what we are seeking – the truth.

That night as I am getting ready for bed a knock comes at my door. There is a note from Chance by messenger. The note reads:

Dear Harry,
    A picture about a lunatic lost on the plains is not what I had in mind. Press him about Indian wars.
                                        Sincerely,
                                        Damon Ira Chance

16

Chance's curtly dismissive note about the McAdoo interview recounting the thunderstorm on the prairie and his playing pig for the Indians leaves me feeling idiotic and abashed. It worries me even more when the next week's worth of transcripts is passed over unacknowledged and uncommented upon. I am not pleasing Mr. Chance.

I berate myself for my stupid assumption that words on the page can convey what I have learned about McAdoo. Which is that he has something he needs to tell. What this is I can't say, but I sense the weight, the pressure of it behind everything he said that night. Words on the page are not capable of communicating this. It had been the burial, the drawing in of night, the incessant wind, the way McAdoo held himself in the chair, the flick of the boot slamming closed the stove door, the sudden darkness, the voice playing scales in the darkness, beginning flat as dictation, then growing troubled, self-questioning. All this I suddenly see as more important than what he said; the *feel* of the night was its meaning.

That's why what I've given him seems to Chance inadequate, pedestrian, a labour of diligence rather than imagination. But I am not just an unimaginative stenographer. I am not. To use Chance's favourite word, I have intuited whatever is to be got from McAdoo will not be got for the asking, simply, easily. It will have to be won.

Shorty McAdoo is no braggart. Chance could find a hundred cowboys here in Hollywood who, in a few hours, could tell enough colourful lies to fill any number of movie screens. But Chance's ambition is to go beyond entertaining lies, to make a great film, a truthful film. That is what he has set his heart on. And I want to tell him only delicacy and patience will extract the truth from Shorty McAdoo.

I have my pride. It galls me that Chance might have written me off, that I might be underestimated, unappreciated, misunderstood. I need to meet with him face to face and explain all this, or at least talk to him on the telephone.

The problem is I can't reach him. When I phone his office, his receptionist says he is busy and can't speak to me. I'm beginning to suspect Fitzsimmons has given her orders not to let me talk to Chance.

I need some kind of breakthrough with McAdoo. So I buy the pistol.

～

"What's this?" demands McAdoo.

"What does it look like?" He refers to the revolver I bought in a pawnshop in L.A., hoping it would be useful in coaxing a revelation out of him.

"That ain't what I mean. What I mean is, why you showing it to me?"

"I want you to teach me to shoot."

"Put that away before somebody gets hurt."

"Come on, Shorty. You know about guns. That first day I came here, the day you went back to the bunkhouse and put your jacket on – I saw the pistol in the waistband of your pants."

"You wouldn't have, I didn't intend you to. And in case you didn't I showed it to you. Remember?"

"So it was a warning?"

"I'm a careful man."

"Teach me to shoot."

"I ain't a shootist. Never was."

"You said you intended to knock those Indians off their ponies. What did that mean?"

"Means I was in fear of my life."

"Sounds like fancy shooting. Sounds like a shootist to me."

"That close, you just point and squeeze. It's much of a muchness to pointing your finger." He points his finger at me by way of illustration.

I proffer the revolver to him. "Show me." For a moment, I'm sure he is going to refuse point-blank, but he takes it, weighs it in his hand. Then he sweeps the muzzle up and down in broad strokes, like a painter running a brush up and down a picket fence, smooth and calculated. Repeating this action several times he says, "Wait here," and strides off. It is obvious from the length, the deliberation of each step that he is pacing off a distance. I begin to count to myself, seven, eight, nine. McAdoo halts, swings back to me. "Don't you move now, Harry," he warns me.

The sharp, flat crack, the spray of dirt pattering on my right pant leg seem simultaneous with the movement of the pistol barrel. Again, the glint of the barrel travelling through the hot sunshine, the loud pistol report, the eruption of dirt by my left boot.

I stand locked to the spot, a weightless sensation in my bowels, my head dizzily adrift. His voice snaps me back into focus. "Just point and squeeze," he says mildly. "Point and squeeze."

"For the love of Christ, Shorty!"

McAdoo casually ambles back to me, the pistol dangling loosely by his side. My eyes don't leave the revolver until we are face to face again. "There's your lesson," he says, holding up the gun innocent in the palm of his hand. "Take it."

I take it because the weapon seems safer in my hands than in his. My tongue is cracked leather in a dry wool sock.

"I ain't no shootist," he says quietly, "but here's a fact. A carrying piece has got but one business. That business is man-killing."

I am having trouble with my tongue, it feels numb.

"This gun ain't about fancy shooting, it's about stomach. This gun ain't got but one earthly use but dropping a man. A man who can see your face and whose face you can see. It ain't no play toy. I knew boys could shoot the pips off a playing card with one of these, boys could dance a tin can around a yard like it was on a string. Hotter than slick shit in July as long as nobody put the wind up their ass." He takes me by the shoulder and points to the scarecrow Wylie has planted in the garden. Ragged overalls and a pillowslip stuffed with straw on which a lopsided face has been scratched with a piece of coal. "I just put a little wind up your ass. Now point and squeeze," he says.

I shake my head. I don't trust my trembling hand.

"You wanted this fucking lesson. Learn it, Vincent."

I raise the gun. Immensely heavy, a great weight dragging on my arm, it is as if I am trying to lift the scarecrow staked in the garden on the tip of the gun barrel, uproot it from the earth. I fire, the pistol springs in my hand, a small captive animal struggling in my fist.

"High and to the right," says Shorty drily. "Point and squeeze."

The quaking in my hand has spread, run up the length of my arm to vibrate in my shoulder. I try to fix the bead in the centre of the overalls but it twitches with every beat of my heart. Clenched muscles cannot overrule it. Another shot. A puff of dust dances in the field beyond the garden.

"Squeeze," says McAdoo, "squeeze."

I snap off two more shots as quickly as I can; I want to be done with it, the gun kicks in rapid recoil, the smell of expended powder worms up my nostrils. Then I am pulling the trigger of a gun dead in my hand, the hammer clicking repeatedly on empty chambers, the scarecrow leering at me untouched. Shorty's hand closes on the barrel and pushes it down to my side.

"Learn anything?" he asks.

Over Shorty's shoulder I spot Wylie running hard and awkward in his riding boots, knees pumping high, shoulders thrown back. Passing the burned house, he snatches a piece of lumber from the ground and hurtles on toward us.

"Lose the gun, Harry," Shorty is saying. "It ain't for you." Then he senses something, breaks off, turns and catches sight of Wylie. "Christ," he says, "here comes the cavalry."

The cavalry is upon us now. "I heard them shots, Shorty! I come to see!" he cries, breathless. "You okay, Shorty?" He holds the two-by-four wrapped in a two-fisted grip. A large rusted spike protrudes from it.

"Calm down," says McAdoo. "Everything's okay."

Wylie's eyes jump suspiciously from McAdoo to me. He has spotted the revolver in my hand and it seems to have stirred muddled outrage in him. "Why you shooting that gun?" he yells at me. "Shorty says you try to make him talk about stuff he don't want to talk about." He takes a menacing step towards me. "You leave him alone. He don't have to talk to you."

"Climb down off of him, Wylie," Shorty orders. "I was just giving Harry a shooting lesson."

Wylie clamps his top teeth over his bottom lip and sucks it, seeking solace and consolation even while his eyes narrow resentfully. "Whyn't you give me a lesson, too?" he complains to Shorty.

"Yes, Shorty, whyn't you give him the lesson you gave me?"

"He don't need that particular lesson," says Shorty.

"Please, Shorty, I ain't never shot a short gun but once or twice. Leave me do it, Shorty."

"Wylie don't need no lesson like you did, Mr. Writer. You seen him coming to the rescue like hell in a handcart with nothing but that piece of lumber in his hand. He was ready to pulp somebody." He gives me a wolfish grin. "No wind up Wylie's ass."

"That's right," agrees Wylie hesitantly, unsure what the conversation is about, "I ain't got no wind up my ass."

"Going to save old Shorty's bacon, wasn't you, boy?"

"I heard them shots. I say, There's maybe trouble, maybe Shorty's in trouble, and I run like the wind."

I hand the pistol and a box of cartridges to McAdoo. "Give him his lesson," I say.

"Show me, Shorty," Wylie pleads. "I can do her, Shorty."

McAdoo doesn't say anything. He simply breaks the gun, feeds cartridges into the chambers, slaps it shut. Before giving it to Wylie, he says sternly, "Point your finger."

"At what, Shorty? Where?"

"There. At that goddamn scarecrow you made, Wylie."

Wylie does.

"Say *bam*."

"Bam," says Wylie.

"Put your hand down."

Wylie does.

"Now up and *bam* – all together."

"Bam," goes Wylie.

"All right." McAdoo smacks the gun into his palm. "Do the same with this, point her and squeeze the trigger."

Wylie hefts the gun in his hand, the brightness of the weapon pulses up his arm and into his face. He beams. The gun flies up. It goes *bam*. The overall shudders from the impact of the bullet. The next two shots flap the cloth as they tear through the denim, twisting the scarecrow askew.

"See?" says McAdoo to me. "Nothing to her." He turns to Wylie. "Like shooting fish in a fucking barrel, ain't it?"

Wylie grins, face shining. "Easy," he says, head bobbing. "Easy."

"Try for the head," says McAdoo. The words are scarcely out of his mouth when the barrel glares in the sun. I hear three shots, so quick they stutter, and the head of the scarecrow tosses like a buggy whip.

McAdoo and I stand silent while a few wisps of errant straw float lazily to the ground. Wylie has drilled a hole in the scarecrow's leer and two more, one through the right eye and the other two inches above the left.

"Jesus Christ," mutters McAdoo.

"Bam," goes Wylie with the empty gun. "Bam, bam."

"The gun's his," I say. "I don't want it. Let him keep it."

I walk away, quickly. Wylie is standing with the gun, swinging it from target to target, going *bam*, louder and louder. He shoots the windmill, the bunkhouse window, a fencepost. I take one last glance back after I've cranked the car into life. Wylie has me in his sights. "Bam!" he shouts. "Bam! Bam!" He is laughing. McAdoo jerks Wylie's arm down as I duck into the car.

17

The fording of the Milk was a good deal easier than the Marias – no fool and blind white horse to save from drowning. Once across, they shucked their wet clothes and hung them in the willows, built a fire and breakfasted buck naked while their duds dried. Finding themselves north of the Milk seemed to lighten the boys' mood, they were now beyond reach of the Choteau County sheriff, the United States Marshals, the army, or Indian agents. On the Canadian side of the line there were no meddlesome lawmen of any stripe whatsoever.

And the health of their spirits might have owed something to the fact that all trace of the horse thieves was now well and truly gone. Pure relief, the Englishman's boy guessed, noting how the knot in his own gut had loosened over the last day when it became clear they had lost them. Biggity talk about what you were aiming to do to Indians was one thing, the prospect of delivering on it was another. There were some hard cases in this crowd, but even hard cases got second thoughts when their mouths fell shut long enough to allow a spell for thinking.

Hardwick let them linger over morning coffee; with the trail dissolved into thin air there was no point in hurry. The thieves might have skedaddled in any direction – maybe they'd even doubled back south. But Hardwick had decided to gamble that they were bound for the Cypress Hills, fifty miles to the north, prime hunting grounds for the tribes. And not just for the Cree, the Saulteaux, the Assiniboine, and the Blackfoot who gathered there to dance, to hunt, to make war, and to chop lodgepole pine, the slim, arrow-straight, nearly branch-less trees prized for teepee and travois poles. Because also folded in among the hills were bands of Métis who had given the *montagne de cyprès* their name, buffalo hunters who supplied the Hudson's Bay Company with the pemmican to feed its factors and servants in the Northwest. And traders, too. Only the year before, according to Vogle, that Bay bastard, Isaac Cowie, had packed out seven hundred and fifty grizzly pelts and fifteen hundred elk skins despite the Company's monopoly being broken by independents trading the bad whisky the Company refused to sell. The thought of whisky of any kind, bad or good, and the prospect of a long swallow had helped cheer the boys remarkable, too.

Nigh ten o'clock, Hardwick ordered them into the saddle and they forsook the camp by the Milk, winding up and over and through gaunt, brooding hoodoos the colour of cured hides, riding out onto a rippling plain contoured like a washboard. The heat of the previous day had eased a little, but the wind had struck up fierce, gusty. As far as the eye could see, the short curly grass writhed and shuddered under the invisible lash of the shrilling wind. The Englishman's boy rode leaning into it, like a man shouldering through swinging doors, his bowler hat battened down tight around his ears. Handfuls of sparse, sombre cloud sped overhead, spinning shadows on the glow-ing, rolling grass like coins tossed carelessly across the lamplit baize of a saloon table. An occasional faint spit of rain accompanied the dark shadow, then suddenly disappeared, the sun pouncing back on them, quick and hotblooded as a cougar.

To the left of the Englishman's boy, Scotty rode with a stiff smile pasted on his gob. At first the boy had wondered if the wind wasn't twisting up the corners of the Scotchman's lips, curling them like the tips of a waxed moustache; now he figured it had nothing to do with the wind but with the Scotchman's mind. Out of the corner of his eye, he watched him talking to himself, a brief mumble of words, a puppet-like bobbing and wagging of the head on the stem of the thin neck signalling agreement with his own propositions. And each time he ceased jabbering, his smile was stretched even wider across his face until the Englishman's boy feared the mouth might rip at the corners; each time the smile seemed frozen a little harder and more unlikely ever to thaw, a toothy grimace as strange as that fixed, blue, teary shine in the Scotchman's eyes.

The boy bounced his heels on the horse's ribs, left the Scotchman making faces and muttering to himself, and jogged ahead to the trio of James Hughes, Charlie Harper, and Ed Grace. Better to get shut of that lame duck while the getting was good. He'd had enough of lame ducks to last a lifetime. First, the Englishman Dawe, who'd sickened and died on him, then sorry-ass Hank, now this crazy-grinning Scotchman. He had enough to look out for, looking out for his own skin.

Hughes, Harper, and Grace rode hunched in their wildly flapping coats, Hughes shouting over the roar of the wind. "Hardwick'll land us at Farwell's post. If he starts flying his kite there, he'll soon forget about them horse-snatchers. We'll do a few days' drinking, turn around and head for home. That's all she wrote."

"The hell he'll forget," said Harper. "Those Arapaho took him captive in Wyoming put a burr under old Tom's foreskin when it comes to Indians. I don't know what they done to him, but he's got one bad hate on for our red brothers. You heard what happened in the Sweet Grass Hills last April. He scattered lead on a bunch of Assiniboine riding in under a trade flag. That's bad business, shooting the customers."

The Englishman's boy gave close attention to Ed Grace. Grace was a quiet man who didn't bandy opinions, but now he seemed to be studying some thought, slowly shifting a wad of tobacco from cheek to cheek. A tall, raw-boned man with a strong hooked nose, hooded eyes, and a balding head, Ed Grace was nicknamed the Eagle. He shifted in the saddle, crooked his neck, and squirted a stream of tobacco juice over his shoulder, downwind. "Beating up on Assiniboines is one thing," he offered in a hoarse voice. "Assiniboines are a scrubby, poor sort of Indian. Short on horses and nothing but sawed-off Hudson's Bay flintlocks for guns. But I figure there'll be Blackfoot camped in Cypress. There were last year. Caught sixty Cree braves collecting spruce gum and rubbed them all out, didn't spare a one. The Blackfoot got no shortage of horseflesh – even the squaws and brats ride fine ponies – and they own plenty of rifles, good rifles, Henrys and needle-guns. The Spitzee Cavalry didn't do anything to keep repeaters out of their hands and they aren't the least bit shy about turning them on whites. The dose of the smallpox they caught lately didn't do anything for their sweet temper or our popularity. I don't care how much that burr under Hardwick's foreskin is bothering him – he better not go taking any potshots at Blackfoot or some of our hair will be dangling from their belts."

The Englishman's boy could see what Grace had said didn't go down well – with Hughes in particular. He wasn't about to swallow it. "Ain't no goddamn Indians ever going to get the drop on old Tom," said Hughes. "He's a foxy one. No Indian's going to outfox the fox."

"Anyway, we got Eagle here to protect us from the Blackfoot," said Harper, giggling through his bad teeth, the fool. "This side of the line Queen Victoria owns the Indians. Eagle being a Canadian, it's up to him to be hospitable, see that we Yankee boys have a good time and don't have our hair troubled by no British Indians. Eagle's the Queen's rep'sentative. Ain't you, Eagle?"

"God only knows what I am," said Grace, "but I assure you I'm not happy. Not with this situation. I ask myself why in hell I'm here. There's no percentage in it and that's the truth."

"Why, you're here for friendship's sake, ain't you?" Hughes hollered into the wind. "We all of us seen the winter out together, didn't we? We all been good partners, thick and thin. Friends is duty-bound to stand by friends, ain't they?"

"Who was Farmer Hank's friend?" asked Grace. "Who stood by him?"

Hughes and Harper threw one another troubled glances.

"Not me," the Eagle answered, "and not you either." He pointed to the Englishman's boy. "Ask him if he's riding with us for friendship's sake."

Hughes and Harper swivelled in their saddles and squinted hard at the Englishman's boy as if they were seeing him for the first time, as if they were striving to plumb his heart, his mind, his soul for some dark motive. Grace had to smile, seeing the way the Englishman's boy stared back at them, like a stray alley cat outfacing a pair of mangy, slat-ribbed dogs.

Harper said, "The kid's riding with us because he had to pull foot from Benton after he stabbed that hotel man. He don't want to face the music. He scared off out of there."

"That's right," said Grace. "Fear landed him here. Same as us. Only we're along because it's Hardwick's got us shitting yellow."

"Hell," said Hughes peevishly, "I don't appreciate that remark. Why you go putting such a complexion on things?"

"I'm not putting on a complexion. Complexion's there. I know it for a fact and you know it for a fact," said Grace. "We're all of us afraid to cross the Green River Renegade."

"He don't like that name," warned Hughes.

"Why?" said Grace. "He worked hard to earn it."

Harper had been working on his righteous indignation until he'd puffed up like a tom turkey. "I ain't afraid of Tom Hardwick. Any man says I am is a liar."

"That's right, he ain't," confirmed Hughes. "And I'm a gent cut from the same rough cloth. Jimmy Hughes ain't afraid of any two-legged creature walks God's green earth. I got myself out of tight corners Tom Hardwick couldn't have spit out of."

"That being the case, you brave boys sure as hell don't belong in the company of two cowards like us," said Grace. He paused. "So why don't you heroes piss off out of here and go pin a medal on each other." Grace leant back in the saddle and spat over his shoulder in summation. The gesture, the tone of voice, were two slaps in the face, bald contempt on bald contempt. Hughes swore, savagely jerked the reins of his horse, the bite of the bit hooking open its mouth, flinging back its head, popping its eyes.

Grace and the Englishman's boy kept on, didn't bother to look back. Hughes and Harper were cursing them, the wind wiping away whole words and phrases, like a cloth smearing chalk on a slate. The Englishman's boy strained to catch their threats. "Bastard . . . don't ride away from me . . . you'll answer . . . Jimmy Hughes . . . don't forget . . . we'll settle for you . . ."

The Eagle gave no sign he was listening, only passed a clumsy hand back and forth over his face like he was brushing off flies. "Maybe I ought to have held my peace just a little longer," he said. "But I might have bust. Passed the worst winter of my life, shacked up with that bunch of whoreson rascals. I thought once we reached Fort Benton I'd get shut of them, and then five mile out of town those plaguy Indians scampered off with our horses. I always was a fellow scanty on luck. I got a ten-per-cent share in twenty-five-thousand-dollars' worth of wolf pelts and you can bet how much of that I'd see if I'd told Hardwick I didn't intend to help get the horses back." He fell silent, absent-mindedly rummaging about in his jacket pocket as he contemplated hard luck and mischances. A piece of soiled candy came up in his fingers. "I got no use for this," he said, turning it over and over. "Bad teeth. But a youngster likes his candy."

He passed the sweet. The Englishman's boy popped the smudgy peppermint in his mouth. "I ain't no kid," he said, sucking hard.

By early afternoon, Evans suggested they call a halt, but some time between breakfast and then Hardwick had undergone a change of plan. He had ditched the notion of leisurely travel and demanded they press forward. Evans did not argue and no one else asked for an explanation; they knew Hardwick better than to question the man's decision. For the next five hours they pushed on, then paused to water the horses while the men ate a little biscuit and jerked meat. After twenty minutes, Hardwick signalled them to mount again, there were miles to be made before dusk fell.

As they advanced on twilight the wind died down, but heavy, grape-coloured clouds were louring in the north, gloomily dragging toward them. They and the wolfers met on the spine of a ridge in the last vestiges of tinted light, the world displayed behind smoked glass. A slow, steady rain began and with it night descended, a swift black sword. The men dismounted and the few with waterproofs wrestled into them, the rest crouched miserably under tented coats and blankets, passing a glum hour watching water puddle around their boots.

As abruptly as the rain had begun, it ended. Men, soaked and chilled to the bone, threw off soggy blankets, groaning as they shook and stamped free joints which had locked while they hunkered under cover. They hobbled about in the darkness, doing what needed to be done, unsaddling and picketing the horses, spreading bedrolls, breaking out biscuits and dried meat, dim wraiths, shadows of routine. Soft, impersonal curses, the clink of metal buckles and the creak of leather, someone's dry, hacking cough were the only sounds. A few damp buffalo-chip fires began to fume and stink. Tonight Hardwick had relented and said they might smoke and build fires – if they could find anything dry enough to burn. A long, cold night threatened. Grace and the Englishman's boy were muffled up in saddle blankets still warm with the body heat of horses. They sat before a small fire started from a bundle of kindling the Eagle packed for just such emergencies. The boy was toasting a stack of damp buffalo chips on a stick, drying them so they would burn. That was Grace's idea. He had a handle on things, a practical turn of mind. Some of the pissers and moaners would rather stay wet and complain than do something to make themselves as comfortable as they could. The two of them were getting on though, doing just fine.

Or perhaps he should say the three of them because the Scotchman had crept up to the cheer of their fire like a woebegone dog. There he sat hugging his knees, three or four feet off where the flames licked at the night, his face wavering in and out of the black in tune with the beating heart of the fire. He wasn't talking any more, to himself or anybody else for that matter, but he was still smiling, although the corners of the smile appeared to have wilted and run a mite in the rain.

"I don't know what the point was – hurrying us all along," said the Englishman's boy. "It didn't get us nowhere in particular, except under a cloudburst."

Grace sat wrapped in his horse blanket, the firelight applying a yellow varnish to his face. His bald head was tied up in a big blue-and-white spotted bandanna. Earlier that day the wind had snatched off his hat, blown it to Kingdom Come like a tumbleweed, no point in even giving chase. Simply gone. The Englishman's boy had taken steps to prevent a similar misfortune; his derby was lashed down to his head with a rawhide thong passed through the hat brim and knotted under his chin. He looked a bit like an organ grinder's monkey.

"I figure this is Hardwick's reasoning," said Grace as he rolled a cigarette. "He wanted to pull within ten mile of Cypress before making camp. That gives us a short morning's ride to the hills. In full light, nobody can take us by surprise, ambush us. We can put out scouts in the timber so we don't stir up a hive of Blackfoot on our way to Farwell's post. We went fast today so we can feel our way tomorrow. Not a bad plan." He lit his cigarette on a brand from the fire and passed the makings to the boy. "Hardwick's a funny case. He can think things through good enough – to a point. He's a cool customer – to a point. But he's like the man who woke up in a house-fire and started to climb into his pants. When they were halfway up he began to feel the heat and decided to hell with the pants, it's time to run. In the heat of the moment, Hardwick sometimes trips, pants around his ankles."

"You think that'll happen?" the Englishman's boy asked.

"Anybody's guess. But I'll tell you one thing, son. If it gets hot, nobody in this bunch is going to pull my fat out of the fire."

For the first time, the Englishman's boy thought the wary tilt of the Scotchman's head might mean he was listening. The kid shook a buffalo flop off the stick into the fire. "So what you going to do about it?"

"Do?" said Grace. "Nothing to do."

The boy was staring into the fire, the fitful convulsing of flames. "You stand by me – I'll stand by you."

Grace stretched his wet boots out to the fire, a faint steam rose from the leather. "I don't know you but a little," he said matter-of-factly.

"Fine," said the kid. "I ain't begging."

"You're right," said Grace. "I was raised better than that. Who am I to cold-shoulder a courtesy?"

Nothing more was said. Their two faces danced in the glare of the fire. The Scotchman's mouth grinned maniacally out of the blackness, receded, grinned again. The boy felt a sense of occasion, his father had been a ceremonious man, gravely polite in a backwoods fashion. The kid laid aside his stick, and with his blanket hanging off his shoulders like a cape, shyly held out his hand. Grace shook it three times, emphatically. The boy returned to his place and began to vigorously thrust more buffalo chips into the blaze.

18

$\sim$

On a quiet Sunday afternoon Rachel and I cross the sun-flooded lawns where patients recline in striped canvas deck chairs or, shepherded by attendants in white, shuffle the brick pathways which wind among flower-beds and hedges. Rachel has been accompanying me on visits to the Mount of Olives Rest Home ever since she learned my mother was a patient there. There is nobody else I would have admitted this to but Rachel. Her own utter lack of reticence is what gave me the courage. She has no qualms about telling anybody anything. I've heard it all, blow-by-blow accounts of her two marriages, intimate details of her frequent, calamitous affairs.

The barricades I had built up over the years had to be taken down piece by piece the night of my confession. The telling was a hard struggle, with myself, with memory, even with Rachel. The final struggle was to hold back my tears, but that struggle was no more successful than the others had been. I sat in a chair weeping and then she wrapped me in her wiry arms, pressed my head tight to her flapper's bosom where with every sob I gulped her fragrance: tobacco smoke, cologne, the comfort of warm, tired flesh. It was, I suppose, the moment I knew I loved her.

For years my mother has been withdrawing further and further into a dense mist of apathy, eating whatever is put in front of her, going to bed when told, getting up when told, seldom speaking, never smiling. It is as if the rest of us are ghosts, shadowy presences whose existence she cannot quite credit. Except for Rachel Gold. She is the most solid, the most real to my mother. That much was clear from the beginning.

The first time Rachel came with me to Mount of Olives we found Ma in her room, standing in front of the window, occupied with the only thing she ever seems interested in – cleaning the glass with her handkerchief.

"Ma," I said, "I've brought you a visitor." She did not turn to see who this visitor was. The handkerchief continued to squeak in tight little circles.

"Mother, it's Harry."

For a second, the circles stopped, then began again, more rapidly than before.

"Mother, stop that. Come and say hello."

The circles whirled on the glass, faster and faster.

"I know you can hear me, Ma."

She began to whimper softly, the handkerchief spinning more and more frantically. Her head, bobbing with the effort, shook loose a few stray strands of hair from her bun.

I was about to speak again when Rachel touched my sleeve, stopping me. She lit a cigarette and then crossed the room, her customary boiling, decisive energy leashed a little, but still capable of making her skirt snap, and took up a position by my mother at the window. Ma did not acknowledge her presence; she continued doggedly polishing the glass, her eyes pinned on a vast tree spreading its branches directly outside her window.

Rachel said, "I'm a friend of Harry's. The name is Rachel Gold and I give a very decent manicure. If you do a lot of windows one thing you've got to look after is your hands. And you've got nice hands, very shapely. Unlike Harry, who owns a set of bricklayer's mitts. Besides, he's the nervous type and chews his nails. Anyway, if you'd like, the next time I come to visit I could do your nails for you.

However you'd like. If you're the conservative type we could go with a little clear polish. If you feel like kicking over the traces, fire-engine red. And we'll chat while I do it. It's a very relaxing thing, to get a manicure and make small talk. Would you like that?"

My mother stopped rubbing at the window, she turned and intently searched Rachel's face.

"Well, Harry," said Rachel, "I think your mother and I have a date."

When we said our goodbyes that afternoon, I saw that Mother's eyes never left Rachel; they followed her out the door. I hadn't seen that happen before.

So the manicuring sessions became a ritual. I noticed a change in Ma, nothing miraculous or earthshaking, just a tiny heightening of attention. In the past, I had only hurled bits of stilted conversation at her: How was she feeling? Wasn't that a nice rain last night? Weren't the flowers in the grounds beautiful at this time of year? Hard little pellets of desperate talk which rattled off her solitude like cold sleet off a tin roof. Nothing but racket.

But what Rachel did was different. A kind of girlish conspiracy grew between them, a conspiracy which revolved around small luxuries and attentions which had never been part of my mother's hard life – manicures, chocolates, the cosy beauty-shop conspiracy of women.

Rachel plays it like an actress, for my mother, for me. She plays the professional beautician, mimicking the beautician's professional chatter. But, underneath, it is more than a performance. Under the guise of gossip, she is telling my mother things about me, and me about myself. It is like a beauty-parlour séance. Rachel the medium, through which Mother and I, the world of ghosts, commune. For a long time I didn't see the point of telling Mother anything about myself. I tried to reach her by asking about her. But now, if she is listening – and I am growing convinced she is – Mother is learning who I, this stranger, this ghost, have become since her illness.

This Sunday, Rachel is up to her usual tricks.

"You know, Tillie, I think Harry's beginning to reveal a side of himself neither of us ever suspected."

A faint smile plays across Ma's lips as she sits absorbed, watching Rachel work on her cuticles with an orange stick.

"Which side's that?" I ask.

"His ambitious side. I don't know what you think, Tillie, but I find it surprising. Because, frankly, since he signed on to the script department he hasn't exactly been the picture of vaulting ambition. He didn't show much push, wasn't a go-ahead guy. To tell the truth, I don't think he much cares for the work. Not to say he wasn't grateful when I put a word in for him, got him the job, but it seemed to me he was grateful for *a* job, not for *the* job. I always got the impression it was all the same to him, short-order cook, tram conductor, hod carrier, photoplay dramatist."

"I do my job."

"Of course he does. Better than most. Better than Wilson, or Dermott, or poor Ehrlich. Harry can write title cards in his sleep; for him it's merely a case of filling in the blanks, like doing a crossword puzzle. For a bright boy like Harry it's easy enough. What the camera can't convey he puts on a title card. The trouble with the aforementioned Unholy Trinity is that they're too stupid to recognize the blanks. If you can't find the blanks you can't fill them. Tillie, you wouldn't believe what I caught Ehrlich doing the other day. He was writing a title for a scene in which hero and heroine are wound around one another, osculating. Ehrlich writes, 'Emily and Tom kiss with inexpressible desire!'"

I can't help laughing. Mother actually smiles.

"For the Dermotts, the Ehrlichs, the Wilsons of the world, contributing to the literature of the silver screen is stating the obvious. But not Harry, not for our Little Truth Seeker, Tillie. No," she says, shaking her head, "he's too pure to yearn for vulgar success in the movie game. He thinks that to succeed in the business is proof positive of idiocy. He has contempt for what he does."

"Look who's talking."

"He has a point, I suppose, Tillie. But my contempt has limits. I may have contempt for the idiotic pictures I write, but I keep going because I want to get somewhere. Gal to gal," whispers Rachel to Ma, "some day I'm going to direct a picture."

"And I'll play Hamlet."

"You know, Tillie, in the early days, in the days of the one- and two-reelers, there were women directing pictures. Because the money boys didn't think it mattered. Budgets were small, a thousand dollars, so the stakes weren't big. And you could take a picture of a wagon-load of horseshit and sell it to the public. As long as the flies on it could be seen to move. People just wanted to see *moving* pictures. What did it matter who directed horseshit? But now the studios say picture-making has got too technical for women to handle. Not like the old days, one stationary camera, point it and shoot, painted back-drops, no rough location shooting. They say big crews of men won't take orders from women. And they say women don't have the money sense to handle a big budget – unlike that paragon of fiscal responsi-bility, Erich von Stroheim. You'll love this, Tillie. Do you know what Erich did on *Foolish Wives*? He insisted, on the grounds of authen-ticity, that the actors playing officers wear monogrammed silk under-wear. Which the camera couldn't photograph. There's hard-headed business sense for you. Yet Stroheim's excesses are genius. A woman's would be whim."

"What are you whining about?" I say. "I'd like to make the kind of money you make. You don't strike me as so hard-done-by."

"He's not listening, is he, Tillie? Because I'm not talking about money; I'm talking about power. And I think Harry is after power, too. But here's the difference. I come right out and say what I want and Harry hides behind this polite, fastidious English facade –"

I correct her. "Not English."

"All right, Canadian. Excuse me if I can't see the distinction. It's not a bad thing, politeness, I suppose, if it's genuine and you don't take it to extremes. But isn't it just a little hypocritical, too? Of course, maybe Harry's undergone a sea change, maybe he's not really nice any more. After all, he's made himself indispensable to one of the most powerful men in Hollywood. He and Mr. Damon Ira Chance are apparently as thick as thieves."

This digging sarcasm is irritating. "What the hell do you know about it? Nothing."

"Understand, Tillie, I'm only drawing conclusions from the evidence. Mr. Chance has a general factotum by the name of Fitzsimmons who guards the master's door like it was the entrance to the Holy of Holies. And who gets admitted? Occasionally a big-name star. Occasionally a big-name director. Who else? Your boy. Seems he's making good. Very good. Out of the blue, a lowly seventy-five-dollar-a-week title-writing drudge penetrates the Holy of Holies, is admitted to the Presence. Smells like ambition, if you ask me."

"This is pretty lame stuff, Rachel, this routine."

"Or maybe Harry really isn't ambitious, maybe he's just a guy adrift on a great green sea of wanting. You can get carried a long way from shore when you're adrift."

"What the hell is that supposed to mean?"

"I know where I want to go. Do you think Harry does?"

She's made me really angry now. "If you've got something to say, say it. To me. Not my mother."

Rachel looks up from my mother's nails. "All right, Harry, I will. Here's what I've got to say to you. You're an intelligent man, Harry. And a nice one. One of the nicest I've met. Did you know I thought that?"

"No." Then I qualify it. "Maybe."

"I want you to remember that because now I'm going to say something you're not going to like. I'm afraid for you, Harry, because you don't know what you want and you're weak. You lack the courage to take responsibility for your intelligence. You actually prefer writing title cards rather than scripts because then you're not responsible for the end result. That makes you a blank-filler. You use your intelligence to find the answers to questions other people ask, but never to find answers to questions *you* might want to ask. A good man for cross-word puzzles. Is that what you're doing for Chance? Crossword puzzles? The intellectual odd jobs the Irish moron isn't up to?"

"What is it you resent so much, Rachel? Me? Chance? Or our idealism?"

"As far as I'm concerned the jury is out on Chance's idealism."

"I told you. He wants to make the great American movie."

"Sure you told me. But do I believe it?"

"He's an eccentric, Rachel. But so is anyone who tries to do something big. Edison is. Alexander Graham Bell. Nobody can really explain them. Chance happens to believe movies are the art form of the future. He thinks they can capture the American spirit the way Shakespeare captured the spirit of Elizabethan England. Speaking of ambition, it may sound megalomaniac and preposterous, but that's his aim. I don't hear anybody else talking that way. Everybody else talks dollars. Not Chance. He talks art." I wait for this to sink in. "What you say about me is likely true. Maybe I'm nothing more than Chance's blank-filler. But let me put the question to you, Rachel. What's better? To be a small part of something big, or a big part of something small?"

She ignores my question and fires back with one of her own. "And what's the American spirit, Harry?"

The best I can do is one word. "Expansive."

"Oh, that nails it, Harry. Just expansive?"

"And everything the word implies. Energy, optimism, confidence. A quicksilver quality. Like the movies themselves. Chance says the movies are the only thing that can capture the American spirit because they are like America herself. It makes a kind of sense to me."

"Quite the theory, Harry. But for myself, if I want a dose of the American spirit I'll go to Whitman, Twain, or Crane before *Rebecca of Sunnybrook Farm.*"

"You're missing the point. Chance wants to make films that are the artistic equal of *Leaves of Grass.* He might fail but he's got the guts to try. Besides, how many people have read *Leaves of Grass* in

Mencken's Sahara of the Bozarts? Or anywhere else in this country for that matter? And what about the tenements and the ghettos? Immigrants can't read English. Whitman is for the elite. But everybody goes to the movies. It's the movies that have the chance of making everybody – the immigrant, the backwoods Kentuckian, the New York cab driver, maybe even the Ivy League professor – all feel the same thing, feel what it means to be American. The Constitution and the Declaration of Independence are all very well, but constitutions make states, they don't make a people."

"And you're a Canadian, Harry. So why is a Canadian so concerned about teaching Americans how to be American?"

"Because I chose this place. And I'm not the only one in Hollywood. America's Sweetheart, Mary Pickford, was born in Toronto; Louis B. Mayer came from Saint John, New Brunswick; Mack Sennett was raised in Quebec. Canada isn't a country at all, it's simply geography. There's no emotion there, not the kind that Chance is talking about. There are no Whitmans, no Twains, no Cranes. Half the English Canadians wish they were *really* English, and the other half wish they were Americans. If you're going to be anything, you have to choose. Even Catholics don't regard Limbo as something permanent. I remember when the ice used to break up on the South Saskatchewan. We'd be woken up in our beds in the middle of the night by a noise like an artillery barrage, you could hear it all over the city, a great crashing and roaring as the ice broke apart and began to move downriver. At first light, everybody would rush out to watch. Hundreds of people gathered on the riverbanks on a cold spring morning, the whole river fracturing, the water smoking up through the cracks, great plates of ice grinding and rubbing against the piles of the bridge with a desperate moan. It always excited me as a kid. I shook with excitement, shook with the ecstasy of movement. We all cheered. What we were cheering nobody knew. But now, here, when I listen to Chance, maybe I understand that my memory is the truest picture of my country, bystanders huddled on a riverbank, cheering as the world sweeps by. In our hearts we preferred the riverbank, preferred to be spectators, preferred to live our little moment of excitement and then forget it. Chance doesn't want Americans to forget to keep moving. I don't think that's ignoble."

It is then my mother says a surprising thing. "Home." Loudly and distinctly. Both Rachel and I are taken aback.

"What, Ma?"

She points to the window.

"What, Ma?" I ask. "What?"

"Home," she says one more time before retreating into silence.

19

The wolfers rose at first light, ate a quick meal of pemmican and biscuit, saddled their horses and rode out. The morning air was sharp and bracing after the night's rain, the sky a clear crystal-blue, cloudless. Hardwick, Evans, and Vogle took the lead, the rest bunched in a squad behind them, surrounding the pack horses and remounts. There was no straggling this morning, no one spoke. In the cool air, the horses moved briskly across the platter-flat prairie, Hardwick setting the pace, a sharp trot alternating with short walks to allow the horses to recoup their wind. The sun swung up in the sky as they headed north; a few mares' tails began to stripe the blue crystal bowl, brush-marks of white.

In an hour or so, Grace pointed the Englishman's boy to the Cypress Hills lying athwart the brown horizon, a low bench of hazy blue, darker than the sky. By mid-morning they had reached the foot of these hills miraculously heaped on the prairie, an astonishing blue-green elevation on a sallow plain. Hardwick called a brief halt to admonish his men to look sharp, keep their eyes peeled for the Blackfoot, Saulteaux, Cree, and Assiniboine, for whom the hills were a favourite hunting ground and haunt. As he talked, the men fingered their guns, eyes warily scanning hills darkly shaded with green bands of spruce and lodgepole, interspersed with the paler green of newly leafed poplar and willow. Then they began to climb, steering to open uplands spattered with yellow cinquefoil, avoiding the spreading skirts of timber that might hold raiding parties of Indians ready to pounce. This slow procession winding its way to the Power Trading Company post run by Abe Farwell on Battle Creek moved more cautiously, more watchfully than before, the wolfers flicking their eyes right and left, a few twisting round in their saddles to toss hurried glances back over their shoulders.

At noon, the scout, Philander Vogle, spotted a single rider on a treeless ridge and raised the alarm. Hardwick's troop bunched in a meadow a hundred yards from the nearest timber. All around him the Englishman's boy could hear the click of rounds being levered into firing chambers. He did the same as Hardwick studied the horseman on the ridge.

"Make for cover?" Vogle prompted.

"If it's a war party, it might be a trap," said Hardwick. "They might be trying to drive us to the trees. If they've hid a party in the bush and they open up on us point-blank, from cover, that'd brown our goose but good." He pondered some moments, his lips rolling a stub of cigar from one corner of his mouth to the other. "We've got an open field of fire here," he said at last, decisively. "If it's a small band back of that ridge, they ain't going to come at us across the flat. If they're in force and they charge us, we'll break them with a volley, then high-tail it for the trees."

They sat their horses, watching the motionless figure silhouetted against the sky, watching them. Nobody moved. The Englishman's boy could feel the tension stiffening the faces all around him, feel the plumb line of midday heat bobbing up and down on the clustered heads. The figure began to move, the horse switching daintily down the ridge, breaking into an easy lope when it won the level.

"He ain't an Indian," observed Hardwick. The man's blue capote had identified him as a French half-breed. On the rider came, reins draped high in both hands to show he was concealing no weapon. He braked his horse before Hardwick with a cavalier flourish, a slightly built man with a wisp of straggly beard and shocking blue eyes, evidence of a distant Norman ancestor, startling, exotic in the dark face.

Cinched at his waist was the red sash of his people; a brilliantly beaded fire bag hung from it.

The two men nodded to each other. "You parlez the Anglais?" demanded Hardwick.

The man smiled, held up forefinger and thumb gapped an inch apart. "Bit much," he said.

"Devereux, get your Frenchifying ass up here!" Hardwick roared. "Parley this fellow!"

Hardwick set the questions, Devereux translated. The man's name was Hector Desjarlais and he lived in a Métis settlement close to the trading posts of Moses Solomon and Abe Farwell. He told Hardwick there was a band of Assiniboine led by Chief Little Soldier also camped there on the Battle Creek. The Assiniboine were in an ugly mood, spoiling for trouble. They had warned their half-breed brothers they intended to kill Solomon, burn his fort, and feast on his oxen. Solomon sold bad whisky. When it came time to rub Solomon out the Métis were to keep their noses out of this business or they might find them cut off. Desjarlais said this talk of butchering the traders made the Métis nervous. They were friendly with the whites but . . . He lifted his shoulders expressively. Anything could happen. Little Soldier's talk might not be whisky talk. Just a month ago, Indians had killed a white trader, Paul Rivers.

"Which Indians? What tribe?" demanded Hardwick.

Desjarlais said he didn't know.

"The bastard's lying," said Hardwick. "Assiniboine are a shoddy kind of Indian. No guns to speak of. If anybody's killing whites its Blackfoot. I figure Frenchie here thinks we're scouting us a situation for a whisky post. All these Frenchies freight for T.C. Power. This boy's trying to put the fear into us about wicked hostiles. He's calculating we're competition for Power and he wants to scare us off."

Devereux shook his head. "I t'ink dis boy telling de troot," he said.

"Well, if he is, and there is a big camp of Assiniboine on the Battle, could be that's where our horses is at. Maybe a couple of young bucks needed ponies to buy themselves a bride. It's spring, ain't it? Time when a young man's fancy turns to love?" He rubbed his chin with the back of his hand, thinking. "But if what Brother Frog says is true and they see twelve brave boys ride into town, they may speculate we've come in strength to get our horses. I wouldn't want to show our hand too soon. Maybe I ought to ride up to Farwell's post on my own, one lost and lonesome pilgrim, and smell out if any bucks been parading horseflesh don't belong to them. If it turns out they have, then I ride back here with the lay of the land in my head and we plan how to get the jump on them. If there ain't no horses, I ride back, give you boys the all-clear and we take ourselves off to Farwell's to sample some of Father Abraham's whisky. How's that sound, John?"

"How long you figure to be gone?" said Evans.

"I'll stay the night. If I don't keep company that long and leave early it might tip our hand."

Evans looked doubtful. "It don't please me to overnight here, like a chicken without a henhouse. Not with Indians on the prowl."

"Not to worry. Have Vogle scout you a treed slope he's sure is clean of Indians." He swung round in his saddle and pointed to one. "That there looks promising. You don't want to get caught in the open in the dark; if they come in strength they'll scatter you and ride you down. Get up in the timber at dusk and post pickets. If any hair-lifters try and sneak up on you, you got the high ground and plenty of cover. Don't light no fires. I'll be back tomorrow morning."

The Métis watched Hardwick as he gave his orders to Evans. When Hardwick finished, he turned to Devereux. "Tell this orphan I'm going to make him a present of tobacco for his news," he said. "Tell him to keep his mouth shut about us and I'll buy him all the whisky he can drink at Farwell's. Tell him that."

Devereux did. Hardwick passed Desjarlais a pouch of tobacco but when the Métis offered his hand to shake, Hardwick ignored it. The Englishman's boy saw the briefest of smiles twitch the Métis's lips, then he ironically and gravely saluted Hardwick, wheeled his horse around, galloped back to the ridge and disappeared behind it.

⌇

After Hardwick left for Farwell's the men dismounted in the meadow, tying a rein to the foreleg of each of their horses so if they were surprised they could unhobble at speed, mount up and ride. Evans set one man on each of the points of the compass to keep watch. The rest of the wolfers sprawled in the grass to pass the time until dusk summoned them into the trees. Everyone was uneasy. The Englishman's boy could feel it in the way they put their heads together, talking quietly in churchgoing voices; he could see it in the way eyes switched nervously to the surrounding hills, the wall of trees which shielded and hid God knew what. They all laid their rifles beside them, didn't let their horses out of sight, making sure they didn't stray beyond easy reach in an emergency.

The Englishman's boy was gnawing a piece of jerked meat, staring at the split toe of his right boot when Ed Grace joined him, making himself comfortable on the ground. The bandanna he'd tied around his head was soaked through with sweat. For a conversation opener, he said, "Well, son, God help us, but I smell shit in the wind."

The Englishman's boy moved his shoulders in the big tweed jacket. "What kind of shit?"

"To start with, Indians full of bug juice if the half-breed wasn't lying. Second, politics."

"I don't know nothing about politics," said the boy.

"Then you better learn and learn quick, because you're plumb in the middle of politics." Grace dropped his voice. "Take a look around you. All these boys are I.G. Baker men. There's two parties in these parts – T.C. Power men or I.G. Baker men. Those two trading companies run this part of the world. They're God's own governors of Whoop-Up country."

"I ain't never heard tell of Whoop-Up country."

"You're in it, citizen. Whoop-Up country runs a hundred-and-sixty-mile stretch between Fort Benton and the meeting of the St. Mary and Oldman rivers north of here. Once you cross the Milk River, you leave the States and John Law behind. Out here nobody can touch you. Indian agents, sheriffs, U.S. Marshals, their jurisdiction stops at the Medicine Line and north of the Medicine Line the treaties say you're in Canada, but they're dead wrong. You're in Whoop-Up country. Up here the Democrats and Republicans are the T.C. Power Company and I.G. Baker Company, clawing each other for booty, clawing to carry off every pelt of fur, every buffalo hide they can lay hands on. As you might guess, it don't make them the best of friends." He plucked a stalk of grass and chewed it. "Hardwick's taking us to a Power post and all these are dyed-in-the-wool Baker men. They get goods from Baker on credit or they work for him as freighters. He's got them in his pocket. A year ago they were the next thing to being at war with Power." He tilted his head toward Evans who was laying out a game of solitaire on a blanket. "Just over there you have Mr. John Evans – Grand Panjandrum and Chief of the Spitzee Cavalry himself."

"Spitzee Cavalry?"

"You haven't heard of the famous Spitzee Cavalry?" said Grace, scratching his head through the bandanna. "There's innocence. Last year Evans and Kamoose Taylor got it in their pointy heads they were going to regulate trade in these parts because guns were being sold to the Blackfoot. So they put together a posse of regulators and started to lean on anybody trading firearms to the tribe. They said it wasn't healthy for white men if guns got into the wrong hands. Now the trouble with their regulating was the only people they regulated were traders who bought supplies from T.C. Power. It was a put-up job to drive Baker's competition from the field. Fifteen or twenty of them would ride into some post and threaten the factor that if he didn't sign a pledge to stop trading guns they'd burn him out, or worse. Most of the little outfits signed. They didn't have a choice but to knuckle under.

"Where they put their foot in the pisspot was when they tried to shake down Johnny Healy in Fort Whoop-Up. Healy had had the sand to go deep into Blackfoot territory and risk his skin with those white-hating heathen when nobody else would. His first kick at the cat he knocked together a few log cabins and a picket fence that a crew of drunk Blackfoot burned to the ground. The next time he built, he did himself proud. He raised a square timber fort, quarters with dirt roofs so they couldn't be fired by hostiles, put iron grates on the windows and in the chimneys so unfriendly red monkeys couldn't come climbing into his front parlour, hung oak gates and put brass cannon on the walls.

"Then one fine day the Spitzee Cavalry came riding up to Fort Whoop-Up to lay down the law like the lords of creation. If old Johnny Healy had a mind to it he could have stood on his strong walls and pissed down on their hats, but he had more style than that. No, sir, he invited them in for a good sit-down meal and a palaver. After they'd eaten hearty of all John's good food, one of the Spitzee boys stood up at table and read a charge they'd written out against him for trading guns to the Blackfeet and asked him how he pled, guilty or not guilty. They say Healy just tipped his chair back on its hind legs, took a long look at this dirty, jumped-up prosecutor wearing his rags and his stink like glory, and laughed in all their faces. He said it'd be a frosty Friday in hell the day he recognized the right of I.G. Baker to hold court on his doings and judge him with a jury of yellow, contemptible cowards the likes of them. It wasn't his habit to confess to anybody but a priest, and since he hadn't bent the ear of one of them for a good five years maybe he'd lost the knack of it entirely. He believed he had. No, the only thing they were going to get from him was what they already had – full bellies at his expense and forbearance for their damnable impertinence.

"Now the Spitzee Cavalry had come to take their make-believe lawyer papers and themselves so serious – dropping "whereas" and "How do you plead?" and "I charge you" like so much pig shit in the pea patch – that they rose up full of wrath at being told to go piss up a rope by the likes of Johnny Healy. Evans pulled his pistol first and the rest unholstered too, covering Healy in his chair where he was sitting unarmed in his suspenders. 'If you hold us so cheap,' says Evans, 'we'll return the favour and send you to the Devil. You can kiss his arse for me.'

"Healy didn't turn a hair, just sang out in a loud voice, 'Mr. Reese, if you please!' and the kitchen door flew open and the Spitzee Cavalry got a tooth-puller's look into the mouth of one of Johnny Healy's brass cannon, Mr. Reese standing over the wick with a staff of burning pitch pine in his hand. 'Now, gentlemen,' Healy said, 'that cannon has three coal shovels of nails and a good sample of river pebbles crammed down its craw. It is primed with powder and sports a fuse shorter than John Evans's little dick. And I'm prepared to kiss the Devil's arse if you send me to him, but just remember, I'll be standing in line behind the rest of you to do it. Now you can listen to reason, or you can listen to my cannon's roar. Which is it?'"

The Englishman's boy laughed appreciatively.

"That turned the mood of the jury fast; they voted to a man for acquittal on all counts. Healy thanked them for their wise decision and commended them for their interest in seeing justice done. He said if they ever cared to hold court in front of Judge Brass again, Judge Brass would be pleased to accommodate them. They weren't eager to take him up on his offer. The Spitzee Cavalry disbanded shortly after. Healy was the end of them."

The Englishman's boy had taken his knife out of his boot and was jabbing it in the sod. He looked up at Grace. "What you telling me? You don't like being left with Evans in command?"

"Hell, no. At least Evans showed some sense faced with a cannon. All winter I've been listening to Hardwick rag him about turning tail. He says the foreman of the jury ought to have seen to a guilty verdict – Judge Brass or no Judge Brass. Shoot the bastard where he sat, Hardwick says."

"And get blowed to scraps?"

"Hardwick does things hot-iron," was all Grace said.

The Englishman's boy twisted his knife in the earth. "So what is it you saying?"

Grace glanced around him to make sure nobody was listening, tapped the boy on the knee. "What I'm saying is that you and me are like that half-breed – he isn't white and he isn't Indian. It's a tough place, betwixt and between. I'm not a Baker man and nor are you. Maybe we're going to get caught in the middle at Farwell's post," he said significantly. "The only reason I'm here with this godforsaken crew is to protect my share of the money from those wolf skins. You're here because Fort Benton's too hot for you. Neither of us has any reason to get shot for I.G. Baker. I'm not a man who has a taste for blood. Hardwick is."

The Englishman's boy wiped the knife blade on his pants.

"We could light out tonight," said Grace urgently, "when Hardwick's gone. Evans won't follow us."

"You do what you like," said the Englishman's boy.

"There's no point going on my own. In this country, a man needs someone watching his back. Two repeating rifles are better than one."

"And where we going to go? I ain't welcome in Fort Benton."

"There's whisky forts spotted all over this country. We could make for Fort Kipp, Fort Slideout, Fort Conrad, Fort Whisky Gap, the Robbers' Roost – you name it."

The Englishman's boy remained stubbornly silent. His reaction altered Grace's mood; when he spoke again the pleading tone was gone, replaced with a sad resignation.

"I was born in old Ontario," he said. "My mother had a piano in the parlour. We had books. One of them had a picture in it of a centaur –" His head bobbed up. "You know what a centaur is, son?"

The boy shook his head.

"A being, half man, half horse." He stopped, began again, explaining. "I've been knocking around this country ten years – it changes a man. But I'm not all the way there yet. I'm not Tom Hardwick. I'm betwixt and between – half civilized, half uncivilized. A centaur."

The Englishman's boy waited for Grace to go on, but he was finished. "If I was a centaur, I could ride myself out of here," the boy said. "But I ain't. I'm mounted on Tom Hardwick's horse. If I ride out of here on his horse, that makes me a horse thief. Horse thieves hang. I'd sooner take a bullet than have folks gawking at me while I kick and dangle."

"So you won't go?" The question was a formality.

"I won't go. But if you want, the deal we made still holds."

"It holds," said Grace. "We'll watch each other's back."

At dusk, they filed into the trees. Grace said it was a quarter to nine by his pocket watch, but the sky still held a little light. They climbed

191

through a stand of lodgepole pine, winding amid the slender limbless trunks, straight as spear-shafts, which culminated in crowns of branches which lent the pines the appearance of bottle-scrubbing brushes. There was little undergrowth and the forest floor crackled dry and sere under the horses's hooves. The air held no taint of rot, of fungus, of mould, was odourless, except for the occasional furtive, astringent whiff of sap or pine needles.

Earlier, Vogle had discovered a deadfall that formed a natural breastwork and it was behind this they camped, unsaddling and hobbling their horses, unpacking gear, spreading blankets in a hushed, deepening gloom. Evans nominated two men as advance pickets for the first watch, and two more as reliefs. The first sentries glided off down the slope, flitting through the trees and ashen light like spectres.

Needing a piss, the Englishman's boy strolled away from the camp to politely make his water. Despite the lateness of the hour, everywhere birds were calling to one another in the treetops, a cascade of urgent, piercing cries, succeeded by sombre, dolorous chirps which seemed to float, prolonged, thirty feet above where the lodgepole pines waved their heads in the breeze.

He stopped to listen. The shoulder of the hill acted as a windbreak; down here all was dead calm, the air still warm with the heat of the day, but overhead the pines whispered and sighed like a sickroom. It recalled to him the hotel room in which the Englishman, John Trevelyan Dawe, had surrendered up his spirit.

The boy shook himself free of that thought, drifted on, moving farther and farther from camp. The widely spaced pine grew blacker by the minute as the light died in the sky, turning into columns of ebony. Darkness was gradual and sudden both, a stealthy movement turned peremptory – simply *there*.

He arrested himself in his tracks, fidgeted his pecker out of his pants. Above the hissing of his water on the ground, off in the distance, he heard a burst of duck squabble. Was something else besides himself moving in the night? Indians? A grizzly?

Now that he was still, he heard the thin whining of mosquitoes, like an itch in the brain, and their stings prickling his back, his face, his hands like the touch of nettles, a savage cloud inseparable from darkness itself, a cloud against which he could only blindly flap his hand and curse. He buttoned up in haste, and began to blunder back to camp, stumbling over the tree roots veining the ground. Once he cast his eyes up to the forest roof and there was the moon, bouncing along in step with him, jarring and bobbing its lunatic face at him through the treetops.

He tripped and fell, scrambled to his feet with his Colt drawn. He could hear himself panting, hear his feet slithering in the slippery pine needles as he turned a circle, the barrel of his pistol holding the trees at bay. That's when he saw it. An old gullied washout running straight and true like a well-worn wagon track down the slope. The moon's onslaught of pallid light was turning the tide of darkness – or maybe his eyes were only accustoming themselves to it. He stared hard, until it seemed to shimmer in the dimness.

A road offering itself. But he knew better'n to take an offered road. There weren't no straight tracks out of the trees, only the path you won yourself, squeezing and dodging, twisting and turning, doubling and backtracking, slipping through where you could. That was all, slipping through where you could.

The Englishman dead. Only God Almighty himself might know how that sorry-ass Hank had ended. Today he'd seen Scotty scribbling in that writing book, like Dawe had done, going so blamed quick you wouldn't believe it. Writing ever so much faster than ever any man could even think. So what was he writing?

And Grace. Grace with his head tied up in a hanky like a bandage, asking him to take flight with him. Grace pretending there was some straight road the two of them could sashay down. Grace would have him hanging straight, straight down on the end of a rope, like the geese his Pap used to string up to age, hang until they dropped off at the neck.

There it was still, a road pointing off somewheres. Right enough, it give him a clutch in the throat. It hurt him with its straightness and its promise. It hurt him with its moonlight prettiness. But he knew it one better. He knew there weren't no straight roads.

And so he slipped away, fugitive amid the pines, the passage of an animal, sure and deft now, his feet no longer awkward, but moving soft and certain in the soft and uncertain forest mulch.

He woke to the drumming of a woodpecker. Dawn was breaking. He stood up in his clothes and went to the breastwork. In the trees farther down the slope, he could see fine ground-mist unwinding skeins of white yarn. All around him men lay completely swaddled in blankets, even their heads were covered. It had been a bad night. Even in the midst of a swarm of mosquitoes Evans had allowed no smudges to be lit for fear of giving away their position. All night men and horses had suffered torment, the horses having the worst of it. The Englishman's boy had listened to them stamping their hooves in frustration, the wild, hissing rustle of their whisking tails. After four or five hours, they had begun to groan hollowly, a deep, sonorous, dumb complaint against their misery. When the Englishman's boy crawled out of his bedroll and went to his mount, he could see its eyes rolling wildly and flashing in the darkness. A comforting hand run down its neck came away wet with blood.

He did what he could. After he saddled the gelding he took the two blankets of his bedroll, wrapped one around the horse's neck, draped the other over its hindquarters. Then he lay back down on the ground in his clothes.

He might have slept as much as an hour. Leaning now against the wind-toppled timbers of the natural barricade, he could feel how puffy his face was, his left eye almost swollen closed by the insect bites.

Someone was hacking and spitting behind him, someone else muttering. The wolfers were rousing themselves. He smelled match sulphur and pipe tobacco.

Soon they were back on the flat, where Hardwick had instructed them to await him. One hour, two hours passed; they acquired a discouraged and sullen air, like a school party abandoned in strange surroundings by their teacher.

Then someone shouted. Hardwick was coming.

Hardwick had not seen any of their horses in the Assiniboine camp. They would spend Sunday at Abe Farwell's post.

20

From Chance's quarter all is silence. I am beginning to wonder if I haven't blown a golden opportunity, spilled the milk. The problem is I don't know because I can't get in touch with him. That is the frustrating thing, the uncertainty. Two nights ago I drove up to his house in the hills intending to beard the lion in his den, but when I got there I found the iron gate to his grounds was locked. Although I thought about it, I knew it would be too ridiculous to leave the car in the road and grapple my way over the gate to get into the property. Given my leg, probably it was impossible.

Yesterday I called his office again and asked to speak to him. After a brief interlude during which I could hear papers being shuffled on a desk, the receptionist said, "Your name is not on the list of people from whom Mr. Chance will accept calls."

"You tell him Harry Vincent is on the line. He'll take my call."

"Mr. Chance is occupied. I'll put you through to Mr. Fitz-simmons."

"I have nothing to say to Mr. Fitzsimmons. I wish to speak to Mr. Chance."

"That is impossible. Perhaps you would care to leave a message?"

"Here's my message. Give him two names. Harry Vincent and Shorty McAdoo. If I were you, I'd see that he gets them."

I sat down to wait for Chance to return my call. He didn't; Fitz did. He was ready to skin me alive.

"What did Mr. Chance tell you? Keep it fucking confidential. And you, you asshole, you throw McAdoo's name at a receptionist."

"I thought it might catch his attention. Nothing else has lately."

"Don't go *thinking*. You ain't paid to think. You're paid to do what you're fucking told. And another thing. When Dorothy tells you Mr. Chance is unavailable, understand what that means. It means you are to get the fuck off the telephone – Mr. Chance doesn't have time for you."

"Or maybe it means you gave Dorothy orders not to put my calls through. I heard mention of a list. What's the list about, Fitz?"

Fitzsimmons ignored this. "And where do you get off telling Dorothy you don't want to talk to me? That's an insult. You're an insulting little prick, Vincent. For one-fifty a week, you talk to me. You got that?" He paused. "I tried to tell him you was an insufficient man. Insufficient in every way. But he had one of his –" he searched melodramatically for the word "– one of his *intuitions* about you. But you don't produce results, do you?"

"Who's complaining? Mr. Chance? Or you?"

"Maybe both of us."

"You make it sound as if the two of you are one and the same thing."

"Near enough."

"Then how about if I submit a letter of resignation? See if it makes Mr. Chance as happy as it would obviously make you."

I could hear him breathing ominously into the mouthpiece of the phone. His delay in answering made me think it hadn't been a bad tactic to call his bluff. Very quietly, each word weighted with emphasis, he said, "No, you ain't going to quit."

"Why's that, Fitz?" I asked, feeling I had gained the upper hand.

"Because it's inconvenient for you to quit. That's why you ain't going to do it."

"Inconvenient for who? You?"

"Maybe inconvenient for your ma in that expensive nuthouse. She wouldn't like it in one of them state-run hospitals. I know. I had a cousin worked in one. The stories he used to tell."

How did he know about my mother? It frightened me. Then I got angry. "Don't go putting my mother in your gob-shite Irish mouth, Fitz! Do you hear me?"

All he did was laugh his rasping, gravel-grinding laugh. Transmitted over telephone wires it was even more terrifyingly expressionless than delivered in person, in the flesh. "Or what?" he said. "What you going to do, Vincent? You're all yap, like one of them little lap dogs. A little pussy-warmer pup, that's what you are. Yap, yap, yap. Don't make me sick. You ain't going to quit on us because we ain't going to let you. Besides, think about Ma Vincent. Think about your Jew girl friend."

"Think what about Rachel?"

"Those Jewish dollies don't like boys without a nickel to their name. You heard it here first."

I spoke very carefully. "Don't think that Mr. Chance isn't going to hear about this."

"You bet. I'm going to tell him."

"Don't leave anything out. I don't intend to. Be sure to pass on your remarks about my mother and Miss Gold."

"What's this? Hurt feelings? He don't give a fuck for your feelings."

"Are you sure? Maybe I read him better than you do. We've talked. Maybe about things beyond your comprehension, Fitz. He seems a civilized man. Are you sure he doesn't give a fuck for my feelings?"

"I'll tell you what he gives a fuck about. In order of importance. Him. Me. Because I can be trusted to look out for his interests. When I am told to keep my mouth shut about a man named Shorty McAdoo, I keep it shut. When you are told to collect information about Indians and suchlike from that selfsame McAdoo, you don't. Whose feelings is he going to worry about? You give him nothing. I wipe my ass with your nothing, Vincent."

"There's a reason I've got nothing yet. That's what I want to explain to Mr. Chance."

"Fuck the explaining. *Do your job.* I get paid to look after his interests. So do you. Same locomotive pulls us. So let's get behind it. Let's get going where the locomotive wants to go."

"I'd be pleased to, Fitz. But I want to make sure I'm hooked behind the right locomotive. Because I haven't seen it for some time. Too many bends in the track."

"Ever hear of being too smart for your own good, Vincent?"

"There's many a man who might imagine he's the locomotive when he isn't. Just like there's many a man with his hand in his shirt who thinks he's Napoleon. If you get my meaning?"

"Fucking right I do. Thank your lucky stars I'm not there in that room with you."

"Well, you aren't. And I don't know which locomotive is pulling me. Do I?"

"There's not a man on the studio lot who doesn't know I speak for Mr. Chance."

"That's for the small-time pictures, Fitz. This is closer to Mr. Chance's heart."

"Just do your job," said Fitz. "That's all he wants from you."

"He's a lonely man. What about friendship?"

"Don't press your luck, Vincent. He's got friendship. You get him Indians."

"I think the time has come for us to lay our cards on the table," I say to McAdoo.

He is emptying the box of supplies I brought from town. A kerosene lamp is lit against the falling dusk and it sends tall shadows leaping up and down the walls as Shorty stoops and straightens unpacking his bacon, his beans, his coffee, his sugar, his crackers, the box of ammunition for Wylie's revolver. When the cartridges hit the tabletop Wylie snatches them up and bolts to his bunk where he breaks the pistol open and starts excitedly loading it.

"It's too dark to go shooting now, Wylie," Shorty warns him.

Wylie's dismayed face shoots up. "It ain't too dark. It ain't hardly too dark at all."

"Leave off until tomorrow."

"I disbelieve it's too dark, Shorty. I'm pretty sure it ain't."

"It's blacker than Toby's arse out there," says McAdoo. "I ain't telling you again. Get it out of your head."

Wylie gives a downcast tuck to his mouth but doesn't argue, only commences mournfully emptying the pistol with the lovesick air of a young girl plucking petals from a flower. One by one he carefully stands the bullets in a line on the floor, looks at them, and then takes each bullet up in turn, mysteriously sniffing its blunt lead nose before returning it to its place in the ranks.

"What the hell's he up to?" I ask.

McAdoo shrugs. "I ain't going to lay a guess. God himself don't know what goes on in that boy's head. I don't reckon that gun was such a good idea. He's shooting the property full of holes."

Now Wylie is rearranging the cartridges in an X, extending the arms of the X with new ammunition recruited from the box, blissfully sucking on his bottom lip as he fusses with the alignment of the bullets like a little boy playing with his lead soldiers.

"What about these cards you want to lay on the table?" says McAdoo, as he watches Wylie tinkering with the cartridges.

"It needs to be said, Shorty. Don't take it wrong."

"Say it."

"This crap you've been handing me doesn't cut it. You've got to do better. My job's at stake."

I wait for Shorty to take the bait. He doesn't.

"At first I thought, Shorty needs to get to know me. I have to establish confidence and trust before he'll open up to me. I told myself, The money you're paying him now is just seed money. Think of it as seed money. But where's the crop, Shorty? I can't wait forever for the crop."

Shorty holds a can of beans in his left hand. His eyes avoid me.

"I think maybe I ought to lay the cards on the table for both of us, Shorty," I say. "I've got a sick mother in the hospital. You want to take this boy to Canada with you." Wylie glances up from his bullets when I mention him, eyes distrustful. "You and I have people depending on us. We have responsibilities. Responsibilities that require money. But nobody gives money away to get nothing in return. My employer is not getting what he wants, Shorty. Soon he'll cut our water off."

"Let him cut it."

I raise my voice, turn McAdoo's head with it. "That's not good enough, Shorty. I deserve better from you." I point to Wylie. "How're you going to get him to Canada without money? And what the hell are you going to do for money when you get him there?"

McAdoo doesn't respond. His face is set, emotionless.

"I am telling you a fact. There is a chance you can carry a substantial amount of money to Canada with you – if you tell me something I can use. But if you have nothing to tell, we are wasting each other's time." I pause. "You know what I am asking."

"You asking me to put money in your pocket."

"If it was just a case of money, don't you think I could look out for myself? I'd sit down, make up a story, sign your name to it. I know what he wants and I can give it to him; I'm a writer. But more than money's involved. There's respect. I respect the man I work for. He's trusting me to give him the truth and I'll give him that or I'll give him nothing. I respect you, too, so I won't put your name to a lie. Because I don't believe you're a liar, Shorty."

"No, I ain't." He records this as a fact, in a courtroom voice.

"I'm glad to hear it. Because if you aren't, that must mean the things that are said about you are true."

"I can't answer on that. Depends on the things." It comes out hard, a rebuke.

"They say you were an Indian-fighter."

He smiles stiffly, mouth twisting lopsidedly with effort. "They say all the real Indian-fighters is dead. Like Custer." He isn't convincing.

"But if they aren't? That makes a survivor damn valuable."

He keeps smiling, his grin the rictus of a corpse.

"You a survivor, Shorty?"

"I done some surviving."

"You ever fight Indians?"

He stares at me for a considerable interval. "Some," he admits at last. The smile has vanished.

My heart is beating fast. I know I am getting close but I'm not sure how to finish. "Now was that so hard?"

"What you want, Vincent?"

"Not what I want, what he wants. He wants Indians. Indians plus the truth."

"He don't want no fucking truth. Not your man."

"I assure you, he does."

Shorty laughs sourly.

"Claiming he doesn't want the truth gives you an out, doesn't it? Because then you don't have to bother telling it."

"I know it. He don't want my truth. It ain't to his taste."

"That's what you say. I say different. Let's see who's right. Tell it."

"For the money."

"Money – for whatever reason you want."

Shorty puts the can of beans down on the table. "Wylie," he barks in a no-nonsense voice, "take your blankets, take your gun, go wait outside."

Wylie squirms uneasily on the bed; he scoops up the box of cartridges in one hand and a fistful of blanket in the other. "Why I got to go outside, Shorty?"

"Because you're the best shot here and I'm giving you the job of looking out for us."

"Who's it I'm a-guarding you from, Shorty?"

"You'll know the bastards when you see them. Don't let nobody close now. I'm counting on you."

Wylie gathers pistol, cartridges, and blanket. "I'll know them when I see them?" he asks doubtfully.

"They're Mexicans," says Shorty. "You see a Mexican, shoot first and ask questions later."

"Christ, don't tell him that."

"Mexicans," says Wylie to himself. "Mexicans."

"Build yourself a fire," Shorty tells him. "You going to be keeping watch a goodly spell."

"How do I know if they're Mexicans?" says Wylie.

"By the big fucking hats. Mexicans are big-hatted bastards. Sombreros. Look for the hats." Shorty holds each of his hands out a couple of feet from his head.

Wylie nods and goes out full of purpose.

"What's that about?" I say.

"He don't need to see and he don't need to hear."

"See and hear what?"

"Us fattening on the dead."

"I don't know what you mean."

"That's what you and me are setting to do. Fatten us up on the dead." McAdoo's smile is beyond cold; it is a raw, self-inflicted wound. "What's a dead Indian bring nowadays? Ten dollars a head? Fifteen?"

"I don't follow you."

Shorty sits down at the table. "Well, I'm just trying to put a price on what you asking for. Calculate the going rate. What's he going to give me for a story about Indians, this boss of yours? What's the price of truth?"

"If he likes your story, wants to use it, he has to buy it from you. You negotiate."

"Rough figure? I reckon we need fifteen hundred dollars to set us up handsome in Canada."

"I want to make this clear, he hasn't given me authority to make deals for him," I qualify. "But I think that if he likes the material a figure of fifteen hundred dollars would not be an unreasonable expectation on your part."

"For the truth?"

"Of course, for the truth. There's a premium on the truth."

McAdoo spreads his hands on the table and gazes down at them, thinking. Scarcely above a whisper, he says, "I been thinking on this business for a long time. Ever before you came. I thought it in Mother Reardon's boarding house. I thought it making them fool pictures. For a long time, I never thought it at all and then it starts on me. My daddy used to say you think a thing and think a thing, you can't shed

203

it, that means you going to be called to answer on it. My daddy believed in all kind of second sight." He looks up at me. "I been thinking on this for a goodly time, but I didn't want to believe what my daddy told me. I said it weren't going to happen. Then you came along." He sits quietly, his chin on his chest. "You got your pencil and paper out?"

"Yes."

"Fifteen hundred dollars," he says. "Now I know the going rate on a dead Indian. Near fifty dollars a head."

⌇

Shorty McAdoo must have been thinking on it for a considerable time, just as he said. He knew exactly what he wanted to say and would frequently request me to read back to him what I had written in my shorthand notes. He listened very intently and then he might add or omit some detail. Occasionally he would get up and go to check on Wylie; sometimes I would accompany him to the window. We could see the boy beside the big fire he had built, the sparks churning up into the sky like fiery confetti, the flames blowing and seething in the night wind, the light swaying across the figure draped in a blanket, staring out into the darkness, forearm propped across one raised knee, gun hanging ready.

It was a long, long night. Several times I asked if we couldn't continue tomorrow but he said no, this was like amputating a leg, you didn't stop in the middle, pick up the saw in the morning. He never permitted himself a rest; even when he stood at the window watching Wylie his voice went on, growing slightly frayed and raspy, hoarse from hours of talk. He talked as he made coffee at the stove to keep me awake. He talked as he paced up and down the room.

We finish about dawn. He asks me to read aloud the part about the girl. I do and he listens closely, his head cocked to catch every word. Then he asks me to read it again and listens as closely as he did the first time. "Put her down for fifteen," he says, judge rendering a decree. "She mightn't have been fourteen like I said first. I'm more comfortable going high than low."

"All right." McAdoo gets up and stands at my shoulder, watching me make the change.

"What did I say?" he asks me.

"What did you say?" I am tired and don't grasp what he means.

"I said the truth wouldn't pleasure your boss. Am I wrong?"

I shake my head. "I don't know." I really don't.

"Your man wants it, he takes it all. She's all of a piece. Nobody's going to cut it up like an old coat, for patches. The girl stays."

I say nothing, collect my notebook and pencils, wiggle my last cigarette out of the package and light it before going out. It is a strange dawn, the overcast sky diffusing a tea-coloured light over everything, like tint in a Griffith picture. Wylie has finally given up his watch and dropped asleep. He lies cocooned in his blanket, the fire subsiding into ashes and tendrils of grey smoke, the gun fallen to the ground beside him. McAdoo picks it up, wipes the dust from it as fastidiously as Wylie would himself.

"There was a number of us had the second sight," he says. "We knew what was coming. The only mistake is one of us never shot him in his blankets when he slept."

"Jesus, Shorty," I say, "that's a little cold-blooded, don't you think?"

He aims the pistol at the sleeping Wylie's head to make his meaning perfectly clear. "We could have shot the snake in his blankets. Before he bit," he repeats. Then he puts the gun up like a duellist prepared to step off ten fatal paces; his ten paces carry him over the threshold and into the bunkhouse, walking like a somnambulist.

～

Mr. Chance's office at the studio is the very antithesis of his house. It is cluttered. Or rather I should say the walls are cluttered. Hardly an inch of them isn't covered by black-and-white publicity photos of actors and actresses who have starred in Best Chance productions. I am certain that most of these people have scarcely had more than a handshake from the reclusive Chance, yet that hasn't stopped them from autographing their pictures to him with the most intimate and saccharine effusions, each signatory striving to outdo his rivals in the fine art of Hollywood ass-kissing. Directly above the door of the office, Webster DeVilliers, a.k.a. Walter Digby of Pass Creek, Indiana, smiles toothily down on me. His mug is inscribed with the words, "To Mr. Chance, 'Our Star' from the East! Lead Kindly Light! Yours for Best Pictures, W. DeVilliers." Anyone who knows Walter Digby of Pass Creek also knows that no irony was intended by this inscription. There are many, many more testimonials to Mr. Chance's genius. Perhaps a hundred. "To Dearest Mr. Chance, The Genie in the Bottle of Motion Picture Art, Twyla Twayne." "To Mr. Chance, Good, Better, Best Chance!!! Roger Douglas Braithwaite." Have the big game mounted in this trophy room volunteered their stuffed heads? Maybe yes, maybe no. But this smells like Fitz's idea. I can imagine him making the rounds like the grand vizier of some oriental satrap, extorting tributes. "Pitcher for Mr. Chance. Write something nice. Get it back to me by tomorrow."

Mr. Chance is seated behind a big teak desk, commanding a corner where two floor-to-ceiling windows meet, Venetian blinds closed to deflect the stares of the curious. His manner smacks of the principal welcoming back to the old school a former pupil who has made good.

"This is top drawer," he says, flourishing the transcript. "Absolutely top drawer."

"I'm glad you're pleased, sir."

"Oh, I'm more than pleased. Much more than pleased. You are to be congratulated, Harry. We have our picture. It's all here."

This strikes me as overstating the case, but if the boss is happy, Harry is happy.

Chance's tweed suit and sparse hair are both rumpled with childish excitement. He speaks in short, emphatic bursts. "The story of a great battle. Obscure but nevertheless great. Both are important.

Obscurity *and* greatness. Novelty and awe. You see? Think of Custer – famous in defeat because he fought against overwhelming odds. But this, this is much better. *Victory* in the face of overwhelming odds. America needs this example, Harry. The strength of isolation. A dozen souls pitted against hundreds. The magic of the number twelve. It's almost as potent as a seven, don't you think? Twelve disciples, twelve jurymen, twelve tables of Roman law, twelve months of the year, twelve days of Christmas – can you think of any other significant twelves?"

"No."

"No matter," says Chance. He is scrawling a lengthy note on a piece of paper now. His face shoots up. "About McAdoo," he says eagerly, "can he act the part?"

"Part?"

"Part, Harry, part," he urges brusquely. "You're in the business. You know what I mean. Does the man have presence?"

I consider a moment. "He's not very talkative. On the other hand, when he says something . . . I think people are inclined to listen."

Chance nods. "And this quality would be conveyed in interviews?"

"He won't do interviews."

"Why not?"

"Because he'll be afraid of looking ridiculous. Like Buffalo Bill."

"No one thinks Buffalo Bill is ridiculous. Besides, people don't refuse their moment in the sun."

"He will. To him, it's not the sun."

"You're sure?"

"As sure as I can be."

Chance writes something on his pad. "That is unfortunate. But if he refuses to conduct himself as a hero, then for our purposes he is better off dead."

"Dead?"

Chance laughs. "Not literally dead, Harry. I was thinking more along the lines of an announcement of the great plainsman's passing – the timing would have to be nicely calculated. You, as friend and biographer, could represent him to the press. That might do very well indeed. There are heroes more compelling dead than they ever were alive. Custer, for instance. Not a man to survive close scrutiny, Custer. Tied to his wife's apron strings and very foolish. But he made a heroic corpse."

"And what if Shorty McAdoo doesn't want to play dead?"

"Well, as I said, it's a question of timing. You say he has expressed a desire to relocate to Canada. For our purposes, Shorty McAdoo in Canada is as good as dead."

"And if he changes his mind about Canada?"

Chance lays his little gold pencil down on his desk. "Then it must be changed back."

"You mean money."

"Of course, money. Or other persuasions if necessary."

"Such as?"

"In the past, Mr. Fitzsimmons has proved useful in such situations."

"Fitz's tactics – they wouldn't work on a man like McAdoo. In fact, they're likely to produce the opposite effect."

Chance smiles. "I will take that under consideration, Harry. But perhaps we are putting the cart before the horse. We don't own the rights yet, do we? The rights must be secured. Do you have any idea what we might get them for?"

"He wants fifteen hundred dollars."

Chance taps his desk blotter with his pencil. "I don't see that as a problem."

"Who's buying them might be. To keep your name out of it, I told him I was working for a publisher. McAdoo doesn't have much love for the movies."

"Many people disapprove of the movies. Three-quarters of the authors who sell us rights to their novels claim to despise the pictures. But they swallow their disgust and take the money happily enough. I don't expect McAdoo will be any different. I don't intend to have this picture blocked because it costs me a few thousand dollars more. Do you understand?"

"I understand, Mr. Chance. But will McAdoo? He may point-blank refuse to have anything to do with a film."

"Then," says Chance, "the contract will need to be framed delicately. My lawyers can draw up the proper phrasing. Something like, 'for the sum of X number of dollars, all rights to portray Mr. Shorty McAdoo's life story in any and all forms of artistic expression shall reside in the sole possession of –'" He stops in mid-sentence.

"That's right," I say. "If you name Best Chance Pictures, or yourself, the cat is out of the bag."

Chance barely skips a beat. "'Shall reside in the sole possession of Harry Vincent, his heirs, assignees and or partners as the aforementioned party so assigns and determines.' Mr. McAdoo is not a legal sophisticate, I think something such as that should satisfy him." Chance composes his hands on his desk. "And once the contract is signed, you will sell me the rights for the sum of a dollar. Agreed, Harry?"

I cross my legs, take my glasses off, pinch the bridge of my nose.

"Reluctance, Harry?"

"Not so much reluctance," I say. "I know it's not a question of your cheating him . . ."

"What then, Harry?"

"But shouldn't it be his decision – whether or not his life is made into a movie?"

"And if he says no?"

"I'm not sure."

"Harry," says Chance, "artists don't compromise. They pay whatever price is required for their work. Tolstoy exploited the most intimate details of daily life with his wife. Do you think that matters when weighed against *Anna Karenina*? I'll have McAdoo now – or later. The interviews are my property, I paid for them. If necessary I'll wait until McAdoo dies and then make my movie. But what good would that do him?" He waits, offering me the opportunity to refute him. "You know how these cowboys end. They live one day at a time and then finally when they're crippled or sick, the day of reckoning arrives. When it comes, they cannot pay the bill. You know he is certain to spin his last days out in abject penury."

"I know," I say. "But . . ."

"What would you do if you were appointed Shorty McAdoo's guardian angel? See him handsomely paid for his story, or get nothing? Those are the two choices." Chance sits there, question hanging. The question not only of Shorty's future, but his, too. He clears his throat. "I am willing to have you fill in a figure on the contract. You can write the number in, Harry. I trust your fairness."

"I sold him on the truth," I say. "He expects the truth to be told."

"Harry, you and I are going to work together very closely on this picture. Who knows the truth better than you?"

"I want four thousand for him."

Chance falls back in his chair, makes a steeple with his fingers and smiles ironically at me over it. "It's a rare privilege to play philanthropist with somebody else's money. But since I offered you the opportunity, I can't complain. My lawyer will deliver the cash, along with documents for signing, to your apartment by eleven o'clock tomorrow morning. Get a receipt from McAdoo when the money is paid."

Suddenly I need to explain. "I feel an obligation to him. He needs the money. He's taken this pathetic creature Wylie under his wing –"

Chance holds his hand up, stops me. "Harry, I can live with it."

I am still apologizing. "I know there were moments recently when you had doubts about me, Mr. Chance, but I hope that –"

"My confidence in you has been amply rewarded. Never a second's doubt."

"That isn't what Mr. Fitzsimmons suggested."

Chance raises his eyebrows. "I think you must have misread Fitz. Being a man of action he is naturally impatient of delays. Impatience is the key to his character. What you must remember is that feelings often run high in our business. It is a business which attracts people of temperament. All three of us are people of temperament. That is why it is so important that we learn to forgive and forget." He gets to his feet. "And get on with the next picture."

There is no real difficulty getting McAdoo to sign the contract. Chance is right, he is not a legal sophisticate. What makes him suspicious is all the money.

"Bounty on Indians gone up?" he says.

"I bargained hard for you" is all I tell him. I believe it.

He walks me to my car, we shake hands, I urge him to keep well. He promises he will. He tells me that now he's flush he intends to put in a supply of good whisky. Whenever I feel inclined I should drop by and take a dram. I am welcome. I tell him not to forget Canada when he's drinking his whisky, to make sure to get there before the money's gone.

I leave him then, a gaunt old man whose hollow eyes look every bit as corroded and blackened as the suicide's farmhouse. I expect this will be the last I'll ever see of him. He looks no lighter despite his confession.

21

The twelve horsemen kept the Battle Creek between them and the Assiniboine camp as they approached Farwell's trading post. The Englishman's boy was numbering the teepees; he tallied forty-nine and then lost count. At two hundred yards the lodge-skins resembled fine parchment, parchment written upon with yellow suns, red and blue horses, black bear tracks. Indian magic. Behind the camp, a stand of dark-green timber hung like a stage curtain.

Three young boys of eleven or twelve herding ponies down to the creek for water were close enough for the Englishman's boy to see plainly – the narrow brown chests, the shoulder-length blue-black hair. One of the youngsters who sat a brown-and-white paint pony drinking from the stream started to mark off the wolfers with his quirt as they passed. The action struck the Englishman's boy as mighty sassy, vaguely threatening.

Women were bending over black iron cooking kettles in a haze of blue smoke, stooping to prod and encourage flames with a stick. A number of girls ran out of camp to watch the wolfers pass. The camp dogs followed after them, howling and yapping and barking at the white men as if they had sniffed Old Nick himself. The girls hung by the creek edge laughing, their buckskin dresses soft and inviting as yellow cream in the morning sun. Several were a mite unsteady and a trifle loud; the Englishman's boy thought they looked like they'd had a cup or two of bug juice for breakfast.

To the northeast, on the wolfers' side of the Battle Creek, stood Farwell's post, and directly across the stream the establishment of his competitor, the weathered peeled logs of Solomon's fort looking like they'd been rolled out of clay. The Englishman's boy could see a man in a red shirt chopping wood there; the blade of his axe winked semaphore flashes in the sun. The man paused in his work as the wolfers reached the walls of Farwell's trading emporium and dismounted. It was eleven o'clock on a Sunday morning. He mopped his brow and returned to splitting wood.

Farwell's was no Fort Whoop-Up, just a ramshackle whisky post with a palisade of shaggy-barked logs ringing it, a stockade that inspired no confidence it could so much as hold off an attack by the hens scratching dirt at its gate. The trampled grass and beaten earth the riders swung down on was littered with refuse, scraps of hide and animal bones which the chickens had pecked clean. A black cloud of flies rushed up into the face of the Englishman's boy when he trod near an elk head where the hens had left one clouded, staring eye undisturbed.

He looked around. Six Red River carts rested tipped on their shafts and through the spokes of the high wheels, half-breed children peered out shyly at the strangers. A few log outbuildings with sod roofs sprawled haphazardly about the post: a small stable, a summer kitchen with a rusted stovepipe, a chicken-house with a chopping block dabbed with little white feathers glued in dried blood. A rail corral held half a dozen horses and a gaunt milch cow bellowing to be milked.

Three or four hundred yards north of the post, the Englishman's boy could make out faint chimney-smoke rising from squat cabins like steam from a kettle. The smoke came from the Métis settlement straggling along Battle Creek. The appearance of the wolfers had already been noted there; a broken file of men, women, and children could be seen making their way up to Farwell's post.

"Gentlemen," said Hardwick, "the Lord took his rest on the seventh day. Let us follow his wise example."

There were raucous guffaws as the men pushed through the gates of the stockade. An Indian woman stood outside the post door with a pan of shelled corn in her hands. Hardwick raised his hat to her, smiling sardonically. "So good of you to greet the wayfarer, Miz Farwell," he said.

"No drink," she said loudly. "No drink Jesus day."

"We shall see, ma'am," said Hardwick, shouldering open the door, his men crowding into the post at his heels. Inside was dark and cramped and at first the Englishman's boy found it difficult to see. But as his eyes adjusted, he discerned a counter of raw planks laid on barrels and behind it steel traps, muskets, axes, and hatchets hung on nails driven into the log wall. There was also plenty of rough shelving stacked with wool blankets, tea, sugar, flour, and calico. Chests on the floor, lids propped open, enticed customers with misty hand mirrors and gimcrack trinkets, cheap beads, rings guaranteed to turn black after a day's wear, little pots of vermilion and ochre. It was a carnival of smells, some good, some bad.

Hardwick rapped the countertop sharply with a coin. "Mr. Farwell, sir!" he called.

After a brief delay marked by several nervous coughs, a stout little man pushed aside a blanket hung in the back-room door and stomped his way to the counter. He had a leonine shock of prematurely white hair and arched eyebrows as black as his hair was white. He did not seem pleased by what greeted him.

"Hardwick," he said, "I didn't expect to have the pleasure of your company again so soon. You just rode out of here a couple of hours ago."

"Well, Abe, I reckon I'm the bad penny that just keeps turning up . . . and this time I brought you a pocketful more. Twelve, all told."

The wolfers snorted gleefully, shuffled and scraped their boots appreciatively on the plank floor.

"And what can I do you?" said Farwell, lifting his sooty, shrewd eyebrows.

"Me and the boys would like a supply of whisky to start. And not that shit you remedy up for the Indian trade – red ink and cayenne pepper and raw alcohol. Real whisky, if you please."

Farwell brushed the palm of his hand back and forth over the countertop in a manner which conveyed his reluctance to oblige. "I cut them Assiniboine off this morning – I told them no more whisky. They been drinking for four days and every day they get uglier than Auntie. They got nothing left to trade and now they expect me to parcel them out bug juice on tick. I had to let on they'd drunk me dry."

"Well, you ought to be heartened by the sight of paying customers then."

Farwell shook his head. "I can't sell you whisky. On account of the Indians."

"What's Indians got to do with us?" said Hardwick. "Last I looked, my boys weren't wearing paint. Last I looked, my boys were wearing pants with two legs. Last I looked, we were all genuine white men or close enough to pass. Now, in this howling wilderness one white man has a duty to provide aid and comfort to a fellow white man." He waited, allowing this moral obligation to penetrate Farwell's thick head. "So why don't you kindly sell us the comfort which we require, Father Abraham?"

Farwell shifted uncomfortably behind his counter. He thought of correcting Hardwick on the small point that his name was Abel, not Abraham, but decided against the wisdom of it. Hardwick may have spoken with an air of easy jocularity, but only a fool could miss the harsh, dark current running beneath the words. Farwell attempted to elucidate his position. "They see me selling whisky to you boys – they ain't going to like it. That's all."

"Now what do you care if you're liked by a bunch of naked savages, Abraham? What does their opinion count with you? What you want is to be respected, not liked. An Indian can smell weakness. They smell shit in your pants and take advantage of you." He paused, stretched his arm across the counter and tapped Farwell on the arm with his forefinger. "Now, if you're quick fetching the whisky, I won't charge you for that lesson."

From a shadowy corner someone brayed laughter.

"Damn it, you don't know the situation here," said Farwell angrily. "The old chief, Little Soldier, can't rein in the young bucks.

They're proud and uppity as a nigra in a new suit. Yesterday, a man working for Solomon by the name of George Hammond had his horse stolen. The brave who stole it offered to sell it back to him for a bottle of whisky. Hammond didn't want to do it, but Solomon persuaded him. He told Hammond peace at the price of a bottle of whisky was cheap. No point in stirring up the anthill."

Hardwick turned to the men in the packed room. "Hell, boys," he said, "if the traders in these parts allow Indians to put on airs – is that our fault? Are we supposed to suffer for it? Besides, ain't we just as proud as any dog-eating Assiniboine? And ain't we owed some consideration on account of our complexions? And ain't one of them considerations a drink after a long ride?"

Sniggers ran round the room. "You lay down the law, Tom," said Vogle. "Hold his nose to where the bear shat in the buckwheat," encouraged another.

"Produce them bottles," Hardwick said quietly to Farwell, "because me and my boys ain't going to stand for being treated like we was a bunch of bare-assed nitchies."

For a moment, it appeared Farwell might refuse, then he shrugged, entered the back room, and returned with six bottles. As Hardwick tossed money on the counter with a devil-may-care air, laughing his careless laugh, the Englishman's boy felt a hand close on his shoulder, heard Ed Grace whisper, "Let's clear out of this."

The escape of these two was unremarked except for the thirty-some-odd Métis patiently waiting outside the stockade gates for a closer look at the strangers. The men stood propped against the Red River carts contentedly sucking on stubby pipes, the stained legs of their buckskin trousers casually crossed one over the other, their eyes impassive as their faces. Ranged behind the men, the women kept an equally tranquil and silent vigil, their print dresses a field of tiny, bright, becalmed flowers. The hair of the young women was braided or coiled on top of their heads, the hair of the old women was hidden under blue and red kerchiefs. No one moved. They made the Englishman's boy think of a mob he had seen in Sioux City crowding around the body of an old man who was slowly dying after being hit by a runaway wagon. Like that day, only the children made any noise. The Métis kids were gathered some way off, counterpointing the unnerving quiet of their elders with shrieks and excited shouts as they played some game on a blanket.

Grace was saying, "I don't know what your feeling is, son, but I think you and me need something to eat a damn sight more than we need something to drink."

The boy assented with a disinterested bob of his head. He wasn't really listening; he was watching the watchers. What were they waiting for – news, a glimpse of unfamiliar faces?

"Goddamn," Grace said, rubbing his hands together at the thought of victuals, "what I could use is some fresh meat. A bit of broiled venison, a bear steak, something doesn't want to break your pearlies when you bite down on it." For the first time, he seemed to see the Métis, ranged like a sombre Greek chorus loitering in a tragedy. "These half-breeds more'n likely have some fresh game on hand," he said to the Englishman's boy. "One of the women might cook us a Sunday dinner if we paid them. What do you figure?"

"Maybe."

The Englishman's boy watched Grace as he approached woman after woman, watched the women shake their heads, or stare at hands knotted in the cloth of their skirts. This would take some time, he calculated. He wandered over to scout what sport the brats were up to. Judging by their squealing, it was a dandy.

When his gruesome shadow fell across the blanket a dozen pairs of eyes lifted. At the sight of him a baby began to cry; her sister boosted her onto her lap, shushing and clucking. The Englishman's boy stood solemn and flint-faced, looking like a spark could be struck from his chin with a steel, a shred of newspaper he'd stuffed in the sweatband of his derby dangling on his forehead like a grimy kiss-curl, smudgy and grey as his hard, stony face. He had left his Winchester parked in his saddle-scabbard, but he still wore the two bandoliers of rifle cartridges crossed on his breast, and the holstered Colt cinched tightly at his waist. Whenever he took a step, travel-dirt made his pants flap stiffly as tent canvas. One of his boots was hanging just short of complete and utter disintegration by a few waxed threads. Only a year or two older than the eldest child there, nevertheless he looked wizened, forebodingly ancient.

They stared at him with naked, undisguised wonder, and he stared back, fingering a cartridge in a bandolier. "What you looking at?" he said suddenly, making an impatient gesture to the blanket lying on the ground. "Get on with your game."

It was impossible to say which they understood, his English or his peremptory gesture, but a boy of thirteen or fourteen with clever grey eyes and a broken front tooth swept the blanket in a matador's pass over his knees, snatched up three white smooth knucklebones off the ground and, grinning a jagged-tooth challenge at the Englishman's boy, began rattling the bones in cupped hands. His torso wove from side to side; his hands darted in and out from under the blanket, flew behind his back, cut passes underneath the noses of the smallest children, who shrieked with delight when his quick, lithe hands fluttered at their faces like birds against a window. All the while he sang a chant to the scudding hands; the same phrase repeated over and over, like a rosary prayer.

The chant suddenly stopped and the hands froze closed, the singer slowly twisting his shoulders to hold up his fists to the Englishman's boy. The Englishman's boy figured he was to guess where the bones were, how many in each hand. It weren't no mystery to him; he'd been studying hard the didoes the bone-boy had been cutting up.

He tapped the back of the Métis's right hand and held up two fingers. The bone-boy slowly opened his fingers – nothing. There was a sharp intake of breath around the blanket. He uncurled the fingers of his left hand. The three bones lay like little white eggs in a nest.

A great shout, a great hubbub; they smote the earth with their palms, beat it like a drum, even the baby struck her knee in imitation of the others. They all pointed, wagged their fingers derisively at the Englishman's boy, chanting the player's chant, a taunt, an insult.

He wrinkled his nose with distaste, blushed scarlet, drew himself straight as he could. The half-breed kid was laughing at him, brown eyes flashing, that broken tooth looking sharp as a chisel. The Métis dashed the bones to the ground with a flourish and scooped them up again in a single, unbroken, flowing movement. Then he was off chanting and rocking on his haunches, hands feinting, white bones juggling from palm to palm, fists leaping behind his back, under the blanket, wrists twisting and fingers flickering, chant rising and falling like last night's wind hypnotically swinging the treetops.

The Englishman's boy felt his face burn like it had a touch of sun-scald. Backwoods boy at a one-donkey circus, fooled by a fast talker with his pea-and-shell game. Fooled by a little snip like him. But he'd watch right smart this time. He'd track those bones like a hound.

The song broke off. The grinning face with the sharp tooth was tempting him with the offer of doubled fists again. The Englishman's boy had spotted that last little skip, that dodginess at the blanket edge, the roll of the white bone between the deft fingers a split-second after the song had stopped. When everybody's eyes were supposed to pass on to the brown imp's face.

The ring of children were waiting for him, faces tight with sus-pense.

Might be, this time, he'd wipe that scoffing smile off his face. Look at him, proud as Lucifer for owning a pair of pickpocket's hands.

He could hear Ed Grace halloing him. He daren't look away – that scamp would switch those bones on him in an eye-wink if he did. He held the half-breed with his eyes, slowly, deliberately drew his pistol. The muzzle wagged back and forth between the clenched fists like a water-witch's wand, then pointed. Water here, it said.

Two could play this kind of game. It produced a different kind of stillness. He tapped the hand with the barrel and stuck up three fingers. "Three," he said.

She was quiet as a prayer. All but for Ed Grace ramping at the fort for him to come along now. Did he hear? But the Englishman's boy had a piece of business to finish first. He was going to see that smart half-breed scamp chew feathers. The kid's eyes were melting on him; they were going to puddle soon.

"Open," he said. He opened and closed his own hand to show what he meant.

The half-breed shook his head like he had a bee in the ear. The rest of the brats were huddling back.

"Open."

No sharp tooth showing now, was there? He weren't no fool. They'd learn it now, by glory. Learn it if he'd have to break that young one's fingers open.

"Open your goddamn hand!" He saw his own hand when he shouted, the cords on the back of it standing up rigid like bones in a hen's foot, the thumb hooked white on the hammer of the Colt. He caught the boy's wrist, wrenched it viciously. The face twisted, he saw the broken tooth gleam from under a curling lip. Reluctantly, the hand fell open.

It was empty.

When the Englishman's boy let go the wrist and quickly straightened up, he went light-headed. Showed up for a fool.

They read his face, white, seething, violent as a blizzard.

His head swivelled like a turtle's in its shell, a painful, awkward seeking. Where was the voice? The horizon swam, the post buildings wobbled, the blood surging in his head submerged the voice in foam like a boulder in a rushing river. Then he located the source, Ed Grace, calling, beckoning him up by the fort.

His thumb pressed down hard; the hammer locked and all the heads around the blanket jerked and then locked too, bug-eyed, open-mouthed.

The Colt slowly drifted up as if it were rising on its own, then locked steady too. Everything seemed to freeze, even the buzzing of the flies. He jerked the trigger. The baby started on her sister's lap, wailed.

Ed Grace waved back. All right, he understood. He'd been heard.

The Englishman's boy lowered the Colt which had put a bullet in the belly of the sky, fishing in his pocket as he addressed the bone-boy's face, tilted at him like a plate on a plate rack. Eating crow wasn't his dish, never had been. "You beat me cold – twice," he said. "I don't know how you done it, but you done it." He'd found what he was searching for, one of the Englishman's precious silver dollars. He held it up. "Loser pays. Right?"

The bone-boy lifted his wrist and pressed it to the side of his face.

"You catch my drift?" asked the Englishman's boy.

The bone-boy gave no sign he did. The Englishman's boy hesitated, dropped the coin on the striped blanket, strode off purposefully.

The bone-boy didn't move. The other children pushed their heads in to admire the silver dollar like moths closing on lamplight.

22

We begin to thrash out our picture in meetings at Chance's place in the hills. These meetings have a bad-tempered, testy air because James Cruze's Western, *The Covered Wagon*, has recently been released and everyone is hailing it as a masterpiece, speaking of it in the awed tones previously reserved for *The Birth of a Nation*. Its success is eating away at Chance, maybe because the triumph is so unexpected, the picture always having been under a cloud. Only a short time ago, rumours abounded that Mary Miles Minter had turned it down flat and Hollywood insiders were of the opinion its stars, J. Warren Kerrigan and Lois Wilson, didn't have the box-office appeal to carry the film. There were budget overruns and enormous difficulties on location – heavy snow, dust storms, breakdowns of equipment, trouble supplying cast and hundreds of extras with food in the wilds – disasters which came near to duplicating the trials and hardships of the original pioneers themselves. Besides, it was the received wisdom that the public's love affair with the Western was over, movie audiences were growing more sophisticated, demanding classier entertainment than horse operas; even the great William S. Hart's pictures were flagging at the box office. And yet, despite frequent setbacks, Jesse Lasky stood by *The Covered Wagon*, ploughing more than eight hundred thousand dollars into a picture everybody was certain was doomed.

Hollywood loves disaster. Hollywood loves success. But it loves disaster more. Everybody was anticipating a catastrophe on the scale of Mayer's and Thalberg's *Ben-Hur*, a production running up an unprecedented string of disasters in Italy. During the filming of a spectacular naval battle two men had been killed; then an entire fleet of Roman galleys resting at anchor had sunk overnight. Production had been disrupted by disturbances linked to Benito Mussolini's new Fascist government and now the whole production crew was packing up to be shipped back to Hollywood to reshoot the picture.

Everybody had been sure a similar fate was staring *The Covered Wagon* in the face. They were wrong. The dodo bird flew. It flew beautifully, and on its back Lasky and Paramount were soaring too.

The Covered Wagon gnaws at Chance. When it crops up in his conversation it is always with the implication he has been cheated, robbed, swindled of what was his alone, the right to make the first Western epic. Fitz tries to coax and jolly him out of brooding, arguing the success of *The Covered Wagon* will play neatly into our hands, prove good for business by stoking public interest in the Western, but Chance isn't mollified. It isn't profit he is interested in, it is glory, and he resents having it snatched from under his nose. *The Covered Wagon* has raised the stakes in the glory race, and Chance is determined not to be beaten on territory he considers his own. A good deal of the praise lavished on Cruze's picture has been for its documentary qualities – the endless wagon train crawling across the plains, the thrilling fording of the River Platte, the use of locations along the original wagon route.

All this stokes Chance's mania for authenticity; like his idol, Griffith, he demands historical accuracy in every detail. It is a consuming passion that isn't satisfied cheaply.

"We need Indians, Fitz. Three hundred. Maybe four. Make it four. And *real* Indians. No Mexicans in wigs on this picture."

"Where the hell am I going to get real Indians?" grumbles Fitz.

"Lasky got real Indians, that's all anybody's talking about. Where the hell did he find them?"

"Colonel McCoy got them for him. Two trainloads. But McCoy has connections with the Board of Indian Commissioners. He's got pull."

"Then hire Colonel McCoy."

"Paramount has him sewed up. He's running that Indian song-and-dance number at Grauman's Egyptian Theater and once that's done he's taking a boatload of them to Europe to promote the picture there. The Colonel ain't available."

"Then find us an equivalent. Call McDavitt in Washington and have him get in touch with somebody at the Bureau of Indian Affairs. I didn't put money into President Harding's campaign for the good of my health. Pull some strings. Somebody owes me a couple of hundred Indians."

"Indians are more goddamn trouble than they're worth. You don't want nothing to do with them bastards. It's easier to herd cats than Indians. Most don't talk no English; they show up for work with dogs, squaws, papooses. Before you know it the bastards are into the firewater and stealing props. You got to negotiate a separate deal with each of them. One wants a cowboy hat for services rendered, the next one wants five dollars. Then they get jealous about what the next chief got and the dickering starts all over again. Cruze had to hustle up an army uniform for one of his bucks or he threatened not to do the big scene. You want a dogfight each and every day of the week, hire Indians."

Chance isn't listening. "And another thing," he says. "Hire me an Indian woman who can act. None of this 'how' stuff either. And make sure she's good-looking."

"You ain't asking for much," says Fitz. "I ain't never seen a good-looking Indian."

"And we'll need another Indian who can act to play the chief."

"Christ, what's the matter with Wallace Beery? I seen him in *The Last of the Mohicans*. He fooled me."

"I don't want any iodine-stained Wallace Beery. What's the name of the Indian in Griffith's *Mended Lute*? Young something or other. Young Deer? Try and get hold of him. Give him a screen test."

But Young Deer is not to be found; reports have it he is in France directing pictures for Pathé. Indian actresses don't come a dime a dozen either. Mona Darkfeather, a Seminole who worked for the Bison Company in the early days, is too old for the part, as is the other well-known Indian actress, Dove Eye Dark Cloud.

Chance is like a man who claims to want to build a cathedral but spends all his time on the gargoyles. We have no director or scenario yet and here he is worrying about casting. When I suggest my time might be better spent writing a script, he dismisses the idea. "The scenario will be written in due course. But first, the essential elements must be put in place."

What are these essential elements? Indian artifacts for one. He wants all the Indian artifacts Best Chance can lay hands on. Buyers fan out across the country, chequebooks in hand, to dun private collectors, to seduce destitute reservation Indians who might be persuaded to part with Grandpa's medicine bundle, coup stick, or eagle war bonnet for a pittance. Three artists are sent to Washington to sketch Plains Indian costumes in the collection of the Smithsonian. A Chicago stock-buyer is commissioned to purchase Mr. Chance his own herd of buffalo.

Every day he thinks of something new; pelts will be required, lots of them, and somebody must be immediately sent to fur auctions in Canada. Location scouts accompanied by still- and motion-picture cameramen are sent north to survey prospective sites and report back on possibilities. Even before locations are settled on, he insists Fitz hire Mexican workmen to build an authentic adobe fort. He also reminds Fitzsimmons if clay isn't available on site it will have to be shipped in by train, by the boxcar-load. A working riverboat, a stern-wheeler is needed. And don't forget to clear landing strips at each location so he can fly in on a regular basis to supervise production.

Fitz comes and goes, relaying orders and seeing the work gets done, while I keep Chance company beside the pool, or in the study, or eat lunch with him in the long dining room hung with Flemish tapestries, a convenient ear into which he can pour his thoughts about the picture.

Soon wooden crates begin to arrive packed with wampum belts, beaded rifle-scabbards, leggings, scalp shirts, buffalo-bull-hide shields. Delivery is not to the studio wardrobe department but directly to Chance's house, where I crowbar off the lids and he fingers the booty, nods bemused, then leaves the room, never to give them another glance.

Has Fitz heard from Washington about getting Indians from the Bureau? Call again and keep calling until there is an answer. The right answer. Any likely candidates to play the girl? Why not? The chief? Why not? As soon as they arrive bring me the drawings from the Smithsonian. I'll choose the ones I want and then you put the order in to wardrobe to run up costumes. Immediately. Even if it means putting production of another picture on hold. I want to see costumes here, in the house, on models, not mannequins. I want to be satisfied as to how they hang, how they move on a body.

It is four weeks before he even raises the obvious question of who will play Shorty McAdoo. Fitz, predictably, lists the names of the most popular cowboy stars.

"No," says Chance, indignantly shaking his head. "To the public Tom Mix will always be Tom Mix and nobody else. Just as Hoot Gibson is Hoot Gibson and William S. Hart, William S. Hart. These gentlemen are personalities, not actors. The personality of a Tom Mix is like a force of nature, it simply is. When the movie-goer looks up at the screen and sees Tom Mix he cannot also believe he is seeing somebody called Shorty McAdoo. An elementary law of physics states that two objects cannot occupy the same space at the same time. This is a psychological truth also."

"You don't want personality," says Fitz, "how about Richard Barthelmess? I didn't recognize him when he played the Chink in *Broken Blossoms*."

"Not right. Dickie is too effeminate."

"Okay, you want to put a big set of balls on McAdoo – Donald Crisp."

"Too old."

"Richard Dix?"

Chance hesitates before making a note. "How many movies has he made?"

"Three, four."

"Perhaps DeMille hasn't done him irreparable damage yet. Cecil has such a pronounced taste for ham. Get Dix in for a test."

"Monte Blue."

"No. He can't act."

"You want acting, what about that guy you went so nuts about when we were in New York, the one in *Hamlet* – John Barrymore. He's a new face. Break him into pictures in a big way. All he's done so far is that *Dr. Jekyll and Mr. Hyde.*"

"You must have lost your mind, Fitz. Apollo in chaps? The famous Barrymore profile against the background of an elegant drawing room may resemble a chiselled cameo, but on film, in a Western, it would caricature the scenery – hoodoos, mesas, chimney rocks. No, not John Barrymore."

"Raoul Walsh then."

"I thought he was directing now."

"For the right kind of money he could learn to be an actor again."

And so the names roll by, Roy D'Arcy, Jack Holt, Bull Montana, Henry B. Walthall, Rockcliffe Fellowes, Neil Hamilton, Arthur Dewey, none of them satisfactory.

Then I say, "Noah Beery." It is the first time I have dared to speak. Both of them look up at me.

"Fuck, he must be forty. I thought McAdoo's supposed to be a kid," says Fitz.

"You're right. Bad idea." I shrug. "But Noah Beery feels right. He reminds me of McAdoo, that's all. A fighting cock."

Chance leans back in his deck chair under the umbrella and sips his tomato juice. "Let me think about it," he says. "After all, art is elastic not rigid. The spirit of Shorty McAdoo is what we must capture. If Harry says Beery, then perhaps Beery it must be." He toasts me with his tomato juice. "Intuition, Harry. I'm inclined to trust it. For the moment," he qualifies.

Chance requests I accompany him to a showing of *The Covered Wagon* at Grauman's Egyptian Theater. It surprises me he hasn't seen the movie yet. Is he afraid it is as good as everybody says it is?

We take a cab, not the Hispano-Suiza. He doesn't want to be recognized. He orders the hack to stop a few blocks from the theatre and we walk the rest of the way. Chance is in disguise, muffled up in a dark overcoat with a flat cap balanced on his head like a stove lid, the spitting image of a hardware-store owner out for an evening of wholesome fun.

Grauman's Egyptian Theater was the precursor of the more famous Grauman's Chinese Theater, where stars have been plunking down their hands in wet cement for the past thirty years. But the Egyptian came first, influenced by the craze for things Egyptian set off by the discovery of King Tut's tomb. Grauman certainly pulled out all stops building a sideshow. Before the entrance there is a spacious forecourt, lined on the right with massive columns supporting a tile roof. The doors to the cinema are modelled on the massive gates of a city of antiquity, flanked by gigantic plinths crowned with the busts of pharaohs. To the left of the entrance an impressive stairway rises to the roof where potted palms stand in relief against the evening sky. The front of the building is covered with green, red, blue, rust, and purple hieroglyphics, golden scarabs, paintings of hawk- and jackal-headed Egyptian divinities. Over the entrance, stylized wings of green and red and blue bear a yellow-horned scarlet moon with vipers curled like apostrophes on either side of it. The lobby of the theatre is more of the same, more painted pillars, more hieroglyphics, more Isis, Osiris, Anubis, and Ra, more decorative hyperbole.

The program is well advanced when our usher directs us to our seats. The twenty-piece orchestra has played the overture, selections from *Faust*; "News of the Week" and a short Chaplin comedy have been shown; Colonel Tim McCoy has put his live Arapahos through a war dance on stage as a warm-up to the main event. Now the feature presentation is ready to begin and twenty-five hundred men, women, and children sit, a respectfully quiet congregation.

Thirty years later it is difficult to remember how pictures used to speak to us then, in a more primitive, uncomplicated language of image and music. But I recall the opening of *The Covered Wagon* like it was yesterday, the close-up shot of a young boy picking the strings of a banjo, and from the orchestra pit the ghostly twang of that simple instrument, sounding lonely and tentative in the vastness of the auditorium, sounding as it might have in the emptiness of the echoing wilderness. Then, on the boy's face, a shot of sheet music is slowly superimposed and, as the notes and words to "Oh, Susannah" become clear, on cue the whole orchestra springs into action, twenty instruments like a burst of hope in the heart, and beneath the surge of music an insect hum is heard, the audience murmuring the familiar song. Next, a shot of Lois Wilson framed by the canopy of a wagon, a portrait of American womanhood, sweet, chaste, shyly smiling to you and you alone as "Oh, Susannah!" dies to a faint whisper, a sad, tender signature tune for the girl lovely under the arch of canvas.

The Covered Wagon has something. Hundreds of prairie schooners creeping across a limitless expanse of earth under an infinite sky make the gigantism of Grauman's theatre seem shabby and hollow. The scenery has a reality, a conviction, that Ra and the pharaohs – long-dead god and long-dead men – can't compete with. It's true J. Warren Kerrigan with make-up crinkled in his crows'-feet and his face as white as a geisha girl's is every bit as dead as a California Tutankhamen, but the leathery faces of the extras aren't; men and women like them are living in plain wooden bungalows all over L.A., you see them every day of your life. More important, you can believe they *did* ford the River Platte, *did* lay the bullwhip to the oxen, *did* tramp mile after mile in billowing clouds of dust. The honesty of certain faces, the honesty of the land itself.

Every once in a while I cast Damon Ira Chance a surreptitious glance. Throughout the picture he sits absolutely still, flat cap laid primly on the coat folded over his knees. He sits that way through the buffalo hunt, the Indian attack, the settlers falling to their knees in the snows of Oregon to give thanks, never moving a muscle until the last frames of the picture when he rises and taps me imperiously on the arm, a sign to follow him out.

Here and there, under streetlamps, young men with brilliantined hair are smoking and eyeing girls who strut by holding themselves sexlessly erect like models on a runway, only to collapse sexily against one another, whispering and giggling, once they have steamed by these islands of maleness and light.

Chance walks quickly, face set. Whoever he meets on the sidewalk, man or woman, has to step aside or risk collision. He simply doesn't see them. Every few steps he takes, a hand flies up to his spectacles like a gadget on an assembly line, and jams them into his face, hard. With my bad leg, it is an effort to keep up. We go along like this for five or six blocks when he stops suddenly, grasps my shoulder, drags me closer. "Facts are of the utmost importance, Harry. If I can convince the audience the details are impeccably correct, who will dispute the interpretation? The truth of small things leads to confidence in the truth of large things. That is indisputable." He looks at me anxiously, chewing his bottom lip. "'The blood of America is the blood of pioneers – the blood of lion-hearted men and women who carved a splendid civilization out of an uncharted wilderness,'" he intones contemptuously. "Recognize it? It's one of the titles from the picture we just saw. As soon as people start piously throwing around the word *civilization*, you can be sure they're whistling in the dark. Civilization has always drawn enemies like rotten meat draws flies. I hate the word."

Two girls are walking toward us, flapper dresses moving provocatively in the dusk like Victorian shifts glimpsed by gaslight. They lean together, deep in private conversation, and when they go by, one of them laughs, a low bubbling laugh like the cooing of a pigeon.

Chance follows them with his eyes, his hand tightens on my shoulder. He leans into me as the girls lean into one another. "They were laughing at me," he says, "because of how I am dressed. Details again, Harry. Details are how most people read the world, the simple letters of their idiotic alphabet. They spell crude and literal meanings such as 'clothes make the man.' Most people don't have what you and I do, Harry."

"What's that?"

"The gift to see beyond a flat cap, or beyond small facts."

I can see how tired he is, his face looks jaundiced in the lamplight. He presses his shoulder to the lamppost and lifts his face to the light. It looks exhausted, drained. I follow his staring eyes to a delirium of moths whirling thickly around the electric light. Like the details chasing around in his head.

"Start work on the scenario, Harry," he says.

23

Grace finally persuaded an old woman, Granny Laverdure, to cook them their Sunday dinner. She led them off to her son-in-law's cabin, one of the most substantial in the Métis settlement. The logs were peeled and soundly chinked with clay, the walls standing twelve timbers high and set with three small windows of scraped fawn skin which shed a soft, tawny light into the quarters. Most impressive was a waterproof roof, canvas stretched over poles and topped with squares of sod.

"Snug as a bug in a rug," Grace pronounced when he dipped his gangly frame through the low doorway.

The Englishman's boy had to give the breeds their due. The cabin was stout as his own Pap's. Except the breeds had a cast-iron stove where he and his kin had done their cooking and roasting in a fireplace chimbley. The breeds ate at a table, on benches, too; no Indian squat when they took meat. The floor was packed dirt swept with a spruce bough, you could smell spruce in the air and see the scrape-marks of the branch left in the dirt.

Along the walls more benches served as beds, piled high with Hudson's Bay blankets, buffalo robes, grizzly skins; two youngsters sat on one of these, cheeks bulging as they chewed with frantic intensity.

Close to the iron stove, a few shelves holding flour, tea, a little dried fruit, roots, and meat were pegged into the wall. In a corner where a bitch lamp burned there was even a picture; he could see it from where he sat. One of them Cat-licker Jesus pictures. Him prying his chest open and showing his heart on fire.

He and Ed made easy at the table drinking boiled tea, black as coffee, while Granny clattered at the stove. A little twig of a girl of two, with gold rings in her ears, Rose Marie, stood clinging to the table leg, watching Grace wide-eyed. Every time he winked at her, she hugged the table leg all the harder.

"Those six bottles'll be gone in an hour," said Grace. "I spent a winter with those lads and experience has taught me liquor doesn't lighten their dispositions. Put a pint of liquor in any one of them and they're apt to turn quarrelsome. They'll be fighting each other before the day goes out – or anybody else who's handy. I'd just as soon not be handy. No, we're better off where we are, drinking strong tea out of harm's way."

The Englishman's boy couldn't take his eyes off the two kids on the bench, jaws working like steam locomotives.

"Goddamn, Eagle," he said, "what them boys over there chewing? They're making my head hurt watching them."

"Over there," said Grace, squinting across the room, "is the ammunition manufactory. You know that lead foil the tea packets come wrapped in? They chew it to make bullets for their Northwest guns. A Métis kid'll spit round shot for a five-eighths-inch bore like it came from a bullet mould."

The smell of elk steaks frying and bannock baking put a glow of contentment and goodwill on the Eagle. He stretched his legs out comfortably under the table. "I tell you, son, once I lay hands on my share of that wolfing money I'm heading for the Red River country. This Whoop-Up country's too wild for me. A betwixt-and-betweener prefers things by halves. Half-wild country. Half-wild women. I reckon those Red River women fit the bill. Half-French, half-Cree. Half-housebroke and half-wild, half-pagan and half-Catholic. I like a roof over me and a good bed under me, but on the other hand I'd sooner shoot my meat than raise it. I like to turn footloose in the summer when the sun shines and nest in a cabin in the winter when the wind blows cold and the snow flies. And those gals are handsome women, some light-skinned as any white women, and a few even have curl to their hair, or blue to the eye. I believe they'd suit me just fine."

The food was ready. The boys hopped down off the bunk and put their feet under the table. Granny said grace and everybody but the Eagle and the Englishman's boy crossed themselves, even the baby. They all set to with a will and an appetite, piling their tin plates with elk steaks and a stew of buffalo and wild parsnip. Everybody had a side bowl of boiled and sweetened saskatoons for bannock dipping and as much scalding-hot tea as they could drink.

In a bit, the Eagle had coaxed the little girl up on his lap and was spooning food into her from his plate. Soon she was clambering all over him like a squirrel, patting the bandanna on his head with her chubby hands.

"*Aimez-vous*, the pirate? *Aimez-vous*, the pirate?" he squawked at her. When she tried to speak French to him, he made a droll, rubbery face and said, "No *comprenez-vous*." Every time he reiterated this, she laughed louder and harder than the last time.

It wasn't long until he had a game of "creep mousie" going with the child, cautiously stealing his fingers up her arms, breathing, "Creep mousie, creep mousie, creep mousie," into her ear, and then with a sudden cry of "Right in there!" burying a finger in her armpit, tickling her until she squealed loud enough to raise the roof.

Then, suddenly, he stopped the game dead, finger poised. An apparition darkened the doorway. The Englishman's boy made an involuntary movement to the pistol at his side, but the Eagle caught his hand. "No," he said, pulling the child protectively to his chest.

The figure in the doorway was sniffing the air, swaying, grunting to himself softly. He shambled a few steps into the cabin and halted.

The Englishman's boy had never dreamed himself such a bogey man as this. The bogey man had shaved the top of his head bald and rolled the hair on his temples into balls so they resembled bear ears. His face was painted blood-red and down each cheek the paint had been scratched away to the skin, leaving claw-marks. The eyes and mouth were circled in black and a bear-claw necklace swung from his neck. His skin shirt was daubed thickly with ochre and hung in bedraggled yellow shreds; long cuts slashed the front, and holes were punched the length of the sleeves.

Now his face was lifted to the ceiling and he was casting back and forth with his nose, the way the bear does when it rises on its hind legs to take the wind for danger. He lowered his head and shuffled toward them, grunting.

"He got a knife in his hand," warned the Englishman's boy. The knife was broad-bladed, double-edged, and fixed into the jawbone of a bear.

Grace signalled him by dropping his eyes to something beneath the table. The Englishman's boy caught his meaning. Grace's pistol hung between his knees.

The bear stalked around the old woman's chair. His nightmare face descended to the part in her grey hair, snuffled the hollow of her wrinkled neck. She sat like a stone. He stalked over to the boys, scented each of them in turn, panted *huh, huh, huh.*

When he swung clumsily towards the Englishman's boy, the boy said loudly, "You ain't sniffing me, you bastard."

The bear stood swaying, then jerked and rolled his shoulders so the distinctive hump of the grizzly rose up menacingly on his back under the torn shirt. The Englishman's boy did his best to stare him off like a dog, but these weren't the eyes of a dog. They were the black fierce lights of the bear the Indians called the real-bear, the grizzly, beside which all other bears were nothing. This was the bear that broke the body of the hunter in the bushes, killed the women and children when he found them stealing in his berry patch; this was the bear who crushed your bones as easily as he did the bones of a salmon, who tore your guts with his claws. This was the bear with the great hunger, the bear who, in his rage, could eat the world, all its fruits, all its fish, all its flesh.

And he was in the room with them.

"Yes, you will," said Grace quietly. "You will let him sniff you."

The bear came forward, the vermilion on his face shining with grease, the charcoal eyes and mouth shafts leading into some terrible inner darkness, a darkness out of which he groaned hollowly, out of which he laboured to walk on his hind legs, like a man.

Then he was in the Englishman's boy's face, inches from it. The boy could smell meat on the panting breath, smell the bear grease twisted up in the balls of hair on either side of his head – smell something else, musky, slightly skunky, which snagged in his throat, coating it with old, rancid fat. The bear peered into his face, nose to nose. Sniffed him.

Death was smelling him to see if he was ripe; Death was looking him in the eyes to see how they would answer. When the grizzly caught you, you best play possum.

Don't you try to eat me, old bear. I ain't big, but I'm more'n you can swallow. I might stick in your throat and choke you. I might slide down your gullet like a straight razor, slice you stem to stern.

The bear was leaving him, swinging his head toward Grace. The two black eyes bored across the table to where the child clutched Grace's shirt pocket, mouth hanging open with terror. The Englishman's boy thought he could see a little picture of Grace holding that babe tight sitting in each eye of the bear. Slowly, the bear wrinkled his lips and bared his teeth. Slowly, he backed across the room to the door, his moccasins whispering in the dirt as he smiled his yellow, carnivorous grin for Grace and only Grace. Then he was gone.

The Englishman's boy glanced at the Eagle. He was staring at the yawning door, clasping the child even closer.

"Eagle."

Grace didn't answer.

"Eagle."

He turned to the boy, kissed the child on the head, set her on the floor between his feet.

"What the hell was that, Eagle?"

Grace stood up. "Assiniboine Bear Cult man. One of the chosen few the bear visits in a dream to pass bear medicine to."

"So what the hell was he doing here?"

Grace was watching the door, as if he expected the bear to shuffle back in any minute. "I don't know. But it can't be good. A bear man always means bad luck. They never prosper. Their wives die and their children go hungry. The spirit of the bear brings trouble and death. They have a reputation as touchy killers like the grizzly. Maybe these people know what it means, but I don't." The family sat solemn as owls, watching Grace as he spoke. He put money beside his plate, more money than he should have. "I've got a bad feeling. I think we better get on back to the post and warn the boys. Maybe it's nothing but it stinks like something." He turned to the old woman. "We're obliged for the hospitality. I'm obliged to have sat in a house on a Sunday. When we're gone, bar the door."

Leaving wasn't so easy though; when she realized he intended to go, Rose Marie wrapped herself around his leg and hung on with all her might. The Eagle pried her off, screaming, and passed her to her granny.

Stepping out the door the Eagle drew his pistol and signed for the Englishman's boy to do the same. The door closed behind them and they heard the bar fall with a solid chunk behind them. It was hot and still. The sun glared on the surrounding cabins. There was no smoke rising from the chimneys. A great silence reigned. Grace cocked his head, listening. Nothing but insects playing jew's-harps in the grass. Even the dogs were mute. Not a soul moved outside the cabins. He could feel eyes pressed to the chinks between the logs, watching him.

He narrowed his eyes against the painful light, attentively swept the field from right to left. It was empty. No sign of the Bear Cult man. He had disappeared, maybe into the willows down by the creek. Maybe across the creek and up the bench rising to the north of Moses Solomon's fort. He prayed God he wasn't lying up there with a gun, sighting them now.

"Let's move," he said.

He broke into a trot and the Englishman's boy fell in beside him. The gophers squeaked and dove for their holes at their approach. The Englishman's boy didn't know why they were running, but suddenly, like Farmer Hank, he had no intention of being left behind. The taut look on the Eagle's face persuaded him that if the Eagle said move, they'd better move.

The Eagle had bottom, he never let up until they reached Fort Farwell. The Métis were gone. Across the creek the Indian camp might have been a painting, except that now and then a dog or horse moved, spoiling the picture and the conceit. The only living thing outside the walls of the fort was Scotty hunched on a wooden bucket; Scotty smiling to himself, scribbling like mad with a stub of pencil in a cracked-spine journal.

"Where's Hardwick?" Grace asked him.

Scotty didn't look up.

Grace took him by the shoulder and shook him. "Goddamn it, where's Hardwick?"

Scotty stared up with a dazed, angelic smile. He shaded his eyes with a hand. "Why, in Hades," he said sweetly, then returned to writing.

The Englishman's boy tapped Grace on the shoulder. A rider was coming toward the post at a gallop. George Hammond in a lather of high excitement. "That thieving red son of a bitch stole my horse again!" he shouted. "Same son of a bitch I paid a bottle of whisky yesterday! Same horse! I'm riding over yonder to get him back!" He pointed wildly to the Assiniboine camp as his horse champed and spun. "I regret to say there ain't no men at Moses Solomon's post with the guts to support me, but I heard tell there's a fellow here by the name of Tom Hardwick who has a reputation for being a man! I rode over to see if he's as big as his brag! I rode over to see if he'll back a fellow recovering his rightful property! I rode over to see –"

"Goddamn right he will," said Hardwick, stepping through the gate of the stockade. "Goddamn right he will." He walked toward the mounted man with his arm outstretched. "And here's his hand on it."

24

Chance set an absolute deadline for delivery of a first draft of the photoplay. I've been working day and night for two weeks, surviving on sandwiches, coffee, cigarettes, and nerves. Fifteen years ago a scenario was a bare-bones sketch, often written in a day, a crutch which director and actors used as a guide to improvise a picture. Photoplays have become more detailed, but they're still expected to be quickly written, rough-hewn scenes, a blueprint for a shoot. Maybe I've got too close to the material. It's tough to convey the feeling of McAdoo's story without dialogue, because I keep hearing his voice, the way he *told* it. I'm fighting to capture his emotions in images which will foreshadow the last scene, the awful conclusion to the picture. And while I'm doing this I have to keep in mind Will Hays, remember that what happens to the girl can't actually be shown, has to be suggested in some way which won't offend the proprieties of the censors but conveys to the audience the stark horror of her fate. Some scenes I've rewritten five or six times, trying to get a slow build to the fire, a suggestion of stealthily crackling flames which finally burst up in a raging conflagration. But instead, the writing feels like a forced march through a bog, every step forward sinking me deeper in a mire of confusion and uncertainty. Maybe Rachel is right. Maybe I am nothing but a blank-filler, a title-writer. After fourteen days of floundering I need help so badly I call her at home.

"Rachel?"

"My Little Truth Seeker! To what do I owe the honour of this call?"

Her pronunciation is a little eroded around the edges, liquor having rubbed away enough clarity for me to know she's been hitting the bottle heavily. And it's only seven o'clock.

"I need help."

"What kind of help?"

"Help with a script."

"You need help? I'm the one who needs help with a script. Bloody Gibson. You know what he's got me working on now? Do you?"

"No."

"Another Identical-Twins-Separated-at-Birth Saga. A real doozy," she proclaims. I can hear the sound of a glass clinking faintly against the telephone receiver as she pauses to take a drink. "It's based on a novel written by the spinster daughter of an English vicar. What else is new?" She takes a deep breath as preface. "Anyway, diabolical aristocratic parents give birth to identical twins. So as not to complicate inheritance and title, noble parents decide one is a keeper and the reject is set out in swaddling clothes to perish in the forest. Sherwood presumably. Disposable son is found by cretinous peasants who rear Boy Scout in uniform of swineherd – deeply attached to simple life, his hogs, and the Village Virgin whom he hopes some day to deflower within the bounds of holy matrimony. Then, one day, pig boy stumbles upon noble brother slaying deer in the forest. 'What is this I see, as in a glass darkly?' exclaims the Dispossessed One, smeared in pig shit presumably, but nonetheless smelling sweet as any rose. You know the rest. Evil brother plots swineherd's murder. Caretaker of pigs overcomes all odds, gains title. Huge wedding in white in castle."

"Who are they thinking of for the swineherd?"

"Fairbanks."

"Village Virgin?"

"Pickford."

"Sounds like a piece of cake."

"Yes and no. After writing a hundred of these, mounting self-revulsion can cramp your style. Besides, our glorious story editor has decreed one fundamental change in this anodyne numskullery. He's ordered me to make Douglas Fairbanks a shepherd rather than a swineherd. According to Jack, sheep are more sympathetic than pigs. It's a well-known fact. Especially lambs. Everybody loves lambs. He feels the English spinster's dark vision of life needs tempering with plenty of shots of gambolling, fleecy lambs. I told him, 'No fucking chance, Jack. It's got to be hogs or nothing. My artistic integrity is hanging in the balance.'"

"What did Jack say?"

"He said he'd put somebody else on the project. I said you were the only person innocent and naive enough to write this picture with all the mindless conviction it deserves. Harry Vincent, Little Truth Seeker. But, unfortunately, you aren't available. You have a higher purpose. Since it falls on my shoulders, drastic action may be called for."

"Such as?"

"There's a new operation for scenarists. They suck out half your brains and then you can write again."

"Surgery's a serious business. Don't make a decision under the influence of alcohol."

"Is that a criticism or a witticism, Harry?"

"Just a warning."

"Oh, fuck warnings."

"Maybe I better let you get back to what you were doing."

"Harry," she says, "please come back to work. I miss how your freshly scrubbed and shining brow furrows with serious purpose and concentration each and every time you read another English spinster's novel for Rachel."

"Really? I thought you had Mr. DeShane to provide amusement."

There's a pause on the line which alerts me I've made a mistake. "Fuck you, too, Harry," she says, a slight catch in her voice.

"What's up?"

"I'm not seeing him any more. Not since the accident." She's trying hard to recover her sprightly air.

"What accident?"

"We had a car crash."

"God, Rachel, you're not hurt, are you?"

"No. Not a scratch."

"And DeShane?"

"Mr. DeShane hit the windshield. His nose got broken. He didn't take it well. He thinks it was his best feature. He blames me because I was driving. Somebody had to. We were both drunk and I won the toss."

"Oh, Jesus."

"That's the trouble with pretty men. They put too much store in their looks."

"I'm sorry."

"Well, I should know better, shouldn't I? So much for a thing of beauty is a joy forever. Joy with DeShane only lasted weeks."

"Is that the reason for your condition?"

She avoids answering the question. "You really ought to come back to the office, Harry. You cheer me up. We're the only ones who prefer Thomas Hardy to Scott Fitzgerald. When you're living the jazz age why would you want to read about it, too? But nobody else gets my point."

"You better get some sleep, Rachel."

"Maybe. But you had a reason for calling. Something about help?"

Now is not the time. "It can wait."

"Come on, Harry. Shyness is one of your endearing traits but you can overplay it."

Then I recall the book Chance gave me. He even marked passages with a red pen. Georges Sorel's *Réflexions sur la violence*. The only problem is I can't read French.

"Look," I say, "Chance gave me a book to read while I work on the script. But my menu French isn't up to deciphering it. From the number of times the words *prolétariat* and *socialisme* crop up in it, I thought it might be up your alley. If I sent it over, do you think you could give me a précis?"

"I could give it a whirl."

"All right, then. Thanks."

"Come back to the office, Harry."

"Soon," I tell her.

〜

I am not entirely satisfied with my photoplay, but I've got close, and the deadline for the script is tonight, nine o'clock. Rather dramatic in its precision, but that's Chance. However, I fear some mistake has been made. The driveway is filled with vehicles parked bumper to bumper and the house is lit up like I've never seen it before, brash yellow light streaming from every window on every floor, and the tinny, nasal sound of gramophone jazz trumpeting inside. Lately, Chance's nerves have been badly frayed. A mix-up over still photographs of prospective shooting locations earned Fitz the dressing-down of his life. I can still see the big Irish moron standing on the carpet, head hanging down like an illustration from a Sunday-school paper – the boy caught pinching nickels from Mother's handbag. Maybe in the midst of all the planning for the picture, the deadline has slipped Chance's mind.

Nothing slips Chance's mind.

Feeling uneasy, I decide to ring the bell, hand the envelope to Yukio, and get the hell out of here. However, in a brightly lit window I see three women with cocktail glasses in their hands – Mary Pickford, Gloria Swanson, Pola Negri. Change of plan, I'll go around to the back. To dance attendance upon such a big party of celebrities, he'll have hired caterers. I'll give the envelope to the kitchen staff and avoid encountering any of his classy guests.

I begin to fumble my way to the rear, brushing past rosebushes emitting a thick, heady fragrance, hugging the darkness like a housebreaker, dodging the splashes of light on lawn and shrubbery where the shadows of Chance's guests dart, fishes in a pond. From the house, laughter spills, mingled with mirthless shrieks. Blindly feeling my way among the flower-beds I sneak glances at the lighted windows, catch glimpses of revellers inside. Clara Bow, Colleen Moore, Barbara La Marr.

Turning the corner of the house, a constellation of Japanese paper lanterns blazing against the night sky surprises me. Yukio teeters on a stepladder while Chance stands on the lawn directing the positioning of lanterns on a cord strung between two palms. An intruder, I instinctively freeze to the spot.

"Now the red one," says Chance, "next to the green."

In the warm glow of the lanterns, Yukio's face shines like rubbed brass. Beyond the two men, the swimming pool gleams intensely green in a blanket of soft light, liquid jade. A woman is swimming in the pool, sinuous water rolling smoothly over her shoulders, the surface of the pool undulating faintly behind her as she plies the breaststroke. Completing a length, she turns without a splash, glides back. Chance pays her absolutely no attention; face raised and forehead lined with attention, he studies the lanterns dangling like coloured concertinas drying on a clothesline.

I clear my throat and he wheels around, peers hard to where I stand one foot in the shadows, one in the light.

"Harry!" he exclaims. He comes forward eagerly, pointing to the manila envelope tucked under my arm. "That's it?"

"That's it."

He checks his watch. "Punctual to a fault," he says, taking the envelope. The girl in the pool begins another lap. The water flows around her thickly like heavy green syrup. A burst of laughter rings out from the house, followed by the sound of breaking glass. Chance ignores it, or doesn't hear.

"Let's go in," he says.

"No, really, I don't want to crash your party."

Chance puts a hand on my shoulder. "But the party is for you, too. A little treat for working so hard."

"I'd feel out of place among such a distinguished crowd."

Chance throws back his head and laughs. "That's right. Don't spoil it. I get your meaning." He steers me to the rear entrance. Over my shoulder I peek at the woman in the water. It is as I thought; she's stark naked.

He leads me through the kitchen, past a number of rented waiters in dinner jackets toiling over trays of canapés, and down a passageway which delivers us into one of Chance's empty, blank rooms. A very odd setting for a party, just a few ladder-backed chairs marooned on a parquet floor. A waiter is serving drinks to two women; a man's muffled shouting can be heard further back in the house. The two women are Gloria Swanson and Clara Bow.

"It's a very small affair," explains Chance, completely ignoring two of Hollywood's greatest stars. "By coincidence some of Fitz's boon companions from New York are in town and I indulged him by inviting them along. Fitz is like a boy with a new train set; he wants to show it off." He taps the envelope. "I'll take this up to the study and give it a look. It's quieter there. Until I need you, consider yourself to have been given the keys to the city. Miss Lillian Gish is dying to meet you." With that cryptic comment he exits the room. As soon as he leaves, Gloria Swanson and Clara Bow advance on me, heels clicking like castanets on the hardwood. It's now I become aware that Gloria's sequinned dress, skeins of pearls, and beauty mark are right, but her chin isn't. It's pronounced, but not pronounced enough. Seen up close, Clara Bow, the "It" girl, isn't It either. The eyes are set too close together and the eyelids don't droop the way the Jazz Baby's do in the pictures.

I laugh with pure relief.

"Is it a man, or a hyena," snarls Gloria.

"Be nice," cautions Clara.

"The rest are hyenas, why'd he be any different." Gloria tips her glass and drains it.

"So what is this? You girls doubles? Stand-ins?"

"That's rich – stand-ins. We don't do much standing." Gloria consults her companion. "More like lay-downs, wouldn't you say?"

"Lay-downs," giggles Clara and then covers her mouth coyly with her hand. Some of her teeth are rotten.

"What is it with this Chance?" asks Gloria, gloomily surveying the barren room. "He run out of money before he got the decorators in?"

"You're a card, honey," says Clara. "A regular card." She appeals to me. "Isn't she a card?"

"How come nobody's interested in La Swanson?" demands Gloria, sullenly angry. "My stock falling with the movie-going public?" She turns on me. "What about you, sport? You interested in a little movie magic?"

"Just have another drinkie and relax," Clara advises.

Gloria wants nothing to do with relaxation; she's obviously spoiling for a fight. "Come on, big spender," she says. "Don't just stand there. Show us a parlour trick."

"What kind of parlour trick?" I ask pleasantly, a feeble ploy to smooth her ruffled feathers.

"Parlour trick. Parlour trick," she rasps. "The big palooka in the other room showed us how he could balance three silver dollars on his cock. Be a sport. Go for four."

Just then Fitz crashes into the room, dragging a cringing Lillian Gish by the wrist.

"Speak of the devil!" shouts Gloria. "Here's Mr. Show-off now!"

"Shut the fuck up," says Fitz, "or I'll fucking shut you up."

Gloria looks like she is going to answer him, then thinks better of it. Fitz is sweating, his face puce. "Harry Vincent, guest of honour," he says introducing me to Lillian Gish. "Treat him right, he earned it, Mr. Chance says." He shoves the girl at me. "Here's your fucking treat, Vincent. Suck on this little candy cane, you're so special."

"Hey," says Gloria, "we seen him first."

"I told you to close your cake-hole. Miss Gish is compliments of Mr. Chance. Keep your nose out of it." The girl is rubbing her wrist. "Miss Gish is Harry's favourite actress. Mr. Chance remembers stuff like that. Don't he, Harry?"

"Apparently."

Fitz prods the girl forward with his thumb. "Take the golden boy Vincent upstairs."

"Maybe I don't want to go upstairs," I say.

"I wouldn't look a gift horse in the mouth if I was you," says Fitz.

The girl snatches at my arm like it's a life raft and she is drowning; she's hardly bigger than a child. "Please," she whispers, "do like he says." Her plea unmasks a terror so naked, so compelling, it would be cruelty to refuse. She pulls me from the room, fingers biting my forearm; my last glimpse of Fitz he's clumsily fingering Gloria's pearls with one hand, a breast with the other.

Upstairs, the girl drags me into a bedroom and locks the door. Something tells me it is Fitz's. There's an unmade bed, a dresser with a bottle of bay rum on top of it, pictures of Gentleman Jim Corbett and Kentucky Derby winner Man o' War on the wall.

The girl offers a smile meant to be provocative but isn't. It's a grimace – whistling in the dark. "My name is Miss Lillian Gish. How do you do?"

In some respects it is true. She succeeds as Miss Lillian Gish in a way that the tawdry Gloria Swanson and Clara Bow fall short of their models. The resemblance is astonishing. She has the wrought fragility of the original, the delicate bird-like bones, the cupid mouth, the large eyes, the fine tousled hair which now, with the light of a lamp behind her, blazes like a heaven-sent aura. Unlike the others she isn't dressed in glamorous party clothes – just the opposite – she's wearing a paisley shawl and a long dress with a conspicuous patch on the skirt.

"You girls – just who are you?"

She smiles shyly, a real Lillian Gish smile this time, and makes a stab at resuming her performance, "My name is Miss Lillian –"

I interrupt. "What the hell's going on here?"

She says, "The greatest gift it is in an innocent, pure girl's power to give is yours for the asking." It sounds like a recitation at the Christmas concert.

I drop down in a chair; she remains standing uncertainly in the middle of the floor. After a moment's hesitation, she begins to unbutton her dress.

"Stop," I say.

Her hands slowly open the dress front, cup her breasts and hold them on timid display. They are exquisite.

247

"Why are you doing this?"

Consternation and confusion struggle in her face. "I'm supposed to do this," she complains.

She begins to toy with her nipples; voyeuristically I watch them stiffen. An uneasy, violent lust ripples in me.

"Don't do that."

"You don't like that? What would you like me to do?"

"I want you to answer my questions. *Who* said you were supposed to do this?"

She bites her lip, throws a nervous glance to the locked door. "Him."

"Fitz? The man who dragged you into the room downstairs?"

"He came to Mrs. Kirkland's and hired us all. For the night."

"Mrs. Kirkland's?"

"You haven't heard of Mrs. Kirkland's?" She can scarcely believe my ignorance. "It's the deluxest establishment in the city. Mrs. Kirkland says everybody dreams of making love to a movie star. I thought everybody had heard of Mrs. Kirkland's."

"Sit down."

"Very deluxe," she repeats, still standing. "We have a splendid piano player, you should come just to hear him. He plays all the latest tunes. Daddy would die if he knew – the piano player's a Negro."

"How the hell old are you?"

My question pleases her. "How old do you think I am?"

"You look fifteen."

"Just like Miss Gish," she says proudly. "She played a fifteen-year-old girl in *Broken Blossoms*. That's where I got the idea for my costume, from *Broken Blossoms*." She touches her skirt. "Do you like it?"

I say nothing. She falls back on the bed in an artless, maladroit pose of abandon. "Are you ready?"

"No."

She sits up, a picture of concern. "Why? Because of your leg? I saw you limping. Does your leg hurt?"

"Not because of my leg. That was hurt a long time ago."

248

"Poor baby, how did you hurt it?"

I don't explain.

"It wouldn't hurt if I sat on your knee, would it? Let me sit on your knee."

"Please don't."

She is standing over me. With one deft movement she hikes her skirts, straddles one of my thighs. There is nothing to her, it is as if a cat bounded up and settled down on my leg. She throws her arms around my neck. I try to pry her off but her arms tighten, she lowers her face to mine, the tiny lips part slightly. With solemn fervour, she says, "Miss Lillian isn't wearing underpants tonight." She slides back and forth against my leg, rubbing like a cat. "That feels nice. Ever so nice." Large eyes dizzy me. She lifts her hips, takes my hand and slips it between her legs. "When you're fifteen you'd like somebody to touch it – but that's wicked. You'd like to show it to somebody – but that's even wickeder. Shall I show it to you?" she whispers, breath warm on my throat.

"No," I say, choking on the lie.

She nestles her head into the hollow of my neck and shoulder. "Let me take you out," she says. "Please. I feel so wicked."

When her hand fumbles at my fly I catch her wrist and twist it away. Her face writhes. "You're hurting me," she says.

"This is over. Get off me. Now."

"Please," she says, "you have to let me do it. He paid."

"I buy my own whores."

She shudders, the porcelain face cracks, I feel the doll's body go limp. "Why do you want to get me in trouble? Can't you be nice? He warned me. He said if I didn't, too bad for me. I know he means it. Look what he did already." She holds up her arm. There are bruises left by Fitz's fingers. "I had to let him take a pair of nail scissors and trim me. So I'd look fifteen, he said. He laughed, the son of a bitch. Couldn't you feel how he trimmed me?" She clutches at me desperately, begins to squirm in a mechanically provocative way. It feels like despair.

I shake her. "Stop it!"

She freezes, fine hair fallen loose about her shoulders.

There's a sharp rap at the door. "Harry! Harry!" It's Chance. I shove Miss Gish off my lap. She staggers backward, eyes running wildly round the room, rabbit seeking a bolt-hole. "Get on the bed," I hiss. "On the bed. Throw up your skirts." She clambers up on the bed and does as she is told. I get a glimpse of Fitz's handiwork before facing the door and calling out, "Just a minute, Mr. Chance." I unbuckle my belt and then unlock the door. Chance peers impassively over my shoulder into the room as I ostentatiously do myself up.

"Satisfactory?"

"Yes," I say, stepping into the hallway and pulling the door closed on Miss Gish.

"I wish I could say the same of this. I went directly to the ending and skimmed it – it's an abomination. Dreadful." His tone is aggrieved, hurt.

"Well," I say, taken aback, stumbling, "it's only a first draft, Mr. Chance. A rough approximation –"

He cuts my explanation short. "I thought you were a man worthy of opening my mind to, a man with the intelligence to understand what is at stake in this enterprise. And then you give me this –" He breaks off. "The girl," he says sharply, "the business with the girl just won't do. It misses the point completely."

What is the point? "But I wrote it exactly as McAdoo described it – at least as much of it as the audience could stomach and we could get past Hays's people. I assumed it wasn't possible to go any further."

"Yes, you wrote it *exactly* as McAdoo described it. But where is the artistic intuition? You've assembled the facts like a stock boy stacking cans on a shelf. You must reach beyond that. The last scene, the most important scene in the picture, is all wrong. Disastrously wrong," he pronounces contemptuously.

I scramble to apologize. "I realize it isn't as good as it should be. I want to make it better. Please, just tell me what's wrong and I'll do my best, make every effort to fix it."

"Wrong?" His eyebrows lift. "The psychology is all wrong. Absolutely wrong."

This only confuses me more. "Psychology?"

"I want the girl to start the fire," he states. "Surely you see she must start the fire."

"The girl?" I say, stupidly.

His severity relents a little in the face of my obvious bewilderment. Assuming the manner of a kindly, patient teacher he begins to lead me through the lesson, step by step. "What the picture must convey, Harry, is the psychology of the defeated. And what is this psychology? A diseased resentment," he says implacably. "The sick hate the healthy. The defeated hate the victor. The inferior *always* resent the superior. They sicken with resentment, they brood, fantasize revenge, plot. They attempt to turn everything on its head; try to impose feelings of guilt on the healthy and the strong. But our film will not fall into that trap. Our film will be a celebration of spiritual and physical strength."

My mind, confused, clumsy, doesn't really believe it can be following what he means to say.

Chance smiles persuasively. "The resentment of the weak is a terrible thing, Harry. The inferior always refuse the judgements of nature and history. They are a danger to the strong and to themselves. Resentment blinds them to reality, blinds them even to their own self-interest."

"Self-interest? I don't know what you mean."

"The judgements of nature and history are impersonal," Chance says calmly. "But the weak refuse to accept them. Think of all those quixotic lost causes of history. The Jews furnish a perfect example. All those futile, petulant rebellions against the Romans. A sick resentment drove them to become the authors of their own destruction."

I stare at him dumfounded. Suddenly my face is hot, my belly cold.

"That is how we must present the girl," he says. "I envision her as a sort of Indian Samson. To destroy his captors he pulled down the temple on his own head. If she were to set fire to the building, that would be entirely in keeping – psychologically speaking – with the point we must make."

"Which is?" I can hear an undercurrent of challenge in my voice. The private falling back on what the army calls dumb insolence.

Chance doesn't notice. He's too absorbed in his lesson. "That the Indian tribes, like the Jewish tribes, would not face facts. Think of the Sioux uprising at Wounded Knee. No different than the suicidal Jews at Masada. But let us not be sentimental about what they brought down upon themselves. The weak wish the strong to be sentimental because they know it undermines their strength. But in the world we face at this moment, we must keep strong. Only the strong will survive."

"But the girl didn't set fire to the post," I say stubbornly, clinging to the irrefutability of fact.

Chance's mouth twists with impatience. "Don't be wilfully obtuse," he says angrily. "I have explained to you. This picture is about psychological truth, poetic truth. Poetic truth is not journalism."

"But it's not a lie either. It can't be a –"

He cuts me off brutally. "This discussion is at an end." And he walks away from me. Doesn't let me finish. I start after him, determined to have my say. Down the hallway he strides, fists clenching and unclenching at his sides.

"Mr. Chance!" I shout.

Down the staircase he goes, feet quick on the steps, nimble despite his stoutness, fleeing me as I clump awkwardly in pursuit. He rushes past the costumed girls and Fitz's friends in garish suits who greet him with drunken familiarity. One room and another room and suddenly there is nowhere further for him to fly, we've washed up in the chamber with the French doors overlooking the garden, the room with the single hardback chair placed like an altar under a cut-glass electric chandelier. Chance halts under this fixture, stands bathed in harsh, stunning light which fractures his shadow into a spiky asterisk on the marble floor.

Now I have him cornered, everything I meant to say suddenly evaporates. The best I can manage is, "Mr. Chance, I did as you told me. I wrote the facts."

This claim only agitates him. He begins to pace the marble floor, flexing and unflexing his fingers like an arthritic. "I spoke of the dangers we face and you refused to hear. In Italy, Europe brings forth a new man, with a new rallying cry. '*Avanti.*' Advance! '*Ne me frego.*' I don't give a damn! The artists, the Futurists, anticipate. They carry pistols. The poet D'Annunzio leads an occupation force into Trieste. And we sleep. *I* lived abroad, *I* read the foreigner's books, *I* listened to his music, *I* ate his food. But not as a tourist, no, not as a tourist. As a spy. Like Attila the Hun did when he was held hostage in Rome, I put my time to good use, I studied the enemy. Like a Hun seer I read the future in the scorched bones. I saw the danger in the bones of Europe scorched by the last war. Look at the Bolsheviks in Russia, hard men every one of them. The Asiatic brutality of the face of Lenin. And the Germans? Do we expect the Germans to lie down with the lambs? Never." He rattles on, unstoppable. "The war to end all wars was a sham, a lie. Eighteen million dead – only the beginning. The League of Nations offers Sunday-school morality while the hard men gather outside our door." He quits his pacing to confront me. "And the danger is not only outside America, but inside also. Two years ago Congress adopted a new immigration policy. Each European nation is allowed a quota of three per cent of the number of its nationals living in our country. But what of the millions we have already let in?" He moves to my side. "The only solution, Harry, is conversion. Convert the strangers with lightning! The way Luther was converted in the thunderstorm! The lightning of pictures! American pictures! Make the Sicilian living in New York American. Make the Pole living in Detroit American. Convert all those who can be converted – damn the rest!"

He stares at me intently. I want to look away, but don't have the guts. His fierceness hypnotizes. "That is my argument with the Laemmles, the Mayers, the Goldwyns, the Warners, the Zukors," he says. "The Jews will not convert. They are too full of resentment. They remain Jews first and always. For two thousand years they refused every overture. Whatever society, whatever country they inhabit, the worst of it sticks to their coats like a burr. The Russian Bolsheviks are all Jews. Like Trotsky. Trotsky commands the Red

Army, refines Russian brutality as only a Jew could. The Jew Laemmle carries Teutonic burrs to us on his dirty coat, German sentimentality and kitsch taken to new heights of vulgarity. And so on. The examples are endless."

Somebody is fiddling with the volume of a gramophone, jazz spurting and sinking like the jet of an erratic fountain. My mind is jerking and starting, like the music. Rachel, I think. Walk away, I think. But a chilled fascination roots me to the spot. And fear. I'm frightened now. Of this strange, eerie house. Of Fitz and his brutal friends, crashing about upstairs. Of Chance. Say something, I think. But I don't. And this is the thing that frightens me most.

Chance's gaze sweeps the room. "Do you know something, Harry?" he says, suddenly subdued. "This is my favourite room, the room where I think, imagine. Here I imagine myself on a train, a train which carries me to every corner of America. I imagine myself speaking from the back of it, at every whistle-stop, to the heart of America. Because when you speak from the heart to other hearts – even imagined hearts – the truth slowly dawns on you. Then the lightning crackles in your mind, pictures flash . . . something profound, something original is born. You *see* what is really there." His voice has sunk to a whisper, but it is a hot whisper, coals settling in a grate. "Turn out the light," he whispers, rapt.

For the moment, his puppet, I do. A little starlight and cloud-swaddled moon steals into immediate darkness through the French doors. Chance clambers up on the waiting chair, sways, corrects his equilibrium, rises erect under the baubles of the chandelier, pale grapes glistening in the pale moonlight. The gramophone falls silent, someone is changing a record. In that moment everything freezes. So do I. "What I have to say gives me no pleasure," he states. His voice, low and confidential, spreads like a soft carpet over the cold marble to every corner of the room. "My friends, I wish I did not see so clearly. I tell you, the age of the hard men is upon us. That is the *Zeitgeist*. The Italian mimics the Roman centurion. The German worships blood and iron. The Bolshevik murders the Czar and his children. They leave us no choice but to be hard too. Remember the frontier – how savagery answered savagery? Picture the lonely cabin in the forest, the eyes watching from the trees, waiting for their opportunity. The lonely hunter on the plain, naked in his solitude. The children hatcheted in the corn patch, the mutilated man in the grass. The wife raped. The barn burning, the cattle slaughtered, the carrion crows descending. We did not fail that test."

The gramophone starts again. People are dancing upstairs, the chandelier shivers in sympathy.

"But the strangers among us have no memory of this – the fired roof, the women taken captive, the lurking, painted nightmare. The unseen enemy everywhere, at the turn in the river, behind the bluff, hidden in the long prairie grass. They know nothing of that."

Someone in the back of the house screams. It is followed by shrieks of laughter.

Chance pleads with the surrounding darkness. "If Mussolini exalts the spirit of the Roman legions, the German the Teutonic knight, the Russian the pitiless terrorist, surely we are entitled to do the same. The picture of the rawhide frontiersman is entitled to hang in the mind of every American. To hang illuminated by lightning – the cold eyes, the steady hand, the long rifle revealed in brightness. Europe returns to wilderness and returns us with it." Seconds pass as I stare up at him. "A Frenchman noted that the profound contempt of the Greek for the barbarian is only matched by that of the Yankee for the foreign worker who makes no attempt to become truly American. So be it. Was the Jew there when our forefathers knelt by the window in fear for their lives, watching the woods? Was he with us when we rode out on the broad plains under the eyes of savages? Can he understand us? Argue our case to the world? I know what you are thinking, my friends. Do not insult the Jew, you think, he repays every insult with interest. He . . ." Chance trails off, holds himself perfectly still on his pedestal. "No matter. The lonely house must be protected. The wilderness encroaches on the fields we have cleared, the wilderness stirs abroad. It is coming. *They* are coming. I walked among them. One day soon a face will peer in your window, the face of a Blackshirt, or the face of a Bolshevik. They who resurrect the savage ghosts of their past must be challenged with the savage ghosts of *our* past. I will help, I will raise up our ghosts. Steel yourself. Meet strength with strength." His neck turns stiffly like the turret of a tank, testing every corner of the room for opposition. He is done. "Help me down," he says.

I take the groping hand. The palm is the hood of a mushroom, stickily moist. He steps down abruptly, clutching at me to keep from falling. He hangs on my shoulder. "You see, Harry?" he says, face close to mine. "Rewrite it. Change the girl. The enemy is never human."

25

With the addition of George Hammond, the party that approached Little Soldier's camp tallied thirteen. This made the Englishman's boy distinctly uneasy; they were back to the bad-luck number they'd suffered before Hardwick cut loose Farmer Hank. Now he felt as if Farmer Hank had changed shape, remounted, and was spurring himself across Battle Creek with them.

The Englishman's boy stuck close to Ed Grace. They rode side by side, knees almost touching; the strong-boned profile of the Eagle with its powerful hooked nose was stoical, as pale as the marble bust of a Roman senator. He looked neither right nor left, but kept his eyes fixed dead ahead as if they were fastened on stern duty.

Hardwick had given the command to go forward at a walk, in good order, so as not to give the impression they were attacking; nevertheless every man carried a rifle at the ready, butt planted on hip. The camp stirred excitedly at their coming; the wolfers could hear the strident, hysterical barking of dogs, could see figures dodging in and out of lodge entrances, young boys hurrying to catch ponies in the pasture, women snatching up children on the run. In a matter of minutes, a phalanx of fifty or sixty warriors had assembled on the outskirts to meet them.

Hardwick halted his men three hundred yards from the camp, waved a white handkerchief in the air to announce a parley and rode forward, accompanied only by George Hammond. The fierce afternoon heat warped the air between the two parties like a flawed and wavy windowpane; sweat slid out from under the derby on the Englishman's boy's head and trickled down his face.

Some of the welcoming party were drunk, had the same slack-jawed whisky belligerence written on their faces as the majority of wolfers Hardwick had left waiting behind him. Yet a goodly number of the Assiniboine were stone-faced and sober, waiting so profoundly, so mutely still, the only discernible movement in their ranks was the flicker of a feather when a gust of hot breeze licked it. Their faces were painted red like the Bear Cult man's, except their eyes were circled in white instead of black. The warriors' hair was hacked short over the forehead, daubed and smeared with white clay, drawn back in long, thick queues trailing down their spines. Many wore ear beads, and those who went shirtless displayed two black stripes of tattoo running from their throats to their bellies. The red of the faces was repeated in red flannel breechclouts and leggings, black and crimson trader blankets which many of the old men wore draped around their shoulders.

The only firearms Hardwick could spot were Northwest muskets. The Indians without guns were armed with lances and horn bows.

Hammond leaned across his saddle-pommel to draw Hardwick's attention to a tall, lean Assiniboine in a round wolf-skin cap, the owner of a ferociously lupine face extravagantly pocked with small-pox scars and looking like an adobe wall riddled by a blast of buck-shot. "I know that bird," he said. "He's a bad one. Killed two Blackfoot outside of Fort Kipp last year. His name's First Shoot, and he does."

Hardwick nodded, then began to speak, demanding to see the chief, demanding to see Little Soldier. He spoke a childish English, scolding them for stealing Hammond's horse and saying if the Assiniboine didn't want heap trouble, Little Soldier better make the bad Assiniboine return the pony pronto.

He had just launched into this pidgin peroration when Abe Farwell galloped up from the fort on a saddleless mule, legs flapping against its ribs. On second thought he had decided the stakes were too high to sit this one out; if there was trouble with the Assiniboine, a post full of trade goods and a winter's cache of furs and buffalo robes would be placed in jeopardy. He was offering himself as interpreter and mediator.

"Which one of these rascals is Little Soldier?" Hardwick wanted to know.

Farwell quickly scanned the crowd. "He ain't here."

"Then you tell one of these monkeys to fetch him. On the double."

"You want the horse back, there's your man," said Farwell, pointing out First Shoot. "He's head of the Agi'cita, the Soldier's Society – Indian police. If Hammond wants his horse back without bloodshed, you ask First Shoot to get it for you."

Hammond's jaw was working angrily under a wiry black beard which crawled so high up his cheekbones it stopped just short of his eyes. "I ain't asking nobody," he said. "I ain't begging for what's mine. I paid once to get my property back to keep the peace, but they turn around and steal it off you again. I ain't asking any more, I'm telling."

Hardwick was studying First Shoot. His face betrayed he understood a little of Hammond's speech.

There was a disturbance at the back of the warriors. The crowd parted to make way for Little Soldier, blind drunk, leaning on his Sits-Beside-Him wife for support. A big American flag was tied in a bib around his neck. Looking like a grey-haired baby taking his first uncertain steps, he stumbled forward to greet Hardwick.

"There's your chief," said Farwell, under his breath. "Think you can talk any sense into him?"

Little Soldier began to orate.

"What's he jawing on?" Hardwick snapped.

Farwell translated. "He's saying he brought the Star Flag to show you how good a friend Little Soldier is to the Americans. They gave him this Star Flag because he never kills Americans – only Peigans. The Peigans kill Americans all the time. Maybe sometime you'd like to come with him and rub out a few Peigans. Maybe you'd like to make him a present of needle-guns so he could kill the Peigans for you and save you the trouble."

259

"You tell him my trouble right now is a horse. That's my only trouble. You tell him George Hammond's horse was stole by one of his people. You tell him a couple days back Indians stole nigh on twenty head of my horses. You tell him I'm losing patience with redskin thieving ways and I'm of a mind to do something about it. You tell him that."

"I ain't telling him no such thing. You can't talk to him like that in front of his own people."

"You tell him what I said – straight out – or I'll make my point by riding over and ripping the flag off that lying old rogue."

Farwell, looking uneasy, addressed Little Soldier. Before he was finished, Little Soldier interrupted him, speaking wildly, flailing an arm, teetering back and forth on his heels.

"He says nobody from his band stole Hammond's horse. Maybe Hammond's horse wandered. Horses wander. Maybe some bad Peigans took the horse. He knows Hammond's horse. A sorrel horse. Look for yourself; there are no sorrel horses anywhere in Little Soldier's camp."

"No," said Hardwick, "there ain't never no stolen horses in an Indian camp. That goes without saying. Shit."

"He says to show Hammond he speaks the truth, he will give him two horses of his own. They will be hostage horses. When Hammond finds his wandering horse again, then he can give the ponies back to Little Soldier. If he doesn't find his horse, he can keep them. That's fair, he says. Two horses for one. Let them shake hands on it and then when Hammond brings him a bottle of whisky they will be friends."

"I don't want two goddamn starving, bag-of-bones Indian ponies for my horse," blurted Hammond. "My horse is grain-fed and fat. He's got thoroughbred blood in him. I ain't horse-trading with no son of a bitch of a pilfering Indian. I want my horse back and that's the end of it."

Farwell said a few words to the chief. He answered.

"He says he can't give you what he doesn't have. You might ask him for the sun, but the sun is not in his power to give. He will give you what he has to give – two horses for one. Be happy with what he has to give – the Assiniboine are poor Indians. They came to the Cypress Hills to escape the hunger in the north. The hunting is good here but they are not fat yet. They need horses to run the buffalo, but he is willing to give George Hammond two horses so there will be no bad blood between them. George Hammond should take his horses and be happy. There are young Assiniboine men with no horses who would bless Little Soldier's name if he were to make them such a generous present. He says take the horses or you will make the young men angry. He cannot be responsible for young men when they are angry."

A queer smile flitted across Hardwick's lips. "I believe I just heard a threat," he said.

"No, no," soothed Farwell, "it ain't no threat – it's the truth. Take the goddamn horses, Hardwick. This is a mighty poor band. He's making you a big gift. Big enough it hurts. I don't think they own more than a dozen horses. He's trying to smooth things over. Be polite – take them."

"Tell him I piss on his horses."

Farwell heeled his mule in front of Hardwick, strategically blocking the old man's view of the white man's sneering face. Little Soldier smiled broadly while his wife clutched his elbow, steadying him as he rocked back and forth on his heels.

"Tom, I ain't going to say that. Don't go hot-headed on me now. Some of these young bucks are full of Solomon's whisky. Don't go poking the hive with a stick. Let it rest."

Hardwick stood in his stirrups and shouted over Farwell's head. "I piss on you and your horses! Understand? I want Hammond's horse! Give us Hammond's horse or take the consequences!" Uncomprehending, Little Soldier grinned foolishly back at him, but First Shoot understood enough English to grasp Hardwick's meaning. He began to angrily shout and a discomfiting murmur arose and spread through the ranks of the warriors. Stepping forward, he flung his buffalo robe to the ground in a passionate gesture. Others followed suit, stripping off their clothes. Farwell trotted his mule back and forth between the two white men and the Indians, holding up his arms in supplication, doing his best to cajole them in the Assiniboine tongue.

"They're getting ready to fight," said Hammond anxiously. "Throwing off their clothes so if they take a bullet it'll be a clean wound. We better pull stakes."

The Assiniboine were nearly naked now, taunting the whites, brandishing muskets, making the air whine as they whirled poggamoggans threateningly above their heads, shaking bows and lances as Farwell desperately pleaded with them.

"Farwell, clear out!" shouted Hardwick. "Clear out or, damn your hide, I'll fire anyway!"

"Don't you do it!" screamed Farwell. "Not with a white man between you!"

Hardwick and Hammond, carbines levelled, were backing their horses away from the shrieking Assiniboine. Suddenly, Hardwick's horse reared. Hammond had fired.

A frantic scramble to suck leather, clawing to keep his seat. The horse slammed back down on its forelegs, hard, popping him up, skidding his boot out of the stirrup. He heard the dull pop of a musket discharging, caught the dazzle of the haunch of Hammond's horse, spinning in a tight turn. Farwell flew by him, wide-eyed and screaming, clinging to his mule, slashing it into a clumsy, slew-footed gallop with his reins. Fumbling with his boot to retrieve the lost stirrup, fumbling with the Henry, without aiming Hardwick squeezed a shot off over the flank of his horse. Then he was pounding after Hammond and Farwell, flattening himself low in the saddle, brutally slapping his pony's rump with his rifle barrel. A spasm of muzzleloader fire erupted at his back. He shrank down further, pinching himself as small as he could. His neck tingled with the expectation of a bullet.

With the white men between them and the Assiniboine, the wolfers sat their pawing, stamping horses, holding fire. The Indians pursued on foot, little patches of black musket-smoke puffing into the air as they ran and fired, ran and fired. They were reloading fast, shaking powder into the barrels of their guns and spitting bullets into the muzzles, in their haste omitting to use wadding, so their shot did not carry far or accurately.

Hammond reached the wolfers and bellowed, "Run for cover, boys! The coulee! The coulee!" as he galloped by, heading for the narrow gulch which lay like a wound in the breast of the prairie. But the nervous wolfers held their ground on whinnying, panicked horses.

A row of tense white faces shimmered sidelong in the eye of the Englishman's boy. He heard harsh, whispered curses directed at no one; shouts of encouragement to Hardwick that Hardwick could not hear. Distance and time were mirages, bending and shimmering like the hot air. Closer yet farther. Sooner yet later.

And then Hardwick and Farwell *were* upon them. Hardwick waving them back to the coulee. The line swung as one, as prettily orchestrated by terror as a practised cavalry manoeuvre on a parade-ground square. They whipped their mounts into a headlong gallop which in moments brought them churning down into the cutbank where Hammond cowered, a cataract of heaving horses, clouds of dust, men jolting in saddles.

By the time the Englishman's boy dismounted, the narrow confine of the crevice was ringing with rifle-fire. He picked out Grace's blue-handkerchiefed head and ran to him doubled over, jerking his horse down the shallow coulee bottom after him. He could hear someone screaming, "They're coming! Lord Jesus, they're coming!" He flung himself down beside Grace. Here the coulee was only four feet deep, forming a natural rifle pit.

Dragging himself up on his elbows, he surveyed the ground he'd just covered in precipitous retreat, an open expanse dotted with clumps of wolf willow and sage. Over this the Assiniboine were advancing from patch of cover to patch of cover, firing their muzzle-loaders, reloading, then skittering and zigzagging their way forward to discharge another shot. Behind them the camp was emptying, women rushing children and infants into thick timber which, once it closed on them, resumed its placid front.

Already the Englishman's boy could count three of the attacking

Indians lying broken on the landscape like dolls hurled to a nursery floor. Ten yards from the lip of the coulee Farwell's wounded mule lay on its side, its head rising and falling as the strength bled out of it with every pump of its heart.

"Your mouth's hanging open," Grace said. "Close it and fire."

In that instant, the Assiniboine let loose a volley and swept up out of the willow and grass with sharp, piercing cries. Fox-fast and fleet, they shredded the screen of gun-smoke issuing from their muskets with their charge.

The Henrys began to bark up and down the coulee like a pack of hounds on the scent. The Englishman's boy was firing fast, the sweat pouring into his eyes in a blinding, stinging rain. For a terrible second, he believed the Assiniboine were going to pass unscathed through the hail of bullets, pour into the coulee stabbing and clubbing. But the attack ripped apart, like rotten cloth. The abrupt sprawl of men into the sage stunned the Englishman's boy. They dropped like all the deer he had ever shot cleanly and fatally. The attack stuttered, hesitated, the Indians withdrew in confusion. A cheer went up in the cutbank.

The Englishman's boy slid down the face of the slope, pulled off his derby, mopped his brow with his sleeve. His mouth was bone-dry. He'd tried to draw a bead on those twisty, slippery figures but they'd leapt and dodged so as to freeze his finger on the trigger. In the end, he'd only pointed and fired, pointed and fired. He didn't think he'd got himself one.

Hardwick was walking up and down the trench, asking each man, "How many rounds you got left? How many rounds?"

Grace answered tersely, "Enough."

Hardwick took one glance at the bandoliers looped over the shoulders of the Englishman's boy and passed on.

John Duval was calling for water. Hardwick shouted, "Nobody drinks yet! We don't know how long we're going to be pinned down here! Water's rationed!"

The Englishman's boy dug a pebble out of the side of the cutbank, put it in his mouth to suck. The blistering heat roiled in the coulee.

The wolfers pricked their ears. Out there, someone was chanting. It ran toward them like a wave, washed over them, receded, swept forward once more.

"Death song," said Grace to the boy.

The men crouched in the coulee, gripping their guns, listening to a man preparing to die. The chant rose and fell, rose and fell. Suddenly it stopped. In the distance, a man stood up out of the scrub, straight as a lodgepole pine. It was First Shoot in his wolf-skin cap. The wolfers began to fiddle with their sights, adjusting them for the range. First Shoot didn't give them time enough to sight him. He pumped his musket to the sky three times, sprinted forward. The Soldier's Society soared up out of the grass like a covey of birds. A second force of hostiles gushed up behind them, older men not so fleet, not so agile as the first, all of them whooping.

This time, the Assiniboines did not skirmish forward, discharging their weapons. It was a pell-mell assault, a dash of supple swiftness, a foot race to the coulee. The speed, the audacity of it stunned the men huddled there. The Assiniboine came pelting forward, leaping sage-brush, veering and twisting like a hunting wolf pack, quick, terrible.

A sheet of flame scorched the air. The death-song singer did not break stride; it was as if the muzzle flashes were a curtain of beads, insignificant, to be brushed aside. He drove on, hot, direct as fire burning down a fuse to a powder keg. Fifty yards, forty.

Then the powder keg exploded. The curtain refused to part. His heels skidded out from under him, kicked up, flesh fountaining in a spray of blood. The white men worked the levers of their rifles madly, shot swinging through the warriors like a heavy scythe mowing hay, everywhere the human grass shivered when it met the sharp blade, wavered, fell in a windrow of bodies.

The Indians broke and fled.

A shout went up in the coulee, punctuated by rebel yells. Random shots spat on fleeing backs. An Assiniboine fell, staggered to his feet, was scythed again.

The surviving Indians retreated to an opposing coulee from where they began to lay down fire. Now in a defensive position they had time to prime and load with calculation. The use of wadding gave them greater range and accuracy. Despite smooth-bore, single-shot weapons, their numbers made for a steady, debilitating sniper fire which penned the wolfers in the coulee. Whining, whistling shot kept them ducking. A ball struck a stone near the Englishman's boy and he felt a sting of splintering lead on his cheek. It began to drip blood.

They knew they were trapped. The sun glared and burned, roasted them. Fear sank its claws in their tender, smitten skins.

26

"I 've got to get out of this picture," I say.

Rachel Gold and I are sitting on a blanket gazing at the Pacific Ocean and a stretch of beach which once doubled for the Red Sea in Cecil B. DeMille's *The Ten Commandments*. It isn't really a day for the beach – overcast, the water riding under the horizon line grey and mud-coloured, but today I want her undivided attention and an empty beach offers few distractions.

"Jesus, Harry," she says, "you scheme your ass off to get this job and then you want out? What's this about?"

"I can't do it."

"Do what?"

"Write what he wants." I can't get into explanations. I can't confess how scared I am. I can't tell her that if I write what Chance wants, there's every likelihood I'll have a hand in attaching Shorty McAdoo's name to a lie. After Chance's bizarre performance at the party, I can guess at the savage, distorted, paranoid lens through which this picture is going to be shot, guess at what crazy, politically "visionary" message he thinks the movie will deliver. As he's said all along, this picture isn't *supposed* to be just another Western. To do what he requires wouldn't just be a betrayal of Shorty, but of Rachel, too.

And myself.

Rachel is being her usual hard-headed, practical self. "You're not Leo Tolstoy, Harry. You're a scenarist. Somebody hands you the

267

measurements and you cut the cloth. This shouldn't come as news to you. Write what he wants, for Christ's sake, and have done with it."

The shore is deserted, not another soul in sight. The breaker-washed sand gleams like hot asphalt packed by a steamroller, flat, smooth, oily-looking. Waves monotonously assault the glistening beach, rolled banners unfurling liquid flags to a steady, muffled drum-beat. Sitting on the blanket with her feet tucked up under her, Rachel is tiny, porcelain-white and serious, a Victorian doll.

"Chance is nuts," I say.

"This is news? Everybody who runs a studio is nuts. You've got to be. Mack Sennett has a bathtub in his office. Carl Laemmle's son follows him around with a lard pail in case his old man needs a piss. Lasky and Thalberg hire a scenarist who thinks the filming of *Ben-Hur* is the fulfilment of a prediction by Nostradamus. Need I go on?"

"This is different."

"Different how?"

I shrug and announce, "Politics." Immediately I wish I hadn't.

"What, politics? You vote Democrat and he votes Republican? These are not irreconcilable differences, my friend. I don't hide I'm a socialist and he hasn't fired me yet."

I don't mention the Jew-hate. I don't know how to tell her about that.

"I've been thinking of quitting," I announce.

"What can I say? If your artistic sensibility – which I've yet to see any evidence of – is getting seriously bruised, quit."

"What if he won't let me quit?"

"Let you? What's let you? We had an Emancipation Proclamation in this country. He can't stop you from quitting."

"I have this feeling he's not going to let me out of this. He's always been very secretive about this project. Only three of us really know what it's about. Chance has been getting more and more paranoid about this picture."

"You're scared of him."

"Goddamn right I'm scared of him."

"You leave him so he puts it out you're unprofessional, a bad writer. Who will listen? Everybody in the business has him pegged as a joke. He gives you a bad report card – it's likely to come off as a glowing recommendation."

"You forgot Fitz," I say. "That son of a bitch is capable of anything. Fitz might get something into his head. He's like the crazy, loyal servant in Murnau's *Nosferatu*. Devoted to the master." I look out to sea. The waves are rolling forward in relentless reiteration, repeating themselves over and over, like my worries of the past few days. The sky is turning denser, greyer, like cheap blotting paper, fibrous with skeins of cloud. Around me I can feel the air growing heavier, moister, closing in. "Chance sent me away to rework the scenario. But now I've seen the picture he wants to make through his eyes – I can't do it. It's a hallucination, not a movie. A Western *Nosferatu*. It won't work. And when it doesn't, he's going to want somebody to blame. I'll be the candidate."

"Then maybe you're right to quit before your name appears in the credits. In this town, a writer's first picture goes bust, it's likely his last."

"Yeah, but I've got to consider my mother. What do I do? Quit my job and when the rent comes due at the nursing home let her get pitched into the state asylum? I've investigated. They're worse down here than they are in Canada."

"Find another job."

"Where am I going to find another job pays one hundred and fifty a week? Nobody is going to hire me for that kind of money. Maybe nobody is going to hire me at all. With my responsibilities I've got to consider that." I rummage nervously in the picnic hamper I've packed; not for a sandwich, for the gin. I offer the vacuum flask to Rachel first. "Drink?"

She shakes her head.

"You're turning down a drink?"

She studies the leaden ocean. "I've been feeling out of control lately," she murmurs.

I take a swig. "I thought you were the lady who said she liked feeling out of control."

"It could be I didn't say exactly what I mean. I do like feeling out of control. I like excitement. But if you're out of control all the time then maybe something is controlling you. If that makes any sense."

"Maybe. I'm not sure I don't feel the same. Out of control. Or in somebody else's control. But I'll tell you one thing, whatever it is, I don't like it. It feels bad."

"Don't make so many plans, Harry," she says. "In my experience, plans have a habit of hoisting you on your own petard. Too much calculation can get you into trouble. If everything doesn't fall into place, you fall out of it."

I sit with the flask of gin in my hand. "That book Chance gave me – did you read it?"

"In a manner of speaking. My French is not as good as you assume it is. And this book, it wasn't light reading. Very philosophical, in the French fashion."

"I thought it was politics," I say.

"Politics of a peculiar kind. The Western world is rotten, degenerate. Action is required. Myths are the only spurs to action."

"Go on."

"Not Greek myths – Apollo, Zeus, Hera. Myth in a sociological sense. Myth as a complex of pictures which express the deepest desire of a group. Sorel talks about the French working class and their belief in the myth of the general strike, the great violent paroxysm which will bring the bosses to their knees, destroy the bourgeoisie, and usher in a new age. According to him, the myth doesn't need to have any grounds in reality, or have any possibility of being accomplished; it's there to motivate people, provide the impetus for violent action. Because violence is the only means of invigorating a degenerate society. Your friend gave you an indecent book to read, Harry."

I don't bother to answer. A fine drizzle, scarcely more than a mist, is drifting down upon us. We are floating, soiled angels wrapped in a dirty cloud. The sea blurs; Rachel's face shines luminous behind a veil of moisture. Like gauze on a lens, it softens her.

Before I know what I am saying, I tell her I love her.

She lights a cigarette, the flame cradled in her hand. "This isn't like you, Harry," is her only comment.

"You said not to plan so much. It just came out. Maybe I've adopted your style – out of control."

"Or maybe you just want somebody to take over for you. Tell you what to do." Her gaze is fixed on the beating waves. "I can't do that. What I am willing to do is take care of the bills for your mother until you settle this thing."

"I'm not broke yet," I say.

"All right, then *do* something. Don't play helpless." She stubs out the cigarette. "I'm going for a swim. Think about it. Decide."

I avert my eyes, listen to the rustle of her disrobing. Each article of clothing she discards, the strength of her perfume increases. Then the scent of her is gone, the void filled by the poorhouse-soup smell of the Pacific, suggestively warm, vaguely salty, vaguely vegetable. I wait, but not as long as I should have, stealing a glimpse of her as she covers the last few yards of sand to the waves, her outline bleary in the rain, delicate, moving – a small ghost.

I had wanted to reach out and touch her. For an instant, I had half-believed she wanted to be touched. But a moment's cheap daring fails, even in the mist. Do something, she said. But what? Ambiguous. Wasn't it?

So I do something. That night I go to my office in Best Chance Studios and clean out my desk, sit down and type out a letter of resignation. My letter isn't righteous or impolite, it simply treats what happened at the party as if it hadn't, like a fart at a formal dinner. Not a mention. The best exit I can manage from a bad situation. I only hope it will work.

> Dear Mr. Chance,
>
> I regret to inform you that I am no longer able to continue in your employ. Our last meeting impressed upon me that I have neither the talent nor the experience to undertake a scenario for

a picture of the scope, breadth, and magnitude you envision. I am sorry that I have failed you in a project which is so near and dear to your heart, but I am also confident you will find someone who is far better equipped to undertake it than am I.

I have left the keys to the car in my desk, and the car in the lot. All interviews, notes, and the carbon copy of the rough draft of the scenario in my possession will be returned to you under separate cover by registered mail. Please consider my resignation effective as of this date. I am sorry I could not have been of greater service.

Yours sincerely,
Harry Vincent

Closeted in my apartment I wait to see what Chance's reaction to this will be. No letter, no ringing phone. I haunt my window, watching the street, expecting Fitz, but Fitz doesn't come. Young women in cloche hats parade back and forth on the sidewalk, walking furry handfuls of dog straining on leashes fine as fishing line. Mexican gardeners trim little squares of lawn in front of the apartments lining the street, their lawn mowers tossing spumes of green. The milkman, the postman, the iceman come and go. By noon the sun roasts the road and makes the softening asphalt smell like bad meat cooking, everybody but me pulls down their window blinds to hold the heat at bay. I leave mine up so I have warning of Fitz's arrival.

A little after six the telephone operators, the hairdressers, the manicurists, the waitresses, the salesgirls bustle by. In the passageways of my building girls heft packages and struggle with keys. Doors bang shut, radios start to squawk, the tantalizing smell of frying pork chop and hamburger reach me as I sit smoking at my window, cocking an eye for Fitz. Time passes and turns the road briefly golden, the sky a turquoise swimming pool of bliss. The sun dips, the boulevard slides into grey, the horizon blushes pink before freckling itself with pale evening stars. I doze in my chair, jerking awake to every sound outside, my head turning to the street before my eyes have opened. No Fitz.

After four or five days of this, I begin to think maybe he isn't coming, maybe I'm getting away with it. I start to look for another job. But I'm still a nervous kid playing hooky, looking around corners, half-afraid of bumping into the truant officer, Denis Fitzsimmons.

I know one or two people at most of the studios, but they are lowly types without the pull to snooker me employment the way Rachel Gold did. I make the rounds at Fox, Metro, Goldwyn Company, Louis B. Mayer Productions, Universal, Famous Players–Lasky, United Artists and Warner Brothers. Sure, I have experience, but experience writing titles. Any hack can write titles, titles are work for burned-out, boozy newspaper has-beens. The studios want creative types. Somebody with ideas. Somebody with zip. Sell me a story, they say. If you can't sell me on a peppy story, I don't need you.

I try, but when I push some story idea the hysterically false enthusiasm of my voice prompts such shame and embarrassment that gradually my improbable and idiotic scenarios falter, trickling away into the censuring silence of my auditor like a weak stream into desert sand.

"What's this, kid?" they say. "No cigar."

They aren't interested in me, but they *are* interested in Chance. What's going on with him? Rumours are obviously surfacing. Rumours of a big Western. I learn that things are moving rapidly with the picture we had dawdled over, moving fast.

Somebody at Universal informs me Chance has suddenly hired a lot of "pioneer types," grizzled, hard-faced men who could give you nightmares with a glance, men whose reputations are worse than the way they look. He's cleaned out a reservation of Sioux, loaded them on a train bound for Montana, men, women, children, cost no object. It seems that shooting has already begun. Chance must have doctored the script himself.

And I learn he hasn't cast Noah Beery in the lead as I'd suggested, but a punk of seventeen by the name of John Bean who has the manners of a reform-school inmate. Bean can act, they say, but he isn't box office, too much meanness in his eyes to make hearts flutter or to melt an audience like an ice cream cone on a hot day. He's been in trouble with the police in Los Angeles, some claim it was drugs. What the hell is Hays going to say? What the hell is my former boss up to? they want to know. What's he doing with this zoo? I only shrug non-committally and grin weakly, play stupid, and keep my mouth tightly zipped. If anybody's going to get anything on Chance it isn't going to come from me.

Day after day I beat on doors without getting so much as a sniff of interest from any of the majors. I decide to swallow my pride and turn to the small studios and independents referred to as Poverty Row, operations which teeter on the precipice of bankruptcy and take small profits from quickie one- and two-reelers to plough back into more of the same.

Six long weeks after my resignation from Best Chance Pictures, I find myself in the office – really a glorified outhouse with a pepper tree out front stickying up the porch – of a man called Herbert Farnum, who rattles off cheap Westerns and Mack Sennett copycats. I've hardly finished trotting out my credentials when he slings his big feet up on his desk and says, "So you used to work for Best Chance Pictures. What's the dope on this Western Chance is making? They say he's throwing big bucks into it."

"That all started after I left," I say. "I don't know anything about it."

"I've heard he's going to direct," Farnum says. "All of a sudden I hear he directed pictures in the East before the war. Made one- and two-reelers when things were just getting off the ground. But he didn't use his own name so's not to embarrass his old man. A rich boy's hobby. I'd call that news. You know anything about that?"

"Not a thing. But I doubt it's right."

"Talk is that's how he and his monkey Fitzsimmons got together. Back in the days that the directors in New York used to hire tough boys from the Irish gangs – Plug Uglies, Hudson Dusters, the Whyos – to protect them from Pinkerton detectives who smashed their cameras and kicked the shit out of their crews for ignoring the Motion Pictures Patent. Sounds like for a society boy Chance liked the low life and the rough stuff."

"Who told you that?"

"Word gets around," he says vaguely. "Some little birdie's been singing. As the man said, your past has a habit of catching up to you. And besides, he's got to have a taste for the bad boys if he's making a movie about that fucking Shorty McAdoo. You know Shorty McAdoo? Mean little cock-sucking bandit. He worked for me once and he didn't do nothing but stir up trouble with the cowboys. Haley Carr, my star, told the director to fire him. When McAdoo found out why he was getting his walking papers the little son of a bitch climbed on a horse and chased Carr all over the lot until he roped him. Then he dragged Carr down Gower on his belly. Carr was so scabbed up we had to take him out of the picture and stick somebody else in. We had a day of retakes on account of that fucking McAdoo."

"Well," I say, hopping quickly to change the topic, "this is all very interesting but what I came here about is a job."

"Job?" he says, annoyed to be reminded why I'm here. He considers for a moment, lips puckered. "Could be if you write scenarios I like, I'll buy them fifty bucks a pop. Westerns. But it's strictly free lance. I don't pay writers to loaf at my expense."

I get to my feet. "All right."

Going out the door I can hear Farnum muttering to himself. "Fucking McAdoo. Imagine somebody making a picture about that no-good grifter."

I stand on the porch steps, my shoes sticking to the adhesive pepper-tree sap that has dripped on the boards. How will McAdoo take the news of his immortalization?

∽

It's not until a month later that I find out. Bound for Poverty Row with another dopey scenario to flog, I see the two of them a block up the street, headed my way. I consider crossing the road to the other side, but my limp is conspicuous; I'll be spotted. Better to face the music.

There's no choice but to hang on the sidewalk, waiting. Already I know Wylie has seen me, he stoops to pass on his news to Shorty, one hand flicking in my direction, his great height crooked over McAdoo. Shorty doesn't appear to be listening, he just keeps coming on with deliberation, not a hitch or hesitation in his bandy-legged strut.

This morning McAdoo's wearing a bleached blue denim shirt and pants and an obviously new seal-brown stockman stetson shading a face that shows no willingness to break into a smile of welcome. Wylie's balancing a new hat on his head too, a big white Carlsbad which raises his altitude in the neighbourhood of seven feet and makes him look like he'd blow over in a gentle zephyr.

"Take a look at the mangy dick-licking dog," Shorty says to Wylie as they come up. By the scowl on him, there's no doubt Wylie is in complete agreement with McAdoo's opinion of me.

"Nice to see you, too, Shorty," I say. "I take it you've heard the rumours."

He doesn't answer at once. His eyes, pitted in dark, brooding flesh, are unflinching as they study me, but there's something else in them too, weariness, perhaps even a touch of sadness. He looks older, more tired, than the last time we met.

"I told you once, I'm an old whore who's been rid hard," says Shorty. "But I don't know if ever I been rid this hard before, Vincent."

"Shorty says you sold him body and soul. That's what Shorty says. He says that," Wylie chimes in excitedly.

McAdoo makes a cutting motion with his hand. "Shut up, Wylie."

We're standing in front of a diner with gingham curtains in the window. "Let's discuss this," I say. "Let me buy you a cup of coffee."

Shorty squints scornfully up the street. "What makes you think I'd set down with you?" he says.

I pull open the door. A little bell tinkles inside. "Come on. Hear me out."

For a second, he seems bent on refusing but then brushes by me, Wylie following, his forehead wrinkled with disapproval because Shorty has accepted my invitation. We choose a booth and sit in tense silence while we are served. The two of them blow into the steam rising from their mugs, identical judgements.

"I thought you would be in Canada by now."

Shorty puts down his mug and begins to roll a cigarette. "I guess that's what you was banking on – old Shorty out of the way."

"You didn't get cheated. Nobody else could have got you as much money as I did. That's a fact."

"Fuck the money."

Wylie's eyes fly back and forth between us. He raises his mug to sip, changes his mind, glances at Shorty's mug resting on the tabletop and thumps his own down, face screwed up like he's sniffed poison in his coffee. "Fuck the money," Wylie says, seconding the motion.

"Where do you think the money came from for your new hat, Wylie?" I say.

Wylie rips off his big white hat and presses it defensively to his chest. The Carlsbad is a fine one. Best beaver felt.

"You leave him out of this," says McAdoo.

"Then tell him to mind his own business."

"Shorty says you sold him down the river. Shorty says them pitcher people going to make him a laughing stock. They going to put some beauty boy in a big white hat and call it him. They going to make him wear his pants stuffed down in a pair of hand-tooled boots. They going to make him set on a silver saddle and ride a horse that's all mane and tail. That's what Shorty says. We going to stop that – Shorty and me."

"Drink your coffee," Shorty tells him. Wylie does, obedient for the moment. McAdoo turns back to me. "I spent but little of the money. I want to buy my life back. Get me in to see him. I asked to see him but he won't."

I shake my head. "I don't work for him any more. I quit over a month ago. Besides, you can't stop it now. I hear shooting's started."

"Don't hand me no more fucking lies, Vincent."

"No more lies," repeats Wylie.

"Look, if I misled you, it's because he misled me. As soon as I understood that, I quit."

"Too bad for me you didn't understand sooner."

"Listen to me, Shorty," I say. "I know you've got no reason to trust me, but trust me on this. Stay away from Chance."

"It's my life, Vincent."

"That's right. And I'm telling you to take the rest of your life north. Take it north and stay away from him."

"And what about the girl?"

"Christ, the girl's dead. *Dead*, Shorty."

"I sold the girl, too," says Shorty. "I got no right to sell him the girl if he ain't going to do right by her."

"It's a little late for you to be developing a conscience about her, isn't it?"

Shorty picks up his spoon, studies it, lays it back down carefully. "Well," he says, looking up at me with those black eyes, "I'm an old man now, Harry. Lots of things I wish hadn't happened – but everybody looks to keep his own precious hair. You drop the cat in boiling water he's going to claw his way out or cook. I didn't never intend to cook. So I clawed. I don't make no apology for it. You'd have done the same. But what happened with the girl – there weren't no excuse for it. There weren't no excuse to scald the girl."

Wylie leans across the table. In a voice low, husky with emotion, he says, "Shorty taken care of me. He did. I do the same for him. Remember that." Then he sits back, satisfied, a self-righteous smile on his lips.

"Settle yourself, Wylie," Shorty says quietly. "The milk's already spilt. Now I got to see how much I can spoon back into the bottle, dirty or not." He lifts his eyebrows. "Isn't that right, Harry?"

"Believe me, there's none of it you can spoon back in," I tell him. "Don't think you can."

"Oh," says Shorty, "I ain't going to rest until I've tried. I wouldn't talked to you but you promised me the truth would be proclaimed."

"He promised me the same. Otherwise I wouldn't have done it."

"Then it seems to me the two of us is obliged to try put the milk back in the bottle," says Shorty with a flat, terrible authority.

27

The wolfers remained pinned down in the coulee, forced to trade shots with the Assiniboine. The mathematics of that was not in their favour and they knew it. Although they had taken no casualties as yet, it was clear to everybody that with each passing hour their situation grew more dire. Their hunted, desperate faces announced that knowledge. One or two of them had already had to shamefacedly scurry further down the ravine to relieve themselves, terror proving a powerful purgative. Hardwick called a council of war, his lieutenants Evans and Vogle hunkered to the right and left of him. He began with an attempt to put some heart into his men. "Well, boys, we burned their asses good. I counted at least fifteen or sixteen dead Indians lying out there and not a one of us with a hair harmed on our heads. And we're safe here for the time being. They can't shake us out. But, on the other hand, we ain't going to shake them out neither. If we try to skedaddle for the fort, they're likely to pick a few of us off while we cover open ground. If we squat here, we cook in our own juice, seeing as we're low on water, and ammunition ain't going to last forever and a day. Also I'm thinking, could be there's more than one band of Assiniboine in these hills. Could be they already sent a runner to round up the relatives and bring them in."

A ball sizzled overhead; everyone flinched. Hardwick glanced up at Trevanian Hale, the lookout. "How's she hanging, boy?" he said. "Got them eyes peeled?"

"That one near peeled my scalp. Them bastards got our range."

"Well, look sharp. And take your goddamn hat off."

Hardwick turned back to the sombre circle. Vogle said, "I elect we make for the fort. Take our chances."

It sounded like drawing straws on death. The men looked at one another.

"I don't know," said Evans. "They're organized now. Organized as an Indian gets. If we raise up out of here, they'll put thirty, thirty-five ball at us. If we all get clear of that, dandy. But I don't figure we'll all get clear of it. Somebody's going to get winged."

"Then what the hell we supposed to do?" said John Duval. His red little eyes were angry. The way he spat was angry.

"The war taught me one thing," said Hardwick. "Take high ground wherever you can. Then hold it. There's a promising little rise to the right of us. If we get a good covering fire on them from here so as to keep their heads down, we can get some men up top that knoll. Couple of men with repeaters blazing down in that coulee can do a heap of damage."

No one dared speak. Finally, Duval put the question no one else would. "Who?"

"I told you boys I hate a slacker," said Hardwick. "I ain't going to shirk. I'll go." He shifted on his heels. "What about you, Chief?" he asked Evans. "You game?"

Evans didn't lift his eyes from the ground. "All right."

"She's settled then. Leave us a minute to collect our hosses. When I give the word, you boys let fly at them. Don't skimp on the lead. Keep the red bastards ducking."

The men dispersed to the lip of the gully. Evans and Hardwick led their mounts to the end of the coulee where it rose in a gentle, gradual slope to merge with the prairie. At a signal from Hardwick they sprang up on the horses, spurred them out of the ravine with the cry, "Give 'em hell, boys!", a cry which triggered a fusillade to flash and crash the length of the coulee.

They galloped breakneck for the rise, dismounted on the run, and scrambled up the hillock. In minutes they had gained the top, fell prone, and began to pour deadly repeater-fire into the enemy below while their compatriots raked the top of the coulee with an enfilade. A gauze of blue gun-smoke hovered in the still air, a lethal miasma.

Suddenly Grace shook the shoulder of the Englishman's boy and pointed to five figures emerging from the timber the women and children had escaped into, figures which flitted so swiftly across open ground and vanished into the spotty brush at the base of the hill that the Englishman's boy wasn't sure if he'd seen them at all.

"They've flanked Hardwick and Evans," said Grace. "They're going to run off their horses. Cut them off."

Oblivious to the danger at their backs, Evans and Hardwick continued to pepper the Assiniboine position. Grace shouted a warning down the cutbank. "They've got behind Hardwick and Evans!"

Several men rushed to Grace, peered to where he pointed. There was nothing to be seen, not a leaf of the brush moved.

"I don't see nothing," said Duval.

"I seen them," the Englishman's boy said.

"Well, how in Christ's name are we supposed to get out of this mess?" said Duval. "Can't shoot what you can't see."

"Flush them," said Grace. "They'll be in that brush laying plans to steal up on Hardwick and Evans. If we charge, they'll scatter in surprise. Either we run them off or we run them down."

"Fuck you," said Duval. "Hardwick got us in this infernal spot. Let him look after his own hide."

With their leaders gone, the men were indecisive, lost. "That's true. Hardwick did get us in this spot," Grace said quietly. "But I don't remember anybody raising objections to coming along." He paused. "And I don't remember anybody except Hardwick and Evans offering to risk his skin to get us out of it."

No one contradicted the Eagle, but no one was volunteering to take part in the rescue either. The Englishman's boy thought that when Grace turned and walked away from them, that was the end of it. But Grace unhooked a cavalry scabbard from Trevanian Hale's saddle, slung the sabre on his own saddlehorn, sheathed his Henry rifle, broke his revolver, checked the chambers, slapped it shut. "I reckon this is a pistol-and-sabre charge," he said to no one in particular. No one moved. Grace shrugged, put his foot in the stirrup, swung up. "I can't swear to it, but they looked to be youngsters. A little determination should break them." The men stepped aside to let him pass when he kicked his horse into motion. "Cover me," he said.

They did. As rifle-fire crashed about him the Englishman's boy ran to collect his horse and vaulted onto it. Already the Eagle was crossing ground at an easy lope, his handkerchief a dab of blue, his back erect. The Englishman's boy tore after him, his horse's pricked ears bouncing like crazy rifle-sights striving to take aim at Grace's back. Fifty yards off, Grace whipped his horse into a cavalry charge, closing fast on the scrub at the bottom of the hill. When he was thirty yards short of the brush, the Englishman's boy heard a muffled clap which buckled the legs of the Eagle's horse, sledgehammering it in full stride. The gelding somersaulted and Grace bucked over its head, pitching into a dreadful, awkward tumble which smashed him to the ground. He staggered to his feet, left arm dangling broken, pistol gripped in his right hand as two boys burst out of the brush, one brandishing a hatchet, the other a bow. Grace knocked aside the first with a pistol-shot just as the second dropped to his knee and let fly an arrow.

Grace reeled, the pistol fell to his feet, one hand lifted in bewilderment to paw feebly at his throat. At full gallop, the Englishman's boy snapped off two shots, missed with both. The Assiniboine gave a triumphant whoop, darted forward, struck the swaying Eagle twice with his coup stick, and turned to bolt back to cover just as the Englishman's boy slammed his horse into him full tilt, trampling him to the ground. He scrambled up and the Englishman's boy leaned down from his saddle, thrust the revolver into his face and fired.

Throwing himself off the horse he ran to Grace. The Eagle's right hand clenched the shaft of the arrow buried in his throat, a bloody cravat spread down his shirt front. He gave a convulsive twist of the wrist, breaking the shaft off in his hand, stared uncomprehendingly at the markings and feathers, and fell. Grabbing his shoulders the boy dragged him to shelter behind the dead horse. There they both lay, breathing quick and hard. The Eagle mumbled something the Englishman's boy didn't catch. He laid his ear to the panting mouth. "Pull it," Grace begged. "Pull it." Rolling him on his side exposed six inches of arrow protruding from the nape of his neck, revealed the cruel barbs of an arrowhead filed out of an old frying-pan bottom. The Englishman's boy clasped it and drew it in one long, sticky sigh of grasping flesh; when the arrow jerked free blood shot in spasms on his shirt sleeve. He ripped off Grace's bandanna and stuffed it in the wound, the Eagle groaning under his ministrations. Grace made a vague gesture with his hand, his eyes glazing blue like the eyes of a butchered animal, murmured something faintly. The boy lifted his head, nestling it in the crook of his arm. The Eagle gave a long, bloody snore, the blood gurgling in his throat, stretched his legs luxuriously like a man making himself comfortable in his bed. "That's better," he whispered, and died.

The Englishman's boy heard a musket-shot, the woody thud of a ball embedding itself in the body of the dead horse. He flopped across its belly and raised the Colt in both hands; both were shaking fearsome. The leaves of the stunted willow, the buffalo berry, the chokecherry, hung dead and lifeless. He wiped the palm of his left hand on his pant leg, then his right, so as to get a better grip on the ivory handle of the Colt. He could see his horse forty yards off, cropping grass, reins trailing on the ground. Another thirty yards lay between him and the Indians in the scrub.

Five. Grace had said five Indians. He and Grace had done for two. That left three in the bush.

He had the strange feeling of fading out of the scene, standing apart from what was happening to him. Where had this second set of eyes come from? He felt himself floating, peering down from above. He saw old Grace lying dead behind him. The horse dead. The Indians dead. He could see himself scrunched as small as he could make himself. He saw it all. God, but didn't he look small. Didn't old Grace look small. Didn't they all look small. He wondered if maybe he weren't dead too, maybe a ghost, seeing as he could picture it all. He bit his tongue, fiercely, and the salty tang of blood in his mouth told him he wasn't no spectre yet.

They'd started yelling at him from the bush. Indian jabber. You could tell by their voices they were young ones. But a youngster had killed Grace. Youngsters might kill you dead as any buck, give them their chance. The musket clapped again and he ducked and grovelled as it dully smacked saddle leather.

He started to yell back. Every unholy thing he'd ever heard anyone give tongue to in a stable or grog shop. It came out of him like pus from a lanced boil. He yelled until he was hoarse, trying to out-yell the three of them. The blood of his bitten tongue kept welling in his mouth and he had to keep spitting it so as to be able to keep shouting back. The blood was of no account. Nothing was of no account.

Now they were singing the same song the other had in their cracked boys' voices, singing like very angels of death. He commenced to singing too. Roared "John Brown's Body" back at them. He knew when they had done their own song they would be ready to come for him; he was letting them know he would be ready to give them their fitting welcome. He ran through his song beginning to end twice before they give it up. Then he give it up too.

In a long minute of anxious silence, he heard somebody sobbing. Grace? He looked back. No. It wasn't coming out of Grace's throat but his own. He croaked at them to come. "Come on, you clappy whoresons! Come on!" he screamed.

They did. He didn't trust his aim with no short gun. Give it to them at spitting distance. Colt locked steady in both hands, forearms propped on the saddle-seat.

They flew for him, dogs for the throat. One red bastard tripped, picked himself up, gimped after the others, plucky but slow on a sprained ankle.

At five yards he put two shots into the lead runner. The second was on him as he was cocking the hammer the third time. There was only time to stab the Colt against the belly and jerk the trigger. It blew the Assiniboine back over the horse with the weight of the lead, the thrust of expanding gases.

The third one was still coming, hop-step, hop-step like a grasshopper, hunting lance poised in his hand. The Englishman's boy centred the bead on his breastbone, squeezed the trigger. The hammer fell with a click. He cocked and squeezed again. The hammer snapped hollowly. Breaking the revolver, he fumbled a bullet out of his belt. Dropped it. His eyes ran back and forth between the Indian closing on him and the bullet at his feet.

His eye caught the sabre-handle. He grabbed it and tugged. It came hissing out of the sheath just as the Indian thrust, driving the lance through the heavy tweed of his jacket below the armpit, popping open his coat in an explosive spray of buttons. The blade grazed his ribs, snagged in the back of his jacket, wrenched it off his shoulder. He snatched the shaft with his left hand just as the enemy tried to withdraw it, yanked it hard toward him, and lunged with the sabre.

They stood locked together, the Englishman's boy's fingers knotted on the lance-shaft, the Indian spitted on the sabre, his mouth gasping like a fish out of water. In the second before his face altered irrevocably and his legs melted in a slow collapse, the Englishman's boy recognized who it was: the saucy boy who had sat the horse by the creek that morning, counting the wolfers as they passed.

He began to sag on the blade, dragging it down with a great heaviness beyond the tug of gravity, the greatest weight the Englishman's boy had ever supported, a profound dream-like mass which slowly bent his arm like water bends the dowser's wand. The Englishman's boy was fighting it with all his strength, fighting to keep the dying Assiniboine on his feet every bit as hard as he had fought to defend his own life. Because he knew that when his arm finally bowed to the earth, it would bow to a grave.

∽

He'd seen some tough doings in his short life, but nothing to compare to this. When the Assiniboine had finally cut and run, the wolfers crept out of their hidey-hole, sniffed the air like cautious dogs before they commenced to scalping. It was like an egg hunt, Easter morn. They ran back and forth in the grass and bush searching for bodies, cutting and tearing off scalps with one almighty jerk of the arm, foot planted on the body. They whooped and pranced and shook the bloody hair they'd lifted. Vogle, laughing, plunked a scalp on top of his hat and started to sashay like a society lady in a new bonnet. Now and then the Englishman's boy heard shots when they located a wounded Assiniboine in the grass.

They lost some of their swagger when they went down into the Indians' ravine. It had a turn or two in it and maybe some hurt brave was lying around a corner with a musket, ready to take a white man to the Mystery World with him. They had totted up eighteen dead on the flat and found twelve more corpses in the coulee. The five young-sters dispatched in the fight at the hill brought the grand total to thirty-five.

When they came to lift the hair of the Englishman's boy's Indians he swore he'd shoot any man laid a hand on them. Nobody dared gainsay him, on account of the dreadful look in his eye. The boys who had fought in the War between the States had seen men who would go thankful and joyous after surviving some terrible battle while oth-ers went broody, black, and contrary. It didn't do to meddle with the black ones.

Neither did he accompany them when they rode to complete the destruction of the Assiniboine camp; he just sat in the grass alongside Grace, waving the flies off him with his hat. Grace was too big a man for him to lift onto a horse and carry back to the fort. He needed help for that, but Hardwick said they'd take care of that business when more pressing work was finished.

He watched the teepees catch fire and burn like tallow tapers, one by one. A black pall of smoke crawled sluggishly into the sky, show-ing a little yellow in it here and there, like a four-day-old bruise. After a bit, he heard a passel of shots. A little later, he spied Vogle capering about with something stuck on a long pole, maybe a lance. Some of the smoke came creeping his way, sickening whiffs smelling like spilled grease frying on a stovetop. That was Hardwick burning the Indian's store of pemmican. He had said he was going to follow army procedure, destroy their lodges and supplies, so they had no reason to come back.

After an hour, they all rode back in a laughing, lightsome mood for finding Little Soldier in his lodge too drunk to stir when the women had cleared the camp. There he had sat, a bottle of whisky in one hand and himself wrapped up in Old Glory, trusting in the Bluecoats' medicine flag to save him. The joke was they'd pumped a shot into him for every star of the Union. When they had finished emptying their weapons, Vogle had chopped his head off with a hatchet, stuck it on a pole, and marched him up and down through the burning village so he could get his eyes full of the consequences he had wrought by being unmannerly and by trifling with a white man's property.

On their way back to Farwell's, by accident they'd roused a girl of fourteen or fifteen from under one of the banks of Battle Creek. Likely she'd been fetching water when the fight started and ducked into hiding there. The Englishman's boy watched her stumble by, wrists bound in a rawhide rope lashed to the horn of Hardwick's saddle. "Looky at the young hen we caught," Hardwick sang out to him.

"What the hell you want with her?" the Englishman's boy had said in a bitter voice. He was grieved by Hardwick's not having lifted his hat to Grace's corpse, like he should have by all rights.

"Hostage," was all Hardwick offered, and kept on pulling her towards the fort while she fought like a calf being dragged to the branding.

28

I wait by the ruined windmill as he approaches. Wylie in his big
white new hat, riding a big white old horse, the low-slung sun
blazing behind him. The horse comes on at a tottery trot, flailing
the dust with his hooves, rolling onward like an overloaded ship in
breakers. Wylie reins him in, sits scowling down at me.

"Morning," I say.

"What you want?" Eyes sullen and heavy and hostile, a belliger-
ent tuck to each corner of the mouth.

"Shorty isn't in the bunkhouse. Do you know where he is? I'd like
to talk to him."

"Maybe he don't want to talk to you. Go away."

"Maybe he does. Maybe it's his decision."

The horse is a very old horse. His eyes are a blank, stony pink; the
nose bristles like a porcupine, thick with stiff white hair. The yellow
teeth grind the bit despairingly while a grass-green slobber bubbles
over the lips. The legs are scarred; the hooves cracked, broken,
spreading, pie-plates of horn.

"You leave Shorty alone. You made him enough trouble."

"Where'd the horse come from, Wylie?"

The question distracts him. He thinks before answering. "Shorty
ain't too restful lately. Many a times he leaves his bunk and goes to
night-walking – he won't let me go along. I says he's going to founder

in the dark and break a leg but he don't listen. Three mornings in a row he comes back and says he seen a horse a-wandering up and down the roads. It don't sound likely. I never seen no horse by day. Then, first light, one morning he comes along a-leading this here old horse. Somebody turned him loose, Shorty says. Don't want to pay his feed bill."

"I didn't come to make Shorty trouble," I say. "I just came to see how he is."

Wylie shifts in the saddle. The old horse stands like a statue. Wylie casts his eyes anxiously toward the horizon like a man seeking the exit of a burning theatre.

"Where is he, Wylie?"

"He got enough trouble without you," says Wylie. "Shorty boughten himself a new black suit. Every day he puts it on and goes to say his say. Alls he wants is a word. But they don't let him get close to that man. 'Move along,' they say. Shorty says, 'They making a pitcher on me. I got a right.' 'Yeah and I'm the Queen of Siam, look at my yeller tits,' they says and shoves him on. I put a poke in that feller's eye when he said that and now Shorty says I can't come along no more. Keep to home, he says. I'm a-keeping but it ain't proper what they doing to him. Old Shorty standing outside that gate in his boughten suit waiting for that man."

"Listen, Wylie," I say, "there's nobody for Shorty to see. They're away shooting the picture. On location. There's nothing he can do now. It's finished. You tell Shorty that. You tell him it's gone too far to stop. Whatever's going to happen is going to happen. There's no changing it now."

"He's sitting on the step of a morning, dogged out. I say, 'You got to go night-travelling, ride that horse, Shorty, hold to your strength for waiting by that gate.' But Shorty he won't ride this horse."

"Ask Shorty to take you to Canada. Tell him you want to go."

"You ain't getting rid of us that easy," says Wylie. His face is a hard white plaster splendour. "Somebody got to talk to him. He's Shorty McAdoo."

Farnum has stopped buying my scripts. He says I've lost my way, that it isn't up to him to support a sermon-writer. For weeks my savings have been going to pay my mother's bills at the Mount of Olives Rest Home. I have to stoop to taking work as an extra. It's a few dollars and the studios supply a boxed lunch. Then I get a job on a picture about the French Revolution that almost qualifies as acting. A revolution requires mobs of the convincingly crushed and downtrodden and my lameness makes me a natural for a *sans-culotte*. I am to make my film debut as the crippled beggar André. André has to beg alms from a sneering, effeminate aristocrat who thrusts him into a puddle with his gilded cane. Then comes my big moment, a close-up of my mucky face passing from bewilderment to injured pride, to homicidal rage. This, the director has confided, is a critical moment in the picture, the moment I become a *symbol*, the moment I become the embodiment of the French people awakening to the dream of *Liberté, Egalité, Fraternité*.

When I get out of bed at four o'clock the morning of my debut, I don't feel at all well. In costuming and make-up the feeling grows worse. The girl rubbing grime into my face remarks how hot I am. I am, and then again I'm not. One second my scanty beggar's rags are as stifling as a winter overcoat and the next I am shivering and my teeth are chattering. My legs ache. The scene is to be filmed at dawn, on a set with a cobbled street and a Parisian tavern. After standing for an hour waiting for props to deliver the aristocrat's coach my bones feel tender and bruised. A slow stain of misery seeps through me; something is putting brutal thumbs to the back of my eyeballs.

I get the call, the coach has arrived. I wade through harsh, raucous light which skids off the papier-mâché tiles of the tavern roof and into my aching eyes. The director booms at me through a megaphone, the coach lurches around the corner and brakes dramatically at the tavern door. When I hold out my hand and cry for alms, I can feel fingernails scraping my throat.

At a touch of the cane I topple. Acting is not required. However, I collapse on my back, not my face. Somebody drags me to my feet as the director barks for another take. The coach circles the set and rattles at me again, four horses, four madly spinning wheels. The tip of the cane thuds into my chest; I reel down into cold, glutinous muck. But I've forgotten my close-up. The director rages through his megaphone. Where is bewilderment? Where is wounded pride? *Where is the righteous rage of the dispossessed?*

We do it again. We do it four more times. And each time is a greater failure than the last.

Someone takes me back to costuming and strips the soaked and filthy rags from my body. Somebody else climbs into them and rushes out the door and into my part while I sit on a chair naked, shivering. People bustle in and out of the room, the noise makes my head hurt. At last, I order my legs to stand and begin to put on my street clothes. With one hand I steady myself against the wall while the other painfully fumbles with buttons. I don't try to tie my shoes, just shuffle out, laces dragging.

I board a streetcar. At first I hear people whispering all around me, even though the car is nearly empty, then I realize it is the hissing of the tramlines overhead. I've never been so tired in my life. I keep dozing off and waking, disoriented, whenever the streetcar bangs to a stop. The people boarding move in slow motion, sway sickeningly up the aisle. In my desperation to get home I have to stop myself from shouting, "Get a move on!" Watching them lurch unsteadily up the aisle, the hot California sunshine pressing against the glass of the windows, I am on the verge of puking at my feet.

So I close my eyes, struggling to hold the nausea at bay, and miss my stop. Walking the two blocks back to my apartment, everything seems bursting bright: the grass of the lawns a vitriolic, throbbing green, the violent blue of the sky shifting and tilting, making the earth do the same beneath my feet. I stop and vomit beside a fire hydrant. "Drunk," a passing woman says disgustedly.

The longest walk of my life and the stairs in my building the longest climb. I have to rest on each landing, clinging to the banister. My feet are leaden and awkward; they fumble and paw the stair-treads. The lock refuses my key; I have to brace my right hand with my left to insert it. The light swims giddily in my head, I have to draw the curtains in my apartment. But the darkness whirlpools, a vortex sprinkled with sparks makes a whooshing sound like a firehose. I sit on the sofa, clammy sweat soaking my shirt. Now and then I open my eyes and hold up my hands, not sure if they really belong to me, watch the madman tremble, the dim light between splayed fingers shaking in sympathetic agitation.

I sit like this for hours, my head flung back against the top of the sofa. Every time I try to move, I smell and taste my own vomit, the ceiling and floor slant or rear dizzily.

It isn't until I find my way to the kitchen that I recognize my thirst. Lowering my head to the gushing tap I gulp an icy flood until my insides turn cold, until the sweat on my skin shrinks back into my pores. Propped against the sink, water-logged and dazed, I stare at the clock on the wall. It says five o'clock – that isn't possible.

I tear off my clothes and burrow into my bed, weighted with water, weighted with an overwhelming need for sleep. Sunlight shimmers in a slit of the curtains like a candle flame. The flame slowly wanes and I sleep, burning.

I wake with a start. The sunlight no longer stands in the slit of the curtain, the candle has been snuffed. But light is coming from somewhere else; lifting my head I locate a crack of it under the bedroom door, drop back on the pillow. It feels late, the hushed, lonely silence of three o'clock in the morning. Can I have slept ten hours? I feel better, but not well. There's a nasty, scummy taste in my mouth, like I've licked an ashtray clean. The fever is still there, but nearly burned out, restless and fitful, a dying fire. When I move my legs over the sheets, searching for a patch of coolness, they feel strange, weak, the muscles as reliable as ropes of water.

No, I'm not well. Beyond the door I can hear the whispering of the streetcar again. A tramline running in my apartment? Lines overhead, suspended in darkness, rustling with a low insistent rumour. Whisper, whisper, whisper. Monotonous. Was that a word? I thought I heard a word. Now the trolley stops. To take someone on. Who?

Who? Somebody is out there.

"Rachel?"

A mocking voice, a man's voice. "Rachel?"

It's not sickness now, just my heart drumming. I pull myself up in bed. Night and a stranger in your house.

"Who is it?"

"Rachel?" the voice calls again.

"Be quiet," someone says.

Emphatic footsteps. I'm too weak to get out of bed. The door opens and I see two silhouettes cut out of black tin. One of them moves along the wall; I can hear him sweeping the wallpaper with his hand, a faint sandpapery sound. He finds the light switch, my hand flies up to my eyes, but even in that instant of blindness I know who the intruders are.

"Hello, Harry," says Chance.

The two are dressed identically in linen motoring coats which hang to mid-calf like the dusters cowboys wear. Like cowboys, both are burned brown as berries by sun and wind, a fine layer of dust powdering their features. Chance is thinner, his bones rise under the skin, stark in his face. Fitz is leaner too, stands with his arms folded across the front of his stained coat, reclining against the door frame.

"How did you get in?" My mouth is parched by fever; I have trouble forming the words.

"We knocked and got no answer," says Chance. "You ought to lock your door when you go to bed, Harry." He grins. "Not that that would have mattered. Fitz has a way with locks."

"What time is it?"

Chance glances at his watch. "Four o'clock."

Fitz laughs harshly.

"What the hell were you doing out there – in my apartment?" Suddenly I'm angry and suspicious.

Chance looks up at the ceiling, smiles to himself.

"Looking for papers," announces Fitz.

"Papers? What papers?"

"Now, Harry, don't bristle," Chance chides me. "It occurred to us you might have neglected to give us everything relating to the picture.

Research notes, drafts of the script, material we wouldn't want to see circulating, people putting their noses into. We wanted to make sure all the loose ends were tied up. Seeing to legalities, as it were."

"And what did you two detectives find? Nothing. Because I gave you everything, just like I said I did. And speaking of legalities, you happen to be housebreakers."

"Why don't you shut the fuck up," says Fitz.

"Yes, please shut up, Harry, and don't be difficult. I assure you that everything we disturbed is back in its place. Any letters of a clearly personal nature were not read. Besides, we had another reason for our visit. We bring news which is naturally of great interest to you."

"What news?"

"We've finished shooting the picture. Four months of hard work. Harry, you can't imagine the difficulties we had to overcome. And now Fitz and I have been driving day and night to rush film back for cutting. An arduous, exhausting journey. Some of those roads in Montana, Wyoming, and Utah are disgraceful, little better than cow trails. You'll understand if I sit?" He doesn't wait for permission but picks up a chair and places it at the side of my bed, sinks on it with a sigh. "There," he says, "much better."

The thought of Chance settling in panics me. "If you don't mind – I've been dreadfully sick all day – dead on my feet –"

"Do you hear that, Denis? Harry's been sick all day, dead on his feet. Now that he mentions it, I have to say he doesn't look himself. Wouldn't you agree?"

"Looks like shit, you ask me."

"I feel like shit. And you're not making me feel any better."

"I think you'll be very pleased with our picture." Chance eases himself back in the chair, crosses his legs under the spreading skirts of his motoring coat. "In particular, the performance of the young man who portrays Shorty McAdoo. He conveys magnificently Mr. McAdoo's visionary ruthlessness."

"Then he's conveying what isn't there. And so are you. Shorty McAdoo is just an unhappy, guilty old man."

"Yes, but he was young once, wasn't he? Come, come, Harry, no sour grapes. And no false morality either, please. False morality is what I found so disappointing in your letter of resignation. It wasn't that I needed you – I never *needed* you – but to find that the man to whom I had opened my heart and revealed what was at stake could attempt to wash his hands of his actions, that was most disappointing."

"I explained myself in the letter. I couldn't write the scenario because I was too inexperienced, too untalented –"

Chance reaches across the bed to lay an intimidating finger to my lips, stopping me. "There, there, Harry," he says coldly. "I'm not a fool. I know the sort of things that go through a young man's mind. You want to believe you obeyed your conscience. I find that sheer hypocrisy. Because all along you had no qualms about lying to McAdoo, misleading him. Why? I'll tell you why, Harry. Because you have a sick mother in an expensive asylum and I was paying you a lot of money to mislead him. But more important, I think, is that you are an intelligent young man who pulled himself up by his bootstraps, but only far enough to realize that to get any higher you would need help. I was the man who could give it. Isn't that so?"

I refuse to answer.

"I suppose you justified yourself by the argument of necessity. You had to do it. And I sympathize, Harry." He touches my arm in his best bedside manner. "Because I happen to believe that true morality consists in recognizing necessity and then summoning up the courage to act in accordance with it. Which you did – after a fashion. But where we seem to part ways is that I believe this morality is only truly honourable when we follow it to its logical conclusion, and let it be our guide in the large questions as well as the petty ones."

"Large questions? I don't know what you're talking about."

"Was it something I said about the Jews that got you up on your high horse, Harry? Fitz tells me you're romantically involved with a Jewess – Rachel Gold I think he said her name is. Now I have no objections to such alliances when they are purely physical ones. Surrender your body to a woman if you must, but remember to keep your independence and integrity intact. I suspect this woman has been a bad influence on you. The Jews are a sentimental and emotional people, Harry. We need only look at the pictures they make to confirm it. Which is why they are so dangerous. The morality of necessity – of survival – has no room for sentimentality. The Bolsheviks are not sentimental. The Fascists are not sentimental. The Americans who made this country were not sentimental. Far from it. Do you need proof? While I was researching our picture I made a point of reading the diaries and journals of early traders and settlers. One entry in particular made a great impression on me. It was simply two lines written on September 30, 1869. 'Dug potatoes this morning. Shot an Indian.' That was all. It was not accompanied by any tortured self-examination of conscience. Because the diarist knew his enemy would not have indulged in anything of the kind if he had killed *him*. The Indian, we might say, was a Bolshevik in a loincloth. Kill or be killed. They both understood compromise between them was impossible."

"Perhaps it was not up to the Indian to compromise. Ever consider that?"

"What would you advocate, Harry? Offering your throat to the knife because you might be wrong? History deals us our hand and we must play it. We do not choose our enemies. Circumstances choose them for us. I see the enemies who threaten my country. But I refuse to offer my throat to them." He tips forward in his chair, one hand resting on the bed. "I am not preaching anything new, Harry. I am only saying what Christ and Abraham Lincoln said before me, 'A house divided against itself cannot stand.' That is a fact."

"What are we talking about? Immigrants?"

"In part."

"Immigrants like Fitz. Paddies and bog-trotters."

"Fuck you," says Fitz from the doorway.

"Harry, you answer clear thinking with half-baked cleverness. Don't you believe Fitz is capable of writing, 'Dug potatoes this morning. Shot an Indian'?"

The shooting of the picture has obviously taken a toll on Chance; the once plump face has been brought to the brink of haggardness, and the eyes – the eyes are pleading with me.

"The house *must* stand. Lincoln fought a war to keep it standing, pitted blood brother against blood brother. And then Mr. Griffith made a picture, made *The Birth of a Nation*, and reconciled the blood of North and South in the chalice of art. Now it is necessary to go one step further. If Griffith wrote history in lightning, the time has now come to *rewrite* history in lightning. Yes, rewrite the history of the foreigner, erase completely those sentimental flowers of memory and light their minds with the glory of American lightning."

"You mean your lightning."

"Of course, my lightning. And yours too. That is the last thing I came to tell you. You are to have a writing credit for the picture."

"Fuck your writing credit. Keep my name off the picture."

Chance falls back in the chair. He smiles to himself, to the wall, to Fitz. "Harry," he says, "you can't deny your responsibility, pretend you had no hand in this. Even Judas played a part in Christ's teaching. Have you forgotten our conversations? I cannot emphasize enough how important they were to me. To speak to someone with the intelligence to understand what I was saying, someone who could grasp my ideas in a way that Fitz could not – that gave me the faith and heart to continue. And then the way you played McAdoo, discreetly, delicately, so he hardly realized the hook was in his mouth – well, Fitz couldn't have done it and neither could I. I have no doubt that I have you to thank for McAdoo." He pauses for a moment, head tilted back, weighing what he is about to say. "Earlier, when I said I had never needed you – I confess that perhaps that was not quite the whole truth. Honesty forces me to concede that. But when you said you didn't have the talent to write my scenario, you were right. I didn't know that you were right; I only felt betrayed. But your betrayal gave me the resolve to finish what you had started. Put another way: Could Christ have endured the cross without Judas' face hung in the sky before him? And yet I am able to forgive you your treachery, to acknowledge your help and your assistance." He looks directly at me, expecting thanks for his forgiveness. When it doesn't come, his bright blue eyes cloud with obscure emotion, or perhaps it is only a haze of fatigue. "You may wash your hands of me, Harry, but not your part in my picture. That is for the record." He gets to his feet. I sense his reluctance to leave, to finish with me despite his exhaustion. He does not want to let me go. But in the end all he has to say is, "I will see that you are provided with a ticket for premiere night. All of Hollywood will be there. I intend to see to that." He moves toward Fitz and the door.

"All of Hollywood but me!" I shout at his back. "I don't want your ticket!"

He stops, turns back toward the bed. One hand fumbles in the air, trying to summon the words. "But of course you want it," he says at last, mildly. "Because you will want to see what you have done."

Then the two of them are gone.

29

Outside it was full dark. They sat in Farwell's trading room in the wan radiance of a single kerosene lamp turned low and smoking on the counter, shadows towering on the log walls whenever one of them got up and helped himself to the bottle of red eye resting on a hogshead. Now and then a trickle of dirt sifted down and sprinkled the floor whenever Frenchie Devereux shifted position on the sod roof up above where he sat sentinel. Four more men were posted at each corner of the stockade.

Farwell sat perched on a sack of flour, doleful head in his hands. Hardwick had made it plain to him that tomorrow the wolfers were pulling out. Farwell knew if he elected to stay behind he would be killed by the Indians for his part in this day's doings. Moses Solomon was abandoning his post, too. His relations with the Assiniboine had never been good, and his position was every bit as precarious as his competitor's. Some white man was going to have to pay for the thirty-odd corpses the coyotes were picking over. The two traders planned to haul what goods they could back to Fort Benton in Red River carts, burn the posts and any remaining supplies to keep them out of the hands of the Indians. Hardwick's nasty temper had put paid to a winter's work.

The Englishman's boy sat on the floor beside the Eagle's body, which was shrouded in a buffalo robe lashed tight with rawhide thongs. Across the room, crazy Scotty was squeezed in a corner, peering terrified over the top of his writing book. The rest of the men diced on a blanket on the floor, sniggering like schoolboys at the sounds coming from the back room while Hardwick cracked wise. "Lord, listen to that old steam locomotive chug. Maybe you ought to go in there and throw a little coal in his boiler, Harper, so's he can finally get where he's going."

The Englishman's boy would get the invite next. He was considering on what his answer would be. When she was offered to Scotty and he shook his head no, Hardwick took offense. "Why the hell not?" he'd wanted to know.

The Scotchman had hugged his knees like they were his sainted mother, saying softly, "I am a gentleman. The definition of a gentleman is one who never causes pain."

"Don't you go high and mighty on me," said Hardwick.

"I am a gentleman," Scotty whispered back.

Hardwick slapped his face. "Get in there."

"I am a gentleman."

Each time he refused, Hardwick slapped his face again, repeating, "Get in there. Get in there." In the end he even latched onto his collar and dragged the Scotchman scuffling on his hands and knees halfway across the floor. Only when the Scotchman began to weep was Hardwick satisfied and, laughing, let him creep back to his corner, where he huddled himself up sobbing, meek as an orphan.

The Englishman's boy was of a mind to answer the same as the Scotchman, but then he weren't crazy. His twin, the old cold black anger, was sitting up in him touchy as a ripe boil. Hot and sore as the lance gash stiffening on his ribs. Maybe he daren't risk Hardwick prodding that boil with his dirty finger. Maybe he ought to take his walk to that back room, because if Hardwick laid a hand on him he wouldn't go Gentle Jesus like the Scotchman had. There'd been enough blood spilled today. He'd had his sup of it.

The train in the back room was building speed. He'd heard a winter of huffing, puffing racket like that in the whorehouse in Sioux City, Iowa. Late November, cold and starved, he'd knocked at its door because it was such a fine and promising big house. Might be the rich people biding there would let him chore for a hot meal. The woman who answered the door said, "What you want, Raggedy Andy?" He explained and she set him a job of work splitting stove-wood. That wintry morn the axe-handle bit his fingers like cold iron but he hung to it until he'd chopped her a goodly pile of butts and even shaved her a cache of kindling wood. Then she fed him buttered bread, creamed and sugared porridge. He'd swallowed three bowls of it.

That's how he came to work in a knocking shop. For a place to sleep by the kitchen stove and three squares, he chopped wood, hauled washing water for the whores, curried and harnessed Beaky Sal's driving team. Beaky Sal liked to tour around town in a cutter of an afternoon, to blow the smell of spunk out of her nostrils, she said. The only cash money the Englishman's boy had ever touched was tips. Some fancy man might send him to fetch cigars, or a crew of river rats a bucket of beer from the saloon. If he moved sprightly they'd toss him a penny. Once he even run for a bag of peppermints for an old broadcloth pillar of respectability afraid to go home to his wife's roast-pork supper with the smell of sin on his breath.

One thing he could testify, if whores had hearts of gold they was only gilt and flaked easy. Beaky Sal's girls was mostly German whores, and they fought day and night, screeching Dutchy talk until he believed there was a rusty file running to and fro in his ears. Their line of work made them too free and easy in their manners to his taste; some would lift their shifts and squat on the chamber pot when he was sweeping their room.

No, he hadn't found no gold there excepting Selena. Her daddy had sold her to Beaky Sal for twenty dollars when she was but a child of twelve and he was passing through Sioux City, bound for the Montana gold fields. He was a widow man and Selena only baggage slowing him in the race to fortune. He might have kept her, he said, but she was hard of hearing and that was a trial – at his age shouting wore him down.

Selena was skinny as a barked rail, but Beaky Sal figured if she fattened her she could charge the boys a premium for something young and fresh. But Selena didn't fill out and the boys preferred the fat, red, German whores because they would play-act jolly and the best Selena could manage was to look like an undertaker's wife. The boys said she made their peckers droop like wet wash hanging on a rainy day. So Beaky Sal turned her into a whorehouse drudge, boiling sheets and slopping chamber pots. All the whores seemed to think she was their own personal slavey; they'd squawk for this and that, pinch her and cuff her for any mistake she made, sometimes just out of pure cussedness. One afternoon, a Kentucky whore who called herself Beulah Belle started pulling Selena's hair in the kitchen because the washing water wasn't hot enough for her liking. When she was at it, he'd come in with an armful of stove-wood, dropped it in the box and kicked Beulah Belle square in the arse.

Word got around he could kick like a Missouri mule and so the whores let up on Selena some. He supposed that's why she went sweet on him. That and the candies and buttons. She was such a poor and winsome gal he couldn't but help feel sorry for her. Sometimes when he'd got a tip, he'd buy her a pennyworth of hard candy. He knew she had a sugar mouth. Beaky Sal was always slapping her silly for putting her fingers in the sugar bowl.

Selena weren't like him. Every bit of hardness he'd ever been handed, he'd put on the back shelf and stored. But hardness seemed to pass through her like light through a windowpane. She didn't hold a particle of the anger he held. Not a particle. She stored sugar like he stored hate, let the sweetness out bit by bit. Her mouth tasted sweet. She didn't favour you with a smile but seldom, but it was all the sweeter for it. Not one of them broad, false, whorey smiles, just a small and gentle and knowing one. She knew. By Christ, she knew.

He might yet be in that whorehouse if the Englishman Dawe hadn't hired him out of it. He'd been setting on the stoop sharpening Beaky Sal's butcher-knives when the Englishman pulled up in full daylight, arrayed in all his finery, bent on some fun with a sporting woman. He'd stopped at the step on his way in, picked up one of the knives, tested it on the ball of his thumb.

His daddy had said nobody could edge a knife like him. Once he'd whetted a blade you could split a curly hair with it, follow every kink and twist top to bottom. Dawe asked him if he could skin. Skin a grasshopper, he told the Englishman. The Englishman said he was going west to hunt the buffalo, bear and deer and goat, mountain lion and mountain sheep. He was going to carry them skins back with him to old England and for that he wanted a prime skinner and somebody to tote his guns. Gun-bearer he called it. They would have adventures, he said. The pay was ample.

So the Englishman's boy signed on with him. He promised Selena he'd be back for her, back with his pockets full of English gold. She'd have a new dress to sew her buttons on. She'd eat white bread and honey, drink lemonade. He'd carry her out of this place.

He took her for a walk so's he could shout it to her.

"When?" she said. "When?"

"Ever so soon as my pockets are full of English gold."

The way things had fallen out, he knew he weren't going to make it back.

John Duval came out of the back room, settling his suspenders. Hardwick hollered, "All goods satisfactory or money back!"

"I ain't complaining," said Duval, strutting to the whisky like a turkey cock.

"Well," said Hardwick, "age before beauty. Now it's the young-ster's turn. Nothing a youngster likes better than a pony ride." They all laughed. "Look at him over there, stiff as a hoe-handle." They all looked. The Englishman's boy got to his feet. They followed him with their eyes to the back room, watched him push aside the blan-ket, go in.

A guttering tallow candle threw the only light. The naked girl lay sprawled on her belly on a pallet on the floor, her face buried in the blankets. She didn't move, not even to lift her head to see who or what had walked into the room. The place was empty except for a stool kicked over on its side. The Englishman's boy picked it up and sat down on it.

The blue-black hair spread on her shoulders. The soft hollow of the small of her back, the curve of her buttocks had their effect on him. He wished she would make some effort to cover herself, but she lay like a dead one. She weren't though. He could see her rib cage rise and fall like the breast of a dove.

He sat for a short spell and then, so his voice wouldn't carry to the men outside, said softly, "I ain't intending you no hurt. I'll just stop quiet here a short piece." No sooner was it delivered than his explanation made him feel a fool, talking English to a squaw girl who couldn't understand. She didn't stir to his voice, lay like she was deaf as Selena.

He didn't know where to put his eyes, that slim coppery red body roused him something shameful. Glancing around the room, he located her clothes bundled in a corner. He stole carefully over, picked them up. Once they were in his hands he knew it was a mistake, because he dare not go near her to give them to her. He sat back down on the stool and untwisted the dress in his lap.

Five pretty buttons he'd bought Selena for her dress. Shell buttons shining rainbowy. Twisted them up in a scrap of paper found laying in the road, so's to give her the surprise of opening it.

He liked to give her presents. Her face lit like a lamp. She spread them buttons on the table, where the sun danced on them. Counted them into her hand. Closed that hand tight as a strongbox. Smiled and beckoned him.

He followed her up the stairs, three flights to a dusty attic. They stood face to face; he felt a purpose in it. She started to kiss him, lightly, a good many times. He didn't hold her; he didn't know how. Maybe she thought it his preference.

She shucked his pants. Smiling that smile, on her knees, just stroking him, passing her hand lingering and gentle over his buttocks, down the back of his legs, down his calves. Stroking him as he shivered, near swooned, as he tugged his shirt front down to hide from her what was happening to him.

"No, no," she whispered, caught his hand, getting to her feet. She stood and pulled her dress over her head. There was little light but he could see her, pale and thin, stooping to lay her buttons on her dress.

She moved back to him, kissed him, and he held her this time. Soon they was laying on the floor. The sun broke in a frosted window and she burst white in his eyes, white as snow except for the dark twigs of her nipples. He just kissed her; he didn't know what else to do.

She guided him into her. He lay there lost in the pleasure of the slick heat, stunned. He didn't ask for more, only to rest there, sucking her little teats. Something was passing between them in this melting, he felt as if his darkness was drawing light from her body.

She began to flex her hips under him and he hugged her. He could feel her trying to rise up into him, and he yearning to press down into her. He'd heard the rutting men with the whores, groaning as they pushed the need of their bodies into another body, forcing a black shameful exchange. But this was not the same. He was taking light.

A flush was creeping up her white shoulders, her neck, her cheeks. She arched suddenly and he held his breath, what he passed to her, passing in silence into the deaf girl's silent world.

He looked up now and saw the Indian girl had turned her face to him, saw a world silent and blind. Nothing was reflected in the dark, unseeing, empty eyes. When he spoke, her face, like Selena's, registered nothing. Nothing moved in that face except swollen lips, opening and closing, opening and closing.

The Englishman's boy rose from the stool, flung aside the blanket and went into the other room. Hardwick said, "You done your business? We thought you might need help with your buttons. It was silent as a tomb in there."

"I ain't a hog," he said.

"Who's ready for seconds?" said Hardwick. "I always like two pieces of pie myself."

"Scotty don't want his – I'll take it," said Bell.

"I wouldn't if I was you," said the Englishman's boy. Their faces lifted in surprise. It was the harshness of his voice and the wound stoking fever in his eyes, so that they glittered like isinglass in the tormented face. "Look at me." His urgency stilled the rattling dice. "Don't you recognize me?"

They all stared at him. Then Hardwick said quietly, "Who you supposed to be?"

"A curse." He pointed to the corpse on the floor. "Ask Grace. Ask my dead Englishman. Farmer Hank . . . Lord knows his fate." He pitched his voice to the corner of the room. "You know me, don't you, Scotchman? The Scotchman knows there ain't no bad luck blacker than the seed the Devil cursed." He turned to Bell. "Go on in there, lie with her, stir Satan's spunk, let it touch you. See what befalls."

Bell cleared his throat, sat back down on the floor.

"That's right," he said. "You don't want no portion of me. Who did you think I am? Nobody asked my name. I'll tell you who I am. I'm what the black belly of the whale couldn't abide. I'm your Jonah." He looked around the room. "Any of you wants to test what I say, go on in there and mix your seed with mine, see if it's a lie."

Nobody moved. He walked across the room, his shadow breaking on the walls, pushed open the door. The rush of cool air did nothing for his fever, nothing for his lust. He was fumbling with his pants buttons, burning. I ain't no different. I ain't no different. I wanted her every bit as bad as any of them. Quick and savage he used himself, fell back against the wall of the post, ending it like all the rest had, with a cry.

The Red River carts stood stacked with goods, waiting to pull south to Fort Benton. The mounted wolfers were bound northwest, up the Whoop-Up Trail, to pursue their stolen horses. The Englishman's boy had told Hardwick he would not go with him. He would push in the opposite direction, northeast.

"Good riddance," said Hardwick.

"I'm taking the horse," the Englishman's boy said.

Hardwick had only jerked the cinch on his saddle a little tighter.

"I earned it," the boy said.

Hardwick walked away from him.

Now there was only one thing left to do. They had buried Ed Grace under the floorboards of the fort and were going to burn it down over him. If they didn't, said Hardwick, the Assiniboine would find the body, maul and mutilate it so his own mother wouldn't know him.

They all sat their horses in expectation of the torching. Hardwick doused the floorboards with kerosene, came out and splashed the remainder of the can up and down the outside walls. Just as he struck a match, the Englishman's boy darted his eyes frantically over the assembly and shouted, "Where's the girl?"

Hardwick touched the match to the doorsill. There was a whoosh like a passing train and blue flame shot out around the sill, then sucked back into the mouth of the door like a fiery tongue. The Englishman's boy threw himself off his horse and ran to the post, snatched at Hardwick's arm, screaming, "Where's the girl?"

Hardwick yanked his arm free and walked to his horse.

He stumbled to a door framed like a picture in wreaths of fire, tried to drive through it, but the furnace-blast sent him reeling back. He tore his jacket off, held it up to shield his face, and threw himself blind at the doorway. For a moment, he teetered on the threshold, then staggered back whimpering, the tweed singed and smoking. Tossing aside the jacket he peered into the rippling air and curling smoke. She was crouched on the countertop like a cat in a flood, the floorboards beneath her awash in fire. Briefly, smoke glutted the doorway; he lost sight of her. He wiped his eyes. The door cleared. She was drawing herself up to spring, spring down into the flames. He aimed and fired the pistol empty. Reloaded mechanically and emptied it again into the billowing smoke, even though there was nothing to see.

Outside he ran in circles, yelling for Hardwick. The grass, the trees, the creek were his only company and they could not be killed. He sank to the ground and watched the post burn to nothing. When night came down he walked among the glow of the dying embers, boots smoking. Of Grace and the Indian girl he found nothing.

Hours later, he mounted his horse and three times circled the ruins of the post, dabbed here and there with sparks like the sky was dabbed with stars. A dumb, holy prayer for the two of them. Then he turned his horse northeast, like an Indian, to seek in the wilderness.

30

Two days after Chance and Fitz pay me their nocturnal visit I go to see Rachel Gold. It's been a long time since we have had any contact. I think she has phoned several times; the telephone rang so persistently, so doggedly, I concluded it had to be either her or Fitz, and I didn't want to speak to either of them. But now, cornered by my conscience, I ride a streetcar to her pink stucco apartment building with its Spanish courtyard. It's as if when my illness, my fever broke, something broke loose in me too, sending things floating to the surface, things I have to deal with.

My knock gets no answer, despite the fact I can hear somebody moving around inside. I bang the door, loudly.

"Pedlar begone!" she shouts imperiously.

"It's me, Rachel. Harry. Open up."

The sound of rapid, thudding footsteps and the door is flung open. She's wearing a Chinese-looking robe, red dragons on a black satin ground. She is barefoot and the famous black hair is alive. So is her face, registering shock at my appearance.

"God, Harry, where've you been? Why haven't I heard from you? What's happened? You look like hell."

"I've been sick," I say curtly, inviting myself in, walking past her.

She trails concern after me into the living room. "You look like you could use something to eat. I'll make you something to eat."

"No, I don't want anything to eat." I sag down into an armchair. I'm nervous because of what I've come to say; my eyes drift around the apartment, avoiding hers, the anxiety in her face. "This won't take long. I have something to tell you. And a favour to ask."

"Shoot," she says. I hear her settling on the sofa across from me. I'm reluctant to start; a strained, expectant silence forms.

"Harry, look at me."

I do.

"What's the matter?"

I begin, "Remember that day on the beach? When you told me I had to decide? Well, I've decided."

"What have you decided, Harry?"

"I acted on impulse that day and I made a fool of myself. I'm sorry, but I'm acting on impulse again. There's something that's been eating at me. Something I didn't tell you. About Chance."

She shoots me a penetrating look. "What didn't you tell me about Chance?"

I want to make this clear. "I'm not taking revenge on him," I continue awkwardly, "and the last thing I want to do is hurt you, but I think you have a right to know."

"Forget the pussyfooting. Out with it."

"Remember what you said about Fitz in the Cocoanut Grove – that he was an anti-Semite?" I hesitate. "Well, so is Chance. In earnest. I've heard him say things."

Rachel stiffens visibly, someone prepared for a slap in the face. She knows what is coming. "What kind of things?" she demands, voice brittle.

"Don't ask me to spell it out. Take it from me. You don't want to hear."

Rachel draws the robe a little tighter around her shoulders. "A drink might help take the bad taste out of my mouth," she says disgustedly. "Unfortunately for me, I quit drinking." Her lips twist slightly, struggling to summon up an ironic smile. "But looking on the lighter side, maybe this cloud has a silver lining. When I hand the son of a bitch my resignation, I'll be free to write that novel I've been threatening the public with for as long as you've known me."

"Sure."

"But I won't," she says quietly, more to herself than me.

I don't contradict her. We both know she's right on that score. Rachel says nothing else, sits absolutely still and quiet.

"I'm sorry," I say.

She glances up at me. "That's the second time you've said sorry this afternoon, Harry. Don't be a parrot." She moves now, abruptly, leans over and plucks a cigarette from a lacquer box on the coffee table, lights it with a flick of a match. Rachel back to business, the decisive close to a distasteful subject. Chance dismissed like a fly. "You mentioned a favour," she says, shaking out the match, tossing it into an ashtray. "What is it?"

"I want you to visit my mother."

Her eyes lift quizzically. "Of course. When would you like to go?"

"Not the both of us. Just you."

She scrutinizes me closely. "Now what the hell is all this about?"

It seems lately there are no clear explanations. The best I can offer is, "I can't face her right now." I lay my hands on my kneecaps and watch them shake there uncontrollably.

"You're a *mensch*, Harry. A *mensch* doesn't abandon his mother," she says sternly.

That word, whenever she used to apply it to me, would make me angry and envious. I would have preferred to be one of her gigolos. Now it fills me with despair. The debris of a lot of mistakes has floated to the surface in the past couple of days. It seems I have a long history of betrayals. "I let her down once before, Rachel," I whisper without lifting my eyes. "You know what she asked me just before I left to come down here? To buy her a new dress so I could pick her out from all the rest of those drab women on the ward the next time I visited. She sensed I was running out on her. Knew it."

"Or you think she did."

"I'm afraid I'm going to let her down again. My money's going fast. What if she ends up in one of those goddamn state-run asylums?"

"Stop this, Harry," she says.

"But don't you see?" I look up, plead with her to understand. "I can't let that happen."

"I told you before," she says impatiently, "if you need money, I'll lend it to you. Take my word on it."

"She's my mother. My responsibility. I'm going to do my best to take care of her. But I just can't face her now."

Rachel isn't about to relent. "Go and see her, Harry."

"Believe me, she'd rather see you." I'm begging, desperate. "You said I was abandoning her. I'm not abandoning her, I'm just asking for a reprieve, a little time to get things straight in my mind. Is that so much to ask? Look at me, for Christ's sake! Do you think she should see me looking like this?" I hold up my trembling hands as testimony.

She studies my face, my hands. They are the only arguments which have any effect. "Sure I'll go visit your mother," she says at last, gently. "But what about you? When will I see you again?"

I've made my mind up about that, too. No more lingering hopefully for love. It's time to try to get Rachel Gold out of my system. "I don't know. Sometime" is the only answer I can manage.

"Come on, Harry. What are you up to?"

I get to my feet. "Don't you get it, Rachel? I'm ashamed. About my mother. About you. I can't forget Chance once accused you of being an influence on me. He meant a bad influence. What I didn't say is that if you were an influence – it was only for the good."

"Harry, there's no reason for this."

"Listen to me, Rachel. I'm not fit for human company just now. Grant me a little time. Okay?" That said, I start to leave the room.

"Harry," she shouts after me, "this is nuts!"

I pause, momentarily, to look back at her on the sofa. "Give me this one last thing, Rachel. Please. Don't try to find me."

Then I go.

To save some money I sell whatever I can of my household goods and move into a rooming house whose only other boarder is a cadaverous-looking retired Lutheran minister from Minnesota. For the next few months I continue to look for work, but aside from jobs as an extra, everywhere I meet with failure. Evenings, I sit in my landlady's verandah, depressed, worried, fatalistic, waiting for something to happen; what, I'm not sure. Something. In another economy move I've dropped my subscriptions to the movie magazines, but the Lutheran minister's daily newspaper is full of tittle-tattle about the approaching premiere of Chance's epic Western. The chat columns retail gossip, there are full-page ads for the picture, and Chance has obviously forsaken his role as the Hermit of Hollywood. Now interviews with him multiply alarmingly. His mild professorial face greets me at the breakfast table, staring out from the morning edition. A buzz is building around the picture and show-biz reporters, after the success of Cruze's *The Covered Wagon* and rumours about Chance's picture, stoke it with headlines announcing the rebirth of the Western.

Then one afternoon Chance's Hispano-Suiza pulls to the curb outside and a chauffeur in livery comes briskly up the walk with an envelope in his gloved hand. Chance has tracked me down. The envelope contains two passes to the premiere of the Best Chance production of *Besieged*. There is also a note which explains something else the envelope holds, a cheque for five hundred dollars.

Dear Harry,

Enclosed are two tickets to the premiere of our film; bring your inamorata if you wish. I'm sure you have been informed she has left my employ and is now at Metro, but I bear no grudges. I hope you will be able to say the same and lay aside personal prejudices, and judge for yourself whether or not *Besieged* crystallizes the idealistic hopes for American film which we shared in our first conversations. Please come, I would like to hear that you approve of what has been accomplished. Oddly enough, your good opinion remains important to me.

You and I share credit for the scenario. Mr. Fitzsimmons

tried to dissuade me from this step, but upon reflection I knew I could not deny what you have meant to this picture; it is only right to acknowledge your contribution.

Which leads to the delicate question of money. You will find enclosed a cheque for five hundred dollars. I believe this sum is a fair settling of my account with you, if not yours with me. I am sure you are currently encountering financial difficulties, so please note that the cheque is drawn on company finances and not on my personal account. This, I trust, will dispel any notion you might have that this could be regarded as an act of charity. It is, rather, the closing of the books on a debt.

Yours sincerely,

Damon Ira Chance

The premiere is one week off. I put the tickets and the cheque in my night-table drawer, determined to make use of neither. But as the date draws near I find myself wavering; one minute I am rock-solid in my determination never to give Chance the satisfaction of seeing me at his premiere, and the next this determination dissolves like salt in water. One part of me needs to see what Chance has done, another dreads it.

I don't know what is happening to me. One evening, sitting in the sun-porch watching darkness descend, I have the thought that the darkness sifting down into that empty street is like the darkness filling my own emptiness. I cover my face with my hands and cry. And that is how my landlady finds me, as Shorty McAdoo's landlady Mother Reardon found him, in the darkness, his face wet with tears. And like him, I try to deny them.

∿

Tuxedoed, I make my way to Grauman's Egyptian Theatre, two blocks up the street. Searchlights are visible against the blue-black wall of night sky, golden sabres slashing and wheeling, crossing and clashing, bright blades of gleaming light. People overtake me on the sidewalk. Skipping insect-like toward this mesmerizing display, the women utter chirps of excitement as they brush impatiently by me – "Oh!" "Look, Herb!" Little jolts of delighted anticipation set their hips to switching, rattle their heels on the sidewalk; they jerk with impatience. Despite trying to lock down their enthusiasm, the men are the same. Their excitement is proclaimed in the rigid set of their shoulders and faces, a pose of nonchalance. A young man in a straw boater trots by me, pretending to scan the thickening crowd for a friend, and, like horses in a paddock, others infected by his example start trotting too.

Suddenly he stops, his eye caught by a long, luscious limousine crawling up the street. All the rest of the trotters halt too, halt and edge toward the curb for a better look. One looses a low, appreciative whistle and his bird-like call is copied – they all trill their homage as their polished black dream glides by. Then the young man in the boater lifts his head – he's spied another car – and all the other heads turn too, staring up the street, songbirds transformed into birds of prey.

The throng begins to clot, coagulate, as the Pierce Arrows, Stevens-Duryeas, Rollses, Renaults, and Mercedes pour out of the side streets in a parade of luxurious rolling stock running on golden rails laid down on the asphalt by headlight beams. Clusters of star-gazers crane necks for a peek into windows, into back seats. Reports of sightings fly about, fickle breezes which blow heads in this direction and that. "Is that Buster?" "Is that Doug and Mary?" They strain to see, ripple, bend as one, bow down over the curb like tall grass in a gust of wind.

I keep walking, moving as fast as the traffic jamming the roadway, touching shoulder after shoulder to beg passage, beckoned by Grauman's marquee, hundreds of electric bulbs pulsing out a single word, *Besieged, Besieged, Besieged, Besieged, Besieged* . . .

Opposite the theatre, onlookers are packed deep on the narrow sidewalk, bobbing up and down on tiptoes, heads tossing like turbulent waves. Blue-jacketed cops patrol a rope strung mid-thigh at the edge of the pavement, good-humouredly keeping the crowd behind it with fatherly nods and gentle taps of the nightstick, friendly reminders not to trespass on the street.

Young couples with infants tucked in their arms; old couples gripping purses and canes, fragile in shiny black clothes and high-topped shoes and boots, red noses sharp, red eyes sharper; men wearing hand-painted ties and others in work shirts and cloth caps; fast-looking, painted girls and respectable young females whose scrubbed cheeks exude rosy virtue: one happy congregation. With this mingling of humanity comes a mingling of scent, bay rum and tobacco, camphor and peppermints, lilac water and stale sweat, chewing gum and dirty diapers.

Chance's publicity campaign has worked. Despite being no house-hold name, no DeMille, no Griffith, despite having no actors in this picture who are stars of any magnitude, the ordinary people, the giants of the industry, have come.

A great stir of shuddering excitement. The crowd groans, "Charlie! Charlie! Charlie!", a moan of sexual pleasure. Above the roof of the car, a mop of curly black hair, two black eyebrows, and a chunk of black moustache drawn on the alabaster face of a corpse by a cartoonist pops up to stare back across the street at us. It ducks back down to assist a young lady from the vehicle. The young lady is Leonore Ulric. The dapper little man graciously escorts Leonore Ulric out from behind the vehicle to greet us; they wave to us across a river of asphalt, Chaplin grinning impishly. Mad cheering as he wheels Miss Ulric in a military about-face on to the long red carpet running from curb to picture palace, snapping a sergeant-major's salute to the bank of photographers. "This is too good!" "Catch this one!" The camera bulbs pop and blink like muzzle-flashes of distant artillery on a night horizon.

If Chaplin is here, the evening is already a success. But the magnificent automobiles keep disgorging celebrities on the crimson carpet; they wave to fans, blow kisses, strike preposterous poses for photographers. Harold Lloyd and Buster Keaton, Pola Negri and Will Rogers, Douglas Fairbanks and Mary Pickford are all here. With each new arrival frenzy mounts, the mob calls names like they were the names of children lost in a forest; they skitter forward like iron filings answering the pull of powerful magnets. The press of people behind me drives me hard against the rope, it saws at my thighs; there's an elbow in my back, a cane tangled between my legs. The smell of desperation pollutes the air. I start to scramble over the barrier before I get dumped over it on to my face.

A cop catches me straddling the rope. "What you doing, Bub?"

"I've got to get over to the theatre," I tell him.

"Sure you do," the cop says.

"I've got tickets." I stick them under his nose.

At the mention of tickets, a resentful look slides on to his flat face. "You can't cross the road," he says. "We got traffic control here."

"Look," I say, "I've got a bad leg. It can't take much more of this pushing and shoving."

"If you got a bad leg, take it home. Take it home or stay where you are."

I'm prepared to argue when I spot the Hispano-Suiza gliding up in front of Grauman's. I nod to the cop, a tacit promise to stay put. He clamps his jaw with authority, takes a couple paces down the rope, glances over his shoulder to make sure I'm not up to any funny business behind his back.

Chance and Fitz get out of the car. They are wearing tails and silk top hats. The enthusiasm of the crowd dips, they don't recognize these two. The expensive car, the beautiful young girl in the evening dress sweeping forward with a bouquet to present to Chance announce these men are important – but why? Chance accepts the bouquet with a stiff little bow, passes it to Fitz who grapples it clumsily to his chest.

Slowly Chance turns to face us, slowly his hand rises in a hieratic gesture to the marquee. He points and we cease even to murmur, watch in enthralled silence, struggling to decipher this obscure gesture. Now he is shaking his finger at the sign, emphatically, schoolteacher waiting for the answer.

A single voice rises in a shout from the back of the crowd. "Besieged!" Radiant pleasure, pride, happiness flood Chance's features.

He straightens, grows taller. Yes, his body is saying, yes, yes, yes. The finger prods once more, jabbing a smattering of high, thin, involuntary-sounding cries out of the mob. Behind me a hoarse voice, roughened by a foreign accent, joins in, to my left I hear a child's, a woman's. Now Chance's finger is marking time, more voices add to the deep, swelling chorus of, "Besieged! Besieged! Besieged!" People shout it recklessly, happily, making a noise like the noise of empty barrels rolled in an empty street. "Besieged! Besieged!"

Chance raises his hands above his head, clasps them in a prize-fighter's gesture of victory, shakes them at the mob. The mindless roar is physical, a hot wave of breath on my back. I twist around and con-front a wall of faces; a painted midway canvas of freaks, a nickel's worth of depravity, the mouths yawning cavernous and hungry, the eyes blazing.

But now the mad clamouring sputters, fades out, disintegrating into lonesome cries, desultory handclapping. I look back and Chance is strolling up the carpet into a barrage of winking flashbulbs, Fitz walking carefully in the rear, the tall hat balanced on his head, the flowers bundled in a big fist.

Around me everyone subsides into disappointment. It's over now. A sort of post-coital *tristesse* settles on us, a listless shame. We avoid each other's eyes, shrink from touching one another; the knot which briefly held us together is unravelling, people are drifting away like scraps of paper blowing in an aimless wind. Across the street, uni-formed flunkies are closing the main doors of Grauman's Egyptian Theatre, the temple is being secured. It is too late for the picture. I will miss *Besieged*.

For three hours I sit in a café drinking coffee, keep trying to imag-ine what the audience is being treated to up on the big screen four blocks away. Every fifteen minutes I check my watch and light another cigarette. People stare at me because of the tuxedo. At eleven I pay the bill and go out into the night. A fitful wind has sprung up, a wind that seems to nudge me in the direction of Grauman's. Although it feels like rain, I don't turn for home. Instead

I button my jacket, stuff my hands in my pockets, and permit myself to be shoved along by the wind at my back. The self-congratulatory speeches will have ended long ago, the last reel will be playing itself out, soon the theatre will empty. It's a short walk but feels endless. The avenue is deserted and still, the streetlight poles stark, the ponds of light at their feet bright, shallow, sterile. My left shoe rasps on the concrete, hoarsely, monotonously. I drag it past a line-up of parked automobiles, chauffeurs killing time as they wait for the picture to finish. The police have left, the rope barrier is down, but a few stubborn souls still huddle in the wind, waiting. Tramping up the theatre side of the street, I am treated to a star's-eye view of the fans. From this perspective and distance they look small and pitiable, like children somebody has forgotten to collect after a birthday party.

I stop and light a cigarette under the marquee. None of the officious staff raising the green-and-white awning against the possibility of rain tell me to move on. It is the tuxedo. They assume I am waiting for a friend.

All at once there's an excited rushing about of Grauman employees, the doors are opening, the picture is over. The first of the audience spilling out talk animatedly, always a good sign for a picture, while others linger in the lobby, an even more auspicious sign. Out in the fresh air women draw their furs tightly around their shoulders, the men light cigars and impatiently scan the street for drivers and automobiles. One of Grauman's young men beckons imperiously to the line-up, headlights snap on, the cars move forward like dominoes tipping in a chain reaction. The remnant of fans wave autograph books in the air and cry out beseechingly from across the road.

Here a tuxedo can loiter, smoke a cigarette, cast eyes up to the sky for portents of rain. Betty Blythe, star of the *Queen of Sheba*, passes close enough for me to touch, and so do Bessie Love and Colleen Moore. Others troop by, gentlemen and ladies I don't recognize, L.A. businessmen, lawyers, doctors, their wives. People with enough social standing, enough money, to be granted the boon of buying a ticket to a premiere, to be granted the pleasure of rubbing shoulders with Charlie Chaplin, people who fifteen years ago would have dismissed picture people as vulgarians.

I hear bits and snatches of conversation popping up like bright birds in a bush. "Superb!" says someone. "All it needed for perfection was a true star!" is the opinion of another. "Where is he? Where's Chance?"

I spot Fitz, a head taller than anyone else, doing a chain-gang shuffle through the bottleneck of congestion in the lobby doors. Where Fitzsimmons is, Chance will be too.

I'm correct. Once under the awning Chance holds court, greeting admirers. Actors behave like they do before a camera, pantomiming their awe, their delight, their amazement. When actresses seize Chance's arm and cuddle against his shoulder, or raise themselves on tiptoe to plant a kiss on his cheek for photographers, he receives their attentions with awkward, old-fashioned, gentlemanly courtliness.

Chance is happy. He shines with it, happiness suffuses him. Nodding and smiling, he shakes hands, accepts pats of congratulation on the shoulder. Men offer him cigars. I read his lips. Over and over he is saying, Yes, yes, yes.

Now Fitz is guiding him away, escorting him down the carpet. For an instant Fitz's and my eyes lock, and he deftly steers Chance a little to the right to avoid us meeting. They go past. A determined well-wisher importunes them, expressing admiration for the picture. Chance begins nodding again.

It starts to rain lightly, just hard enough to flicker in the light of streetlamps and headlights, sparse and granular, like a shower of rice at a wedding. Across the street, the little covey of devotees, neglected, is breaking up. Someone opens a newspaper over her head. Someone is crossing the road. Someone else is following him.

The first jaywalker moves like a somnambulist, looks neither right nor left, steps into the path of an oncoming car. The pavement is slick with rain, a horn blares, the car brakes, slides to a stop inches from the man's legs. Under the awning people break off conversations to stare curiously. In the glare of the headlights the man stares back, searching the faces.

Shorty in a black suit and white shirt, collar buttoned tightly. His face lit from beneath by the car headlights, the planes of his face like snow, his eyes black and sunken. He looks old, a walking corpse. He steps up on the bumper of the car and surveys the crowd under the green-and-white awning. "Chance!" he shouts. A woman laughs in surprise, as if this were a joke.

Shorty steps down from the bumper, advances. Wylie follows, eyes switching nervously back and forth. The light of the marquee falls full upon McAdoo, carrying himself like an old soldier, wearing his black suit like a uniform. He passes everybody as if they were nothing more than fur coats and evening dress hung on a clothesline for airing. People step aside, make way for him. He looks strange under the electric light; his tan is gone and his face burns with a hospital pallor. Sick, you would think, if the firm, steady tread, the young man's stride which bears the old face onward, didn't belie it.

Reaching Chance and Fitz he says loudly, "I'd like a word."

Chance stands with a sceptical smile on his lips, his head turned ever so slightly to one side, his eyes fastened on the belly of the awning. "If this is business," he says without looking at McAdoo, "you must make an appointment to see me. I do not conduct business on social occasions."

Wylie shifts his feet on the carpet. McAdoo's mouth tightens. "I come to ask you to write to the newspapers and tell them that feller in your picture ain't me."

Chance is still smiling, still refusing to look McAdoo in the face. He watches the awning flutter with gusts of wind and rain. "Of course it isn't you," he says. "Mr. McAdoo is dead."

"Liar!" bursts out Wylie. He rounds on the gaping bystanders. "Don't you believe him! This here's Shorty McAdoo! I know him! Know him good as anything!"

"You're mistaken," Chance says. "Shorty McAdoo is dead and this man is an impostor." For the first time he looks directly at Shorty. "Stand aside," he says coolly, "let me pass."

"Every day he waits at that gate for a word and you drive on by! He ain't waiting no more!" Wylie screeches.

McAdoo grabs Wylie's arm, pulling him up short. "You listen to me," he says with urgency. "Take hold of yourself. I told you. This ain't got nothing to do with you. I come for my say. That's all – a say. I can do my own talking without help from you. Go home."

"Once more," says Chance. "Stand aside."

McAdoo shakes his head. "You've had one walk over me. You ain't going to get two. Not until I'm finished."

Chance gives Fitz a sign and he slips between them. McAdoo runs his eyes up and down him. "So you're the big dog."

"That's right."

"Cock your leg and piss on somebody else," says McAdoo and moves to step around him. As he does, Fitz grabs him by the lapels of the black suit, jerking him off his feet, shaking him, snapping the old white head back and forth in a blur. McAdoo kicks at him, battering the Irishman's shins, boots thudding against fenceposts. That's it. Flying head, flying feet, everything a blur.

Something cracks, hard and sharp like fracturing bone, and Fitz sways with the old man slumped unconscious in his fists. A woman screams, a long aria of terror. A thought lurches in my mind. He's snapped the old man's neck, like a dry brittle stick broken over a knee. But then Fitz's eyes roll upward, trying to locate the source of his own death, the neat black hole drilled square in the middle of his forehead. He falls, a big tree axed, crashes to the carpet, dragging McAdoo down with him.

Wylie is walking forward jerkily, his arm held stiff and straight at shoulder height, my pistol on the end of it, pointed at Chance. I hear people running, feet pounding, there are more screams, shouts for the police, but they reach me from a far way off, a place divorced from this moment. A fine mist of smoke hovers under the awning; the thick oily smell of a discharged weapon startles my nostrils.

Chance stands, a prisoner in the dock awaiting judgement, his lips moving. What looks like prayer is really only Chance repeating, over and over, "Fitz, Fitz, Fitz, Fitz . . ."

"Wylie!" I scream, the name tearing my throat. Recognizing the voice, his face veers to me, the movement tortured. "Christ, Wylie, let him go," I beg. "Don't do it. Don't."

Pronouncing the last *don't*, I understand Wylie is looking at me with cold hatred, that my own death is being debated in his slow, clumsy mind at this instant.

The wailing of a police siren saves me. Wylie swings his head to the sound, swings back to Chance, decision written on his face. "You-you-you ought to talked to him," he says, stumbling over the words. "If you'd just only talked to him. We would been in Canada now. We would been in Canada . . . happy."

Chance's face wears the blank look it wore months ago at supper as he tore the bread, eating like an animal. When Wylie's pistol rises up so do Chance's arms, not in surrender, but in an extravagant gesture of welcome.

The bullet buckles him as if two strong hands from behind had ripped down hard on his shoulders. His legs give way, sinking him to his knees, a flower of blood spreading vivid petals on his starched shirt front. Wylie takes two steps forward, shoves the gun against his chest and fires, the flash scorching Chance's linen.

By the time I reach Chance, Wylie has dropped the gun and is gazing at the rain as it drums down harder and harder, draping a silver blanket on either side of the awning, enclosing the four of us in a lonely tent. I hear its wild thrashing on the canvas roof and, underneath that, the keening of police sirens.

As I prop Chance's head in my arms he snatches me by the nape of my neck, pulling my face within inches of his with a brutal, frantic strength.

"Harry?" he whispers.

I struggle to pull my face away from the dire mask confronting me, but the grip is unbreakable.

"Harry," he gasps, "when we talked . . . you see . . . I could not bring myself to tell you everything."

"What? What couldn't you tell me?"

"The consequences of the truth." His breath rasps short and quick in my face. "Artists . . . visionaries . . . they always find a way to kill us, Harry. Always."

"Who?" I shout down at him. "Who are *they*?"

He is beyond speech. He makes a gesture to the wall of rain, to whomever, whatever, he imagines lurks behind it. The canvas rips, shreds in the wind with a wrenching, desolate sound as I watch his eyes darken, as he struggles for his last breath, as the open pit of his mouth slowly fills with blood, as the frothy pink liquid spills down my arm, marking me.

3 1

I end with a list of names as I began.

Shorty McAdoo, unconscious, was taken by ambulance to hospital. Six hours later, he slipped off the ward and disappeared. I never saw him again. Shorty on the run, just as he had been as a boy. Making for the Medicine Line. I like to believe he crossed it one last time.

Wylie hanged himself in jail. They buried him in the potter's field Shorty and he had saved his brother from.

Two weeks after the premiere I said goodbye to Rachel at the train station. She had come to see my mother and me off to Saskatoon, our fares paid with the five-hundred-dollar cheque Chance had written me as a settling of accounts. A Santa Ana was blowing, the hot wind whipping her electric black hair around her head. The locomotive stood impatiently panting steam while she kissed my mother farewell. When we shook hands she said, "Reconsider, Harry. I can get you a job at Metro. I've got pull there."

Grit and cinders were flying in the wind. I knew I was done with Hollywood. I shook my head.

"Maybe it's best," she said, tugging down the hem of her skirt against the Santa Ana's ferocity. "Maybe this isn't the place for you."

And she was right. Like Shorty McAdoo, I didn't belong there.

The conductor was calling us aboard. As we stepped up into the railway car she cried out, "Don't be a stranger, Harry! Write me!"

Pressed against the window, my mother and I didn't take our eyes from Rachel until the train left her behind, waving.

I never did write to Rachel Gold. A couple of months after I'd settled back in Saskatoon, I landed a job managing a movie theatre. I've been there almost thirty years. Funny, isn't it? Harry Vincent still in the picture business. In 1925 I put a down payment on a little house overlooking the river which runs through the city. My mother lived with me in this house for ten years, until she died in February of 1935.

I never married. It isn't that I've been carrying a torch all these years. I remember being a rookie at the studio, Rachel laughing and showing me a picture of herself in an old central-casting book. It was from the days when she was a bit actress, before she became a scriptwriter. The photograph was of a very young woman, but it was still Rachel. She had a knowing look in her eye.

Later, I pinched the book, took it home, and cut her picture out of it. I discovered it in my wallet a couple of years after I moved back to Saskatoon. Pictures on cheap paper don't wear well. I could hardly make out her face. During one of my walks by the river I dropped it into the water. I have no more idea where Rachel Gold ended up than I do where that photograph did. Both moved out of view.

I accept that. Living beside the river has taught me something about change. Paved white with snow and ice in winter, slack and brown in summer, the river is never the same. As a boy, I had rushed down to it only in its moments of crisis, when it ripped apart and roared, shattered while I stood on the bank, shaking with excitement. The apocalypse has its attractions.

Chance was greedy for the apocalypse. More, he wanted to have a hand in creating it. For thirty years I've stood at the back of my theatre watching men like him in the newsreels. Hitler ranting like some demented Charlie Chaplin; Mussolini posturing on a balcony like some vain, second-rate Latin screen star. Now Senator Joe McCarthy bullies his way through his hearings, the gods and goddesses of Hollywood facing a different kind of public judgement than the box office, frightened, cringing before the cameras they love so dearly.

I can offer no judgement of Chance's picture *Besieged* because I never saw it. Not many people did. It got pushed into oblivion; Chance's murder became bigger than the picture itself. As so often happens in Hollywood, scandal became the story, obscuring everything else. The man who wanted to be another D.W. Griffith, a visionary filmmaker, is remembered today only as the man who got killed at a premiere. A small footnote.

Shorty's story fared no better in the history books I consulted when I got back home to Canada. Searching them, I found a sentence here, a paragraph there. What I learned was little enough. For a brief time the Cypress Hills Massacre had its day in the sun; members of Parliament rose in the House, hotly denouncing the wolfers as American cutthroats, thieves, and renegades. Nobody seemed to mention that among them were Canadian cutthroats too.

Those few paragraphs always pointed to one result of the massacre. The Canadian government formed the North West Mounted Police, sent it on a long, red-jacketed march into a vast territory, establishing claim to it. A mythic act of possession.

Chance believed character didn't count for much in history. But, looking at the river, I remind myself the map of the river is not the river itself. That hidden in it are deep, mysterious, submerged, and unpredictable currents. The characters of all those wolfers, Canadian and American, cast longer shadows than I had any inkling of that endless night in which McAdoo made his confession, crouched on a cot in a desolate bunkhouse, an old man reliving his pain and guilt thousands of miles from an obscure dot on the Saskatchewan prairie.

Each night I stand at the back of my theatre, watch spectres and phantoms slide across the screen. The picture done, the audience gone, I lock the doors, go out into the night.

But the past cannot be so easily dismissed. The faces of Rachel, Chance, and Fitz, of Wylie and of Shorty McAdoo, accompany me on my long walk home in the dark. I cross the black iron bridge, my limp a little worse each year, the water rushing underneath me in the darkness, pulling for the horizon.

32

Pushing hard, Fine Man and Broken Horn had driven the stolen horses a two-day ride to the northwest of the Cypress Hills, making for where their band waited, the band of Chief Talking Bird. Last night they had made camp in the trees near the river, hiding the horses from sight so they might approach their people with the sun on their faces, the horses they brought revealed in the best light of all, morning light.

As dawn broke, they removed their travel-stained clothes, the moccasins worn thin by the long walk south, the shirts they had slept in for nine nights, the leggings cut to ribbons in scrambles over sharp rocks, the blanket breechcloths snagged and torn by wild rosebushes. Naked, they waded into the shallows of the river and washed in the cold water, scrubbing themselves with handfuls of sand while the mist rose like pipe-smoke all around them and the fish leapt for a taste of the sun.

When they had cleansed themselves, they took up hand mirrors and paint. Fine Man divided his face with the strong colours of blood and the burned-out fire, his upper lip and everything above it red, his lower lip and everything below it black. While Broken Horn was daubing yellow stripes on his forearms to record his horse raids, Fine Man stared in the glass and pondered the blue horse which had led the rest of the ponies to give themselves up to the Assiniboine. As he did, the spots where the quicksilver backing of the glass had flaked away began to swirl in his eyes like falling snow. A sign. Quickly, he mixed a pot of white paint, held it to the nose of the roan horse, letting him smell it as he softly explained what he meant to do – dab his blue coat with white spots to make a picture of the night blizzard which four days ago had frozen the wolfers to the ground in sleep, hiding Fine Man and Broken Horn behind a spirit screen of whirling, blowing snow.

As his forefinger gently swept down the neck of the horse, dotting it with white, Fine Man decided he must not ride the blue horse into camp. Better for the horse to move in freedom, as he pleased, like a winter storm.

As he carefully placed each flake of snow on the chest, the ribs, the back of the winter horse, Fine Man's mind was filling with the memory of how he had gone humbly to Strong Bull, the holy man, to ask him to beseech the One Above on Fine Man's behalf when he sought the horses of his power-dream. To have such a man pray for you, to have him ride his horse among the lodges shouting out your name so the people would not forget you were alone and far away, was a good thing.

It was not so very long ago that Strong Bull was the one the young men went to with the pipe, asking him to lead them on their raids. In his dreams, Strong Bull could see where horses would be found, see how enemies would be overcome. All the country between the Missouri and the Saskatchewan was contained in his mind, every bend in the rivers, every poplar bluff, every buffalo wallow. Four times he had received wounds from the Blackfoot that would have killed any other man. But so great was his medicine that when he painted the sun's healing rays around his bleeding flesh, four times the One Above had taken pity on him, closed the bloody mouths of his wounds, restored him to health.

Yet a time came when Strong Bull refused to carry the pipe. Many, like Broken Horn, said that Strong Bull's heart had withered inside him, afraid that if its blood was let loose to flow one more time, it would die. The strong medicine which had brought the Assiniboine scalps and horses was gone and no one knew why. Neither did they know why Strong Bull now played with the white man's drawing sticks and paper like a child. He was a man after all, a man who owned a better gun than any of them, the Many Shoots Gun, the gun the white men called the Henry.

But he bought no bullets for it. It was true bullets were costly, one buffalo robe for three cartridges, but that did not explain why Strong Bull traded his prime robes for drawing sticks and the books the white men made the marks in, the lying marks which told falsehoods about how much you owed the trader.

Where once three buffalo runners had stood tethered before the entrance of Strong Bull's lodge, now there was only one thin horse to drag his teepee poles and coverings when camp moved. Now he walked beside the travois and the sight of a proud man eating dust was like sickness to the young men.

Still, Fine Man could not believe that strong medicine could ever be wholly taken from a man as holy as Strong Bull; that is why he had gone to him to request his prayers. And when Strong Bull had promised his help, Fine Man had asked him another thing too, asked him why it was he spent his days drawing pictures in the lying books.

For as long as it took to smoke the calumet Fine Man had filled for him from his own tobacco pouch, Strong Bull made no answer. Then he laid aside the pipe, drew his blanket about his shoulders, and spoke in a solemn voice. Two years ago his power-dreams had stopped, making him lonely and afraid. Many times he prayed, begging the One Above to send dreams as before, but the dreams remained lost and wandering in the Mystery World.

He decided then to make a great trial of his spirit. He built a raft, anchored it in the midst of a lake, laid himself naked on it. For two days he suffered without shade, food, or water. He lay there with the sun scorching him, his empty belly howling for food, his tongue and lips thirsting for a taste of water, knowing all he needed to do was reach out, cup his hand, and drink. But he did not. Instead, he called to the One Above, his mouth moving like blowing dust, his eyelids glowing red as hot iron from the heat of the sun. And when night fell, he shook like a reed in the cold wind blowing off the lake.

On the second night of this ordeal, a terrible thunderstorm began to gather, the clouds rolling like black boulders down a hill, boulders which struck sparks of lightning all around him. At first the Thunderbird shot only splinters of lightning at the raft, but the darkness of Strong Bull's mind was so deep that these were not enough. So the Thunderbird struck his chest with a blue-yellow bolt, splitting him, opening him wide with a fierce burning. From this wound nothing flowed out but much flowed in. All his other power-dreams were as nothing compared to it.

Strong Bull stopped then and a long, worshipful silence followed. At last, Fine Man found the courage to ask what it was he had seen.

Strong Bull shook his head. What was given to him, he said, was the knowledge of things to come, a knowledge which had filled him with sadness. Perhaps it would be better not to speak of it. "I will only say this," he told Fine Man. "Everything changes. There was a time the Assiniboine had no guns, no steel hatchets or knives, no glass beads to decorate our clothes." He paused. "There was even a time there were no horses. My grandfather told me that when his grandfather's father first saw horses the people did not know what name to give them. Some called them big dogs, some hornless elk. The new beings puzzled the people. But when the Assiniboine studied their natures, we learned they were neither dogs nor elk; we understood that the One Above had given us horses to hunt the buffalo and to carry us wherever we wished to go."

"Yes," agreed Fine Man.

"Everything changes in this world," Strong Bull repeated, "but in the Mystery World all things live as they were before death. In the Mystery World all things wait for us – our grandparents, our dead brothers of the Soldier's Society, our infants who died at birth. And the horses, the deer, the elk, the birds of the air, the buffalo wait for us, too. Someday you will go to the Mystery World and see these things for yourself."

Fine Man nodded this was true.

Strong Bull smiled to himself. "Sometimes I think of our people long ago, how strange it must have been for them to see horses for the first time. Were they frightened of them? Did they suppose horses ate meat like dogs? Everything changes. Perhaps these beings will pass out of this world the way they came into it. Maybe some day there will be no more horses. Or elk. Or buffalo. You and I have seen these beings, but what if our grandchildren have no knowledge of them? I do not want the grandchildren to be frightened when they pass into the Mystery World and encounter beings which may be strange to them. Of course, the black robes who wear the man on the sticks say the spirits of animals cannot enter the Mystery World, but that is foolish."

"Yes," said Fine Man, "very foolish."

"And I have thought something else," said Strong Bull. "If the grandchildren do not recognize these beings, perhaps they will not recognize us either." He reached behind him and lifted up a bundle wrapped in the hide of an unborn buffalo calf, undid the bindings, took out a trader book, passed it to Fine Man. "That is why I draw the pictures – so the grandchildren will recognize us," he said.

Fine Man began to carefully turn the pages of the book. Here was a picture of the women dancing, he knew each one by her dress. Here men were skinning buffalo in the snow. Here was a feast in which Left Hand could be seen passing his plate of meat to Broken Horn with a token stick. This signified Left Hand was bursting with food, and if Broken Horn would eat his portion so as not to insult the host, Left Hand would repay his kindness by giving him a horse. Last of all, he found a picture of himself, Fine Man in his best black leather shirt embroidered with green and white seed beads.

He handed Strong Bull the book and thanked him for the honour he had done him by showing him the pictures. Strong Bull said, "No one has seen this book but you. I have shown it to you because the One Above has given my old dreams, the dreams of horses, to you. Perhaps when I die and pass on to the Mystery World, the dreams of what is to come will also pass to you. When I am dead, my wife will put this bundle in your hands because you know its meaning. It will be for you to keep it safe for the sake of the grandchildren."

Fine Man could hear Broken Horn stirring restlessly behind him.

Horn was an impatient, proud man, and he was eager to ride to the band and tell the story of how they had lifted these horses from under the noses of the white men, to hear the acclaim of the people, and eat the fat pup which his Sits-Beside-Him wife would cook to welcome him home. Only the cannons of the blue horse's hind legs needed to be done, but Fine Man did not hurry, he worked on attentively, with precision. Then, when he was finished, he stood and signalled to Horn it was time to go.

They rode out, Fine Man on a paint horse and Broken Horn on a sorrel he had picked because it was the colour of the white man's new penny. Each man managed a string of eight ponies, the tail of the horse he led knotted to the halter shank of the horse that followed, its tail knotted in turn to the shank of the horse behind it, and so on. The sun was bright and sweet on the skin, but Broken Horn couldn't stop watching the blue horse running beside them, anxious it might escape in the last moments of the long journey. But the winter horse only trotted a short way off, nickering to his brothers and they nickering back. For two miles they rode in this fashion before glimpsing the teepees of Chief Talking Bird's camp. So close to the promise of home, Broken Horn could not contain his excitement and broke into the lead, swinging his file of ponies back and forth in the zigzag by which an Assiniboine party announced a successful raid. A boy on the outskirts of the camp spotted him and ran back to the village calling out their names to the people. Hearing this proclamation, Broken Horn urged his string of horses into a gallop, cracking the line from side to side so that the dust boiled up under their hooves in a cloud which, lit by the sun, glowed in celebration of their arrival.

People began to spill from the camp, shouting; dogs barked and howled while children laughed and galloped in zigzags like Broken Horn and his horses. Fine Man smiled and held his ponies to a trot, the blue horse close, snowflakes gleaming. The sun was a hot blanket across his shoulder and his feet jogged up and down in time with the life of the horse which bore him. Broken Horn had halted now and Fine Man could see the people crowding in to praise the ponies' beauty and strength, crowding in to caress them. A little way back from the crowd he could see his Sits-Beside-Him wife holding the little one in her arms, and his second wife, her sister, waiting to greet him.

He was very near now, his heart big in his breast with pride as the blue horse flew into the surprised eyes of the people, moving like a snow squall too strong for the hot sun to melt. When he reined in behind Broken Horn, the winter horse did not hesitate, but kept moving, head carried high, ears pricked as he trotted by all those who had fallen into silence, awed by the picture he made. Even the jaws of the snarling, snapping dogs snapped shut at the sight of the horse pushing into the ring of teepees, a blizzard with a purpose, hooves sure and certain as they skirted cooking fires.

Then Fine Man understood his power-dream, completely, perfectly, understood why the winter horse had summoned him across all those miles to come to him, understood who it was the horse had wished to give himself to from the beginning.

The drum of the Mystery World, the drum of this world, of the sky, of the earth, of his wives and his child, was beating, swelling in him, throbbing wildly against his breastbone, filling Fine Man with happiness. Sitting his horse, he began to sing a song of praise for the man to whom the winter horse was giving himself.

The faces of the people bobbed up in astonishment and the sun bowed down when he sang the name of the great holy man, the man who lived now for the sake of the grandchildren. Between the lodges Fine Man could see the horse moving like a storm readying to empty itself, blowing from lodge to lodge, searching while he sang.

Then the blue horse stopped. And Fine Man did too.

Acknowledgements

The works I consulted while writing this novel are too numerous to cite, but I would like to make particular mention of several. Paul Sharp's *Whoop-Up Country: The Canadian-American West, 1865-1885* (University of Minnesota Press, 1955); Wallace Stegner's *Wolf Willow* (The Viking Press, 1962); James Willard Schultz's *My Life as an Indian* (Beaufort Books, 1983); and articles in the *Montana Magazine of History*: Jay Mack Gamble's "Up River to Benton," and Hugh A. Dempsey's "Cypress Hills Massacre" and "Sweetgrass Hills Massacre."

I would also like to acknowledge Richard Schickel's *D. W. Griffith: An American Life* (Simon and Schuster, 1984); Frances Marion's *Off With Their Heads!: A Serio-comic Tale of Hollywood* (Macmillan, 1972); Diana Serra Cary's *The Hollywood Posse: The Story of a Gallant Band of Horsemen Who Made Movie History* (Houghton Mifflin, 1975); John Tuska's *The Filming of the West* (Doubleday, 1976); Neal Gabler's *An Empire of Their Own: How the Jews Invented Hollywood* (Crown Publishers, 1988); and Christopher Finch's and Linda Rosenkrantz's *Gone Hollywood* (Doubleday, 1979).

I would especially like to thank my editor, Ellen Seligman, and my agent, Dean Cooke, for all the advice and the assistance they have given me.

∽

Excerpts from this novel, in slightly different form, appeared on CBC Radio's "Ambience" and in the journal *Planet: The Welsh Internationalist*.

Books by Guy Vanderhaeghe

NOVELS
My Present Age 1984
Homesick 1989
The Englishman's Boy 1996

SHORT STORIES
Man Descending 1982
The Trouble With Heroes 1983
Things As They Are? 1992

PLAYS
I Had a Job I Liked. Once. 1992
Dancock's Dance 1996